THE FOILED PLAN

VERONICA LANCET

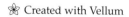

PREFACE

This series is dark. It's **VERY** dark.

No one is a good guy.

Some characters may be **irredeemable**.

Please only read if you are comfortable with the following triggers. The books in the series will get progressively darker.

Trigger Warnings:
abuse, abortion, attempted rape, blood (gore), blood play, death, derogatory terms, death, drugs, guns, graphic violence, graphic sexual situations, depictions of torture, gaslighting, grooming, homophobia, incestuous situations, infertility, kidnapping, knife play, murder, mental illness, non-con/dubcon, necrophilia, ritualistic killing, substance abuse, mentions of suicide.

CHAPTER ONE
RAFAELO

The wind is knocked out of me as the doctor lists her injuries.

"Can I..." I swallow hard, a huge fucking lump forming in my throat. "Can I take a look at her medical file?"

"I'm not sure," he frowns, but a little more coaxing and I find myself in a secluded corner reading through her medical file while the doctor performs the ultrasound.

And what I read has the power to lay me on my ass.

Second and third degree burns on her back.

Fractured ulna.

Fractured tibia.

Hairline fracture on her right hip.

Concussion and swelling of the temporal lobe.

I take a deep breath as I realize why she would have memory issues. Because someone fucking bashed her head so hard they had to add pieces of metal to keep her skull together.

And then there's the worst...

Crushed larynx.

I'm getting sick to my stomach the more I read through the notes, especially when I get to the other observations.

Poorly healed ribs, fractures and other broken bones.

All speaking of ongoing and repeated abuse.

Then there are the internal injuries. They'd had to do an emergency surgery to remove the retained placenta and they'd also ended up performing a splenectomy because her spleen was about to burst.

The more I read, the more I wish to God the earth would open up and swallow me whole. Because as it stands... I don't think I can ever forgive myself for the way I've treated her

As I swipe to the next page, it's to see up close pictures of her battered body and the many injuries she'd sustained.

She looks almost dead, every inch of her a combination of blue and purple. And to think I contributed to that... That those are *my* handprints on her lovely throat...

I close the file, a low tremor going through my body as disgust at myself fills me to the brim.

I've always thought myself a strong person considering what I went through and how I overcame my condition. After all, I went through hell and I came back. And though I suffered horrors during my time in captivity, never once did I shed a tear.

Not like now.

My eyes are misty and I feel a tear roll down my cheek, the thought of Noelle hurt and in pain proving to be my undoing.

I take a moment to center myself, trying to pull myself together and be there for her *now*. Because I may not be able to alter the past—including the fucked up way I treated her—but I can alter the present.

My breathing grows labored as my mind doesn't want to obey me, visions of her slight body so damaged and battered killing me. More than anything, there's a deep anguish at knowing what she's been through and the trauma that no one bothered to acknowledge.

Is this how her own family treated her? How could they?

How the fuck could they?

Surely Cisco must have seen her file. How could he *knowingly* treat her like that when she's suffered what grown men would balk at?

She's so frail...so fucking small. How could she have withstood everything?

How?

Then there's also the other question. What about her baby?

And for that, I'm afraid there's only one answer.

Dead.

The baby must have died.

Anger unlike any other erupts inside of me at the thought of Noelle alone and defenseless, giving birth in that dump that was the *hacienda* without anyone to help her. Without anyone to care for her.

A deep pain that lodges itself inside of me at the thought of anyone touching her—in anger or in *any* way.

"There you are," the doctor shakes me from my thoughts, and giving him back the file with a grimace, I await the diagnosis.

"We found a lot of scar tissue on her uterine walls, and she is currently menstruating, so there is a high chance that is the source of the pain. Regular menstrual cramps combined with endometriosis often result in acute abdominal pain."

I nod, trying to keep my expression neutral as I hear his explanation.

"Has she complained of pain during intercourse?" He suddenly asks and I blink, unprepared for that question. But he doesn't give me the opportunity to reply as he goes on.

"You might want to watch out for that too. Penetration could be very uncomfortable at certain times of the month," he continues to string together some medical terms I've never heard of, but my head whips at him when he says something that fucking kills me.

"There is a chance she won't be able to have children again. There are some surgeries that could help clean the endometriosis, but unfortunately," he pauses, a depressing look on his face. "Her condition is on the extreme end of the spectrum, so IVF treatments might not work."

I keep myself still, his words washing through me and hitting me like a fucking tornado.

"I see," is all I answer—all I *can* answer.

Thanking the doctor, I make my way to her salon.

Still out from the pain medication, she has a serene look on her face.

I move slowly, taking one step at a time until I reach her side. Pulling a chair next to the bed, I take her hand in mine, once more marveling at the size disparity.

How could anyone so dainty survive such horrors?

My mind simply can't wrap around that, and as I continue to watch her, I realize that any attempt at visualizing her beaten, and in a pool of blood, just about sends me off the rails.

Holding on tightly, I let her warmth seep into my skin—evidence she's still alive.

I don't know how much time passes, but I don't let go—I *can't* let go. It's only when I hear her soft voice utter my name that I ground myself back into the present.

"Raf?" her eyes flutter open as she gazes at me in confusion.

Once more, I'm struck by her sheer beauty. Even pale from pain, she still looks absolutely stunning, her eyes big and luminous, especially when she turns them to me.

"How are you feeling?" I ask, my voice clogged with emotion. Still, I try to rein it in lest I worry her too.

"Better now," she sighs, slowly pulling herself in a sitting position.

"Has this happened before?" I inquire gently.

The doctor had suggested that due to the damage caused by the endometriosis, it couldn't have been the first time.

She gives a brisk nod, her expression clouded.

"Not to this extent. I've always been able to bear it before."

"You shouldn't have," I frown. "Haven't you told anyone?"

There's the barest shake of her head.

"I didn't want them to think I was doing it for attention," she shrugs, such a forlorn look on her face that all I want to do is take her in my arms and never let her go.

Our hands are still linked, and her eyes suddenly drop to where our skin is touching, her brows furrowing.

"From now on you have to tell me, Noelle. Tell me when it hurts and we'll deal with it," I tell her gently, and the confusion in her eyes only intensifies.

"Why?" she whispers.

"Because I said so," I declare, leaning back and watching her intently.

"You can still get an annulment, you know," she says flippantly. "I told you that you bought a defective product."

"You're not defective," I grit my teeth, annoyed she'd think that.

But that's a thing I can't fix overnight. I can't change her perception of herself, just like I can't change her perception of me and my behavior towards her.

I'll just have to take it one step at a time.

"Rest," I tell her rather forcefully. "After that we're going back home."

She looks at me wide eyed, but she doesn't argue. So

weary she is from the pain, she doesn't even have the strength to verbally spar with me—our usual pastime.

One thing is for sure though. The moment we reach home, Cisco will have some explaining to do.

———

"I THOUGHT we were going back to the holiday house," she says in a small voice as the car draws to a stop in front of her home—our new home.

At least temporarily.

"No. That's done," I reply, trying to keep my tone neutral.

I shut down the engine, quickly going around the car to open her door.

She seems surprised when she sees me, and for about two seconds she tries to protest as I swoop her into my arms, holding her close to my chest as I head towards the house.

"Greta, where is Cisco?" I ask the minute I spot the housekeeper.

"He's out," she mumbles, her eyes drifting from Noelle to me in confusion.

I nod. "Let me know when he returns. I'll be on the third floor with Noelle."

Not waiting around for her reply, I take two stairs at a time, hurrying towards the third floor.

There's an urgent need inside of me to see her settled comfortably in her bed that nothing else matters.

True to his word, Cisco had done some quick remodeling around the third floor, adding another wall to separate the floor from the rest of the house and give it a more intimate feeling. A makeshift apartment, the floor has two bedrooms, one master bathroom and direct access to the piano room— perfect for Noelle.

Passing by one bedroom, my mind is already quick at

work to think of ways to occupy it so Noelle can't suggest we sleep separately.

If anything, now that the last barrier between us has been broken, there is absolutely *nothing* keeping me from her. Because underneath all my preconceived notions of her, under all those harsh biases that clouded my judgment, there's a ravenous hunger for her.

Lucero's image briefly enters my mind, but I shove it aside.

There will be another time to dwell on that.

"You can let me go," her sweet voice interrupts my thoughts.

I look down to find her shyly staring at me, her beautiful brows furrowed in confusion.

"Not yet," I grunt.

It's only when I reach the master bedroom that I put her down, laying her on top of the crisp sheets.

She releases a soft sigh as she makes herself comfortable, and I waste no time in draping the blanket on top of her frail body, making sure she's covered from head to toe.

She's watching me closely, her eyes following my every move as I ensure that she's not lacking anything.

From water, to medicine and to warm compresses, I try to think of everything she might need. When I've gathered them all, I organize the items on her nightstand for easy reach, from the most important to the least.

"Raf," her hand comes to rest on my arm.

"Huh?"

"What are you doing?' she asks softly.

"Making sure you have everything you need," I answer immediately.

"I can see that. But why?" She tilts her head, studying me.

"Because you're in pain," I simply state.

7

There's a pause as she brings her teeth over her lower lip, nibbling at it in uncertainty.

"Raf," she starts, almost as if she's preparing herself for the worst. "Why do you care if I'm in pain or not? Isn't that the whole purpose of your revenge? To hurt me?"

Her question hits me right into the chest, because I can't imagine even one scenario where I would hurt her.

Not anymore.

Fuck, but the thought of her in pain causes *me* pain.

There's also the startling realization that she's not saying this to bait me, or to start an argument. She's genuinely surprised at my actions, and I only have to blame my brutish self for it.

Me and my fucking prejudiced self.

"What's the joy in kicking someone who's already down?" I shoot back at her, since she's nowhere near ready for the sudden change in my behavior.

Hell, I don't know if *I* am ready.

I'm only aware of this powerful need inside of me to make sure she's well cared for, that she *never* lacks anything and most importantly, that she'll *never* be in pain again.

Fuck me, how I wish I could take away all her suffering.

"I see," she nods, and a flash of disappointment crosses her face.

"Let me know if there's anything else you need," I mumble as I back out of the room, knowing I might do something stupid if I remain in her presence.

Fuck.

CHAPTER TWO
RAFAELO

J ust as I close the door to the room, though, it's to bump into Greta, who lets me know Cisco is expecting me in his study.

Opening the door to his study, I find him lounging behind his desk, a glass of whiskey in his hand.

He raises an eyebrow as he sees me come in, and there is the barest hint of a smirk as the corner of his mouth pulls up.

"Honeymoon cut short?" He asks, his tone amused.

Striding to the desk, I take a seat opposite him.

For a second, all I can do is stare at him as I try to imagine why he'd treat his sister like that.

"We encountered a bump in the road," I say noncommittally.

"Oh, I'm sad to hear that," he offers a fake platitude, that cunning smile still on his lips.

"Noelle had to be hospitalized," I add, watching his expression closely.

But he doesn't slip.

There's not a hint of guilt, not even curiosity as he merely lifts his brows in question.

"Abdominal pain," I continue. "But you must already know that, no?"

"And why would I know that?" he asks innocently, taking out a cigarette and lighting it.

"Because of her history," I grit my teeth.

It takes everything in me to not punch him—or worse, fucking kill him on the spot. Especially as it is clear that he doesn't give a fuck about Noelle.

"Hmm," he intones, and my fists clench in frustration.

"Let's cut the crap, Cisco. I read through her medical file. I know everything that happened to her."

There's a pause as his eyes flash. But he's still sporting the same relaxed look as before.

"So?" He asks languidly.

"So?" I repeat. "Is that all you have to say?"

"What do you want me to say, Raf? You've already read through her list of injuries, so you know the bulk of it," he shrugs. "There's not much more I can add to that," he says with a feline smile.

"How about the fact that you *lied* to me?"

"Lie? Me?" He feigns a look of surprise.

"You and everyone else in the family have been suggesting that she's a pathological liar and that I shouldn't believe anything that comes out of her mouth."

Entirely unbothered, he takes a deep drag of his cigarette.

"You see, that right there is the problem," he smiles. "*Suggestion*. That means you reached that conclusion on your own."

"Cisco," I shake my head at him, barely in control of myself. "You've been treating Noelle like a madwoman from the beginning," I cut to the chase. "Why? She's your sister for God's sake."

"There are some things you don't understand, Raf," his

expression turns serious. "And will likely *never* understand. So do yourself a favor and stay out of it."

"Stay out of it? She's my wife, damn it," I bang my hand over the desk, the sound reverberating in the study.

Cisco's eyes darken, but he doesn't move an inch. He continues to watch me with those mismatched eyes of his.

"So she is," he agrees after a moment.

"That means I'm entitled to know *everything* about her."

"Are you sure you want to know, Raf?" He tilts his head to the side, looking at me through narrowed eyes. "The truth can be a dangerous thing."

"Yes," I reply firmly. "I want to know the truth. I want to know why her family's been treating her like a lunatic. I want to know why you think *everything* she does is for attention. I want to know how the hell it got here, because from where I'm sitting, she's never been anything but a victim."

I'm breathing hard by the time I say the last word, my blood boiling inside of me the more I think of a defenseless Noelle withstanding so much violence and hate—even from her own family.

"Are you done?" Cisco asks in a bored tone as he takes a sip of his drink.

"Tell me," I ignore his previous question as I demand he give me the *truth.*

Or at least his version of the truth, since we've concluded how misleading the *truth* can be.

"If you've read through her file then you must already know she gave birth sometime before the fire," he starts, looking at me intently.

I nod.

"She doesn't know that. She doesn't know *anything* about the day of the fire, and I'd appreciate it if it stayed like that."

"Why?" I frown. "Isn't it in her best interest to recover her memory? Isn't that why you're sending her to therapy?"

He gives a dry laugh.

"Oh, how simple that would be. But no. She's going to therapy for one reason and one reason only," he pauses. "To make sure she doesn't kill herself."

"What..." My eyes widen.

"Her condition is complicated, Raf. And to deal with her I've made some allowances—some rather unorthodox allowances if you will."

"What are you talking about?"

"After she awoke in the hospital, she was hysterical. She remembered everything about the baby and she was inconsolable," he takes a deep drag from his cigarette, releasing a cloud of smoke in the air. "She went through three different suicide attempts. All within the first month," there's a rueful smile on his face as he admits it.

My breath hitches in my throat as I listen to his words, a deep chasm of pain opening inside of me.

"Her last attempt was almost successful. *Almost.* The doctors resuscitated her right in time. After that... her memory was gone. To survive, I think she forgot everything that was too painful for her."

"That doesn't explain *your* attitude towards her," I fire back, even more annoyed she'd have gone through something like that and her own family would treat her like shit.

"Patience, Raf, patience," he shakes his head. "If before she'd been hysterical, then after the last suicide attempt she became almost catatonic. There was nothing we could do to get her out of it." He takes a deep breath. "She had no will to live left, and yet she was still living."

I frown at his description.

"So I did something a little...controversial," his mouth pulls up.

"What?"

"I became her enemy," he simply shrugs. "I gave her a

reason to keep living—if anything, to prove me wrong. I antagonized her at every turn. I taunted her and I made her hate me until she stopped being a fucking statue. It wasn't the best course of action, I admit. Yuyu was against it from the beginning. But I couldn't just sit by and watch my sister fade away. Not after I knew I had a hand in her becoming like that."

"Why would you resort to that?"

I can't wrap my head around what he's telling me. Though to a certain degree it does sound logical, I simply can't understand how he would so easily vilify his own sister —and claim it's for her own good.

"Noelle has always been a stubborn person. Tell her she can't do something and she'll try that much harder to get it done. That is the core of who she is, so I merely took advantage of that. I knew that if I pushed the right buttons, I'd manage to get a reaction out of her. And I did. That she still lives... She needed someone to blame. Someone to hate. And I gave her just that."

"That's..." I trail off, taken aback by his confession. "That's rather extreme, wouldn't you say?" I ask, genuinely confused.

"You didn't see her back then. We tried *everything*, and nothing worked. She was just wasting away." He purses his lips and a flash of emotion crosses his face—one of the few ones I've seen of him. "You can't be a hero if you don't have a villain. Humans work around opposites. There's always good and bad, black and white. But without the latter, the former wouldn't exist. I gave her the bad, so she could nurture the good. It's that simple."

I'm stunned to the spot as I digest his words. I've never heard someone take that approach, especially since he's her brother.

To realize that they've been all playing a role...

"But how long do you intend to keep this up? It's been

two years already, and from where I'm standing, she's *not* doing well."

"She's doing as well as expected, all things considered. Why do you think I've been forcing her to go to therapy? Because memory is a tricky thing. And I don't think the past will stay hidden forever. She needs a backup plan in case she remembers. In case all the safety mechanisms I put in place are broken," he adds grimly.

I grunt at his assessment.

There is, indeed, a logic to what he's saying. Cisco's been manipulating his sister from the beginning, playing psychological games with her that logically make sense. But what about ethically?

Although I understand the gist of his reasoning, there is a line you just don't cross—especially with family.

This new information shines a new light on Cisco, and it serves to make me even more wary about him.

Because if he's capable of doing *this*, then what else is he capable of?

"What happened to her baby?" I ask the question that's been plaguing me all day.

His lips stretch into a thin line.

"Dead," he replies. "We found it at the scene," he frowns, blinking twice. "We did an autopsy, and though he was born prematurely, he was alive at birth. He died later," his voice drops a notch.

"Of natural causes?"

"No," the sound is hollow as it escapes his lips. "He had his skull crushed."

I can't move as I stare at Cisco dumbfounded, that one piece of information hitting me in the chest with the force of a bullet.

"His skull was crushed?" I repeat bleakly. Goosebumps spread all over my skin, my heart beating wildly in my chest as it dawns on me what type of horrors Noelle had been through.

And the fact that I'm only getting a snapshot of it.

"Yes. The baby was killed. So you see why Noelle would go off the rails. Why she would lose herself to her grief? If I didn't act in any way…" he trails off, "I wouldn't have a sister right now. I'd have a shell, or none at all."

"I understand," I nod, a painful lump forming in my throat.

"Good. I hope that means you won't breathe a word to her about what you found out," Cisco raises a brow, which only makes me narrow my eyes at him.

"With all due respect, Cisco. You did your duty as her brother. I am her husband now, and I will do my duty as her husband," I tell him clearly, my voice stern.

The slight twitch in his jaw tells me he understands exactly what I'm saying. That from now on he will *not* have a say in anything that happens with Noelle.

"And on that note," I continue. "From now on I don't want *anyone* to question her sanity, or tell her she's doing things for attention."

"You're getting bolder, Raf."

"No," I quickly reply. "This is not me getting bolder, Cisco. This is me enforcing boundaries and making sure she gets the *best* treatment, including from her family."

"I see," he murmurs, his eyes on me as he brings his cigarette to his lips.

"And that means our plan is off too," I bring up the other elephant in the room.

I'd outlined this particular plan when I'd wanted to kill two birds with one stone—Noelle still being the number one target for my resentment.

But as it stands now, I could never in good conscience allow the plan to move further.

"I didn't expect you to be so sentimental, Raf," Cisco chuckles.

"I'm not being sentimental. I'm being fair. And it's not right to involve her in things that do not concern her." I stand up, ready to leave.

"You sure weren't so considerate when you married her," he calls out, stopping me.

"What are you talking about?" I frown.

"You think I didn't know why you were so keen on her?" the hint of a smile appears on his face. "Do you *really* think I would give my only sister away again without having all the information?"

"What do you think you know?"

"That you spent a good amount of time at the *hacienda* under Sergio. Isn't that right?" His eyes glint dangerously as he looks at me, daring me to deny.

"So?"

"So I assume you had a hidden agenda when you decided to pursue my sister. Which," he pauses, "well done. It took me a while to get to the bottom of your objective."

"Then why still authorize the marriage?"

"Because," he grins wolfishly, "some things are more important than others," he shrugs.

"What are you talking about?"

"My sister is important to me, of course," he continues, "but some things go beyond familiar bonds. I always act for the *greatest good*," he says in a dead voice. "And that may, occasionally, call for a sacrifice or two."

What...

The more I listen to him, the more I realize I'm talking to a madman. Because there's absolutely no way Cisco is right in the head.

"What are you talking about?" I snap, a little tired of his circular talk.

"Ah, Raf. That does not concern you," he gives me a tight smile. "But the deal remains on. My sister is and will be part of the plan as we've talked."

"And if not?" I raise a brow.

"If not..." he gives a dry laugh. "Do you really want to find out? I told you. My sister is important. But there are things far more important..." he trails off, the meaning clear. In order to achieve whatever goals he has in mind, he would sacrifice Noelle in the blink of an eye.

"Is this how it's going to be between us now? Threats?"

"See, Raf. That's the difference between the two of us. You care about people." His eyes turn cold. "I don't. And that means I will always have the upper hand."

"Really?" I drawl. The air is growing tense as the stakes rise. And though we have not raised our voices at each other yet, or resorted to violence, the intent *is* there. "What about your wife, then? What about your children?"

There's a pause where he doesn't answer. He merely looks at me, that intense stare boring a hole through me. His shoulders are tense, his entire countenance deadly.

Then, in the blink of an eye he's relaxed again, leaning back and regarding me through hooded eyes.

"They *are* the reason for everything," he states cryptically. "Don't forget the deal we made. You want your revenge. I want... Well, I want what I want."

"This was your plan for the beginning, wasn't it? That's why you kept encouraging my relationship with Noelle."

"You could say that. You and Noelle have a lot in common. And I knew you would eventually find out about her medical history and you would put two and two together. So you see, I wasn't risking much. I've done an in-depth analysis of your character and you're one of the good guys," he smiles in satisfaction, "which made my decision infinitely easier."

"You're insane," I shake my head at him.

"Maybe," he shrugs. "My methods may not be *fully* orthodox," he chuckles. "But I'm a rather good matchmaker. Just ask your sister."

I merely raise a brow, surprised he'd go there.

"I may come across as heartless, Raf, and to a degree I probably am," he shrugs, leaning back in his seat and looking entirely at ease. "But I never do something without planning at least ten more movements in advance. I care about my sister. But in the big scheme of things..." he trails off, a cunning smile on his face.

"But that doesn't matter anymore. She has you now. And *that* deserves a toast," he grins as he lifts his glass in the air.

"Indeed," I drawl dangerously, looking at him in disgust. "To our women. May they forgive all our faults."

Because I pity Yuyu for the man she calls her husband.

"Amen to that," he smirks.

CHAPTER THREE
RAFAELO

"It's not like you to drink, Raf," Carlos' voice echoes in my ear as he slides in the seat next to me at the makeshift bar we'd built at the warehouse.

"I screwed up," I admit, taking another swig of vodka.

As soon as I'd concluded my meeting with Cisco, I'd checked again on Noelle to see she was fast asleep. Only then did I dare leave the house, knowing I needed to blow off some steam.

Because as things stand... I messed up. I more than messed up.

"What are you talking about?"

"The plan to take out both Noelle and Michele. It back-fired," I take a deep breath.

"What?" He frowns.

The plan had sprung out from a need to prove to myself that Noelle didn't matter to me. That she isn't compromising my focus and my commitment to get revenge.

So I'd reached out to Cisco with the outline, not expecting him to actually agree to it. The plan had been rather simple. I would use Noelle as bait to arrange a private piano recital, hyping it up in select circles by dubbing Noelle one of the prodigies of the modern age. The rumor would go that she is a reclusive pianist and this would be her first appearance in front of a public audience. With Michele's propensity for both grandiosity and classical music, this would be right at home for him and would serve to draw him in the open.

The idea had worked perfectly. As it stands, Michele has already taken the bait. Our last report indicates that he purchased tickets through a third party, with Panchito being able to track the transactions clearly and ascertain that the buyer is, indeed, Michele.

"I don't get what the issue is. Michele's already on board with it," he asks as he pours himself a glass.

"The issue is," I laugh sarcastically, "that I just found out that Noelle is innocent. Entirely innocent."

His eyes widen at my statement, and I quickly go over my findings, including what I'd found out from Cisco.

"Holy shit," he curses, clearly shocked.

"Indeed," I drawl. "So you see, I find myself in a quandary. Cisco doesn't want to cancel the plan, and I don't want to go through with it and risk Noelle's safety."

"If he's threatening you, then the best you can do is make sure she's protected at all times," he adds grimly. "We'll help you with that, and I'm sure Cisco will mobilize his men too. After all, she is his sister."

"Yeah, that doesn't seem to help much where Cisco is concerned," I mutter drily.

"So what now?"

"Now? I don't fucking know," I curse out, taking the bottle and filling the glass to the brim. "Worst of all is that all this time I've been picking on an innocent. Fuck..." I shake my head.

Tipping the glass, I enjoy the burn of the alcohol, the only thing that seems to give me a modicum of peace now.

"Is it only that?"

"What do you mean?"

"I know you, Raf. You wouldn't be here, getting sloshed just because of that. So spill. What else is bothering you?"

"Nothing…" I mumble.

"Raf," he purses his lips. "I'm going to be brutally honest with you, which maybe, I should have been from the beginning."

"What are you talking about?"

"You like her. You like Noelle."

"What…"

"No, listen to me first. You like her. You feel attracted to her. But you're also mad at yourself for that because you feel as if you're betraying Lucero. Isn't that right?"

I can only stare at him, my eyes unblinking.

"I see that I'm right," he chuckles as he fills my glass again before doing the same with his.

"You are," I take a deep breath. "Before, it was easier to deny it because in my mind she was the enemy. Now?" I shake my head, my fingers drumming over the surface of the table. "After I found out the truth, it was like something was freed inside of me. Something…"

"You don't have to justify it. To be perfectly honest, I could see it from the beginning. I could see how you were behaving with her and how she took over your focus entirely. It wasn't normal, but I refrained from saying anything since I was sure you'd figure it out sooner or later."

"Well, it seems it's rather late."

It's funny to hear that everyone around me had been noticing what I was trying to bury. Because they are right. From the beginning I'd been drawn to her—desired her more than I've ever desired another. And *that* was the problem. Because that would mean what I felt for her was stronger than what I felt for Lucero…

From the beginning, my hate for her had been my lifeline. I'd used that resentment to feed my thirst for revenge and keep my feelings for her at bay. But instead of squashing them, I'd only stifled them so that the moment I found out how wrong I'd been about her, they resurfaced a hundred times stronger than before.

"Raf, it's been two years since Lucero died. It's ok to move on. It's ok to feel something for another person. It's ok to let go," he pats my back in a fatherly gesture.

"What you had with Lucero was beautiful and it kept you alive. And because of that I'm sure *she* wouldn't want you to languish away or deny yourself the opportunity to be happy."

"I know that," I start in a strained voice. "Logically, I know that. I'm aware that no one spends their entire life loving just *one* person. Yet in practice? I don't know if I can let myself. There's this guilt inside of me every time I think of a future together—because Lucero never got that chance. She died and she never got the chance to be free..."

"So what are you going to do? You married her. Are you going to keep her at arms' length forever? What type of life is that?"

"I get what you're saying..."

"No, you don't," he intervenes in a stern tone. "You're using Lucero as an excuse. I know you, Raf, and I know that whatever you feel for Noelle isn't a trifle. You're just bloody scared to face it."

Anger shines in my eyes as I look at him. But just as it comes, it's gone, a deep calm settling over me as I admit to myself Carlos isn't wrong.

I want her. I *more* than want her.

I want to lose myself in her body and brand her with my touch so that's the only thing she remembers. I want her to belong to me—only to me.

"You're right," I nod, baring my deepest fear to him. "You're right that I'm scared. Because what if she dies too? What if I'll get her killed? For God's sake," I groan, letting my head fall into my hands. "How would I ever forgive myself if I failed yet another woman?"

"All I can tell you is that you're not going to be better off if you don't take a chance. In our walk of life, death can come any moment. Do you really want to regret not trying at least?"

"You're a very good pep talker," I give him a smile.

"I'm just presenting you with facts," he flashes me a grin.

"And you're very good at it. I agree that I have my own issues to work through. But now that I'm here..." I trail off, looking in the distance. "I can't back down. I'll just have to do whatever it takes to protect her."

"See, I knew you'd see the light of it. If life is presenting you with a second chance at love, you should take it," he winks at me.

"Wait, wait, wait," I put my hand up. "You're jumping the gun. I want her—I desire her. But that's it. I'll do my duty as her husband, and maybe we'll find some happiness together. I'll certainly do everything in my power to make sure she's never harmed again."

"Sure," he nods. "Of course. You *only* desire her."

"Yes, and now that I know she's innocent, there's nothing holding me back."

"Right," Carlos nods, but he doesn't seem convinced.

"I don't see why we can't have a perfectly satisfying marriage. I just need to get her to open up to me," I take a deep breath, realizing I've probably mucked that up.

"Raf," Carlos stands up, pursing his lips in amusement. "You have your work cut out for you, so I can only wish you good luck."

"Thanks," I mutter drily. "I'll probably need that."

———

A LITTLE MORE VODKA THAN I would have cared for and I barely manage to keep myself upright as I enter the room.

Squinting, I try to make sense of the furniture around me so I don't bump into anything.

"Fuck," I utter a low curse as I step on something sharp.

But just as the words are out of my mouth, the light goes on, Noelle's worried expression greeting me.

She's in her nightgown, propped against the headboard, her eyebrows pinched together as she looks at me questioningly.

"Chocolalte?" I call out, but I realize my words are failing me. "Chocolate?" I repeat, satisfied when I get it right.

Lifting the bag in my hand, I wave it in front of her.

"What are you doing?"

"I brought you chocolate," I say as I sway a little before propping myself on the bed.

Dropping the bag in her lap, I turn over to take my shoes off.

"Why would you bring me chocolate?" She asks in a confused tone.

Tilting my head to look at her, I frown.

"Isn't that what girls need on their periods?" I ask innocently, removing my shoes and pushing them under the bed.

"How would you know that?" She seems rather suspicious as she unpacks the chocolate, turning it on both sides to check the seal.

"I read on the internet," I shrug.

Bringing my hands to my shirt, I start unbuttoning it.

"Wait, wait, wait," she puts a hand up, her eyes flashing at me. "What do you think you're doing?"

"Getting in bed?"

"No, you're not. At least not this bed," she waves her pointer finger at me.

"Yes, I am," I state confidently, almost ripping the shirt off my back as I fling it to the floor.

"What's gotten into you, Raf? Why are you behaving like this?" She asks on a soft sigh, and I note the tiredness in her face. "Is this the part where you pity me? Because you saw the scars? Is that why you're acting so nice?"

She raises her eyes at me, and her expression hits me straight to the chest.

There's an aching vulnerability to her. It's in the way she's clutching her blanket to her chest, her brows slightly arched, her lower lip quivering as she looks at me.

And so I'm once more reminded what a total ass I've been to her. How I've hounded and taunted until she doesn't feel safe in my presence.

"I'm not pitying you, Noelle," I tell her, slowly advancing towards her. "Why would I pity you for something that's out of your control?"

She regards me wide eyed, and I note the slight jerk of her body as the bed dips under my weight. She leans back, trying to put some distance between us.

"Then why?" the words are barely above a whisper.

Without speaking, I turn, showing her my back.

"What..." the words tumble out of her mouth.

"You're not the only one with scars, Noelle," I tell her gently.

My back, not unlike hers, speaks of everything I'd been through at the *hacienda* and before. Lashings, brandings, canings and everything in between. There are scars from instruments I can't even name. That and a couple gunshot wounds she should recognize...

There's a brief pause before the tips of her fingers make contact with my mangled flesh. A sudden intake of breath and I tense, her touch featherlike, but searing itself on my skin.

"What's this?" She asks as she traces the mark on my right shoulder. A circle that houses the letter A, it's also the source of most of my nightmares.

"A brand," I reply, my voice heavy with emotion.

"A brand?" She repeats, and I feel the confusion in her voice.

Everything inside of me is telling me to walk away. Pretend this never happened and go sleep in the other room. The mere thought of the brand is enough to send shivers down my back, making me want to bury my memories deep inside and never gaze at them again.

But I can't do that.

If I want us to bridge the gap between us, then it's up to me to offer some honesty as well. Especially after everything I'd found out about her.

She needs to know she's not the only one. If she's ashamed of her marks, then I should be infinitely more.

"Before I came to the *hacienda*," I start, taking a deep breath and steeling myself against the shudder that threatens to overtake me at the thought of Armand. "I was sold to a man. His name was Armand."

"Armand… Why would he…" she traces the A etched in my skin, no doubt putting two and two together.

"He claimed I was the love of his life," I give a dry laugh. "In his delusion, I was there of my own free will and we were one happy couple."

"You mean he…" she trails off, and I hear her soft whimper.

"Yes. He raped me," I say as I turn.

The sight of her, however, almost kills me.

Unshed tears line her lashes, her eyes moist as she barely keeps herself from crying.

"No, don't," I whisper as I bring my hand up, brushing a falling tear from her cheek. "I didn't tell you this to make you sad. Or to pity me," I give her a strained smile. "I told you so we would be on equal footing. I know some of your trauma," I pause, letting my knuckles caress her cheek, "and now you know some of mine."

"But how?" Her brows furrow in confusion. "I don't…"

"I was drugged most of the time, so I was never able to fight him off. I stayed with him until he died, and then I was sold to the *hacienda*."

"I'm sorry," her soft voice soothes me deep in my heart, and without thinking, I bring her to me, my arms coming around her as I hold her to my chest.

She gasps in surprise, but doesn't manage to get away.

"*I* am sorry," I say in her hair, nuzzling my nose in the crook of her neck.

Her scent invades my nostrils—a mix of flowers and cream; a comforting yet spicy sweetness that leaves me wanting more… So much more.

And as my hands move over her slight body, I can't help the way my brain conjures up the pictures I'd seen, the injuries she'd suffered and how close she'd been to dying.

"Can you forgive me?" I ask on a ragged whisper, my voice raspy and full of the emotions of the day.

She keeps herself still in my arms, not pushing me away but not encouraging me either.

"Why?"

"Because I didn't believe you," I breathe out.

She doesn't answer, her harsh breath the only sound permeating the air. I feel her rib cage expand and contract against my chest as she inhales and exhales.

"You… You believe me?" she finally asks, her voice lacking her usual conviction. In fact, I detect traces of wonder in her tone, almost as if she doesn't dare let herself trust my words.

And fuck if that doesn't hurt. It reminds me that everyone's been playing with her, accusing her of lying and making things up for attention.

Everyone, including me.

"I do," I assure her. "I believe you, Noelle."

Her breathing accelerates, and out of nowhere, sobs erupt in the air.

"Shh, don't cry," I bring my hand to her hair, threading my fingers through her silken locks.

It's the first time we've been this close to one another without throwing insults at each other, or engaging in a battle of wills. It's the first time I'm feeling her pliant body under mine and fuck me...

I stifle a groan at the plushness of her skin, the fit so perfect it's like we were made for each other—she's small where I'm big, she's soft where I'm hard.

I'm a fucking bastard for reacting to her nearness like this, but my cock doesn't seem to realize that it's not an opportune moment to make a rather hard appearance.

"Noelle," I taste her name on my lips, but this time it's not in anger. It's not in frustration, and it's not in resentment. No, this time, it's just her.

Sweet, brave Noelle.

Knowing everything that happened to her and looking back at our interactions, I can only feel a sense of pride filling me to the brim. From the beginning she stood her ground, meeting me on equal footing, giving as good as she got.

I don't know why Cisco is underestimating her so much when she's got a core of steel. And that makes me even more in awe of her.

"Thank you," she whispers as she draws back, her eyes red from crying.

"You don't have to thank me for anything," I attempt a smile as I let my fingers caress the sides of her arms.

There's a sudden shyness to her as she regards me, her chin tipped down as she barely finds the courage to meet my eyes.

I lean in, instinct and want threatening to overtake me.

Closing my eyes, I simply breathe her in—her scent, her presence, the very warm air she breathes.

"Raf," she says my name, that throaty voice of hers threatening to undo me.

I move closer, yet not close enough.

My lips ache to mate with hers.

Everything in me wants to reach and seize this moment—turn all my desires in reality.

But I can't. Not yet.

I don't deserve it yet.

Hovering over her lips, I mutter a low curse as I bring my lips higher, brushing them against her forehead.

"Are you feeling better now?" I ask her, my voice harsh. I barely trust myself with this proximity, especially as I'm fighting a raging erection from the contact of her skin alone.

"Yes," she nods. "The pills helped."

"Good. Good," I murmur. "Let's sleep then."

And before she can protest, before she can remind me that my place is not in her bed, I draw her in my arms, nestling her against me.

I'm sitting on top of the blanket. She's under.

The temptation is agonizing.

Yet for now I'll settle to have her near. To win her trust step by step and show her I'm not the bastard she's come to know. That she can trust me with her secrets and her pains.

But more than anything, that I can be worthy of her.

Because if she knew what I did...

CHAPTER FOUR
NOELLE

"Is that all you're wearing?" He frowns at me, his hands quickly working the buttons of his coat before he drapes it over my shoulders.

"I'm fine, Raf, really. You don't have to treat me like an invalid," I tell him, though the warmth of the coat is inviting as I snuggle deeper into it, his scent enveloping my body. As I take a deep breath, it's to feel him infiltrating every pore, every part of me. That dark yet sensual smell of his that speaks of whiskey and cigarettes, of forbidden nights and careless abandon…

"You just got out of the hospital. I'm not taking any chances with you."

"Maybe we should just go back to disliking each other," I grumble under my breath, but a blush climbing up my cheeks betrays my true feelings.

"No can do. That was before and this is now," he states as he leans back on the bench, his gaze towards the river.

No matter how many times he says something nice to me, I don't think I'm ever going to get over the shock of it. He's been nicer to me in the past few days than anyone's *ever* been to me.

But the history we share doesn't let me trust it. The fact that right before that he was promising to make my life a living hell, or kill me, doesn't make me particularly trusting of his motives.

More than anything, I'm afraid to buy into his kindness only to be left bleeding when I realize it's all a ruse.

"I don't understand you, Raf," I murmur softly, turning to him. "Why would you change your behavior towards me overnight? Just because you realized I suffered at Sergio's hands too? What about Lucero, then? You've been blaming me for her death from the beginning, so what changed?"

A grimace appears on his face.

"There has to be another explanation to Lucero's death and why the box of matches was in your hand. You could have very well picked it off the ground," he shrugs. "But as it stands, I don't believe you had anything to do with it."

"Just like that?" I frown.

How can he be so sure when even I am not? My mind is still a battlefield, few memories of my time there trustworthy. I *could* have killed her. In my heart, I know I *did* something. I just don't know what.

"I should have listened to you from the beginning," he takes a deep breath. "I... I needed someone to blame and you were there. I didn't consider you might have been a victim too. I didn't think of anything else but *my* revenge."

"What if I end up remembering and..."

"We'll deal with that when the time comes," he replies.

But that's not an answer.

What if I remember hurting her? What will happen then?

"Raf..."

"I spoke with your therapist," he suddenly changes the

topic, and I frown. "I wanted to check up with her before telling you something that might adversely impact you."

"What are you talking about?"

"She assured me that you are strong enough to bear it, and it might actually help you heal."

"Raf, what…"

"Noelle," he turns to me, taking my hands into his. "I've been thinking about this day and night, and I don't think it's fair to keep something like this from you. God knows…" he trails off, pursing his lips. "At least not this. Because it doesn't only affect your past, but also your present and your future," he takes a deep breath. "Do you know why you're suffering from such debilitating abdominal pain?"

His startling light eyes are on me as he awaits my answer, so I can only shake my head, confusion swimming in my head at his words.

"What I'm going to tell you…" his fingers brush across my cheek as his expression turns tender, "I want you to know I'm here for you."

"You're scaring me," I whisper.

"You have endometriosis," he starts, a grim look on his face as he explains what it is, and that it affects my reproductive system. "But what triggered it…"

I listen to him attentively, but a strange sound lingers in my ears as I realize what he's trying to tell me.

"A child. I had a child," I repeat numbly.

"He was premature," he notes, and I can make the connection. He died because he came too early.

Something snaps inside of me as I hear the rest of the information—that the birth had given me an infection that had spread, and as a result it is unlikely I'll ever have children.

Children…

I'd never given them much thought, mostly because of my age. But hearing that I might never have them?

What's worse is that I already had one that died.

Dead...

Sergio had taken a lot from me, but I never realized he would have taken that too.

"God," the ragged sound escapes my lips.

Suddenly, I feel strong arms wrapped around my body, holding me, comforting me.

My breathing soon turns into soft sobs as I mourn the life I'd never met—that was most likely wrenched from me.

"Shh," he whispers in my hair, and his arms are the only thing keeping me from going over the edge. His strength is there to hold me and keep me warm.

"Why did no one tell me?" I ask as hiccups rack my body. "Why..."

"Your brother didn't think you were strong enough to bear it," he explains, his hand cupping my head and holding me flush against his body. His embrace is so tight, he's not giving me any chance to escape—to hide and lose myself to the sorrow.

"Oh, Raf," I mumble, my thought a jumbled mess. "Why am I so unlucky? Why is everything bad happening to me?" I cry out, accumulated pain making its way to the surface. "How much more do I have to bear..."

"It's in the past," he says in a tight voice. "And from now on you won't have to worry about anything. I promise you. No one will hurt you again."

"You can't promise that..." I shake my head, but he just tightens his hold.

"I can and I will. Because they will have to pass through me to get to you. And I'm not letting go."

"What... What are you trying to say?" I sniffle, blinking rapidly as his words filter through my head.

"That I'm here now and that I will protect you."

His words make me reel, especially as he follows them with his lips, skimming the surface of my forehead. It's the tiniest of touches, but it lights something in my chest and though a hole's been burned inside of me at finding out about a child—my child—there's a levity in knowing he's by my side, that he has the power to fill up that emptiness.

"Why? Why would you do that?" I find the courage to ask, because I am terrified this is just a phase—that it's just his guilt speaking at finding out the truth about my time at the *hacienda*.

"Why do you think so?" He leans back, watching me intently with those baby *blue* eyes of his, and it's like something unlocks within me.

I don't know if this is what déjà-vu feels like, but there's something inside of me that ignites at the sight of those beautiful eyes. Something that becomes so full of warmth and an undefined feeling that I don't want to look closer into.

My mouth parts as I just stare at him. The intensity in his features should scare me—it should terrify me. But why is it that I've never been afraid in his presence? I've been beaten and abused by men, yet his proximity has never sparked even a little bit of fear.

In spite of his proclamations of revenge, or his words full of hate. In spite of his massive body that could easily do me harm.

Never once did I feel unsafe in his presence.

It's a conundrum that may never be solved—the way he can make me at ease even in a hostile environment.

"I don't know," I say hoarsely.

"I want you, Noelle. I want to care and provide for you."

His words sound foreign to my ears, so I can only gape at him, afraid I haven't heard him right.

"I want to protect you from the outside world and make sure you'll never, *never*, have to worry about anything."

My brows are pinched together as even more confusion erupts in my mind.

"But why... Why me..." the words are mere whispers, but I can't wrap my mind around why he would want *me*—someone so defective she doesn't even have her own autonomy.

"Why not you?" he fires back. "You're smart, brave, and incredibly, incredibly strong," he states, his voice full of admiration. "You're also a beautiful woman, so that doesn't hurt," he gives a low chuckle.

"But I..."

"No. You don't get to put yourself down by saying you're defective again. You don't get to put an inferior value to yourself just because some people said so," he states with staunch conviction.

"I admire you, Noelle. And I think there is something between us. Something worth pursuing," he swallows, and a hint of vulnerability peeks through. "If you want that, too."

I'm speechless. The words are stuck in my throat no matter how much I'd like to reply to him. All of the things that are against us flash through my mind, yet even knowing that, I can't find it in myself to deny him.

"I know you feel it too," he continues, taking my hand and turning it so my palm is facing up. "There's an electricity between us," he dips one finger to the center of my palm in a tiny caress. "Something that simmers every time we are next to each other."

I bring my teeth over my lower lip, biting it in uncertainty as I look at him. There doesn't seem to be any deceit behind his words.

But everything is too sudden—way too sudden.

Just a few days ago he was promising me that he would end me, and now he wants to pursue something?

"Raf," I start, my voice shaky with residual emotion. "I'm not good with men. I may have teased you," a smile appears on his face. "But that was the first time I'd done something like that—something so daring. Besides my marriage, I haven't been around other men save for those in my family. So I don't know how to react to this. I don't know how to read *this*..." I trail off.

A small frown appears on his face.

"What if this is another one of your games? Get me to lower my guard, fall for you and then deliver the last blow?"

"It's not like that. I swear..."

"No," I lift my finger to his lips. "You don't have to. It's in the nature of our relationship and the fact that I *am* wary of you."

"We'll take it slow. I'll wait for you," he says with so much conviction in his voice. And to stun me further, he brings both my hands to his lips, kissing my fingers before moving to the inside of my wrists, laying chaste kisses all over the tender skin.

I don't react—I *can't* react.

The touch is feather-like, but it's enough to trigger my soul-deep loneliness, and the fact that no one's touched me with such gentleness in a long time—maybe forever.

"I am aware of your trauma, and the fact that it might take time until you get more comfortable with me. But I'll wait. Just say yes," he breathes, the warm air brushing against my skin and making me tremble.

His gaze is arresting as he sets it on me, and a low tremor goes through my body.

I may not have been around many men, but even then I can recognize that the things he makes me feel are not ordinary.

For so long I've been stuck in the persona relegated by my family—the defective, crazy one. But with him, I don't feel like that, evidence being all the times I've behaved outside of my comfort zone with him.

I've shown him parts of myself that no one has seen until now, and *that* makes me question my own judgment.

Because things seem too good to be true. I'm already drawn to him like a moth to a flame—one step in the grave should he call me there. I recognize my attraction to him for what it is—my road towards perdition. It would be infinitely easy to fall for him—maybe a part of me has already done so. But can I trust that?

"Ok," I find myself answering. "We can try."

A radiant smile overtakes his features and his arms are around me again.

"You won't regret it, pretty girl. I promise you."

Half of me believes his words. But there's also the other half that knows I have just handed him an instruction manual on how to end me.

I may have had my body destroyed in the past, but I don't think the pain will compare to having my soul extinguished from my body.

And now, he's got the means to do that.

The following days we settle into a comfortable routine, and it surprises me to see that his attitude has done a one-eighty.

That doesn't mean his behavior doesn't baffle me, every kind gesture stunning me to the spot and leaving me unable to find a proper response.

Just the other day he brought me breakfast in bed, sneaking in a bar of my favorite chocolate and winking at me when I'd asked how he'd done that since for as long as I can remember our household has had a rule—no sweets before noon.

"It can be our little secret," he'd said sneakily, a genuine expression of satisfaction on his face. It had been hard not to return it, especially as I bit into the chocolate, the flavor erupting on my tongue and making me start associating it with him.

I scowl as I wipe the steamed up mirror of the bathroom.

This is exactly what he wants. Bribe me with small, sweet things and make me lower my guard so he can strike when I least expect it.

The logical side of me *knows* this. Yet there's another side of me that wants to ignore all the signs, simply bask in the moment while it lasts.

I've never had someone spoil me before. I've never had anyone pay attention to my likes and dislikes in such a thorough manner, surprising me at every turn and deriving pleasure from *my* pleasure.

It simply seems…impossible.

And so on the one hand, I know it's too good to be true. But on the other hand, I can't stop myself from enjoying every little thing he does for me.

Wasn't this what I'd wished for from the beginning? For him to show me *this* side of him—the carer, provider and protector.

I'd seen him for what he truly was, even though it wasn't with me, and I'd wished from the bottom of my heart it *could* be me. Yet now… It's happening and I don't know how to trust it.

I purse my lips as I stare at my reflection in the mirror, my freckles accentuated by the wan pallor of my face. Since my short stint in the hospital, I've been looking a little worse for the wear, the pain etched into my very features.

I look and look into the mirror and I wonder what *he* sees…

Does he still see me as the evil *doña*? Though he now

knows the truth, does that image of cruelty he's always had of me still seep into field of vision, making him hate me when he doesn't want to?

The questions are making my head pound.

How can everything be erased when he's hated me for so long? When he's thought of all the ways he could make me suffer—had already implemented some of them. Will our relationship be forever marred by that...I wonder.

From my side, I can't say I can forget everything. My entire being lights up in his presence, something about *him* making me forget myself and my past. Yet there's the dark room, always looming over our heads.

I'd known he was capable of great cruelty just as I'd known he was capable of the sweetest kindness—somehow, from the very beginning I'd known. Yet I'd never realized just how far he was willing to take things until the dark room.

Goosebumps spread over my skin as I remember the terror I'd faced at thinking my will would be taken from me, my body violated in the worst manner...

I squeeze my eyes shut, trying to thrust that unpleasant memory out of my mind.

Yet it's there, another wound on my already battered fabric of existence.

Then what about him? What about *his* memories of me—of the other me? Can he forget that, when his hatred has festered for years? When deep down, he must still hold me accountable for Lucero's death to some degree?

With a heavy sigh, I fasten my bathrobe around me, exiting the bathroom.

"You startled me," I give a small yelp when I come face to face with Raf.

He's sitting on the bed, his dark blazer in his hand, his white shirt popped open at the neck. He's watching me intently, his blue eyes sparkling even in the darkness of the room.

"I thought you were out," I try to fill the silence, my voice soft as I flick the light switch, the room coming to life.

"I just got back," he nods, getting up and folding his blazer on the back of a chair.

A little flustered, I hurry to my vanity, taking a seat and hoping he'll ignore me or go take a shower. Anything to have his searching gaze *off* me.

I'd only allowed myself a quick shower because he'd been out, somehow reluctant to give him an opening when I'd be at my most vulnerable—and most naked. A shudder goes down my spine at that thought. I hadn't done it for his benefit, since he's already seen my bare body before. No, I'd done it for myself. Because I know the moment I see desire flare in his eyes, the moment he invites me for something more than a wrist kiss, I'll lose the war.

With him, with myself. I'll lose *everything*.

At the end of the day, the startling truth is that I've wanted him all along. And with just a tiny touch, he'd realize *how* much…

"You're frowning," he notes, suddenly behind me.

I blink in confusion.

"Are you in pain? Do you need something?" He's quick to ask, his body primed for movement—ready to bring me anything I ask.

"No," I force a smile. "I'm feeling fine," I tell him.

And it is the truth. My period stopped the day before and the pain is mostly gone.

He doesn't move, though.

Behind me, I covertly watch him in the mirror as he regards me wistfully.

"You're staring," I point out, feeling myself unravel under his warm gaze.

"I turned the heat on," he takes a step closer, his hands hovering over my shoulders.

"You...did?"

"I heard the water running. I wanted you to find the room warm," a flash of a smile appears on his face.

Through the mirror, I follow his movements.

He's tentative, almost hesitant as he brings his big hands over my shoulders, lightly running them down the sides of my arms.

"Can I?" he inquires softly, and for a moment I have no clue what he's asking.

I tilt my head to the side in confusion.

"This," he continues, pulling on the towel that keeps my hair together. Immediately, my wet hair falls down my shoulders.

I don't understand what he's trying to do. In fact, I continue to sport a befuddled expression even as he takes away the wet towel, depositing it in the bathroom before returning and running his fingers through my locks.

"Your hair is so soft," he murmurs, and before I can speak, in protest or encouragement, he brings his palms on top of my scalp, slowly massaging my skin.

My eyes fall closed, my mouth opening on a soundless moan of pleasure.

"Relax," he whispers, slowly moving his fingers through my hair as he untangles every lock. And before I know it, he takes a brush from the table, threading it through my curls. He's slow, efficient—careful. There's not one flash of pain—of him pulling too tightly, or too fast. Even I would get frustrated with my mass of hair, and the fact that my light curls would often get tangled.

Not him.

He's so meticulous, I'm having a hard time thinking this is

a first for him. And as that thought surfaces, I can't stop myself from blurting it out.

"Have you done this before?"

"Huh?"

"Brushed someone's hair," I add, a blush climbing up my cheeks.

"My mother's, sometimes," he answers, and my heart does a somersault in my chest.

"You're good," I praise, lest he see the hidden glee at his answer.

"Is that so?" His lips curl up, the back of his hand making contact with my nape in a light caress. I barely hold off the shudder that wants to claim my body. Especially as I look into the mirror, my eyes finding his.

Without realizing, I wet my lips, my tongue peeking out for a brief moment. He emulates the movement, licking his lips as if he's had the most scrumptious meal.

It's warm in the room, but the heat traveling through my body has nothing to do with that.

It's all him...

He continues to tend to me in silence, every now and then audibly gulping down.

I try to ignore that, just as I try to ignore the way my treacherous heart reacts to his proximity.

"Done," he finally says, stepping away.

I take in my appearance, surprised to see not a wisp of hair out of place.

"Thank you, Raf." I give him a tentative smile.

"Any time, Noelle. *Any* time." His smile is sadder.

CHAPTER FIVE
NOELLE

"You look gorgeous, Noelle."

I turn to see Yuyu come into my room.

"Thank you," I murmur, studying my appearance in the mirror.

I'd donned on a black dress that thankfully covered all of my scars. My unblemished legs are emphasized by the cut and length of the dress, and that makes me slightly more comfortable.

"Do I really have to come too?" I ask on a breathless sigh.

For weeks now I'd heard about the ball that Cisco has been organizing, all in an effort to bridge the gap with the other crime families of New York and reinstate DeVille to its former glory. After all, my marriage with Raf had been part of that plan.

My brother has spared no expense in trying to make the event as ostentatious as possible—no doubt trying to dazzle his way into the inner circles.

His plan is simple. Pave the way for closer relations between DeVille and the other big players in the city, all the while undermining Raf's brother's power and making a show of a united front with Raf as his brother-in-law.

But that also means that everyone invited is a criminal. And *that* scares me.

"You know you must be seen." She explains gently, placing a hand on my shoulder. "People need to see the physical evidence of a DeVille-Guerra union."

"I wish I didn't have to..."

"I know, sweetheart, I know. But this will be the biggest event in decades. You know our family has always been isolated from the rest. To have DeVille back at the negotiation table is monumental."

"How do you do it, Yuyu? How can you stand all of this?"

Being Cisco's wife, she has even more responsibilities than me. And I've never seen her as anything but cordial—always with a smile on her face.

"It takes practice," she gives me a tight smile. "You may not be aware because you were too young. But it wasn't easy for people to accept me as your brother's wife. I had to hear their backhanded comments for years. I still do. In the beginning it got to me—it would have gotten to anyone. But at the end of the day, does their opinion really matter? I have your brother and that is enough for me."

I look at her for a second, unable to believe that someone as nice and gentle as Yuyu would willingly marry my brother. He might not be bad looking, but he is *many* bad things. And I know Yuyu is aware of every single fucked up thing he's ever done, yet she's never left his side. She's supported him through thick and thin, and that makes me *really* wonder about the nature of the relationship. After all, I don't think many people would be able to put up with Cisco.

"I'll do my best," I force a smile.

"Good. Because you also have Raf, and I see the way you two look at each other."

"What do you mean?" I frown.

"Oh, come on. He's always looking at you as if he couldn't wait to get you alone and," she pauses, a mischievous look on her face, "have his wicked way with you."

"Yuyu," I exclaim, scandalized.

"It's true. I knew from the beginning there was something between the two of you. He could never take his eyes off you. It's why I told Cisco to monitor your relationship closely, and if the opportunity arose, to approve of it."

"You?" I ask, surprised. But then I shouldn't be since Yuyu is the only person my brother listens to.

"Sometimes, two people are just made for each other." She comes in front of me to arrange the small bow at the top of my bodice. "And when you find that person, you hold on tightly."

"Is that what happened with you and my brother?"

"Yup," she nods, a genuine smile on her face. "I wouldn't be here without your brother. And he wouldn't either," she says cryptically before walking away, giving me a wink as she tells me she'll meet me downstairs.

I spend a few more minutes in the mirror, giving myself a pep talk and trying to will the fear away.

After all, I'll have Raf.

And considering how he's been with me for the last few days...

I shake myself, not wanting to go there.

But in spite of my reservations, he's slowly charming his way into my life.

He's nothing short of a gentleman. He opens my door, he pulls my chair for me at the dinner table. He does every-thing short of feeding me himself—which, granted, would be a little weird. At night he burrows his way into my bed, citing that he's looking out for my health as the main reason.

But I've also seen the small efforts he puts in making sure I'm never uncomfortable.

Since the first night, he hasn't gone to bed shirtless again, making sure he's fully dressed before climbing next to me. He always asks me if I'm comfortable, and has even taken it upon himself to taste my water to make sure the temperature is just right.

Why, he even offers me a massage before bed *every single night*.

His behavior is nothing short of astounding. But I have to admit it also makes me feel warm and fuzzy inside, his regard not going unnoticed or unappreciated.

He's been by my side this whole time, offering to talk about my baby and how finding out about it made me feel. But considering my memory is one giant black hole... I'm not exactly sure how to feel. Still, his support has helped me tremendously in coming to terms with yet another thing that Sergio had stolen from me.

The only thing that surprised me—and I've yet to figure out if positively or negatively—is that he hasn't tried to make a move on me.

Not even one.

He kisses my forehead every night before sleep and he gives me a peck on the cheek every now and then. But he hasn't tried to take it further.

For all his talk of wanting me, he's barely touched me.

Even when we sleep, he always lays on top of the blankets, as if he can't stand for our skin to touch.

Before, I knew he was attracted to me sexually, proof being his visible arousal when we'd be next to each other. Now, though? There's a nagging feeling that he may feel disgusted by what he saw—by the scars on my body. He may feel more protective over me now, but I fear that may have extinguished any desire he had for me.

And that...

I shake myself, focusing on the task at hand and adding the finishing touches to my make-up.

When I'm done, I head downstairs.

He's at the bottom of the stairs, engaged in a heated discussion with my brother. But as he hears me come down, he whips his head around, his eyes going wide with wonder.

The intensity of his stare makes my body erupt in goose-bumps, and a slight blush appears on my cheeks.

Yuyu was right. He does look at me as if he'd like nothing more than whisk me away and have his wicked way with me. And that gives me some hope.

His mouth parts slightly, small beads of sweat appearing on his forehead.

He tugs at his cravat ever so slightly before taking a step forward, offering me his hand. The moment my skin touches his, though, it's like a bolt of electricity goes through my body, starting from the tips of my fingers and ending right into my core.

Heat travels down my neck and I'm aware of my color changing, embarrassment visible from the neck up. Yet he doesn't seem *as* affected. His eyes are fixed on me, his irises a clear blue that seems to shine with intensity.

"You look ravishing," he purrs, his deep voice increasing the voltage in my already electrified body.

And when he takes it a step further, bringing my knuckles to his mouth for a brief kiss, I'm pretty sure an audible sigh escapes me.

"Shall we?" He asks, tugging my hand in the crook of his shoulder.

I nod, giving him a shy smile as he leads me to our car.

Cisco organized the ball at one of our estates upstate— one of those old Georgian manors with a ballroom to occupy the entire ground floor.

In fact, the house itself had been converted as an events-only space. A place where all the raunchy crime talk takes place, no doubt.

Everyone is embarked in a car, and after a lengthy journey, we pull up the road of the house.

"Nervous?" Raf asks me as he helps me out of the car.

"A little," I admit truthfully. "I don't know anyone here."

"Don't worry about it. Stay by my side and everything will be fine."

He lays a kiss on my temple.

"Ok," I nod, clutching on to his arm as we make our grand entrance.

Being my first time at such a grand event, I have to admit I'm not entirely confident of myself. And that confidence seems to wilt the moment I see the other guests.

My eyes are arrested by the sight of beautiful women walking in even more stunning gowns, as well as the dashing gentlemen that are by their side.

"These are all criminals?" I ask in awe, and Raf gives me a nonverbal grunt. "Why is everyone so beautiful?"

Turning to him, I frown when I see his cloudy expression, and the fact that he's watching me with a semi-scowl on his face.

"Is everything alright?" I ask tentatively, afraid I'd said something wrong.

For a moment he doesn't answer as we reach the middle of the dance floor.

But one moment we're heading towards a group of people, the next he has me backed into a corner, his finger on my jaw as he tips it up to get me to look at him.

"I'm not a violent man, Noelle," he starts in a harsh voice —harsher than I've heard coming from him. "But I find that you instill that feeling in me."

"Wh-what? What are you talking about?" I ask in a shaky

voice. Already I'm afraid I've committed a faux pas when it hadn't been my intention to do so. But seeing as my experience in high society is limited at best…

"You don't get to call other men beautiful in my presence and expect me *not* to react," he says, and I blink in confusion.

The color of his eyes shifts, a stormy blue overtaking the previous peaceful one. There's tension in his jaw as he grits his teeth, and I realize he *is* serious.

"I didn't mean…"

"Listen here, and listen carefully." His voice drops an octave and chills spread down my spine. "You're my wife, my woman, *mine.* That means you don't look at other men. You don't acknowledge other men. And you certainly *don't* call other men beautiful. Is that clear?"

"Uhm…" He doesn't let me speak as he continues.

"Now retract your words," he orders, his tone serious.

"What?" My mouth opens in a scandalized o.

"Retract your words, or we'll be here all night." He taps his foot against the floor, his body caging mine like an unrelenting fortress.

"They aren't beautiful?" I'm not sure what he wants to hear from me, especially as he raises a brow at my words, clearly *not* pacified.

"Good," he says in a gruff voice, his breath fanning over my cheek. "Now say it like you mean it."

"I'm sure the others are waiting for us," I try to de-escalate. "They're probably wondering if anything is wrong…"

"The words, Noelle," he states in an impatient tone, and I realize that my best bet is to comply.

"I was wrong in saying the people here are beautiful," I start. "I don't find any of them attractive," I add for good measure.

"Good girl," he purrs like a feline who just had his belly

stroked. "You'll learn that I'm a very fair man until it comes to *this*."

I nod enthusiastically, and a smile pulls at his lips.

"I guess we better mingle with the others," he finally suggests in a cheerful tone, so unlike the one he'd used before. "Keep being a good girl and you may earn a reward," he whispers right before the tip of his finger comes down on my nose in a teasing caress.

CHAPTER SIX
NOELLE

With a mischievous wink, he's off me, my hand once more in the crook of his arm as he leads me towards the crowd.

I expel a harsh breath, realizing I just passed a test.

And as I sneak a glance at his profile—at that jawline that seems to have been chiseled in ice—it's to admit to myself that while the people in this room *are* beautiful, there's no one quite like him.

No one who turns my insides into mush.

Cisco and Yuyu are already deep in conversation with some unknown people, and just as we reach a more populated area, the live orchestra my brother had hired starts playing what I recognize to be Tchaikovsky's fifth symphony.

"Raf? Is that you?" A sweet voice calls, and as we turn around, it's to come face to face with a couple. Black hair, pale face, and startling green eyes, hers is the type of beauty that would have *anyone* staring. The man next to her gives Raf a tight smile, his expression reserved. Still, with his stature and tanned looks he's not any less attractive than the woman next to him.

My hand instinctively tightens over Raf's at the familiarity I detect in the woman's voice, a flare of jealousy spiking inside of me

"God, I haven't seen you in so long." Her eyes widen as she peruses him. "And look at how you've changed."

A tight smile appears on Raf's face.

"Catalina," he nods his head at the woman, "Marcello," he greets her companion. "This is my wife, Noelle," he makes the introduction, and my discomfort is momentarily appeased.

"Pleased to meet you," I respond as I extend my hand for a shake.

"Wife? You're married," Catalina blinks in surprise.

"Yes. It's a rather recent development."

"My, but I'm so happy for you. After what happened with Sisi," she purses her lips, and alarms go off in my head as I hear another woman's name. "And then your disappearance. I was worried about you.

"As you can see, I'm doing fine." He nods before proceeding to discuss some business arrangements with Marcello.

"I never realized Michele could be so cunning," Marcello states.

"No one did. He made sure he was seen as the prodigal son. And because of that, look what happened," Raf adds in a strained tone. "But not for long. Cisco and I are working on it."

"If you need any help," Marcello pauses, patting him on the back, "you need only to ask. You know we see you as family," he mentions stoically.

"Thank you."

I keep to Raf's side as we go from person to person, all indicating their astonishment at his appearance.

It's only when we get a brief reprise that he explains why everyone would be so shocked.

"I used to play a role before. What they saw...was what I wanted them to see," he states going in depth about how he'd portrayed himself as mentally weak so that people would overlook him.

I listen intently to his words, lifting my eyes to meet his.

"Does that mean you're playing a role now?" I ask on a whisper, afraid of the potential answer.

"Does it?" A wolfish grin appears on his face. "Maybe," he chuckles. "We're all playing a role, aren't we? Sometimes, behind a lie you'll find the truth. Oscar Wilde once said *give a man a mask and he'll tell you exactly who he is*," he muses wistfully.

I narrow my eyes at him.

"Then who are *you*, Rafaelo Guerra? Who are you, really?" The question tumbles out of my mouth before I can help myself. He's shown me so many different facets of himself— vicious cruelty and the sweetest compassion. Yet there's so much more to him than meets the eye, so much more he's keeping locked tight within himself.

"A man. I'm just a man, pretty girl." His words hold a certain sadness to them. "A flesh and blood man with wants and desires." He takes my hand, placing it on his chest, right over his heart. "A man with happiness and sorrows, grudges and regrets..." he trails off. "I'm just a man—just an imperfect man."

His eyes bore into mine, the electricity of his stare making the hairs on my body stand up.

"It's just as well that I'm not perfect myself." The corners of my lips tug up. What I don't say, though, is what he'd find behind *my* mask. That is a Pandora box I never want opened. If I'm stuck in this role forever, then so be it—anything but the alternative.

He gives me one of his dazzling smiles and heading to a

refreshment table, he offers me a small glass of champagne. Since he's driving, he can't drink any.

"I heard you have a penchant for alcohol," he adds mischievously.

"Another thing my brother told you, of course," I roll my eyes at him. "It happened once. I only had a few glasses, but I didn't realize my tolerance was so low," I shrug.

"You're a tiny little thing, Noelle," his eyes rake over my body with pleasure, "of course you wouldn't have a great tolerance."

"Are you calling me weak?" I raise a brow.

"No, I'm calling you dainty." He says as he steps closer, one hand in my hair as he twirls a strand of my hair around. "And I happen to like dainty," he whispers in my ear in a smoky voice.

Just as the words are out of his mouth, he's off me, straightening his back and looking entirely unbothered. As if he didn't just cause my heart to jump in my chest, or make me feel hot and tingly...

There's a knowing smirk on his lips, and as I narrow my eyes at him I realize that was his purpose all along. He likes to toy with me knowing that I am attracted to him.

As I'm about to call him out on it, another voice resounds in the room.

"Raf!" Someone calls out, and before I know it, a woman jumps on Raf, her arms around his neck as she gives him a big hug. "I can't believe it's you. Good Lord, but haven't you heard of phones? I've been worried sick about you," she chastises him.

It's only when she leans a little back that I get a glimpse of her features.

She's...stunning.

Light blonde hair paired with a tanned complexion, she

also has the lightest brown irises I've ever seen. A pink-reddish mark on her forehead only serves to complement the rest of her features. Her eyes are slanted, giving her a cat-like look that is enhanced by her heart-shaped face and chiseled jaw.

My hands ball into fists at the display, especially as I note the hidden intimacy between them.

"Sisi, wow," Raf says, looking at her with affection in his eyes.

Sisi. That name...

"I'm sorry about that. But maybe we can catch up soon?" He asks on a hopeful tone.

Already, my mind is going into overdrive trying to decipher their interaction and what they are to each other. More so since I'm promptly forgotten as he directs his entire attention towards her.

Who is she? And what is she to him?

But one moment she's in his arms, the next she's in the air as another man shows up, easily lifting her up and depositing her in *his* arms.

"I believe five seconds of skinship is more than enough, hell girl. I'm going to cash in on that later," he says cryptically as he looks down at her.

"You're such a spoilsport," she mumbles, looking put out with him one moment before a wide smile overtakes her face as she puckers her lips to give him a loud smooch. "But that's why I love you."

In the ballroom.

In front of everyone.

But they don't seem to care. Especially since she seems right at home in his arms and doesn't seem inclined to step down. In fact, she wounds her arms around his neck, making herself even more comfortable.

"You must be Vlad," Raf mentions, extending his hand.

"And you must be Jesus Christ because he's the only one who wouldn't stay dead," Vlad states deadpan.

"Vlad!" Sisi exclaims, quite scandalized.

"What?" His brows lift up in feigned innocence. "Although three days was three years for you." His mouth curls up as he turns to Sisi. "See, they don't make them quite like before. It must be the food."

"Vlad. Cut it out," she gives him a look before turning to us. "Don't listen to him. We're really happy you're back."

"And you're not missing a leg? An arm?" Vlad says as he surveys Raf. "Pity," he shrugs.

"I've heard all about you," Raf comments, not mad at all about Vlad's comment. "Sisi's told me all about you."

"Good things I should hope. Right, hell girl? You wouldn't bad mouth me, would you?"

"Of course it wasn't good things, you dolt. You left me," she pokes him in the shoulder. "And I was sad," she sighs.

"And obviously not in your right mind since you got engaged to him," Vlad pouts as he motions towards Raf.

"I thought we moved past that, Vlad. I'm married to you in case you've forgotten," Sisi shakes her head at him.

Engaged? They were engaged?

I stop listening as I try to digest the words. There's more sparring between Vlad and Sisi before he whisks her away, with Sisi saying something about *reeducation,* whatever that means.

But I barely register that. Not when I just found out that he's been engaged before. *And* he didn't even introduce me to them.

My eyes widen at that particular realization.

Hell... Is he... Did he have feelings for her? He must have at some point if he was engaged with her. Does he still?

My heart stills in my chest at that thought and no matter how much I try to ground myself, I can't.

Isn't it enough that I have to compete with a ghost? Now there's another living, breathing, *stunning* woman I have to measure myself up against?

How is that fair?

The more I ruminate about it, the more I realize that *nothing* is fair. I should have realized that someone like Raf would have his choice of women. Someone with his looks and personality would have a myriad of exes. Just because I only knew about Lucero doesn't mean she was the only one.

And that means...

My head whips up as I take him in. Impressive height. Outstanding looks. Quick wit and tenacity that are only complemented by his remarkable strength. There's simply nothing average about him.

He's currently engaged in conversation with another couple, cracking jokes about the current political climate and discussing business strategies.

That's when I see it.

He's everything I'm not.

Likable. Sociable. *Outgoing.*

He attracts people's attention wherever he goes. Tonight is proof enough as everyone is drawn to him like a magnet.

And then there's me.

Crazy. Unstable. *Defective...*

Suddenly, all the dreams and scenarios I'd cooked up in my head return with tremendous force and hit me right in the chest as everything turns to disappointment.

Why did I let myself believe I had a chance with him? That he might like me? Why, when from the beginning our marriage has been nothing but a business venture and an opportunity for him to take revenge for something he thought I'd done.

Remove either from the equation and...there's nothing left.

I down my glass of champagne before setting it down, quickly moving to another. And another. It's only when I finish the third one that the bubbles have finally gone to my head, a levity unlike any other making its home in my mind.

The orchestra starts playing a waltz, and I turn my gaze to the middle of the ballroom where some couples have already taken the floor, swirling around to the music.

I, too, tap my foot to the rhythm, and once more my mind betrays me as I imagine what it would be like for Raf to swoop me in his arms, move with me to the sound of the music...

A disappointed sigh escapes me as I continue to watch the dance dejectedly.

"A dance?" A stranger's voice filters through my mind, and gazing to the left, it's to see an unknown man extending his hand towards me in a polite gesture.

I still, not knowing what to do.

I'd like nothing more than to dance, too, but I don't know if it's the proper etiquette to accept the invitation of someone I haven't been introduced to.

Turning to ask Raf for permission, it's to see he's not even by my side anymore. A few feet away, he's once more talking with Sisi and her husband, their expressions serious as they seem to debate something important.

I don't know if it's the fact that he's talking with her specifically that has me take the man's hand. I don't know if it's the fact that he so clearly forgot about me. Or *maybe*, it's the fact that he purposefully wanted to forget about me.

I only know that I shouldn't have trusted him in the first place.

"Thank you," I give the man a tight smile as I allow him to draw me closer, his arm on my back as he leads me into the waltz.

"What's your name?" He asks me, and as I gaze up, I study his features for the first time.

Black hair and blue eyes, he's not bad looking.

But it's not one particular pair of blue eyes that's looking back at me. And that makes my heart tug painfully in my chest.

I will myself to enjoy the music and the dance, but I find that it's a paltry imitation for the dance that I *do* want.

Just as I'm about to reply to his question, though, another voice speaks for me.

"Her name is move before I blow your brains."

CHAPTER SEVEN
NOELLE

I watch in horror as the other man scurries away, Raf's cold expression sending a frisson down my back.

"What did I tell you, Noelle?" he asks in a low voice. He's not yelling or raising his voice, but the effect is more potent.

One arm snakes around my waist as he brings me flush against his body.

The music is in full swing and very few people seem to take note of his sudden intrusion.

I make to get out of his hold, but he only tightens his grasp on me, every inch of my body in contact with his.

"No, no," he whispers against my hair. "You don't get to leave. Not when you wanted a dance so badly you'd let someone else put his fucking hands on you."

"*You* don't get to complain when you abandoned me," I hiss at him. "Right in the middle of the ballroom. In fact, why don't you go back to your former fiancée. I'm sure you have a *lot* to catch up on."

"Jealous?" He smirks at me. "Sheathe your claws, my dear wife. Sisi is married, and you just met her husband."

"Right," I scoff. "Is that supposed to comfort me considering you *ignored* me and left me behind to talk to them."

"You're being unreasonable."

"Me? *I am* being unreasonable? You just threatened to shoot someone..."

"And I'll do it. I wasn't kidding. You instill a thirst for violence in me unlike any I've ever known, Noelle," he says in a serious tone. "You make me want to raze down this place just so no one can look at you..." he trails off as his eyes peruse my body, "desire you... The thought of someone stripping you down with their eyes maddens me, *enrages* me," he says as his arm draws me even closer to him.

"Stop it," I whisper.

"Why?" His breath is on my lips as he forces me to look him in the eyes, the embrace of the dance an intimate prelude to something obscene. There are no other words for it as the contours of my body are molded to his, his erection not going unnoticed as he pushes it into my belly. "It's the truth," he purrs at me. "No one but me can see you naked. No one but me can touch you. And sure as fuck no one but me can fuck you. Is that clear?" His tone takes a harsher note as he spits the last words.

I stare at him speechless.

"You're insane," I shake my head at him. "How about this then, golden boy? Have *you* earned the right to fuck me?" I ask as I look into his eyes unflinchingly.

If he thinks to intimidate me with his intensity, then he'll have a surprise on his hands. Because I know that if I let him walk all over me now, it's going to set the tone for our entire marriage.

He narrows his eyes at me.

"I'm your husband."

"In name only," I roll my eyes at him. "And it's not like I married you because I wanted to."

"Aw, Noelle, is this when you tell me you *don't* want me? That you're not dying to have *my* hands on you? I know you're probably dripping right now thinking about my cock pressed into you...sliding into you," his voice is a hypnotizing sound as I find myself lost in his eyes, lulled into a sense of urgency as heat spreads all over my body.

"Shut up," I whisper, mustering all the strength I can to put some mental distance between us.

"You can lie to yourself all you want." The corner of his mouth tugs up in arrogance. "But the truth is that you want me. No matter how much you may hate that."

His words are accompanied by the light caress of his fingertips over my shoulder, that touch leaving a blazing trail in its wake.

"It's purely physical," I thrust his hand aside, struggling to remove the fog that's seeking to cloud my mind. "Isn't that what you said?" I smile when I see him frown. "You're a handsome man," I shrug, "but so are a lot of other people around here. Why, Sisi's husband was quite dashing. There was also the man I was dancing with..."

"Noelle," he grits my name in a strained voice.

"What?" I lift a brow. "Are you going to ask me if I get wet for them too?" I ask brazenly, a need to rile him up and establish some boundaries foremost in my mind.

"Careful, *wife*. You're going too far."

"Am I? It's just a physical reaction after all," I give a low chuckle, his expression telling me he's one moment away from exploding.

Ah, but isn't he just giving me all the ammunition I need to get to him? Who knew that golden boy could be so insanely jealous?

"Newsflash, Raf," I continue in a staunch tone. Jabbing my finger at his chest, I look him straight in the eyes. "Being my husband doesn't give you *any* rights to my person. You're being too outrageous right now. First, you order me to lie about finding the rest of the people here attractive just to appease some primitive male ego thing you have going on, and now you prohibit me from talking to anyone because you might shoot them?"

"Lie," he repeats, his tone dead. "Lie?" he asks again, but this time he forgoes any waltz etiquette as he brings his hand to my nape, bringing me closer to his face and holding me there. Staring down at me, I can see the flare of his nostrils and that twitch in his jaw I've come to associate with his barely in control state. "You lied," he gives a dry laugh. "Do tell then. Who else do you find attractive?" he demands in an ominous tone.

"Why, so you can shoot them?" I snicker.

"Careful, little one, you're treading on thin ice," he mutters, his voice ice cold as I realize he's getting increasingly pissed.

"What? Next you're going to hit me, too?" I shoot back unconsciously.

My eyes widen when I realize my words, but it's nothing compared to how Raf's entire countenance changes, shock written all over his face.

"I would never hit a woman, Noelle," he states bitterly. "I would *never* lay a hand on a woman, so don't go comparing me with Sergio."

"Right. Then what is it exactly that you're doing here? Because from where I'm standing it's not *that* different. All of you want to control me. Tell me how to dress, how to act, and who to talk to. How is that any different, Raf? How?" I ask in an exasperated tone.

I'm sick of being locked in a cage. I'm sick of having my every move scrutinized. I'm sick of always messing up and being branded an embarrassment. And most of all, I'm sick of letting it all happen.

"See, that's where you're wrong. I'm not trying to control you," he drawls, his pupils growing bigger right under my eyes. "I'm telling you who you belong to," he says right as he nuzzles his face in the crook of my shoulder.

"What? What are you doing?" I startle as I feel his skin on mine, his mouth a soft caress that makes me weak in the knees.

"This," he whispers before his lips close over the sensitive skin just below my ear, sucking it in his mouth.

My eyes widen in shock as I realize what he's doing.

"You're being indecent," I half-heartedly chastise him, the heat of his mouth on my skin doing things to me—wicked, wicked things that leave me trembling with pent-up longing.

"Am I?" He smiles against my skin. "I think I'm not being indecent enough," he states in a confident tone right before I feel his teeth bite down on my flesh.

I jerk in his arms, but it's not due to the pain. It's because his hand has already wandered lower, cupping my ass as he sucks on my neck like he's out for blood.

Maybe he is…

The realization is startling as he finally comes up for air, the barest hint of blood on his lips as he beams at me in satisfaction.

"And this," he rasps in that suave voice of his, "is how *everyone* knows who you belong to now."

His tongue sneaks out to lick the drops of blood, but I'm too stunned to react.

I'm barely aware of myself and the fact that everyone is staring at us now, some couples even stopping mid-dance to frown at the display.

Bringing my hand to my neck, I feel for the hickey he left behind, my fingers coming up stained with red.

I raise my head and my eyes meet his.

"You're a bastard," I tell him squarely.

"Oh, contrary to common belief, my parents *were* married when they had me," his lips draw up in an infuriating smirk.

I clench my hands by my side, tears of frustration burning behind my eyes.

Here he is, the man who promised he'd do better—treat me better, the same one who abandoned me in favor of strangers not too long after. And now, the one who humiliated me at my first social event. All in an attempt to lay his *claim* on me like I were some sort of object to be possessed.

"Gee, I'm surprised you didn't pee on me," I mutter drily, masking my growing ire, "since you're so keen on marking your territory."

"Hmm," he intones, his tongue doing weird acrobatics on his lip and thoroughly distracting my attention, "I think that can be arranged." A slow smile spreads on his face. "But it would be something completely different I'd mark you with," he winks at me.

"What are you talking about?" I frown as I realize he's turned the tables on me somehow.

"Wouldn't you want to know?" he pauses, assessing me intently before coming closer and tipping my jaw up. Then, lowering his mouth to my ear, he whispers the most obscene things I've heard in my life.

"I'll fuck you so hard, Noelle, I'll erase all thoughts of other men from your mind." He pulls me closer, the contact bringing his hardness into me. "I'll fill your sweet little pussy so full of my cum you'll overflow with it. And you'll take it like the bad, bad girl that you are—*my* bad girl. I'll watch the pretty pink of that gorgeous pussy of yours stained with the white of my seed and I don't think I would ever tire of the sight. Because I'll know that you're mine. *Only* mine. Fucked, marked and fucked again."

My sudden intake of breath makes him pause, amusement in his voice as he continues.

"But it wouldn't be enough. Oh, no. It would never be enough. I'd paint your entire body with my cum so *everyone* knows you're mine and mine alone. That you take my cock and no one else's. How does that sound?" His hot breath on my skin threatens to be my undoing. "But that wouldn't be enough either, would it?" He muses, his tongue sneaking out to lick my earlobe. "I'll make you choke on my cock so hard, you'll never be able to utter another man's name."

"Wh—what..." the words tumble out of my mouth in shock.

"That's right. You *should* be scandalized, Noelle. Because the things I want to do to you—the things I *will* do to you..." he trails off, and I feel him smirk against my skin. "They will leave you breathless, wordless, but so thoroughly fucked you won't ever think to argue with me again. You'll never question who you belong to, and when my cum covers every fucking inch of your body, no one else will either." He pauses. "You make a savage out of me, pretty girl. And a savage I will act."

To my great surprise, his words don't anger me, they don't leave me afraid. They only leave me...wanting. A rush of heat travels between my legs and I clench my thighs together to find some relief.

He sees it too because he has a smug look on his face, those clear blue eyes sparkling with mischief as he realizes he has me exactly where he wanted me—in the palm of his hand.

"Ah," he cups my jaw, his thumb swiping over my lips. "That expression right there is making me want to take you against the nearest wall," he murmurs as he parts my lips.

The music is playing in my ear, but I can't hear it. I can only hear and see *him*. Him, with his scandalous words and smoldering eyes. My attention is wholly focused on him.

And as he stares down at me, his irises swirling in a kaleidoscope of blue—every emotion reflected in his eyes—I feel myself falling into him.

Like a black hole, he swallows me whole, every corner of my being touched by his.

How is it possible to want someone so much yet *not* at the same time? Because I do want him.

Sometimes I want him more than my next breath.

But I also know that he isn't right for me. If I allow myself to be caught in his web, I won't escape with my life intact.

"You're taking this too far, Raf," I manage to string some words together.

"Oh, trust me, I'm *not* taking this far enough," he gives a dry laugh. "Do you know how torturous it is to sleep beside you but not touch you?"

"Who asked you to sleep besides me," I mumble, though heat travels to my cheeks at his admission.

And here I was wondering if he didn't desire me anymore...

"That's my place as your husband. In your bed. By your side. Between your legs..."

My eyes widen at him only to see him smile in satisfaction. He wants to rile me up, see me turn the deepest shade of red so he can assuage his strange male pride.

"Are you making fun of me now?" I ask in a serious tone. "Is that what it is? You know I'm not experienced with this. Are you trying to make me blush on purpose? Get me out of my comfort zone?"

He blinks at my accusation before his face hardens.

"Yes. I want to make you blush, and I want to take you out of your comfort zone. But I'm not trying to make fun of you, Noelle. Never that," his voice softens. "This innocence that clings to you drives me insane," he rasps. "You make me want to take care of you and surround you in a protective cocoon, but you also make me want to take you over my knee for your impudent tongue."

My eyes flash at him, the memory of his palm on my ass still fresh in my mind. And though I'd never admit it, I liked it. Oh, I liked it far more than I should have. And *that* is the problem. Because how can someone with my history derive pleasure from it? As if reading my thoughts, he continues.

"But don't worry. I wouldn't hurt you. I would *never* hurt you. I'd spank your little ass and you'd moan in pleasure, asking me for more..."

My lips part of their own accord, my breath coming in short spurts. It's enough for him to take advantage and push his thumb in, making me suck on it.

His pupils grow larger—if that's even possible—as he stares at my mouth.

"Everyone thinks you're weak," he comments, shaking his head in amusement. "You're anything but, Noelle. You might be innocent but you're certainly *not* weak. And that's exactly what I admire about you. You're strong despite everything you've been through, and I know you'd be able to take my intensity."

"Raf," I whimper as he draws me to his chest, the waltz seemingly continuing as the attention is diverted from us.

He twirls me on the dance floor, and when my body collides with his, the tightness of his embrace makes me light headed.

"Fuck... You make me feel so out of control," he states, almost mad at himself. "So fucking out of control that I feel like I'm going crazy."

"I feel that too," I whisper, our eyes glued to one another. "But you're also driving me crazy with your hot and cold attitude. I don't know where I stand with you, Raf. I never do. One moment you're nice to me, the next you're back to being an asshole. I can't read you," I tell him, exasperated.

"Hell, Noelle..." He releases an anguished sound as he brings my face close to his, our foreheads touching. The dance etiquette is all but forgotten as we give in to the moment, shaping the waltz with movements of our own.

"It's not my intention to confuse you. But fuck if *I* know what's happening half the time. I've never felt like this...this powerless and this fucking angry for no reason at all."

"Angry?" I blink.

"That you could be gone. That one moment you'd be here and the next you wouldn't. That you'll tell me to go fuck myself for once and for all and I won't be able to do anything to stop you from leaving. That...someone else might come along."

Confused is an understatement to what I'm feeling the moment I hear his words. And for the first time, I feel like I get a peek into the *real* Raf. The not so strong, the vulnerable, the *human* Raf.

And it's like manna for my hopeful heart.

If he's feeling like that, then he can't be indifferent to me.

"Who is Sisi to you?" I muster the courage to ask, needing to hear the confirmation from his own lips. I don't want to be second best to anyone, or even worse, third best. I need to know if there is room for me in his heart—and I won't settle for anything less than *everything*.

CHAPTER EIGHT
NOELLE

"What..." his words are drowned out by a sudden commotion.

We move towards the source of the sound. Cisco takes the stage, a microphone in his hand as he draws everyone's attention. Yuyu is by his side, their hands linked as he addresses the crowd.

"Thank you everyone who decided to attend tonight's event, and trust us not to shoot first and ask questions later," he starts in an amused tone, getting the crowd relaxed.

Raf's hand engulfs mine as he places me slightly behind his body in a protective stance.

His attention is riveted on the stage, and I have to wonder what he was going to say...

"By now you should all be aware of the purpose of this meeting and I've likely met in person with most of those present here."

There are nods all around.

"I want to propose a toast for the union of DeVille and Guerra." He raises a glass towards us. "But most of all I want to take this moment to make our comeback official. DeVille is back. And it's here to stay."

More cheering as the crowd approves.

"And I know we all have a common enemy—Michele Guerra."

"We know that at least half of those present here today have had some type of run-ins with Michele. All unpleasant, I'm sure," Yuyu interjects.

"Indeed," Cisco nods at his wife. "As most of you are aware, he has taken power by force, when in fact it shouldn't even belong to him. Isn't that so, Raf?" Cisco asks, motioning Raf to come towards him.

My hand still in his, he leads us towards the stage as he takes the microphone. I try to make myself as small as possible, the attention overwhelming.

"For those who don't know me, I'm Rafaelo Guerra," Raf starts, and immediately, questions are directed towards him.

Why shouldn't Michele be the head of the family? He's first born.

It's the order of our world. The first son always inherits the power.

Is this for real? What is he trying to achieve?

Raf doesn't seem perturbed by the whispers going around. Instead, he merely gives them a bored look as he continues.

"You are right. As tradition dictates, the first born son has always been the designated heir. Some of you, however, should be familiar with my father's wishes that I be the next in line for the leadership position."

Shushed voices comment on his statement, some criticizing Raf's father, while others saying we should honor his wishes.

Raf merely holds up his hand, and immediately everyone is quiet.

"I understand your concerns. Which is why I've decided to make public a piece of information that my father never wanted revealed. But alas, the dead can't protest," he gives a tight smile.

Everyone's eyes are on him, waiting for him to talk.

One small nod from Cisco, and Raf continues.

"Michele was not Benedicto's biological son," he simply states.

Gasps erupt in the crowd at the pronouncement, and more questions seem to make the rounds as some demand proof of the veracity of the claims.

"I can help with that," Marcello, the man we'd met earlier, interjects. "You'll see a DNA test on the screen," he points to the wall behind us. "That should be proof enough that Michele was *not* Benedicto's son. In fact, his real father was my uncle, Nicolo Lastra."

A few clicks and more pictures appear on the screen, showing different degrees of kinship, including one of Marcello's half-sister, Sisi, who also happens to be Michele's half-sister.

What?

I whip my head to look at Raf, trying to gauge his reaction.

His lips are pursed, his features tense. Still, there's no trace of shock.

He knew.

Michele isn't his brother—not his biological brother, anyway.

And I'm the last one to find this out.

"So now you see why my father was insistent on stripping Michele of his inheritance. Of course, like any proud man, he did not want to make it public that his own wife had been unfaithful," Raf continues, and by now people have quieted down.

As I look at him, I can't help but admire the calm way in which he's relaying the information, a quiet confidence to him that managed to convince everyone of his claims.

"I also understand why some of you would be wary of my approach since Guerra and DeVille have always been at war. Cisco and I have reached an understanding that would benefit both our families in the long run, and, we hope, you too," he smiles as he makes a few changes to the screen.

"You are probably aware that for years now strangers have tried to infiltrate the city and take advantage of its ripe market for their own gain. Our plan is rather simple. As long as we *all* cooperate, we can keep those people out. A closed circuit, if you will." He goes on to explain how some families are already interconnected and their businesses are linked together, so it wouldn't be a hardship to enlarge that network.

"Instead of seeing each other as enemies and competitors, we would unite our forces towards a common enemy —outsiders."

Both Raf and Cisco go over a detailed plan of getting the current big players to cooperate with each other by sharing information and potential customers.

"Think of a supermarket. You go there thinking you need some milk and cereal. But on the way out you also pick some chocolate, some soda and some pop tarts. Did you need them? No. But they were there," Raf explains.

Essentially, by joining hands, each branch would profit from the other.

"And because everyone knows everyone in this room, it will be rather easy to keep intruders out." Cisco concludes.

"You do realize that would make them *more* likely to want to infiltrate. Because from the outside it will seem like a gold mine," Sisi's husband, Vlad, intervenes, his stance laid back as he looks at Cisco with a raised brow.

"I am aware. But together, we also stand stronger if anyone should come knocking," my brother smiles.

There's a pause as Vlad narrows his eyes at him before he shrugs.

"More conflict. I like that. I'm in."

A few more issues arise as people start debating the merits of such a union.

And just as the topic of voting comes up, a loud boom erupts in the room.

Turning, I see something on the screen, the image initially lagging before slowly becoming more clear.

"Cisco..." Yuyu's panicked voice barely filters through my ears as I focus on the video.

A silhouette draped in black appears on the screen. The scene seems to have been filmed in a warehouse as the person walks inside, both hands going to the back, grabbing the hilt of two swords and swinging them in the air. Battle cries resound in the background as men charge at him, all wielding various weapons.

No one stands a chance, though. Not as the person swiftly dispatches one after another. It only takes one contact with his sword for their heads to fall.

"Wow," the words are out of my mouth before I can stop them, and I feel Raf's hold on my hand tighten.

"Stop this," Cisco barks out, storming off the stage and sending some directives to the tech team.

Still, the video keeps playing.

It's a bloodbath as the person in black slaughters every single one of the men around.

Out of nowhere, my brother appears in the frame, a white handkerchief in his hand as he brings it to his forehead to remove a few stains of red.

"All?" he asks, and the black silhouette turns, coming towards him.

"All," he nods.

One hand up, the person tugs on the obsidian mask that hides his features, wrenching it from his face and...

I hear a gasp, but I don't know if it's coming from me or someone else.

"Yuyu..." I whisper, the person's features in full view.

There's a commotion on the side as my brother is trying to stop the broadcasting of the video.

It's all in vain, though, as the video continues, showing my brother and Yuyu engaged in a passionate embrace among the bloody corpses.

Clothes are already starting to come off, and that's when my brother reaches the end of his tether. Pulling out a gun, he starts shooting at the screen in a last attempt to make it stop.

The pixels shift, the image distorted, but the sounds still reverberate in the room.

Until they don't.

"You can't say I didn't learn from the best now, can you?" An amused voice resounds, though the video is already broken. "I merely borrowed some of your tactics, Cisco, since you're not a stranger to public viewings of... R rated content," he chuckles.

"Michele," Raf grits his teeth, his eyes on the screen as his hands are clenched by his side.

"Your brother?" I point towards the broken screen that nevertheless still works.

He gives a brisk nod.

"I decided to return the favor, and let everyone know the identity of the elusive Black Monarch. I don't think there's anyone who hasn't heard of it. Well," he pauses, amused. "Meet the Black Monarch."

Everyone is silent at the proclamation, and one glance to the side is to see Yuyu clutching to her pregnant belly, her face full of shock.

"And you, brother," he tsks. "You should have stayed away. Because *now* it's game on."

The transmission stops.

For the longest time, no one speaks. No one dares to...

Michele just publicly challenged both my brother and Raf.

The war is on.

CHAPTER NINE
NOELLE

"What's going to happen now?" I ask as I sneak a peek at his profile.

Hands tightly coiled around the steering wheel, he's got a harsh look on his face.

Since we've left the venue, he hasn't said a word to me, quietly seething as he turned his attention to driving.

Luckily, most people invited had been supportive of Yuyu and her identity as the Black Monarch, some even going as far as praising her abilities. But it's not them my family is worried about. No, it's the others. Those that will hear of her identity and will come back to ask for retribution.

While none of those present had condemned her or held her previous job against her during the negotiation phase, I know Cisco is worried about the information leaking. And since it had been Michele who'd dropped the bomb... It's safe to assume that come morning *everyone* will know the identity of the Black Monarch.

And *that* means only one thing. People will come gunning for Yuyu. Whereas before she could have taken care of herself

—as the video pointed out—now with her pregnancy she is backed into a corner.

Cisco had also stayed mostly quiet until the event had ended, most likely plotting Michele's death for messing with his Yuyu.

Still, until he gets to Michele, he'll have plenty of people to ward off.

"Your brother might need to move upstate until the birth of the baby. He needs a secure perimeter in case anyone tries something," Raf replies, almost absent-mindedly.

"Does that mean we're moving too?"

"Undecided," he shrugs. "I still have a target on my back, and any hint of disharmony could send the bounty hunters running. If they've been lowkey until now it's only because of your brother's influence. And now..."

"Is the Black Monarch so hated?" I frown.

"More than hated," he gives a sad smile. "There will be a lot of people willing to take revenge for the death of their loved ones, that's for sure."

"I see..." I turn my attention back to the road.

The driveway is empty save for a few cars here and there, the hour too late for anyone to be out and about, especially on this route. There is nothing but forest left and right, the atmosphere gloomy and forlorn.

Silence descends in the car, and though I sneak a look at Raf every now and then, I simply can't gauge his mood.

Is he mad? Is he disappointed?

His brother's appearance, though digital, must have shocked him. Because more than anything, it shows that Michele has been keeping track of Raf's whereabouts and what he's been up to.

"When did you find out Michele wasn't your biological brother?" I ask, thinking back to all the times Michele's name had been mentioned, yet never once had I heard anything relating to this.

His expression turns grim and for a moment he doesn't answer.

"Today," he finally says in an odd tone. Almost as if he *suddenly* settled on that word. Almost as if... I frown as I turn to look at him, and for the first time I note the traces of weariness on his face.

"Today?"

"Sisi told me. She put me up to speed with Michele's involvement in an illegal organ transplant ring a few years back and how they'd ended up finding out the two of them were related." He gives me the gist of it, though his entire discourse is mechanical—no trace of emotion even though the story itself is heartbreaking.

When Michele had been a child, he'd been diagnosed with leukemia, but they couldn't find a match for him. By luck, they'd found one in Sisi. Abandoned since birth at a convent, no one had asked any questions when they'd performed tests and later extracted bone marrow from her.

"Wow, that sounds awful."

"Tell me about it," he mutters noncommittally, his eyes on the road.

"That would have been so weird if you'd actually married her," I force a laugh, trying to steer the conversation towards *that* topic in hopes I can get some clarification on their relationship. "He's your brother, but he's also her brother... Wouldn't that have been a mess?"

"Maybe," is all he answers, barely glancing at me. Why do I get the feeling there's something he's not telling me? Something more than what he found out today?

A few clicks on the car's dashboard and music starts playing in the car—a clear sign to drop the conversation. Narrowing my eyes at him, I can't help but feel he's avoiding the topic of Sisi—or at least trying to. In turn, that makes me become even more obsessive about finding out about them.

Is he disappointed she married someone else?

By my calculations, that would have been before Lucero. Has he been pining for *both* this whole time?

I become jittery the more I think of his past, and what that could mean for *our* future—if we have one. His looks alone would make him a magnet for women, and his confidence makes me think he has plenty of experience in that department. And that makes me wonder how I'm going to be able to keep up with him…

God, just how many have there been before me?

That question doesn't want to leave me alone, jealousy festering inside of the more I think about it.

There are nights when he doesn't come home *at all* and I can't help but wonder if he's not with someone… My mind conjures images of him, naked skin and scorching kisses, and I can't help the way my heart squeezes in my chest.

We've never spoken about fidelity before, and given his initial reason for marrying me, I don't see how he would care about that. After all, his goal was to make me suffer, not mind my tender sensibilities.

He's a man… And I've seen how men in this lifestyle behave. When they have needs, they simply take care of them.

"You're quiet," he notes, startling me.

"I guess I'm tired," I mumble.

"We'll get home soon," he assures me, his hand finding its way on my thigh as he gives a quick squeeze.

"Right," I reply in a strained voice, his touch searing itself in my flesh.

I turn my gaze to the road, trying to take my mind off it, especially as he doesn't seem inclined to move it.

Suddenly, the car swerves to the right, and I barely manage to grab on to my seat.

"What..."

"Hold on," he says, his eyes on the side mirror. "We're being followed."

I turn around, shocked to see at least three cars right behind us.

And as Raf speeds up, so do they.

"Why? What's happening?" I ask in a semi-panicked voice.

No matter how much I try to take deep breaths and not allow myself to give in to a panic attack, as I see guns emerging from the rolled down windows of the car, I simply lose it.

"We're going to die," I mumble to myself.

"No we're not," Raf says confidently. "Hold on tight."

As the bullets start raining on us, Raf makes a sudden turn at the same time as he snaps my seat belt out of place, pushing me down so my head makes contact with his lap. Peering up, I note he has his own gun out, he takes advantage mid-turn to identify his targets and shoot.

He discharges all his rounds at the incoming cars before he makes a U turn, this time steering the car towards the others, and not away from them.

"What are you doing?" My voice trembles as the words are out of my mouth, already envisioning our deaths.

"Trust me." It's all he says as he drives at full speed towards the other cars.

Just as I think we're going to collide against them, it doesn't happen.

The car sails past them, and as I dare to lift my head up, I realize they moved out of the way to avoid the impact.

"Wow... That was awesome," I praise, but Raf isn't smiling.

He's even more focused on the road as he quickly rummages through the compartments, pulling out a couple of guns.

"Take one and put your seat belt back on," he commands me, his voice so stern I don't dare talk back.

I do as he says as I buckle up and I take one gun in my hands, clutching it closely.

Turning to me to check, he opens his mouth to say something.

But nothing comes out as another car nabs us from behind, sending us reeling off the road.

"Hold on, Noelle," he yells at me as the car falls on one side.

A gasp escapes me as I feel the impact everywhere, the force of it almost knocking me out.

It's like everything happens in slow motion as the car continues to move, falling down the hill until it becomes lodged in a tree.

By this point, the airbags have popped out of the board, and they've provided a measure of safety against the continuous impact. But not nearly enough as I feel a gash on my forehead, blood falling down my face and getting in my eye.

"Fuck," Raf groans, but I'm barely aware.

I don't know if it's because I'm terrified or in pain, but I can't seem to move.

"Noelle," he calls out my name. A quick snap of his seat belt and he's on me. "Shit, are you ok?" his hand is on my face as he forces me to look at him.

I blink, his features coming into focus.

"We need to get out of here. Now," he says in a rushed tone, immediately at work to release my belt and get me out of my seat.

"Aghh," I release a small whimper as pain radiates from all over my body.

For a moment, I lose track of what's happening. I vaguely feel him get me out of the car, my head against his chest as he cradles me closer.

"Fuck, you're hurt," he mutters.

Opening my eyes, I do my best to stay awake, though a fog threatens to descend over my mind.

"That's it, pretty girl. Keep your eyes open for me," he says as he takes his blazer off, ripping it into smaller pieces and proceeding to clean my wound with it before wrapping one strip around the circumference of my head.

"Am I going to die?" I ask in a small voice, confusion still very much clouding my judgment.

"No. You're not going to die. I'm not going to let you die, you hear me?"

I muster a nod, my eyes wide as I keep all my attention on him as he tends to my wound.

And just as I thought things couldn't get worse, the sound of an explosion permeates the air.

"We have a short window of time," Raf starts, looking in the distance. "In just a little bit, they will realize we weren't in the car for the explosion. And when that happens we need to be as far away as possible. You get me?"

"Yes," I say as I struggle into a seating position, bringing my hand to my head and feeling for my wound.

"Don't. I tied it together and that should work for now. We'll get help when we reach safety," his tone is brisk and efficient, and I can tell he's been in these types of situations before—the life or death ones.

"Ok," I agree with him, ready to follow him anywhere. "Let's go then."

He doesn't answer for a moment as he looks at me with a strange expression on his face.

"Can you walk?"

"Yes. I am a little out of it, but I'll manage," I say as I get up. A little wobbly, but I find that my feet work fine.

He peruses my form, looking me up and down before shaking his head.

"Yeah, that's not going to work."

I frown, not understanding what he means.

But it's soon clear as he swoops me up in his arms, urging me to put my arms around his neck as he starts walking.

I don't protest. Mostly because I'm sapped of strength, but also because his arms feel so good around me—enveloping me in such a protective layer that I finally feel safe.

"Where are we going now?" I ask, glancing around and seeing only trees.

"I managed to get a look at the GPS before the car got hit. There's nothing around for miles. Our only bet is to lose the people on our trails and find somewhere to sleep for the night. Tomorrow we'll go back to the highway and hitch a ride." He details his plan, and I can only stare in awe at him.

Even in this situation, he's level-headed and calm. It's both a little daunting, but also admirable, and a ball of warmth develops in my chest.

There's an innate strength and resilience that emanates from him and makes him even more awe-inspiring in my eyes. He's almost...larger than life.

We walk for what feels like forever, the night our only cover. But just as it is protective, it's also misleading as we venture deeper into the woods with no idea where we are, or where we are heading. Still, this far, those people should have lost our trail.

A sudden sound, though, makes me whip my head around.

"Did you know there are bears here?" I ask, a shiver of fear going down my back.

He grunts.

"We're around a hunting area."

"In your opinion," I wet my lips, my eyes intent on the place where the noise had come from. "Who is more dangerous?"

"Right now? I'd take a bear over a dozen people with guns," he chuckles.

"Me too," I crack a smile.

But just as the atmosphere becomes lighter, a bullet whizzes past us.

Raf wastes no time in ducking with me to the ground, quickly finding cover behind a tree.

"Shit! I didn't realize they'd follow so quickly," he curses.

"Can we make it?" I blink, looking up at him in worry.

"We can," he nods, taking the three guns we'd taken with us and checking them all for ammunition. "We have enough rounds to last for a while. As long as I don't miss..."

"How likely are you to miss?"

"I'm usually a good shot. But it's dark and..."

"There are too many."

He nods.

"We can do this," I tell him as I take his hand in mine. "I'm not ready to die, and I don't think you are either."

His brows lift up, his mouth curled in a smile.

"That's right," he agrees. "And if I get us out of here alive, I want a boon."

"A boon? What do you want?" I ask, surprised.

His smile still in place, he lowers his mouth to my ear.

"A kiss. A *real* kiss," he says in that suave voice of his, and I find myself nodding.

"Ok. You have a deal."

After all, what is a knight without the promise of a maiden's favor? And to sweeten the deal, I lean in, brushing my lips against his cheek.

"Kill everyone and you'll have a kiss. A *real* kiss."

CHAPTER TEN
NOELLE

H is features lighten and a new determination appears on his face.

Leaving one gun with me, he takes one in each hand as he signals me to stay put behind a tree.

It's a flurry of bullets, the noise getting increasingly louder. All the while, I'm praying that nothing will happen to Raf and that I won't become a widow again.

Clutching the gun, I mentally go over the steps Raf had shown me, making sure the safety is off before I rest my finger lightly on the trigger. Somehow the position isn't wholly unfamiliar. My mind may find it foreign, but my body doesn't as I grasp on to the gun with unusual ease.

Grunts permeate the air, the sound of fighting almost deafening in the dead of the night. My heart thunders in my chest as I think about Raf all alone out there and the fact that I'm so freaking useless I can't help him.

I wish I were like Yuyu.

After seeing the video, a lot of things are starting to make sense, particularly why her and my brother are such a good fit—they're both bloodthirsty.

But in this situation, I find that being bloodthirsty isn't that bad. No, when it's your life on the line, there's only one thing you can do—fight.

Shaking in my hiding space, I barely react when I feel something against my temple, the cold of the steel immediately letting me know *what* it is.

"Don't move," a voice says, urging me to get up and kicking the gun from my hand.

As I stand up, a man sneaks behind me, one hand against my waist, the other holding the gun to my temple as he leads me towards a small clearing.

Sweat gathers all around my forehead, the thought of dying making me hyperventilate.

As soon as we reach the open space, I note Raf and another five men engaged in a standstill.

He has one of the men against him, holding him as a shield as he points his gun towards the other four.

On the ground, there are at least three or four corpses, blood staining the grass and making it look an odd color in the moonlight.

Raf's eyes connect with mine as his nostrils flare in anger at the sight of a gun jabbed against my head.

"You want the girl to live, you let him go," the man behind me spits the words, jabbing the butt of the gun into my temple and making me wince.

A putrid smell wafts from him, and I almost gag, my face contorting in discomfort.

Raf notes this too, narrowing his eyes at me as he peruses my form for any damage.

"You'll kill us both anyway," he says, raising a brow.

"True," the man behind me guffaws. "But at least you won't see her die first," he continues laughing.

Across the small distance, our eyes meet and I can see his mind hard at work calculating all the possibilities.

With four other men pointing guns at him, and me already captured, the odds are really slim.

"One question first. Since I will die anyway," Raf starts, taking a step forward with his own hostage.

The other men jerk back, following his movements closely.

"Who sent you? Michele Guerra?"

The man scoffs.

"I don't know no Michele Guerra," he states. "You're our ticket to a million bucks."

"Right," Raf almost rolls his eyes at the obvious. "But *who* is paying the money?"

"No business of yours," he barks, lowering his head to my cheek, his breath on my skin.

"Compadre, cortala. Ya es tarde y nos costaron dos coches. Mata a la puta y yo tiro al gringo," another calls out. *"Sabes que si no nos apuramos, Gato y sus chicos nos van a delantar."*

"Ya, se. Pero ella no tiene que morir. Podemos divertirnos poquito," he says right as he takes a strand of my hair between his meaty fingers, bringing it to his nose, *"no es cada dia que encontramos una alta dama como esta,"* he laughs, and so do the others, nodding their heads.

Dread fills me to the brim, and I barely register that I understand everything they're saying—me, the girl who could barely string together two words of Spanish.

I don't get to dwell on it, though, as one shot resounds in the air.

My eyes grow wide, my body still in shock as the man next to me falls to the ground.

A succession of shots and one by one the others drop dead, their only shots of resistance hitting the man Raf's using as his shield.

In almost no time, the threat is gone.

And as he drops the body to the floor, he runs straight to me, taking me in his arms.

"We need to move. Fast. I don't know how many others are after us. We can't afford to go back to the highway now."

"Ok," I nod, a relief unlike any other coursing through my veins.

At this point, I would follow him to the end of the earth.

Before we leave, though, he picks up all the weapons from the dead, using one man's shirt to form a makeshift pouch to carry them.

"Let's go," he says, taking my hand in his and steering me even deeper in the woods.

We walk and walk, and while my mind is still firmly stuck on the deadly encounter with those men, I know we have no time to waste with my useless inquiries.

Still, I can't help but be in awe of him.

One moment I'd thought that was it, that they would kill him and rape me, and the next I was staring at a clearing full of corpses. The speed with which he'd shot them had been... Well, quite frankly frightening. But more than anything, it has given me the deep sense of security that I've always searched for.

A glance at his profile—half swathed in darkness, half bathed in moonlight—and I feel my heart skip a beat, my throat becoming dry.

"Are you tired?" He asks as we stop for a short while, but I just shake my head, unable to form the words.

It's only when my eyes finally take him in—all of him— that I realize something is wrong.

"Raf..." his name is barely a whisper on my lips as my eyes settle on his torso.

Instinctively, my hands go up, my fingers brushing against his shirt, the white stained with red in a spot that's becoming increasingly more pronounced.

"Is that... Did you get shot?" I swallow hard at the thought, because in the situation we're in—with no help in sight—this could be fatal.

"No," his hand covers mine. "I'm sure it's just a scratch. I'll see about it when we get to safety. Don't worry about me."

"But..."

Just as I'm about to protest, a loud roaring sound explodes in the sky followed by a sudden downpour.

"Shit," he mutters.

The rain is like a curtain as it drenches us to the skin in a matter of seconds.

"Run," he says, a huge grin on his face—one that I unwittingly share as I take his hand.

A giggle escapes me as we keep on running, aimless and with the rain on our side.

The wind brushes against my wet skin, goosebumps appearing all over as a shiver overtakes my body. But even as I feel the cold hit my body, I can't stop the joy that spreads deep within me. I ground myself in the present, enjoying my hand in his, the rain against our bodies as we run towards the unknown.

I don't know how much time passes. So lost I am in the moment and in *him* that I barely realize he's trying to point something in the distance.

"It's a hunting area. It makes sense that there would be a hunting lodge," Raf explains as he catches his breath.

We walk towards the area he'd pointed at, finding a small hunting lodge.

A one room building with a door and two windows on each side, it looks well kept. Going straight for the door, though, I realize it's locked.

"How are we..." Just as I'm about to ask how we're going to access it, he lets go of my hand, wrapping his fist in a material and banging it against the window to break it.

The more I think he can't amaze me more, the more he does. Especially as not two seconds later he has the door open, inviting me inside.

"This looks so cozy," I breathe out as I scan the small room.

A fireplace in the middle, it has a small station that houses tools, a closet and a one person bed.

"It better be. Since it's where we'll sleep tonight," Raf mentions.

"What?" I whip my head around just as he closes the door.

"We can't wander in the rain forever," he shrugs, moving to the shattered window and using a cloth to cover it up.

"I guess you're right," I mumble as I try to make myself more comfortable.

"They left this fully stocked."

He points to the batch of wood next to the fireplace, immediately starting to tend to that.

"Yeah. There are even clean sheets and blankets," I note as I look through the closet.

I also find canned food and drinking water.

"Do you think they will come after us here?" I turn to see the spark of fire come to life, and Raf feeding it more wood and feeding the fire.

"If they do, we'll be ready for them," he nods to the weapons. "But I doubt they will find us. We're very deep in the woods. I think they will cut their losses this time."

"You're right," I nod. "But..." I frown. "If your brother didn't send them, then who?"

"Someone *very* close to my brother, and who stands to win from having his favor," he answers grimly. "His name is Ortega," he says as he gives me a short account on his partnership with Michele.

"I see," I nod, getting closer to the fire.

My hands are on my arms as I try to banish the cold away, but even the blazing flames don't seem to work very well.

"Take off your dress." Raf's booming voice almost makes me jump.

"What... No." My eyes widen at him.

"Come on. You'll freeze to death otherwise."

"I'm not taking my dress off," I say resolutely, crossing my arms over my chest.

"Noelle," he sighs, "I've already seen you naked."

"Yeah but..." *Not like this.*

He's seen me naked when we were still at odds with each other. When I wanted to prove a point with my nakedness and make him swallow his words.

"Suit yourself," he shrugs, moving away and starting to undress.

I blink repeatedly as he takes off his shirt, his bare chest coming into view. Next, his hands are on his belt, unbuckling it.

Without even thinking, I whirl around, my eyes snapping shut.

"Noelle?"

"Just...put on a sheet or something after you're done," I mumble awkwardly.

"Why? It's not as if you haven't seen a naked man before," he jokes in a playful tone, and I swallow uncomfortably.

"Not...really," I reply in a barely audible whisper.

I must admit that I've had a few peeks at Raf, but I've never seen more than a flash. Other than that... My mind briefly wanders to Sergio and our wedding night. I'd gotten a glimpse of his naked body then, but it had been through swollen eyes as I laid on the floor, bleeding and unable to move. I'd been forced to watched him fuck another woman because I'd dared to refuse his *husbandly* rights. And then he...

"Noelle," Raf's voice is in my ear, his hands finding my shoulders as he turns me around to face him.

I muster the courage to peek at his lower half, glad to see he's still wearing his pants.

"What do you mean not really?" He asks, his hand coming up to cup my cheek in a gentle caress.

"I know I had a child but..." I shake my head. "I don't remember," I whisper, not daring to meet his eyes.

"What do you not remember?" He continues to probe, but I can only shake my head at him, embarrassment overtaking me.

"I don't want to talk about that," I say flippantly, making to move.

Because I don't want to air my lack of experience in front of him. Not when it's already something that's constantly on my mind.

"You never want to talk about that..." He holds on to me, his hands hot from the fire, their warmth seeping into my skin.

"What about you then?" I shoot back, annoyance spearing through me. There's a reason why I haven't wanted to talk about the past. About the fact that I found out I had a baby who died, or that I may *never* have children again. There's a reason why it's barely a comfortable topic to broach with my therapist. Yet he can't say the same about *his* situation.

"You're just as evasive. Every time I question you about your past, you change the topic."

"What are you talking about?" He frowns at me, seeming genuinely confused.

"What's your relationship with Sisi?" I push my chin up as I raise my brow in question.

"What?" He repeats in disbelief.

"You were engaged to her."

"Yes. I was engaged to her. That's all," he shrugs, looking at me as if I've lost my mind.

"Well? Elaborate," I tap my foot impatiently.

"Noelle," he groans, his big hands engulfing my shoulders as he keeps me in place.

"What? Don't tell me I'm being unreasonable again."

"You are. I don't understand why you're so fixated on her. We were engaged briefly. Her husband kidnapped her from the altar and we didn't get married. It's as simple as that."

"So you would have married her if not for that. Did you love her?" My lips tremble as I ask the question.

"Did I.... Noelle, I don't see how that's any of your business," he states resolutely, his expression aggravated.

CHAPTER ELEVEN
NOELLE

I can only stare at him in shock.

"Not my business…" I shake my head, trying to bite back tears. "You're an asshole, Rafaelo Guerra." I push at him with all my strength. "You're a fucking asshole," I say as I bring my heel down on his foot in an attempt to extricate myself from his hold.

Already I feel my lashes coated in tears, and no matter how much I try to, I can't blink them away.

"Where do you think you're going?" He calls after me.

"Let me go," I grit as he wraps his hand around my wrist.

"Noelle, you're…"

"I'm being unreasonable. I know," I add drily. "Just let go of my hand."

"I don't understand why you're so moody."

"Moody?" I scoff, looking at him in disbelief. "Next you're going to call me hysterical, no?"

For God's sake, why did I believe his words when it's clear he's just like my brother. After all, that's all I am— unreasonable, moody, *crazy*.

Wrenching my hand from his grasp, I don't even think as I open the door, dashing into the downpour.

"Fucking hell, woman! Where do you think you're going?" He yells after me, and in no time I find myself flush against his naked chest.

"Look at me, Noelle."

"Let me go," I whimper. "Just please let me go."

"Where do you want to go? There's nowhere you can go, pretty girl," he says on a gentler tone, his palm spread over my neck, his thumb pushing my chin up as he forces me to look at him.

My teeth are clattering, my entire body freezing as the cold rain hits my skin, but I don't let that stop me.

"As far away from you," I manage the words out.

"Damn it, Noelle. Why do you have to be so stubborn?" he grits, the tension in his jaw clear as he barely holds himself together.

"I don't know why you tried being nice to me," I start, willing myself to stay strong. "I don't know why you changed your behavior overnight, but I don't want any part in it."

"Noelle…"

"No, Raf," I press my lips together in an attempt to ground myself and stop shivering. "You're actually driving me crazy," I force a laugh. "And not in a good way. You're absolutely infuriating. You threaten to make me miserable and kill me. Then you do a one-eighty and promise you'll always protect me. But I don't know where I stand with you. I really don't." I take a deep breath. "I just… Let me be. Just let me be," the last words are on a breathless whisper.

His light eyes are shielded by the night, only a slight glint visible among the moon beams. The intensity in his eyes should scare me—it should terrify me.

But it doesn't.

Not when I find myself lost in them—a labyrinth I never want to escape.

His nostrils flare as he looks down on me, aggression rolling off him in rippling waves.

We're both breathing hard.

Inhale. Exhale.

The sound of the marauding rain dims and dims, suddenly a distant echo.

There's only my heart thumping.

His heart thumping.

Because somehow I can hear it. Somehow I can hear all those conflicting emotions within him.

And then it stops.

"Fuck it," he curses out, and before I know it, his lips are on mine.

His hands cup my cheeks as he forces me into him, his mouth opening on top of mine.

Lips against lips. Teeth clashing against teeth. Yet it's the feel of him—his taste, scent and touch—that does it for me. It makes me melt into him, the rain completely forgotten as the shelter of his body provides me with everything I ever wanted.

He's the cure I didn't know I needed, and deep in the recesses of my very soul, I feel him with an intensity that scares me. One that shakes my dormant essence awake, spurring it into *being* instead of existing.

Just like that. One touch of his lips and I see stars erupt, universes being formed, and me... I see myself taking shape as never before, a part of me emerging to the surface, ready to meet him on common ground.

One hand moves lower, to my rib cage and the curve of my waist, his fingers grabbing on to me and bringing me even closer, molding our bodies together as he feasts on my mouth like a starved man.

I don't know what I'm doing.

One moment I'm about to push him away, the next I'm holding tight, wounding my arms around his neck and raising myself on my tiptoes to meet him halfway.

The kiss is explosive—everything I would have ever thought a kiss should be and more. And in spite of the coldness of the night, I only feel heat.

Hot, scorching heat low in my belly, the sensation making my toes curl as I seek to close the distance between us even more—though it's not physically possible. An increasing need takes shape within me, one that dictates I should merge with him, that my place is only with him—become one with him.

One moment the world is within my grasp, the next it's gone. I feel bereft to my soul at the absence of his touch, his lips no longer mine.

"What…" I mumble as I open my eyes to find him staring at me.

"Collecting my boon," he whispers, brushing aside a wet strand from my face.

His expression is a mix of awe and confusion as he continues to look at me like he's never seen me before.

But I can't ponder that. Not when I feel too lightheaded from the kiss.

Swooping me in his arms, he brings me back to the cottage, closing the door behind him and setting me on the small bed.

"I want you to take your dress off and put this on." He hands me a small blanket. "I won't look if that's what you want. But you need to take off the wet clothes so you don't catch a cold. Understand?" His tone is gentle yet firm, and I find myself nodding.

Maybe I am still reeling from the kiss, but I don't protest as I quietly remove my dress and fashion the blanket around me in a Grecian style by tying it around my shoulders. I take off everything that's wet, including the scrap of material he'd used to bandage my wound. Feeling for the gash, I realize it stopped hurting, so I leave it alone.

His back is to me as he awaits my signal, and I feel touched by his regard.

"You can turn," I say softly.

"Good," he notes approvingly as his eyes survey my form. "Now I'm going to take my pants off," he warns, raising a brow at me. He's both telling me to turn away and daring me to look at the same time.

Alas, I've never been able to say no to a challenge.

"Go ahead," I try to act unbothered as I urge him to undress.

As I snuggle deeper in the heat of my blanket, a frissons still travels down my back as I follow his movements closely.

His hands on his belt, he first takes that off before moving to his zipper, slowly lowering it. My breath catches in my throat as I watch him pull down his pants to his ankles before getting out of them. He's wearing a pair of black boxer briefs and…

I gulp down, whipping my eyes to his face.

An arrogant smile pulls at his lips.

"I shouldn't leave anything on," he declares in an amused tone, his hands on the band of his boxers.

I immediately turn, heat burning in my cheeks. Because I peeked—for far longer than I should have.

His laugh echoes in the room and in no time he's by my side, a blanket draped around his shoulders. The barest hint of his chest is visible, but something catches my attention.

It's bare. There's nothing. *No necklace.*

He's worn that necklace religiously until now, and to see him without it…

My eyes meet his, the question written all over my face.

"Scoot over," he tells me.

I do, though I keep silent, my thoughts a whirlpool of confusion.

Staring at the fire, I think of the best way to approach this, since clearly any question about Sisi pisses him off. The topic of Lucero should be even more off limits…

"I messed up," he starts in an apologetic tone. "I didn't realize how important it was for you to know."

I open my mouth to say something but he shushes me.

"Sisi was my friend. We were never anything *but* friends. We only decided to get married because she got pregnant."

"Wait. You got her pregnant?" My eyes must be the size of two saucers as I stare at him.

"What? No, of course not. Not me," he rolls his eyes at me as if I just spouted the biggest nonsense, and that alone puts me more at peace than anything. "She was having some issues with Vlad at the time. Anyway, our marriage was supposed to be one in name only. I've never seen her as more than just a friend."

"But she's very pretty," I counter.

"She is. But I'm not attracted to her. I never was. At the time, she was an easy solution to get my father off my back. He was pressuring me to marry and it sounded like the best option."

"See, you could have said that from the beginning. I don't understand why we had to fight over it."

"My, my," he smirks. "You *were* jealous, weren't you?"

"So what if I was?" I raise my eyebrows at him. "It's your fault for not clarifying it."

"Now you understand what I feel every time I see another man hover around you," his voice changes to a raspier cadence.

"You're still an asshole," I pout, nabbing him in his side with my elbow.

"Fuck," he groans out loud.

"Come on, I didn't hit you that..." I pause mid-sentence as I realize I hit him in the same place he'd been injured earlier.

"I'm so sorry," I quickly say, getting to my knees in front of him to check on his wound.

"How did I forget about this?" I mutter to myself as I pull on his blanket, revealing a cut between his ribs.

"Stay put," I order, sure I'd seen a first aid kit somewhere.

"It's not a big deal," he calls out, but I ignore him as I rummage through the closet, finding a small white box with a red cross on it.

"It will be if it gets infected."

Holding my blanket together, I assume a position between his legs so that I'm on eye level with his wound.

And when I push his blanket more to the side, I realize he kept his underwear on.

"I didn't want to make you uncomfortable," he mumbles, the hint of a blush on his cheeks.

My mouth pulls in a smile at his thoughtfulness, though that doesn't mean he's forgiven. He needs to understand that his hot and cold behavior doesn't work on me. I want us to set straight terms that we will abide by.

"Let me see," I push his hands aside as I squint to get a better view of the injury. "It's not too bad," I note.

"See, I told you it was just a scratch."

"Good thing we have this so it won't become a problem later," I add as I wave a bottle of disinfectant. As I pour some over his chest, his eyes close, his mouth parting slightly as he holds in the pain.

Focusing on the injured area, I make sure to clean all the debris before bandaging the wound.

"Done," I quip, satisfied with my work.

When I look up, I find him staring at me with an odd expression. His eyes look glazed with a mix of want and confusion, but most of all an unquenched desire that must mirror my own.

"Why… Why are you looking at me like that?" I make the mistake of asking. As soon as the words are out of my mouth, he's on me, his big hands cupping my midriff and pulling me in his lap. My spread legs go on either side of him, my core making contact with his hardness.

"I'm not the only one hurt," his fingers brush against my forehead.

"Oh, I forgot about that," I admit, raising my hand to feel for the wound.

Keeping me balanced in his lap, he takes some disinfectant and gently dabs at the wound, cleaning it before applying a small bandage to it.

"Why is it that you're always worrying about others first?" He asks after he's done.

He doesn't allow me to move, keeping me trapped on top of him, his body emanating an intoxicating heat that makes me want to purr happily as I nuzzle against his chest.

"I don't know," I give a slight shrug.

"Good that you have me now," he whispers as he scans my face. "I'll take care of you," he murmurs, bringing his face closer to mine.

Our noses are almost touching as I peer at him from beneath my lashes, overwhelmed by the emotions he awakens in me. His expression mirrors my own, the blue of his eyes steeped in turmoil, want and promises of both pleasure and pain.

"One kiss," he rasps, resting his forehead against mine. "Just one kiss… What the fuck are you doing to me, Noelle?"

"I…" I don't know what he's asking of me. Not when my own mind echoes his sentiments.

"I hate this," the vehemence in his voice startles me. "I hate that you make me feel so powerless. That I want you so much I can barely sleep at night. That I want to tie you to me so that you're never hurt, always protected. Fuck, Noelle... I hate that I don't know what you're thinking. If you even..."

"If I what?" I ask breathlessly.

"If you want me as much as I want you," he says quietly, though his eyes burn a hole through me, the fire I see in them only stoking the flames that are already flaring inside of me.

Bringing my teeth over my lower lip, I bite it, my gaze on him.

"I do," I whisper softly. "I want you... So much, Raf..."

Cupping my nape, he swallows my words, his lips on mine in an intoxicating kiss that proves the previous one hadn't been a fluke. No, the same suffocating want bursts inside of me at the contact—one that's never enough. He opens his mouth on top of mine, his tongue probing at my lips, and I tentatively part my lips too, enjoying the taste of him.

I brush my open mouth against his, a tremor going down my body at the feel of his silken tongue as it caresses my lips. His arm snakes around my waist as he molds me to his chest, a sliver of pleasure going through me when I grind against him.

"Kiss me back, damn it!" He leans back, watching me through hooded eyed.

"What do you mean?" I ask softly, dazed from being this close to him, enveloped in his scent and *him.*

"Kiss me back, Noelle," he rasps, his thumb parting my lips as he stares at my mouth. "Put me out of my misery," his voice takes an anguished tone.

"I... I don't know how," I reluctantly admit, lowering my gaze in embarrassment.

"Hey, don't," he tips my chin up. "Don't go shy on me," his tone is gentle, his gaze caressing me with so much warmth a tingle starts to unfurl in my lower belly. "Tell me what you mean by that."

"I don't remember kissing someone before," I whisper.

"Noelle," he brushes his fingers against my cheek, his mouth pulling up in a tender smile. "You never have to be embarrassed with me. Never with me. Ok? I'm not going to pressure you to do anything you don't want to."

"Ok," I nod.

"Good," he smirks. "Now follow my lead," he says as he pulls me in, his mouth open and hovering on top of mine. I comply, opening mine too. There's a tiny space between our faces, our breaths mingling, but we're not yet touching. His tongue darts out to lick my lips before probing deeper inside my mouth.

"Give it to me, Noelle," he demands harshly, and I finally get what he means.

I bring my tongue into contact with his, and a groan escapes him at the first touch.

"Just like that, baby," he speaks softly against my mouth before plundering it.

There's no other word to describe the action as his tongue probes deep within my mouth. I meet it with mine, stroking it tentatively at first before gaining more courage.

A thrill envelops me as I give in to this newly discovered pleasure, the magic of the kiss spreading all the way to my toes. I open deeper, letting him conquer me before I reciprocate, attacking him in a slow battle of give and take. Our tongues waltz around each other just as we'd had on the dance floor—wildly and out of control, proper etiquette all but forgotten.

His hands go down my back, his nails slowly raking over my skin and making me shudder with pleasure. I whimper, bringing my pelvis closer into contact with his just as he sucks my tongue in his mouth, the action positively decadent.

A small gasp escapes me as his teeth start to glide over my bottom lip, alternating between small bites and nibbles. My eyes snap shut and I feel his wet, warm mouth laying open kisses all over my jaw before going lower, down my neck as he continues to suck and bite, leaving his mark all over me.

"Raf," I can't believe the sound that escapes my lips, so full and throaty and so unlike me.

"Fuck. Me," he rasps. "What the hell are you doing to me, Noelle?" he asks, his voice tinged with awe.

I wish I could answer him. There's nothing normal about the way I feel when I'm close to him—when my skin meets *his* skin. One touch and my entire mind goes blank until all I can think of is him.

Raf.

My Raf.

Now, my husband.

Mine.

CHAPTER TWELVE
NOELLE

The single bed is a tight fit. Our bodies are pressed together as he spoons me from behind, his erection digging into my backside. His arm tightens around me, his head in the crook of my neck, and I can't help the sigh of contentment that escapes my lips.

"You feel right at home in my arms," he murmurs as he nibbles at my ear.

"I *feel* at home," I whisper shyly as I let myself melt into him.

"Can you forgive me?" he asks as he lays a kiss on my shoulder.

"Forgive you for what?" I frown.

"For being an idiot and not realizing you were bothered by Sisi," he starts, his mouth on my skin, his breath brushing against me and making me shiver. "But most of all for everything I put you through before."

"Do you mean it?"

He pauses.

"Of course I do. Noelle," he sighs. "I behaved like an ass, I know that. I put you through hell because of my fucking self-righteousness and I can't tell you how much I regret that."

I reach to touch his hand, giving it a quick squeeze.

"Do better in the future," I tell him. "I can't tell you I forgive everything because some things aren't that easy to forget..." I trail off, taking a deep breath. "What you did to me in that dark room... You have no idea how close you were to breaking me, Raf. *Really* breaking me."

"Noelle," his anguished voice caresses my ears, and I just close my eyes, letting myself be surrounded by it. "I don't know how I can make it up for that. But I can promise you to try. Make you feel secure with me and trust me until you can forgive me for it."

"Spell it out for me. What exactly are you proposing?" I ask resolutely, wanting to hear in no uncertain terms what he wants.

"A real marriage." His mouth continues to trail light kisses over my skin. "I want us to have a real marriage."

I swallow.

"Even though I may never be able to have children?"

"Regardless," he answers immediately.

"Surely you'll want them in the future and you know I may not be able to give that to you..."

"Don't. Don't tell me what I want, Noelle. Because, quite frankly, there's only *one* thing that I want and that is *you*. There's something between us...," he pauses, taking a deep breath. "Something incredibly special, and I'm not giving up on you," he states with quiet conviction.

"Raf..."

"Give me a chance," he pleads. "Please."

Turning, I bring my eyes to his, the sincerity in his gaze confirming he *is* serious.

"There *is* something between us. Something I can't

explain," I admit. "That kiss... I didn't know I wasn't whole until you kissed me and put me back together."

"I felt it too," he whispers, cupping my cheek. "From the beginning I've felt something for you. I disguised it with hate because I didn't want to admit to myself that you made me feel things I'd never felt before," he confesses, and more questions arise in my mind.

"Not even with Lucero?" I tentatively ask, immediately beating myself for going there.

I don't want to ruin this moment, but as I watch his expression tighten, I fear I may already have.

He doesn't answer for a moment. But then he shakes his head.

My mouth parts in shock.

"What I had with Lucero was completely different," he smiles ruefully. "But that's in the past. You're my future," he swipes his thumb on my cheek in a gentle gesture, his eyes conveying everything I needed to know.

"Were you..." I try to think of a way to frame my question without coming across as desperate. "Were you ever intimate with her?"

His eyes widen.

I hear the beat of my heart as it drums in my chest, the anticipation for his answer killing me. Because I don't want to be compared to her. I don't want to be in her shadow forever, regardless of his assurances.

"No," he replies, and it's my turn to be surprised.

While I'd asked the question because the curiosity was killing me, I never expected him to say no.

"No?"

"You know how the *hacienda* was structured. I was mostly in my cell, and the few times I was let out I was always supervised. We only met in person a couple of times."

"Then how did you spend time together?"

"We spoke through the wall of my cell. She would often come to keep me company." A smile appears on his face, and I try to rein my jealousy in. "Mentally, she was the only thing that kept me going," he confesses.

I take his hand in mine, bringing it to my lips.

"I'm glad you had her," I tell him sincerely. Though the jealousy is killing me, there is the undeniable fact that few survived under Sergio's care. The fact that he had... I can only thank Lucero for being there for him.

"I don't want you to worry about her. She's dead, and I promise you she's in the past." His voice is full of sincerity, but doubts still plague my mind.

"But the mystery of her death..." And the fact that time and time again he's accused me of killing everyone at the hacienda. How do we move on from that?

"We may never know," he purses his lips. "Maybe you'll remember at some point, but I don't want you to force yourself. More than anything, I want you to know I was wrong to blame you of such heinous crimes with circumstantial evidence at best."

My eyes flare in shock.

"I know it now. You could never be capable of something like that. It's simply not *in* you. And I know sorry doesn't quite cut it, but I will continue to try and make up for my mistakes and my hurtful accusations," he adds sincerely.

I nod, though I am still apprehensive.

"I will be honest, Raf. I am wary about this. I don't want to be second best to anyone. I don't want to put all my hopes into you, fall for you just to realize you'll never be able to match my feelings."

"Don't," his tone is curt. "Don't think that. I told you that everything was different with Lucero."

I wet my lips as I look at him, a little apprehensive about the topic.

"What about before? What about the women you were with before? I told you I'm not experienced. I don't know what I'm doing and I'm afraid you'll end up disappointed with me," I admit reluctantly.

"Hell, woman," he groans. "You blew my mind with *one* kiss. I don't know if it can get better than that."

I blink, taken aback by the vehemence behind his voice.

"You're perfect for me, Noelle. Absolutely perfect," he says as he brings me closer to his body, his lips suddenly on my forehead.

"But what if I don't measure up?" I ask in a whisper, my insecurities getting the better of me.

"You don't have to worry about that, because there's no one you have to measure up to," his breath is on my skin as he skims kisses all over my face.

"What... What do you mean?"

"I haven't been with a woman before," he admits, and I pull away, trying to gauge his expression.

"You're lying," I accuse.

Because *that* is something I can't wrap my head around.

"Not lying," the corner of his mouth pulls up.

"But... But... You're *you*," I say, scandalized.

"Me?" His eyes crinkle with amusement.

"You're handsome, and strong and...." I trail off when I see him watch me with a lazy smile on his face.

"Do go on," he drawls.

"Ugh," I punch him lightly in the shoulder. "You know what I mean."

"I'm glad you think so." He brings my fist to his mouth for a light kiss. "But you don't have to look so surprised. All my life I tried to go under the radar, so women were the last thing on my mind. Then I got sold... And you know the rest."

"But it's been two years," I whisper.

"I didn't have any interest in it." He shrugs, as if he didn't just blow my mind with his revelation. "Until you started shaking that little ass of yours in front of me, that is," he chuckles. "I've been sporting a hard-on day and night ever since."

He's never slept with a woman before... The realization slowly seeps in, and a foreign feeling unfurls in my chest—longing, want, but something else. A sense of possessiveness that's entirely antithetic to my usual self.

He's never touched another woman. And now, he *never* will.

"Then how are you so confident?" I ask, perplexed. I've never met someone more charming and confident than him. And his words... I get the urge to fan myself just thinking about the things he'd said to me on the dance floor.

"I may not have firsthand experience. But I've already fucked you a thousand times in my head," he smirks. "I've dreamed up all the ways I would take you. Hard and fast like an animal," he pauses as his eyes drift to my chest and lower, "slow and passionate..."

A blush travels up my neck before staining my cheeks as I lower my gaze, embarrassed by his words.

"I'll make love to you and treat you like the goddess you are," he says as he tugs a strand of hair behind my ears. "But I'll also fuck you like the bad, bad girl you are," he drags his hand over my face and down my neck, pressing his fingers over my pulse point. "I'll make you scream, and I'll make you beg," he rasps. "You awaken an animalistic side of me, Noelle. One that I never knew I had."

I draw in a swift breath, my pulse quickening.

"But I think you rather like that, don't you?" he drawls in that seductive voice of his, and I have a hard time holding off the shudder that racks my body. "You like to submit to me," he caresses my skin lightly. "You like being at my mercy. You like being *mine*."

Biting my lip, I give a quick nod.

"I *want* to belong to you," I admit softly. It's what I've wanted from the beginning.

"You already do," he smiles. "You'll be the first and *only* woman I take to my bed. Because once you're there, I will *never* let you go," his voice thickens and I bring my gaze to his, my hand cupping his as it rests against my neck.

"I wish you were my first too," I sigh. "Even though I don't remember…"

"I'll be your last," he interrupts. "And I'll be the *only* one you remember," his voice is full of confidence as he tips my chin up. "I'll be the only one to worship your body and care for you like you were meant to be cared for—like a fucking goddess. Because that's what you'll be to me. *My* goddess."

The intensity of his gaze frightens me, but I can't look away.

I don't think anything could make me look away.

"We'll take it slow," he amends, his voice softening— almost as if he doesn't want to scare me. "We'll become comfortable with each other and learn each other's bodies." He brushes the back of his hand down my front. "I won't pressure you for anything. *Ever.*"

"You're so good to me," I smile. "I just don't want to disappoint you."

"You could not disappoint me if you tried, Noelle," he chuckles. "Every little touch you allow me and I'm already a lucky bastard," he winks at me. "Although… I have one question. Call it an errant curiosity," he smiles sheepishly when he sees my confusion.

"What?"

"What did Cisco mean about prostitution charges?"

My features contort in mortification when he brings that up.

"That's so embarrassing," I groan as I place my hands on

my face, hiding in shame. "I swear it wasn't like that," I add immediately, proceeding to explain what had happened. "It was during my small rebellion phase. I only went to this club because I knew it would piss Cisco off. I was in the bathroom, and I saw a few women doing their make-up. Now, I wasn't familiar with clubs and club etiquette, and they seemed to know what they were doing, so I asked them to teach me their ways." I cringe as I say it out loud.

"I gather they mistook what ways you were asking about," he says drily, though as I peek at him, it's to see him hold back a laugh.

I nod.

"They started telling me some stuff, but there was a police bust and everyone was taken to the station. Somehow I ended up lumped with them," I shrug, though that stint at the police station hadn't been entirely pleasant. Especially since it hadn't been my first time there.

"Cisco must have lost it," he muses.

"He did. He started being more overbearing than usual," I roll my eyes. "And in turn I tried to cause more trouble for him. I know it was immature, but it was the only way I could get a reaction from him—from anyone," I sigh.

Suddenly his arms are around me, holding me tight and offering me the comfort of his embrace.

"Was it very hard?" he asks in a low whisper.

"I felt like a stranger in my own body—in my own life," I confess. "I had no one to talk to and I felt like no one cared about me."

Taking a deep breath, I ask something that's been on my mind for the longest time. Something I hadn't wanted to dwell on, but is part of the reality I find myself in.

"Is it bad of me that I don't want to think about the baby? Or talk about it?" He doesn't answer as he waits for me to continue. "Sometimes it doesn't even feel real. I don't remember sleeping with someone, let alone conceiving a child and...giving birth."

I refrain from mentioning there is no way it could have been consensual. And remembering something like that... I don't think I could bear it. It might be messed up, but sometimes I'm glad I can only remember Sergio's beatings and nothing else. But if that wasn't bad enough to forget... God knows what else happened to me.

"Your feelings are valid, Noelle. Never doubt that. I didn't tell you so that you could blame yourself for it, or to cause you unnecessary pain. But you're entitled to know things that still affect your body."

I give a brisk nod. Yet another reason why Raf is so special to me. He's never lied or hidden things from me—unlike my own family.

"I never realized that the pain was abnormal. I guess remembering the past could put a lot of things into perspective. But I'm not sure I want to."

"Then don't," he says staunchly. "Forget the past. We'll focus only on the future."

I give him a strained smile.

If only it were as easy as that. But I don't say it out loud. I snuggle deeper in his embrace, listening to his deep voice and the way it makes my body sing with pleasure. There's something addictive about his timbre and its ability to affect me so.

"Please don't break my heart," my voice almost breaks as I utter the words, giving him a peek into my vulnerability. "I want to give this a chance. But I want it to be a relationship between equals. I know that in our world it's almost unheard of, but I don't want you making decisions for me or keeping me in the dark. So please... Don't lie to me. Don't hide things from me and..." I drift off.

"And?"

"If I'm yours, then you're mine too. No others. Not now, not ever," I imbue confidence in my words so that he realizes I'm serious about this.

I'm tired of being an afterthought. For the first time, I am going to be greedy and ask for *everything*.

I'll give him all of me. But only if he gives me all of himself too.

CHAPTER THIRTEEN
RAFAELO

"**N**o one else," I agree. "You need to understand one thing, Noelle," I tell her in a serious voice. "I would *never* betray you. I would *never* betray my wedding vows. But most of all, I would *never* touch a woman who is not you."

Not only do I condemn cheating for the scourge that it is, but I could never look at another woman the way I look at *her*. She has a unique effect on my mind and body. Even when I hated her, she was all I could think about—fantasize about.

There's something intangible about her that drew me in from the beginning. It's in the way the entire room seems to shrink when we're together; to the point I see only her. It's in her blushes and her small sighs, or the way her eyes twinkle when she looks at me not in hate, but in *not*-hate.

My skin tingles from her mere touch, a spark that starts at the surface of my skin and worms its way inside until it reaches my heart, making it squeeze tightly in my chest.

And then there's her music that has the power to soothe

me—truly soothe me. The only time my monsters go into hiding is when I hear her play—that melody of hers that has the power to put together my fragmented soul.

There's something utterly magnetic about her presence, and sometimes I wonder if the drugs haven't addled my brain. If they haven't screwed my perception of the world to such a degree that I now see fairytales instead of reality. Because only then would I imagine happily ever afters when I look at her.

I've seen the worst the world has to offer. Yet one moment with her and I find hope again.

She gives me hope.

"I'm a one woman man, Noelle," I wink at her.

If there's one good thing my parents taught me it's that real love exists. They may not have been the best people, but they truly loved each other in a way I've rarely seen in our world. They showed me that there's something beautiful out there—something worth pursuing and holding out for. I may have been pretending to be something I was not during my teenage years, but the truth is, if I'd been inclined to, my father could have easily found someone to sleep with me— regardless of my perceived disability. He certainly tried to entice me to do it, finding different opportunities to put me on the spot in his attempt to make me become a *man*.

I didn't want to. Call it idiotic or naïve, but even back then I knew I was waiting for something *more*. For the act to mean something with someone I prized above all. I've never thought myself a great romantic, but looking back on my life, maybe I've been one all along. I couldn't imagine sharing myself with someone I wasn't in love with. Someone who didn't make my body hum with electricity, awakening each and every cell and making every atom with relief at her presence.

That's exactly what Noelle makes me feel.

And it fucking terrifies me.

She wets her lips, peering at me through her lashes and I don't think the sight of her like this will ever cease to affect me. She's too beautiful and too pure for this world, and the thought that I hurt her before cuts me on the inside.

I'd been so wrapped up in everything at the ball that I hadn't realized my carelessness and stupid jealousy were causing her harm. I'd been a fucking idiot and I almost lost her because of that, especially now that I've barely gained some ground with her. After all the pain I've caused her, I know it won't be easy to gain her trust and her forgiveness. And she's right to hold it against me.

Just thinking of the dark room and her tear-streaked face, the way I'd hurt her...

There's no excuse for anything I did to her. And I'll be damned if I know how to fix it.

I've never had a girlfriend. I've never gone on a date, and I've certainly never tried to court a girl before. My one attempt at a date had ended up with me being ghosted by my then best friend, cutting out contact as if we hadn't been chatting daily for *years* at that point.

Hell, even my relationship with Lucero had been completely different in that regard because it had been limited by circumstances. Ours had been an emotional connection, not a physical one. She'd been there for me at my hardest, and in turn, I'd been there for her.

At some point, I might have thought she was my one and only.

Not anymore.

It's a pleasant surprise to realize that thinking about Lucero doesn't pain me as much as before. Most of all, I can see our time together for what it was—pleasant but transient.

She was the right person at the right time. But now, that era has passed. And it's time to truly let go. Whatever I might have felt for Lucero pales in contrast with the feelings Noelle awakens in me.

"Ok," she nods. "I just wanted to make my position clear."

"And I love that, because we are on the same page," my lips tug up. "Never be afraid to speak your mind with me. I want to know your thoughts—your innermost thoughts. I want to know everything about you. Because this," I point between us, "is not just lust."

Her brows furrow as she looks at me in confusion.

"What I feel for you goes beyond mere lust. I desire you, and I might have fooled myself in the past that it was just that. But I know it's so much more," I confess.

"What do you mean?" she asks softly, the question tentative as if she didn't dare believe me.

"I want to experience everything with you, Noelle. I want you to be mine. Completely mine," I tell her, finally uttering out loud what I've been trying to fight from the beginning.

She blinks, her eyes growing wider.

"Ok," she whispers.

"Good girl," I chuckle, "because it's happening regardless of your approval. But I wanted to be a gentleman and ask for permission first," I wink at her. She's mine whether she likes it or not. And if she doesn't, then I'll hound her until she accepts it.

She looks at me dazedly for a moment before a smile erupts on her face, a small laugh escaping her.

"So you ask for permission now," she muses, clearly amused.

"I want you to be comfortable with me. I know I behaved like an ass in the past, and there's no excuse for that. But I want to make amends and show you there are other sides to me. More…civilized ones." The last thing I want to do is scare her. I know she hasn't had the best experience with men, and that makes me wary about overwhelming her.

"I think that has its place," she says innocently, "but I don't expect you to be civilized *all* the time." She flutters her lashes at me suggestively, and I can't help myself as I take her in my arms, rolling on my back and placing her on top of me.

"My innocent wife might be a little deviant, is that what you're trying to tell me?" I raise a brow at her.

Her hands on my shoulders, she raises herself, her legs on either side of me as she sits upright.

"Fuck," I groan when she presses herself onto my erection.

"Oh, sorry," she tries to scurry away, confirming that she's not ready for what I have planned for her.

My hands on her hips, I keep her firmly in place as I take my time to look at her, get my fill of her.

"Don't," I tell her when she squirms in an attempt to get away, "I like you on top of me," I breathe out, though the feel of her pussy on top of my cock is the sweetest torture. And if she makes one more move, I'm pretty sure I'll come in my underwear. After all, there's only so much a man can take.

Fuck, but it feels so liberating to finally admit to myself that I want her. That I *need* her. And that I'll do everything I can to make sure I *keep* her.

If there's anything I've learned about Noelle, it's that she has a hard time trusting people. Every time she's done so in the past, she's been let down. So I know I have *one* chance with her and I have to make it count.

She's skittish, but not without reason. And that makes my work harder.

I have to make sure she falls so totally and utterly in love with me that she'll never leave me—that she'd never *think* of leaving me.

"You're so beautiful," the words roll on my tongue. "So fucking beautiful," I say in awe, lifting my hand to her face and caressing her cheek. She's not just beautiful on the outside. She also has a beautiful soul—a beautiful, battered soul. There's a purity that clings to her in spite of her past, and I can't help but be in awe of her strength.

The mere fact that she's willing to give me a chance after everything she's been through is a miracle. Me, the asshole who taunted and mocked her at every turn. Me, the bastard that dared to make her cry. And for every tear that she shed, I'll fucking prostate myself at her feet until she forgives me.

I feel a sharp pain in my chest at the thought of every-thing she's suffered, and how she's only ever seen the worst of humanity.

My sweet and kind Noelle.

Damn it all to hell, but how could I have thought her capable of harming anyone?

Most of all, how could I have *ever* thought her an experi-enced seductress? I should have seen through her false confi-dence from the beginning. Though her words were daring, her actions were anything but.

"You've gone quiet," she says after a while, startling me.

"I was just thinking of the past."

"Why?"

"Because you amaze me. Your strength and resilience amaze me."

"Flatterer," she blushes.

"No. I'm only telling the truth, Noelle. Everyone in your family is a fool for not realizing what a gem you are. And it's their loss. I promise I'll cherish this," I tell her as I place my hand over her heart. "I won't give you any reason to doubt my loyalty."

Her smile lights up her entire face, and in that moment I

vow to myself that I'll do whatever it takes so she never has to worry about another thing again.

No one will harm a hair on her body. Because no one will get close enough to do it.

Releasing a tired yawn, she brings her head to my chest, snuggling into me.

"Sleep, pretty girl," I caress her hair, the heat of her body seeping into mine.

"You're mine now," I whisper when I hear her regulated breaths.

That's when I finally breathe out relieved too.

I haven't messed this up.

The entire night, I've had to keep myself in check in case I said or did something wrong—again.

There's something seriously wrong with me when it comes to her, and sometimes I'm afraid I might scare her away with my intensity. There's this sick need inside of me to *own* her though I know she cannot be owned.

I want her more than I've wanted another thing, and for the first time, I have to admit that Carlos was right.

I want her more than my revenge.

There are times when I can't help myself, the scene I'd made at the ball being a prime example. When I'd seen her in the arms of another man, I'd been out of my mind with jealousy and rage—pure, unadulterated rage. And so I acted in an unlikely fashion.

But that's the issue. There's something about her that makes me act in the unlikeliest of ways. I've always been level-headed and calm. Yet with her, I see red.

Now, more than ever, I need to rein myself in. I need to show her I'm not an animal she should be scared of.

I'd seen the way she had reacted to my outburst at the ball. How she'd been embarrassed to be seen with me because of my caveman-like behavior, and how strongly she'd resisted me.

Which brings me to my current dilemma.

Civilized.

I need to pretend to be civilized. I need to court the fuck out of her and show her I can be *soft*. That I can be a gentleman.

That's what someone so dainty and delicate like her needs. Someone to take it slow. Not someone who wants to fuck the shit out of her until she's raw and bleeding, screaming my name both in pleasure and in pain...

Fuck. Those thoughts are dangerous... Too dangerous.

I close my eyes, trying to count to ten.

Civilized. Yes, I can be civilized. I've been civilized my entire life before her.

How hard can it be?

———

"I'm glad to see you two returned in one piece," Cisco's lips stretch in a languid smile as he peruses us, but there's no emotion behind his words.

Like I've come to expect from him.

At this point, I'm pretty sure the man is a psychopath. He talks like a human, acts like a human, but I'm getting increasingly sure he's not one. Not with how he's behaving with his own sister—as if he couldn't care less about her.

Except he does care—as long as she's beneficial to his plans.

That's the thing with Cisco. He *never* does anything that's not to his advantage. And it's also the reason why I'm always second-guessing his actions.

"Noelle, go upstairs and take a hot bath," I tell her.

She gives me an odd look, but doesn't argue.

Ah, my sweet girl is a natural submissive. There's no doubt about that. And the mere thought of getting her alone and doing things to her has my blood pumping downwards. Alas, there will be time for that later.

"I'm surprised to see you're still here," I raise a brow at Cisco.

He merely shrugs, motioning me to his study where he hands me a glass of scotch.

"Yuyu is packing. We're leaving for the summer house and we'll be taking most of the guards with us," he dives right into the crux of the issue.

"I see," I nod, keeping my expression neutral.

"We'll stay there until after the birth. You're welcome to join us, but..."

"No, thank you. We'll stay here. I still have business in the city," I interrupt him.

His offer had been reluctant at best but I think Noelle would benefit from not having her family around for a while.

Though Cisco's couldn't have been more clear—we're on our own. He will probably leave us *some* guards, but other than that he won't care if something were to happen to us.

Just like he doesn't seem in the least worried about last night.

"Marvelous," his lips stretch into a wide smile. Bringing his glass to his mouth, he downs it in one go before slapping it on the table.

"Keep me updated. We'll have video conferences every night, and I'll come down to the city every so often," he says, going into a quick outline of how to change our plans around the new developments.

Just as I'd thought, Michele's reveal had already made the rounds around the city and beyond, and already Cisco is fearing for the worst.

"Just how many people could possibly come after her?"

"You have no idea," he gives a dry laugh. "Yuyu's been my sword while I've been her shield for over twenty years. Yet it seems I've failed her," he shakes his head, his façade cracking. "And in this case, whatever can go wrong, will likely go wrong," he says vaguely.

Giving me a list of emergency contacts, he also tells me that the house is equipped with a panic room.

"If the worst was to come, you know what to do," he says before taking his leave.

The reality is that Michele had done a number on us. By revealing Cisco's weakness to the public, he's effectively taken out my protection. And without that...

Both Noelle and I are in danger.

What are you planning now?

Last I'd spoken to Panchito, he hadn't been able to locate Michele anywhere in the city. He's like a ghost with his movements, and his body doubles are not making our job easier.

On the other hand, Panchito had been able to hack into one of Michele's phones and track some of his exchanges with a foreign number—one that belongs to a burner phone.

But that had been short lived too, since Michele had somehow figured out we'd infiltrated and promptly changed his phone.

Still, the conversation with that unknown number had raised a few alarm bells. While it had been sexual in nature, and the exchanges had been filthy and degrading, there had also been the slightest trace of affection in the way he addressed her—pet.

And so it seems I may have a new lead—and a new mission. Find Michele's mystery girl and beat him at his own game.

I make a few phone calls to make sure Carlos and the

other guys are safe and aware of the latest developments, and then I finally head to our suite.

The moment I step inside our room, though, it's to hear a melodious hum from the bathroom. The door is ajar and I take it as an invitation to push it open, stepping inside to find Noelle leaning against the back of the tub, her eyes closer, her lips opening and closing as she sings a quiet melody.

The water reaches her clavicle, bubbles all over the surface hiding her glorious body from my sight.

Alas, I can forgive that slight since she took my advice to heart.

My fingers immediately go to the buttons of my shirt, snapping them open before laying it on a counter. I discard my pants, but I keep my underwear on since I'd promised both myself and *her* that I'd take it slow, and I don't want to frighten her with my desire—not yet.

I move stealthily towards her, all the while letting my eyes greedily roam over every bit of exposed flesh.

Suddenly, I'm reminded of a similar situation. When I'd behaved like the worst bounder, insulting and degrading her at every turn. And I'd topped it off by trying to kill her.

My hands had held her down, waiting for her to draw her last breath.

And even then, when her death should have pleased me, it hadn't.

I'd looked down at her—her eyes open, her expression calm and resigned—and I'd lost myself.

I'd lost everything.

Something had snapped within me in that moment—an explosion of surreal magnitude that had woken me up to reality.

I couldn't do it. No matter how much I thought I hated her, I couldn't kill her.

I'm by the side of the tub when she opens her eyes,

looking at me unflinchingly. For a moment, I fear that the old Noelle is back—the cold one whose arctic stare could freeze my goddamn heart. And if she decided to go back to treating me like a bastard, it's not like I wouldn't deserve it.

Have I done anything right?

I don't deserve her forgiveness, and I sure as fuck don't deserve her attention.

But I'm going to take it regardless.

Chapter Fourteen
Rafaelo

"What are you doing here?" She asks calmly, no trace of her previous shyness.

"What do you think?" I raise my brows in question, taking a seat by the tub and swirling my hand inside the water, destroying the bubbles so her flesh can peek through.

"Are you here to kill me again?"

"Maybe," I answer as I hover my hand over her body, moving it and watching the water ripple around.

I move higher until my hand reaches her tits.

"But it will be a different kind of death. The type you'd welcome." The corner of my mouth curls up as I watch a slight blush color her features.

She takes a deep breath, her chest expanding as she inhales, her nipples protruding through the mist of the bubbles.

"Are you being indecent, dear husband?" She asks in a sultry voice. But then again, everything she says sounds like a *fuck me*, her husky voice going straight to my cock and making the bastard stand to attention.

"Indecent?" I smirk. "I'm the model of decorum, *dear wife*,"

I retort, my tongue between my teeth as I stare at the beauty in front of me.

Fuck, but it should be illegal to look like that.

Her tawny skin is the perfect contrast to the white of the foam that surrounds her. Her freckles are more pronounced against the blush that mars her cheeks and fuck if I don't want to kiss each and every one of them.

Soon…

Her eyes are framed by thick lashes, and as she turns towards me, the light hits them at an angle, one more brown, the other a deep green. Her full lips part as she inhales before swallowing audibly, evidence that she's not unbothered for all her cool appearance.

And I can see why too. Because my pretty girl is being daring. Raising herself into a sitting position, I watch in awe as the water drips from her chest, the perfect swell of her breasts coming into view first before her mounds become completely visible. Two perfectly formed globes hang full and heavy, the sight bewitching and oh, so inviting my mouth is already salivating for a taste.

The little witch has other plans, though.

She raises one finger to my chest, her nail on my skin as she grazes it lightly. A shiver goes down my back, the gesture so erotically charged I almost come in my pants.

I catch her hand just as it skirts the band of my boxers.

"You're courting danger, Noelle," my voice comes out rough and thick.

"Am I?" She wets her lips, batting her lashes at me.

Before I know it, my hand is wrapped around her wrist as I pull her towards me, her wet body sliding against mine. She releases a soft gasp of surprise as she finds herself in my arms, but I don't give her time to panic.

Swooping her up, I lead her to the shower stall in the back, bringing both of us under the warm jet of water. The foam washes away from her body, her gleaming skin revealed for my perusal.

And damn if it doesn't affect me.

"Raf," her soft voice caresses my ears. "What are you doing?" she asks as she turns to face me, her eyes wide with inquiry.

"Taking care of you," I tell her, letting one hand trail down her front. "Spoiling you," I smile at her curious expression. "Making you happy."

The corner of her mouth curls up, her face threatening to explode into a huge grin. But she reins it in as her eyes twinkle mischievously.

"Please proceed," she urges me, and I can read the silent dare in her words. She's testing me—wanting to see how I aim to make her happy.

I can already see that her brain is hard at work, probably trying to anticipate my next move. She thinks she has me figured all out—that all I want from her is the pleasure that her body can provide.

She's partially right.

My cock is nearly bursting from being so close to her, the thought of burying myself inside of her body bringing me closer to insanity than ever before.

Though our attraction borders on animal primitivism, this isn't *just* lust.

If it had been, I could have fucked her already.

For all her apprehension about her inexperience, once she's in my arms she turns putty. Like a haze covering her mind, she loses herself in the moment and I know I have full control over her.

Every interaction we've ever had could have ended with her on her back and my cock buried deep in her pussy. I know that, just like I know that while she'd give herself in the moment, she would hate herself and *me* afterwards.

My mission is to make her happy. But that doesn't *only* rely on giving her pleasure. For that to happen, I need her to see herself like I do. I want her to shed her insecurities and doubts.

Twirling her around, I bring her back to my front as I situate ourselves in front of the wall-sized mirror.

"This," I rasp as my hand wraps around her throat. Her spine instinctively arches, her eyes droopy as she gives in to the embrace. "This is how I want you, pretty girl." I lower my mouth to her ear, bringing my tongue over her ear lobe and nibbling at the bit of flesh.

"Sweet. Biddable. *Mine.*"

A shudder goes down her back, her lips parting on a low moan.

"All of you," I whisper, "I want all of you. Your perfects and *imperfects.*"

The last word gets a reaction out of her, and I already feel her panic rising, her eyes closed as she avoids looking at herself.

"Look at us," I command her, and her eyes snap open to focus on the mirror, widening as she takes in her state of undress.

Her chest expands with every breath, her tits bouncing with each move.

I bring my hands lower, to her tapered waist, cupping her from behind before bringing my palms forward and spreading them over her stomach—over her scars.

"You're beautiful, Noelle," I tell her, and her slight flinch doesn't go unnoticed. "You're more than beautiful to me."

"How?"

That one syllable is uttered with so much anguish and confusion mixed together, her expression suddenly shifting. No longer is it playful and seductive. She's looking at herself in the mirror like she's about to cry, her lashes already damp with unshed tears.

And *that* is the crux of the matter.

I need to drill into her how beautiful she is—how exquisite she is. I need to make her see that her scars don't make her any less of a person. On the contrary, they enhance her beauty by emphasizing her strength and her resilience.

Because I know exactly what she feels like. The only difference is that I had time to cope and heal. She's been closed in a bubble that didn't allow her to come to terms with herself and the past.

After I'd escaped the *hacienda* I'd been skin and bone, my entire body riddled with lash markings and other scars that had gotten infected—some well on their way to putrefaction. I'd been lucky that Carlos had taken me in and offered me help. And while the physical wounds had healed, the mental ones had not. For the longest time, I kept seeing myself as that scrawny man on the brink of starvation. I'd look in the mirror and though my muscles were well formed, I'd only see hollows.

It had taken me a long time to get here, so I know the struggle. But I'd faced my demons head on for that to happen.

Noelle hasn't.

If anything, she's been stifled by everyone around her. In trying to protect her, they harmed her even more.

"What do you see, Noelle? Describe to me what you see," I demand.

Her throat works up and down as she swallows apprehensively. Put on the spot, her anxiety is palpable as her eyes roam over her body, her mouth pressing in a thin line.

For the longest time, she's silent.

"Tell me," I urge her more gently, leaning into her and

offering her the heat of my body—the comfort of knowing I'm here for her.

"Pain," the word is barely audible as she bites her lip.

My eyes meet hers in the mirror and she doesn't look away.

"Humiliation," she continues.

I don't speak, merely letting her get everything out.

"Desperation," she breathes out, a strangled sob escaping her body.

"Tell me," I repeat.

"Shame," she whispers, a tear finally making its way down her cheek. "I see shame."

"Why?"

My arms tighten around her when she doesn't answer.

"Why do you feel shame, Noelle?"

"Because I'm never good enough..." she finally answers, her throat clogged with emotion. "I'm never...never..."

"You are," I bring my mouth to her shoulder, kissing it lightly. "You've always been good enough. They just didn't realize it," I tell her gently.

"He used to say I was useless. That the only thing I was good for was to get him mad and make him lose his temper," the words start pouring out of her.

On a ragged voice, she tells me. How she would behave like a robot to avoid getting him angry. How she'd reshaped her entire persona around him—because only then could she avoid his fists.

"I didn't know who I was anymore... I still don't," she says, and my heart fucking breaks for her.

For this beautiful girl that was given to a monster who nearly destroyed her. For the pure soul that had to witness the worst humanity has to offer.

But my heart also swells with pride. Because against all odds, she made it.

"You do. You know who you are. You just got a little lost along the way," I murmur against her skin. She shakes her head, trying to deny it.

"Where is the brave woman that took me head on? Where is the persevering woman who didn't back down no matter what?"

"It was a mask," she states vehemently. "It was all a lie."

"Then lie to yourself. Lie until you believe that you're the strongest, most courageous and valiant woman. Lie to yourself until there's not a sliver of doubt."

"I can't," she shakes her head.

"You can. Because I already believe it."

She stills in my arms, her features contorted in pain.

"You know who you are, and you know your worth. Otherwise you would have let everyone walk all over you. You would have let Cisco lock you away and brand you insane, because you would have believed it. You would have *never* questioned anything he, or anyone else said."

Her pulse quickens, low tremors racking her body as she tries to regulate her breaths.

"That's what I see when I look at you, Noelle. I see a beautiful woman who, in spite of all the hardships that came her way, kept herself and her integrity intact. The world said you were crazy, but you sought to prove it wrong."

"But what if I *am* crazy?" The ghost of a question stills in the air.

"You're not. And you don't believe that either, do you?"

Her head moves from side to side in a no. Swallowing deeply, she raises her eyes to meet mine in the mirror.

I can see the unshed tears, just as I can see her damp cheeks.

"This," I trail my palms over the scars of her stomach, "is the visible proof of your strength."

Slowly, I move my hands up, brushing over her breasts

and her neck as I reach her head. Cupping it from side to side, I hold her still.

"But in here," I whisper as I come closer to her, molding my cheek to hers, "is the invisible. They may not understand, pretty girl. But I do. I *see* you. I see your pain, and I share it. But I also see your strength and your resilience..."

Her breath hitches, and before I can say another word, she turns, wounding her arms over my neck and pressing herself into me.

Hot tears pour down her cheeks before transferring to mine.

"I want to believe you Raf," she whispers between sobs. "I want to be that woman. But when it's all said and done I feel like an impostor."

"Don't. If you are one then so am I," I breathe out. "The pain never goes away, Noelle. You learn to live with it and accept it as part of who you are. I see you. But do you see yourself?"

She tightens her hold over my neck, her muffled cries echoing in the bathroom.

Slowly, though, they begin to ebb.

She leans back, her tear-streaked eyes gazing at me. And on her tiptoes, she raises herself up, gently pressing her lips to mine.

It's shy and tentative, and I can taste her tears on her lips.

Her tongue makes contact with mine and it's enough for me to see stars, the force of the kiss making me reel.

Just like the first time, there's a tightness in my chest at the feel of her lips, as if they were the sweetest poison, beckoning me towards death but granting me salvation instead.

My body recognizes her on a level that is beyond mere mortal understanding. I hold on to her tighter than I've ever held on, the urge to merge her to me too overwhelming.

Like two parts once separated but finally reunited, she

has the power to make me feel at peace—for the first time ever.

I don't know if it's the fact that we're so alike—both in our suffering and in our healing. Or maybe it's the fact that her mere presence in the same room causes a static that makes my body respond on an atomic level.

Though invisible to the naked eye, there's a palpable connection between the two of us—a red thread of fate that binds us together in an ineffable way. Something that goes beyond basic feelings of hate, love, or desire. Because at every stage, it felt like so much more.

She moans against my lips, her eyes closed as she gives herself to the kiss.

Cupping her ass, I lift her up and she wraps her legs around my waist.

I groan low in my throat when my cock lodges right between her pussy lips. It doesn't help that she keeps grinding herself against me, gliding up and down like a born seductress.

"Fuck, Noelle," I mutter a curse as I hold tighter on to her.

In just a few steps, I kick the bedroom door wide open, laying her on clean sheets.

Naked and in the middle of the bed, she looks like a painting come to life.

Her lashes flutter as she looks at me, her eyes wide and full of wonder.

I take a step back, wanting to memorize her like this— spread out for me and waiting for my touch.

She brings her teeth over her lower lip, and a sudden shyness overtakes her as she tries to cover herself.

"No," I rasp. "Don't."

Grabbing on to her ankles, I pull her down, her legs opening up to make room for me at the same time as I take her lips in another kiss.

"You're mine, pretty girl," I say as I swipe my tongue over her lips. "No one else can see you like this."

She gives me a small nod, her eyes already glazed with pleasure.

"Say it," I demand.

"Only you can see me like this," she whispers.

Momentarily satisfied, I trail my lips over her neck, going lower until I reach her tits. She inhales sharply, her eyes on me as I bring my tongue over one pebbled nipple.

She's so soft and sweet, unlike anything I've ever imagined before.

"Agh," she whimpers, arching into me.

"You like that, pretty girl?" I ask as I take her nipple in my mouth, my eyes on her and watching the play of emotions on her face.

She nods enthusiastically, her pupils two big black circles that keep on expanding.

"You taste so sweet here," I speak against her skin as I lavish all my attention on her nipples, sucking and biting until she's going crazy in my arms.

Her breathing becomes more erratic, and as I switch focus to the other nipple, she's already moaning loudly, her hands going to my shoulders, first to push me away, then to draw me closer.

Only when she becomes frantic and on the brink of pleasure do I move, going lower and hovering on top of her stomach.

Flat, but pebbled with the evidence of years of abuse, it's a mosaic that speaks of her history and her pain. I bring my mouth to her skin to kiss each and every one of her scars, mentally grateful that none of the wounds ended up being fatal. Instead, they made her into who she is today.

She survived, and that's enough for me.

"Never feel ashamed of these, Noelle." I raise my head to

see her watching me with an odd expression. Her eyes are downturned, and even through that initial haze of desire, there's the slightest hint of *more.*

"From now on I'll kiss them every day," I murmur as I lay a soft kiss on top of a cigarette burn. "If I love them, maybe you'll learn to love them too."

Her eyes sparkle with unshed tears.

Lifting one hand, she brings it to my face, a tremulous smile pulling at her lips.

"You're one of a kind, aren't you, Rafaelo Guerra?" She muses, her expression a mix of sadness and something else— something I can't put my finger on.

"Only for you," I smirk at her before laying a kiss on top of her mound.

If until now she's been relatively bold, as I reach the top of her pussy, she suddenly tenses, her breathing harsh.

"What… What are you doing?" She asks on a whimper, her legs closing around me.

"What does it look like I'm doing," I raise a brow at her, my mouth tipped up in a shameless smile. "Do you know how long I've been waiting for a taste of this?" I ask as I bring one finger to her pussy, swiping some of her arousal and bringing it to my mouth.

Sweet. So damn sweet.

"Do you know how many times I've imagined my tongue deep in this pretty pussy of yours, Noelle?" I rasp out, raising my gaze to find a deep blush enveloping her features.

She gives a quick shake of her head, her lip between her teeth as she looks at me.

So fucking beautiful, the sight of her spread out for me like this is only making me harder, my balls drawn so painfully tight in hope for release.

It's even worse as I close my eyes and inhale. Her musky

scent invades my nostrils, making me want to bury my face between her legs and never leave.

Fuck, but I've been imagining this for far too long, dreaming of her taste and of my tongue so deep in her pussy, my name on her lips as she screams her release... Yet nothing compares to the real thing—to her scent, her texture, and everything else that's just *her*.

On her elbows, she's peering at me with the slightest hint of trepidation.

Desire speared by anxiety clings to me as I take my time to look at her and memorize all her features. I have to make this good for her. Despite my lack of experience, I want to make sure she gets so much pleasure from me she comes screaming on my tongue.

But as much as I want to simply dive in, I need to rein in my aggression and this lust that's seemingly taken over my body. I need to take it slow, learn what she likes and then do it all over again. After all, I have to remember that this is as new to her as it is to me. I sure as fuck don't want to scare her off with what I want to do to her—not yet, at least.

"Trust me to make you feel good, pretty girl?" I ask her in a gentler tone, wanting to dispel any worries from her side. I need her to give herself to me of her own volition because I know how important that is for someone with her past.

Today is all for her. Worship her body and show her *she* matters—that her pleasure matters.

"Ok," she nods, and that one word hits me right in the chest, making me breathe out in relief.

I'd like nothing more than to tie her up and take her hard and fast, squeeze so much pleasure from her body she'd beg me to stop. But I can't do that now. I can't do that while she's still apprehensive about intimacy.

And her express consent is quite possibly the best sound I've ever tasted.

My hands settle on the back of her knees as I drag her closer to me, my tongue making contact with her pussy as I give her a long lick. Her taste hits my tongue, coating it with the full flavor of her—sweety, tangy, and just a little spicy.

Just like her.

Fuck, if this doesn't feel like the beginning of an addiction —one that threatens to unman me.

Her pussy is so fucking soft, her wetness velvety in texture as it gushes out.

As I tease her clit, she startles, almost jumping out of my grasp.

"Shhh, this is my pussy now, Noelle. Mine to kiss," I say as I lay a kiss right on top of her clit. "Mine to lick," I swirl my tongue around it, that one movement already making her writhe under me. "And mine to fuck," I blow hot air on her clit before wrapping my lips around it, sucking it into my mouth.

Her hands in my hair, her thighs are already tightening around my head as her breathing intensifies, low whimpers escaping her.

"Wh-what... Raf..." She becomes a wordless mess as I lick and nibble, seeking to learn all her pleasure spots.

"Do you like this?" I raise my head to watch her expression, noting her half-closed eyes and the way she's biting her lip to keep from crying out. She gives me a pained nod, and I get increasingly bolder as I start exploring her pussy, licking and nibbling and watching for her cues.

"What about this?" I ask just as I thrust my tongue into her opening. She's so fucking wet, her juices washing over me and drowning me in the sweetest damned thing I've ever tasted. "Do you like my tongue fucking you, Noelle? Do you like the way you can feel me all the way inside you?" I ask just as I push my tongue even deeper inside of her, feeling her walls clamp down on me.

Men talk. Growing up, they certainly didn't censor themselves in my presence, often teasing that it was a lesson for the future. They would make lewd jokes about what it was like to go down on a woman, have her juices flow down your mouth and feel her pleasure as your own. As an asocial teenager bullied for my speech impediment, my last worry was oral sex. Whenever they'd mention it, I would blush and look away, a fact that would promptly trigger their amusement. Still, in my head, I couldn't comprehend the notion of deriving pleasure from pleasuring your partner. More than anything, I couldn't imagine putting my mouth on someone's private parts.

The man I am now, though, wholly approves of their approach to life.

Noelle needs only be in the same room with me and I'm salivating for her pussy. Now that I've gotten a taste? I don't think anyone can stop me from becoming a regular customer —for life.

"Please," she moans, the sound settling on my tongue and acting as a double agent—increasing my arousal and providing me with unspeakable pleasure.

The taste of *her* mixed with the taste of her voice is the most potent combination I've ever known, and my entire body is reacting to it.

My dick is painfully stiff, pre-cum already beading the tip and staining my boxer briefs. At this point, I'm not even concerned about that, because the outcome is clear. Whether I want to or not, I *will* come in my underwear.

It's impossible not to when every little sound she makes has my cock twitching and ready for release. And though my mind is focused on making her feel good, her pleasure is *my* pleasure. There's no doubt about that. Not as her grip on my head tightens, her hips jiggling around the bed as her muscles tense, her release almost imminent.

"Please what? What do you want? Tell me, Noelle," I demand as I give her another lick, wanting to hear the words from her.

Needing to hear the words from her.

"I..." her back arches, her mouth open as she can't seem to catch her breath. "Please help," she yelps as I continue to nibble on her clit.

"Help with what?" I smile mischievously against her pussy, licking her at leisure, but making sure I keep her on the edge until she gives me the words.

"Help me come. Please..." she barely finishes her words as I apply more pressure on her clit, sucking on it until she's screaming my name, her fingers in my hair as she pulls hard.

"Raf..." she whimpers, the sweetest sound I've ever heard.

Just as she's about to come down from her high, I bring two fingers to her opening, slowly pushing them inside and testing her tightness. She's so fucking wet and tight that my cock weeps with jealousy. And as I start pumping them in and out, my tongue on her clit once more, she starts coming again.

"I can't..." she cries out, but I prove to her that she can.

Only when she's wordless and entirely spent do I stop. Placing a quick kiss to her pussy, I trail more kisses as I move up her body.

"Mhmm," she purrs, opening her arms for me and drawing me closer to her. Exhausted, her eyes are closed as she puckers her lips, inviting me for a kiss.

I chuckle as I take her offering, sneaking my hand behind her nape and bringing her closer to me.

She opens her mouth, tasting herself on me. But instead of pushing me away, she draws me closer, moaning as she wraps her legs around me.

There's a glow that clings to her skin as she grins

languidly at me, and for the first time ever, I couldn't be happier about taking anatomy courses in college.

"You're so good to me, Raf," she sighs as she nestles in my embrace, and I get a small pang of conscience for my behavior and everything I've put her through.

She's become so used to people treating her badly that the smallest act of kindness has her in awe with me.

"I'm not," I tell her, "but I will be."

CHAPTER FIFTEEN
RAFAELO

I'm going crazy.

There's no other explanation for the fact that I've been pacing around the room for the last five minutes.

Five minutes since Noelle walked out the door, taking almost all the stationed guards with her for her therapy appointment. Five minutes since I assured myself it will all be fine.

It isn't.

In my bid to show her I'm not some raging caveman, I've tried to keep myself from smothering her with my obsessive tendencies—like the fact that imagining her alone in the world is enough to make me break out in a sweat.

It has been particularly harder after Cisco and Yuyu moved out, leaving us alone in the entire house. Suddenly, I was able to let loose and stop having my guard up. But that also meant having Noelle next to me at all times, which in itself is dangerous.

If I were to recap how the last two days have gone by, I would list our fun activities—watching movies, playing video games and composing music—while adding the grim fact that I've been going to the bathroom every hour or so, either for a cold shower, or to jack off.

I've also learned the meaning of blue balls for the first time ever. They fucking hurt.

Noelle is too hot for her own good, and my dick approves too much, fact being the raging erection I have every time she's near. It doesn't help that she's been extremely generous in opening her legs for me for breakfast, lunch, and dinner, the mere taste of her making me come in my pants—another fact that she's not aware of.

At this point, I wonder if she considers me a saint, since I haven't as much as let her touch my dick. But fuck... My self-restraint only goes so far.

The moment she puts those tiny hands on me, she's either going to end up with my cock down her throat, or fucked in every hole until she can't walk anymore...

"Fuck," I curse out loud.

My thoughts are not helping.

Especially now that I know she's out of my reach. Why the fuck did I have to listen to my brain when I decided to behave normally and not smother her?

What the fuck am I still doing here?

There's no point in fighting a losing battle, so I just put my coat on and grab the keys of the car. If I break a speed limit or two, I might be able to catch up with her.

My adrenaline is pumping, but a few close calls later and I find myself behind her car as it turns towards the parking lot of the building.

Following closely behind, I park next to the other cars, taking a bag with me as I exit the car.

"Oh," she frowns when she sees me.

I paint a smile on my face to hide my harsh breathing or

the fact that I might appear on the afternoon news as a prime example for reckless driving.

Am I the same person who could have recited the driving manual and who always preached safe driving?

I've always prided myself on being a prudent person, carefully weighing each argument before reaching a conclusion and *never* diving head first into danger.

Well, screw that. And while I'm at it, screw sanity too.

"What are you doing here?" She comes towards me, her hips swaying from side to side.

She doesn't even realize how sexy she is with that determined walk of hers, and my overheated brain—not the evolved one—is already at its limit as it starts imagining how she'd look pinned to the hood of my car while I take her from behind, work my cock inside of her...

"Raf," she waves her hand in front of me and I swallow, suddenly aware of the setting we're in or the fact that my pants have dents in them.

Damn it.

"You forgot this," I mumble an excuse as I shove the bag in her hands.

Her brows scrunched together, she peers inside the bag, fishing a hoodie from it.

"What..."

"It will be cold tonight. I checked the weather." I continue to put my foot in my mouth, cringing internally at my own words.

"But I'll be in the car," she looks up at me, puzzled. "We have heating."

"That can break down any time. Technology isn't as reliable as old fashion planning," I add confidently, lest she smell the bullshit on me.

And to stop her from talking further, I simply take the hoodie and slip it over her head.

"Arms," I command.

Her eyes are two huge orbs as she stares at me in confusion. Still, she obeys, placing her arms through the sleeves of the hoodie.

Dragging it down her body, I realize it is a size—or two—too big. Almost reaching her knees, it makes her look even smaller.

"Well, thanks." She blinks before she turns on her heel, heading towards the entrance.

Two guards follow suit, keeping a modest distance.

Shaking my head and muttering a string of curses, I follow too.

"Warm now?" I ask as I reach her side, calling the elevator down and helping her inside.

She gives a small nod, but doesn't attempt to make small talk—not a surprise since my attempts seem to be abysmal.

"You can go now," she tells me when the elevator door pings at her therapist's office.

"I might as well say hello to your therapist," I say casually, already thinking of asking Gianna to come to the house from now on—to minimize danger, of course.

A few steps out of the elevator, and I notice that Noelle hasn't moved from the door.

She has an inscrutable look on her face, her eyes on the floor as her small hands are balled into fists by her side.

"Noelle?" I call out, frowning as I see her slowly look up at me.

"You promised," she whispers.

"What?"

"You promised you'd never look at another woman," she grits out, moving towards me with determination. Aggression is rolling off her as she reaches my side, her pointer jabbed in my chest.

She's small—appearing smaller still dressed like this—

and though she barely reaches the middle of my chest, she has the stance of a warrior ready to go to war.

It's only then that I realize that I'm a fucking idiot—again. It had slipped my mind that I'd taunted her with Gianna, never telling her that she is, in fact, my sister.

"Worry not, pretty girl. I happen to share DNA with that particular woman, and incest isn't my thing," I wink at her, but she doesn't laugh at my joke.

"What are you talking about?" She asks, more confused than before.

Grabbing her hand, I simply lead her towards the office, knocking before stepping inside.

"Raf," Gianna stands up, frowning as she takes us both in. "I didn't expect you here," she comes towards us, ready to give me a hug.

"You're his sister?" Noelle's tone is still suspicious as she looks between the two of us.

Gianna purses her lips.

"I'm sorry I didn't tell you before. But I didn't want you to think there was a conflict of interests. In fact, I hadn't seen Raf in more than a decade until recently," she says apologetically.

Noelle is silent for a moment as she mulls over the revelation.

"She's your sister," she repeats, turning to me. Just as I prepare myself for her anger, she surprises me by exhaling in relief. "Good, good," she nods to herself.

"You're not mad at us for keeping this from you?" I ask tentatively, but she just waves her hand dismissively.

"If you had told me she was anyone else, maybe," she shrugs. "But I'll trust that incest isn't your thing." She grins at me, looking entirely too happy by the whole reveal.

My sister is still confused by the whole exchange, and taking advantage of that, I plop myself into a seat, patting the spot next to me for Noelle. She obeys, like the good girl she is, sporting a big smile still on her face.

And as she peers up at me, I note the adoring look in her eyes.

She's…happy. And like a direct reaction, I find my own mouth spreading in a wide smile.

She looks so fucking gorgeous, I don't think I ever want to see her *un*happy again.

We're so lost in each other's eyes that it takes a loud cough for us to break that connection.

"If that's all, you can leave, Raf," Gianna gives me a tight nod, motioning towards the door.

"Actually," I start as I lean back, "I wanted to ask you if it was possible to schedule the next visit at our place. It's not entirely safe for Noelle to be out and about now," I add as I look back to my pretty girl.

She's almost swallowed by the hoodie as she draws her legs to her chest, making herself comfortable in the plush chair.

She merely nods at my suggestion, not putting up a fight —surprising.

"Is that so…" my sister trails off. "Fine. I'm sure that could be arranged," she mumbles before motioning me to the door once more.

"I'll be waiting for you in the lobby," I lean to whisper in Noelle's ear and she regales me with a soft giggle.

"Ok," she breathes out, her eyes practically eating me up.

Fuck. And here I thought I could control myself. But one of her sweet smiles and I'm already hard and ready to burst.

"Raf?" Gianna's voice filters through my head—just barely —and I realize I should go.

"Fine, fine," I roll my eyes, finally exiting the room.

It's with the greatest hardship that I manage to occupy my time until Noelle is done with her appointment, but as I see her exit the elevator, a huge smile on her face, I immediately light up.

I take one step towards her, but she beats me to it as she runs towards me, jumping in my arms and placing her lips on mine in the sweetest, most intoxicating kiss.

"How come you're so lively?" I chuckle, though my own heart is doing weird movements in my chest at the sight of her.

"Because she's your sister. I don't have to worry about her," she murmurs against my mouth, her arms tight around my head.

I lean back, searching her eyes.

"You don't have to worry about *anyone*." I tell her in a stern tone.

Biting her lip, she looks at me unconvinced.

"Noelle, we talked about this before."

"I know," she sighs. "It's just..." she takes a deep breath. "I've seen how men in this life behave. Funnily enough, my brother is an exception because he's only a human being with Yuyu. But everyone else..." she trails off, "there's no such thing as fidelity."

"Don't," I cut her off. "I know you've seen the worst there is," I tell her, because I'd heard the rumors about Sergio and his harem. "But I would *never* cheat on you. I'm not that type of man. I'll just have to prove it to you," I bring my lips to her temple. "Even if I have to do it for the rest of my life."

She gives a brisk nod, tightening her arms around my neck.

Wrapping my arms around her, I take her to the car, driving home with the guards closely on our trails.

But as the days pass, I realize that my attempt at keeping her safe might not be the best.

"I'm not sure this is the best alternative," Gianna takes me aside after her third session at the house. "She's getting restless. You're barely going out anymore."

"What else can I do?" I purse my lips. "We're vulnerable right now."

I'd put her up to speed with everything that had happened and why I was afraid for Noelle's safety outside the house. Not that inside we were completely safe, but at least Cisco's safety mechanisms could buy us time until reinforcements arrived. There was also his panic room, which, should an attack happen, could keep us going for a few days.

"God," she sighs. "I'm not supposed to tell you this. Actually, I'm not supposed to tell you anything," she rolls her eyes at me. "But take the girl out on a date, will you? How do you think she feels locked in here twenty-four seven?"

"But we have fun," I argue in my defense.

And we do.

We already have an established routine of late night movies and cuddling.

I've never been a cuddler, and memories of Armand's arms around me always threaten to make me ill.

But with her? I just wrap my arms around her, holding her close to me, my head on her shoulder as I listen to her soft breathing. Her mere presence deletes everything that came before—she has the power to quiet my nightmares.

"Really?" My sister crosses her arms over her chest as she raises a brow at me. "She thinks you're embarrassed to be seen out with her, Raf. I'm already saying too much, but if you hurt her, I'm going to personally kick your ass."

My brows shoot up at her vehemence.

"Wow, I didn't realize you two bonded so much."

"I'm not joking," she sighs. "Just don't screw this up, ok? You've already done much better than I ever thought you would, so don't you dare break that girl's heart." She waves her finger at me in a motherly fashion and I can't help the smile that spreads over my lips.

"I wouldn't. She's special," I grin. "I'll do my best to make her happy," I try to appease my sister.

"You better," she says right before she leaves.

Opening the main entrance, though, it's to see a huge man waiting for her. A deep scar runs from his brow to his chin, making him look dangerous.

"There you are," she breathes out, throwing herself in his arms and kissing his cheek. "Bass, meet my brother, Raf," she says, and I suddenly remember who he is.

Her former bodyguard. The one she'd supposedly run away with. Now, her husband.

"Pleased to see you again," I shake his hand.

He narrows his eyes at me before his mouth tugs up in an amiable smile.

"Good to see you," he says before he draws me in a hug. "Gianna told me about you but damn," he shakes his head. "You've sure grown up," he chuckles.

We spend a few minutes catching up and making small talk before my sister is off with her husband, once more extending an invitation to come meet their children.

With a heavy heart, though, I tell her that maybe in the future. As it stands, it's too dangerous for us to go anywhere. And I certainly wouldn't want to invite danger into their home.

But as I close the door and head back to Noelle, Gianna's words keep playing in my head.

Have I been too harsh on her?

It's true that we haven't been out in a while. But I thought she was happy to just spend time together, away from everyone else.

We'd certainly managed to get to know each other better. Late at night, we'd share a glass of wine and have random conversations, baring our souls to one another. We've tackled a wide range of topics, from light ones like entertainment and sports, to deeper, more philosophical ones. And to my greatest surprise, I realized that we had more in common than I'd previously thought.

For all her restricted education, Noelle has a bright and inquisitive mind, and she's forged her own path by availing herself to resources on the internet. We've discussed movies and TV shows, and I was quite baffled to find out that we like the *exact* same things.

Her favorite movie is *The Mummy*. So is mine. Her favorite TV show is *Buffy The Vampire Slayer*. So is mine. But it goes beyond that. If we get into an in-depth conversation about pop culture, our tastes match almost to perfection. It's a bit scary to see someone so similar to me in most ways, but still so different. And that only made me gain a new appreciation for her and for our budding relationship.

But Gianna's words echo in my mind, and knowing what an idiot I can be when it comes to her feelings, I decide to get the answer straight from the source.

She's in our room, propped on the bed, pen in hand as she's trying to solve an anagram. She barely spares me a glance before she's back at work.

"I was wondering something," I start, clearing my voice.

"Hm?" She raises her head.

"Would you like to go on a date?"

She blinks, surprise written all over her face.

"A date?" she repeats, her small brows drawn together in concentration. "But it's not safe to go out, is it?"

"We could manage one outing," I assure her.

"I'm not sure," she whispers, shifting so she's sitting with her legs dangling off the bed. "I like it at home." She forces a smile, but I catch the tremor in her voice.

Fuck, but in my tunnel vision, I'd only thought about

keeping her safe and away from the outside world. I hadn't realized that I was harming her by isolating her.

Her family has been doing it from the beginning, and now, I'm guilty of it too.

"I'm a fucking idiot," I mutter to myself.

She raises her eyebrows in question.

I plaster a smile on my face as I turn to her.

"We're going on a date," I state resolutely, not missing the way her whole face lights up.

She doesn't dare show her happiness, but I can spot it, nonetheless. And it makes me feel like the biggest imbecile once more, because she didn't trust me enough to tell me what she wanted.

"Do you have anywhere you'd like to go?" I probe gently. I want to make sure I'm not screwing this up any more by taking her somewhere she doesn't like.

"Hmm," she takes a moment to think, swinging her legs around. She looks so fucking cute I get the urge to bring her to my chest for a *really* tight hug.

But I quench it.

Last time I did that, I almost forgot my strength and smothered her.

Fuck me... I close my eyes as I take a deep breath.

I need a dating manual.

Something along the lines of *how to avoid killing your partner with love.*

"I think..." she starts in an unsure tone, "I think I'd like to go to the amusement park." She immediately drops her gaze to the floor.

"Then that's where we'll go!" I declare, and she whips up her head, surprised.

A big smile spreads over her face and she jumps on me, wounding her arms around my neck and peppering my face with kisses.

"I've always wanted to go," she whispers. "I've seen it on TV and it looks so fun," she releases a dreamy sigh. "But I didn't know if you'd find it too...juvenile."

"Why would I when I've never been? We're going," I kiss her cheek.

CHAPTER SIXTEEN
RAFAELO

The rest of the day goes by in a flurry as I make the arrangements, getting a blueprint of the amusement park and assigning guards in position everywhere for maximum security.

But I don't tell her this. It's better if she thinks she's not being watched for at least one day.

The following day, I dress casually for the occasion, putting on a white polo shirt and a pair of khakis. But as I check on Noelle, it's to have my mouth drop open in shock.

She's wearing a pair of black tights under a magenta-colored pleated skirt paired with a black blouse that's so tight to her chest, her tits are the stars of the show.

I swallow. Hard.

When she spots me in the doorway, she gets a pink blazer and layers it on top before adding her bag.

"I'm done," she quips, coming to my side and grabbing my arm.

"You look gorgeous," I lean down to kiss the top of her head.

And she does. She looks so fucking beautiful and

youthful in that outfit that my heart skips a beat. Sometimes circumstances make me forget our ages. The fact that despite everything we've been through, we are still young—too fucking young to have lived so much.

"You too," she winks at me. "We make a dashing couple, don't we?" She asks, a warm expression on her face as she twirls in front of me.

"We do," I chuckle, leading her to the car.

The entire drive to Coney Island is filled with fun chatter and light teasing.

"If you were able to do anything you wanted," she starts, her gaze out the window. "What would you do?"

"What do you mean?"

"If you weren't born in this life. If you had the freedom to choose anything…"

"A quiet life. I imagine I'd be a university professor, spending my time studying rocks," I joke, since I'd told her I studied geology at university. She'd been very curious about what I'd meant and I promised her I would take her on a rock-searching hike at some point.

"That sounds lovely," she sighs.

"What about you?"

"I don't know," she raises a finger to the window, drawing on the foggy surface. "A pianist? Maybe," she shrugs. "I think I'd like the freedom to travel around the world for concerts and to…"

"Be yourself," I complete her sentence.

She turns, a sad smile on her face.

"And be myself."

"You can be yourself with me," I bring her hand to my mouth for a kiss. "I won't judge you for anything, pretty girl. You know I love your music. It's such a unique part of you, and when I listen to you play I feel like you're giving me the key to your soul."

She blinks, taken aback by my words.

"You get it," she whispers. "You're the first to truly get it."

"That's because you play for my soul, too, Noelle. I haven't told you before, but I have a condition called synesthesia. For me, sounds and colors have flavors. And your music is quite possibly the most addictive flavor I've ever tasted."

Her eyes widen.

"You… You can taste sounds?" She asks in awe.

"That's one way of putting it," I chuckle.

"What does my voice taste like then?" She turns to me enthusiastically.

"Hmm," I smile. "It's like a mix of hazelnut and chocolate. It's a rich gourmet flavor I'll never tire of," I wink at her.

She laughs, the sound so intoxicating I can't help the shudder that goes down my body.

"Let me put it differently," I continue, "I could eat bland, tasteless food for the rest of my life as long as I had your voice in my ear."

The words please her immensely, her mouth spreading into a wide smile as she gazes at me.

"I haven't liked the way my voice sounded since the fire," she confesses. "But you make me like it again," she nods satisfied as she resumes her seat in the car.

I maintain a pleasant smile on my face, though my mind takes me to that time—guilt, guilt, and more guilt accumulating in the pit of my stomach. If she only knew that the person responsible for the change in her voice is sitting right by her side… But she doesn't remember. And for the first time, I thank whatever deities are out there for that mercy. I doubt she would look at me the same if she saw me through the eyes of *that* Noelle—the one I tried to kill with my own two hands.

"I love your voice, Noelle," I assure her, for her benefit or mine, I don't know.

But just as I utter the words, I get a flashback of another voice—a soft, silvery one that had given me comfort. And for the first time, I can't help but compare the two.

Lucero's had been light, a voice I'd often associate with vanilla custard and crème brûlée—the type of dessert you'd have on a rainy day in the comfort of your bed. Noelle's voice, though equally as sweet, has a smokey quality to it, a rich timber that makes me think of decadence and long, passionate nights spent in each other's embrace.

"We're here," she exclaims, startling me from my reverie.

The amusement park is busier than I would have thought given the late fall weather. Stepping out of the car, Noelle jumps up and down as she looks at the different activities, unable to make up her mind about which she wants to try out first.

I give some quick instructions to the driver to be on stand-by for any eventuality, before taking her hand and going into the crowd.

We hit the different rides, trying each one at least once.

"Don't get sick on me," I tell her when she insists on going on the scariest looking ride.

"Don't tell me you're scared, Rafaelo Guerra," she taunts, winking at me as she runs towards the entrance.

Shaking my head, I redeem our tickets, and join her, strapping in just in time for it to start.

Joke's on me, though, because I end up queasier than her by the end of the ride. Fact that Noelle can't stop throwing in my face as she drags me to another stall.

A silly smile on my face, I can only oblige her, the sight of her enjoying herself so much worth everything.

Only when she's a little tired of running around does she take a break to have a sip of water.

"So, what's next?" I ask as I see her scanning the area for other fun activities.

"Hmm," she raises her finger to her chin, tapping it lightly.

Fuck, but such a cute gesture shouldn't be so arousing. Yet I find that with her, she only needs to lift her finger for me to react.

"That," she points towards a shooting stall.

My lips tug up in anticipation, since *that* is something I can do for her.

"Then come on. I'll win you a toy," I tell her confidently.

So happy she is at the mention, that she skips all the way to the stall.

"Wow," she breathes out as I shoot down target after target. The owner seems a little put out with me, no doubt hating the fact that he'll have to hand over one of his biggest prizes.

But as I finish the round with all perfect shots, he reluctantly points us towards the biggest toys on display, telling us to choose one.

"That," Noelle points towards a white, scaly and malefic looking serpent.

I gulp down.

"Are you sure?"

"Yup," she nods, going straight for it, wrapping the giant plushie around her neck as if it had been made for her.

"Then that's it," I nod at the shop owner before we walk away.

"You don't like snakes," she finally says as she looks at my wary expression.

"It's not that I don't like them..." I trail off, threading my fingers through my hair. "They don't bring particularly good memories," I add vaguely.

"What do you mean?" She frowns, biting her lips as she looks at me.

"After I escaped the *hacienda,* I wandered in the desert of New Mexico for a while. And there wasn't much food around," I shrug.

She stops.

"You ate a snake?"

"More than one," I chuckle. "They're not the best," I admit.

"I'm so sorry, Raf," she lays her tiny hand on top of mine. "I can change it for something else," she's quick to say.

"No. Absolutely not. You like it and that's enough for me," I stop her when she tries to take it off her shoulders. "Maybe seeing it wrapped around you like this will make me like it too," I try to crack a joke.

She bites her lip as she looks at me worried, but eventually she just nods.

"You know," she starts, giving my hand a quick squeeze. "I don't want you to always make sacrifices for me," she says in a serious tone. "Isn't a relationship all about compromise? I don't want you to feel like you have to give up things just so I am comfortable."

My eyes widen at her sudden outburst.

"But that's just the thing, Noelle. I *am* happy if you are happy. I'm not giving up anything. What brought this on, pretty girl?" I ask her as I tug her closer to me.

She shrugs, but I can tell there must be a deeper issue. Otherwise she wouldn't have brought it up.

"If you keep putting me first, I don't want you to end up resenting me," she says in a small voice and my heart breaks at the conviction I feel in her tone.

She's still thinking that this is temporary. That at some point I'll tire and get rid of her.

"Hey," I tip her chin up. "That's not going to happen.

When someone is important to you, you do everything in your power to make them happy."

She blinks, her eyes damp.

"I guess I've never been important to anyone before." She laughs nervously, and that one sentence fucking kills me.

"You are now," I murmur as I lean down to kiss her.

Her lips are so soft as they skim the surface of mine, and a groan escapes me when she reaches out with her tongue, lightly touching my lips.

There's something different about this kiss. A residual sweetness that tugs at my heart like never before. And as I wrap my arms around her body, bringing her closer to me, it's to feel her closer than ever.

She's in my head, my heart, my fucking blood. Her presence surrounds me so thoroughly, permeating every atom of my body.

And I never want her to leave.

"You *make* me feel important," she whispers against my lips. "Thank you for that," she strains a smile, though I see the unshed tears on her lashes.

"Let me make this sweeter," I propose as I motion towards a cotton candy stand.

"Hmm, I might be persuaded," she replies cheekily, but her expression is brighter.

"Wait here," I instruct her as I move a few steps over to sit in line.

All the while, my eyes are on her, eating her up and thinking how *she* would be better than cotton candy.

"Sir?"

"Oh, yes. Two pieces, please," I say as I pull out my card to pay.

"Cash only," the vendor gives me a tight smile.

"Right," I mumble, pulling my wallet and rummaging

through it. I hand him a few notes, while he tells me to wait for the cotton candy.

A smile pulls at my lips as I picture kissing her right after she eats the cotton candy, the sweetness of the sugar only intensifying *her* sweetness.

"Here," he says after a while, handing me the cotton candy.

But as I turn around, my smile falls, replaced by a vicious scowl. My feet move of their own accord.

"Come on, sweetheart, just give me your number," a man says as he invades Noelle's personal space.

She's visibly uncomfortable, taking a step back.

"I'm married," she keeps mumbling, trying to put some distance between them. Still, the asshole won't listen.

One more step and I slide between them.

"She said she's married," I raise an eyebrow at him. Turning to her, I place the cotton candy in her hands, my entire body tense from just seeing him in her proximity. "Let me handle this," I tell her gently.

"Don't tell me you're the husband," he laughs derisively. "Why don't you trade, sweetheart. Leave your rich boy for a ride in the hood…"

My fist connects with his face before he can finish his words. Stumbling back, he doesn't seem deterred. If anything, he has an arrogant smirk on his face.

"Damn, her pussy must be hella nice," he continues, and that one sentence just handed him his sentence.

"What did you just say?" I ask calmly, taking a step towards him.

He continues to provoke me by stringing together some obscene words, obviously trying to rile me up.

"What's wrong, posh boy? Worried she might like my dick better than yours?" A few others chuckle at his words, all forming a circle around me.

Sounds dim in my ears as my eyes hone in on them—prey. A twitch in my cheek, and my entire mind goes blank.

My fists make contact with flesh, then with bone. Blood splatters all over my face, but I won't stop—can't stop.

Gasps resound from all around me, but it's only when a pained shrill reverberates in the air that I still.

Slowly, consciousness trickles back in, and I find myself face to face with a barely recognizable mess of a human. Blood is everywhere, pouring out of him, splattered on the pavement and staining my entire body. He's not the only one, all of the other chaps cheering him on are on the floor, moaning in pain while holding on to injured limbs.

It looks like a fucking blood bath, and I find it hard to believe *I* did it.

Getting up, I take a step back, intent on going back to Noelle and getting the hell out of here before the cops show up.

Already, people have formed a circle around us, watching and using their phones to record. Fuck... I'll need to send the guards after everyone and ask Panchito to make sure no video makes it to the internet.

But just as my logic decides to reappear, I realize Noelle is nowhere to be seen.

I push through the crowd, shoving them aside as I look for her.

Seconds turn into an eternity as despair starts clawing at me, another fog descending over my mind.

Where is she?

"Where is she?" I yell.

I must look like an animal. All draped in blood, a desperate expression on my face as I move wildly about the area.

People are wise enough to get the hell out of my way. And it's only then that I see her.

She's crouched on the floor, her palms over her ears, her eyes wild with fear. She keeps rocking from side to side, moving her hands over her knees as she holds them to her chest.

"Noelle?" I call out, my voice coming out hoarse.

She flinches, her gaze meeting mine as she makes to move away.

Like a fucking knife to my chest, I feel a hole forming right in the middle of my heart as I see her fall on her ass, all in an attempt to get away from me.

"Noelle," I try to soften my tone as I come near her.

"Don't touch me," she yells, her eyes squeezed shut, her hands still pressing over her ears. "Please don't touch me," she continues to cry out, her entire body shaking.

"Pretty girl, it's me," I tell her gently, extending my hand towards her.

"No!" she yells, slapping it away as she tries to drag herself away from me.

"Noelle, it's me," I repeat, moving closer to her.

But just as my hand touches her shoulder, she loses it. Flailing limbs and sharp shrieks, she starts hitting me right and left in an attempt to get me off her.

Fuck...

More people surround us, and I realize we don't have the time to sit around waiting for the cops to arrive.

I simply tug her to my chest, taking everything she has to give me as I take her to the car.

"Let me go," she keeps crying out, her small fists landing blows on my shoulder blades.

"Shh. It's me," I repeat the same phrase all over.

It's only when we're in the car and on the way home that she quiets down. Worn down, she falls asleep on my chest.

And though I just beat the shit out of four men, my body is still wound tight with tension.

I failed her.

The horror in her eyes when she'd looked at me had ended me.

I don't think I've ever felt less than human than when I'd seen her eyes, so fucking full of fear and disgust as she'd laid them on me...

"Fuck," I bring my blood-stained hands to my face, wiping some of the sticky substance only to realize my eyes are damp.

I should have thought of her before flinging my fists around. I can't even imagine how traumatic that must have been to see for someone with her past, and at this point I can only berate myself for my idiocy.

Because, somehow, I know things won't be the same when she wakes up.

And I only have myself to blame.

Chapter Seventeen
Rafaelo

"She's fine, Cisco. Just a small scare," I grit out before I hang up on him.

It seems that the doctor couldn't help himself and had to go run his mouth to Cisco.

After she woke up, she started crying out in terror again, thinking someone was going to kill her. My presence seemed to make it even worse, and when I couldn't calm her down myself, I ended up calling both my sister and the doctor Cisco has on his retainer.

My sister tried to calm her down, but that was in vain too. Luckily, the doctor administered her a sedative, and according to both, it was just shock and she should be fine —eventually.

It's already been hours, and she's not fine.

She's anything but fine.

Because I know what's going to happen once she wakes up again. She's going to take another look at me and ask me to never show my face again.

Fuck…

I wish I could turn back the time and *not* react the way I did. But I don't even know what came over me.

I've never once in my life reacted like this—with my fists. Opening my eyes to see myself and the others covered in blood from injuries I'd caused had been terrifying for me, too. Because I couldn't recognize myself anymore.

Is this who I've become now? An animal? Someone who can't control his urges?

Just the idea that my pretty girl could be hurt, or upset, awoke something dangerous in me.

And I don't know if I like it.

I spend the rest of the day in video conferences, trying to take my mind off the incident. And as it gets later and later, I get increasingly apprehensive to go to the room.

Will she scream at me?

Will she try to hit me again?

Though I'm not particularly keen to find out, my feet still take me there.

The entire room is bathed in darkness save for a low beam of light from the moon, but I still note her small form huddled under blankets. Her chest rises and falls with every breath, and for a moment I find myself rooted to the spot.

Did I mess everything up?

I move stealthily as I take a seat on the chair by the window. The bed in full view, I can only stare at her.

Will I still have her in the morning, or will she repudiate me?

She's sleeping on her side, her nightgown slid down one shoulder, the tip of her breast peeking through.

Fuck, but even in a situation like this, one look at her and I'm hard. Still, knowing my time with her might be limited, I allow myself to stare at leisure. Eat her up with my eyes until her image is imprinted on my retina.

My heart tugs painfully in my chest just as my cock hardens at the sight of her.

If before I'd been gone for her, then I have no words for quantifying what I feel now that I've gotten to know her better. And to realize I'm about to lose everything...

She moves, a soft sigh escaping her as she shifts in bed, the blanket sliding down her body to reveal more of her.

Leaning back, I spread my legs as I palm my cock through my pants, her sounds making all my blood pool down in that particular region. And as she stretches lazily, like a pampered cat, I can't help the low groan that escapes my lips as I squeeze my balls.

It's almost painful at this point—watching her and knowing I might never get to touch her again.

The urge to lower my zipper and stroke myself to completion is overwhelming. But I can't do it. I can't have her wake up to me jacking off to her sleeping form and make her even more terrified of me than she already is.

I suddenly stand up, ready to leave. One more second in the same room as her and my self-control *will* snap.

But as I take a step towards the door, it's to find her awake, watching me with curious eyes.

Our eyes connect, and I stop, my limbs frozen at the emotion I find in the depth of those two beautiful orbs.

For a moment, neither of us talks. And as her gaze dips down to the bulge in my pants, she swallows hard, a blush climbing up her cheeks.

At least she's not screaming.

"I'll go sleep in the other room," I assure her, knowing I'm likely not welcome here.

"Don't go," her voice is barely above a whisper, but it's enough to make me still.

"Don't go, please," she repeats, adding more confidence to her tone.

I turn to face her.

She's on her knees, moving towards the edge of the bed, her gown hiked up her legs. The moonlight hits her at the perfect angle to emphasize the contour of her body through the sheer material, and I feel my mouth go dry.

"I'm sorry," she says quietly, and my eyes widen.

"*You* are sorry?" I ask, incredulous. "*I* am sorry. I scared you with my brutish behavior," I tell her, barely fighting the urge to take her in my arms and murmur sweet apologies all night long.

She wets her lips as she peers at me, her features full of uncertainty.

"Not you, necessarily," she adds. "The fighting scared me. The fists…" she trails off, looking away.

"Noelle," my voice breaks, because that one gesture gives away all her pain—all her fucking pain. "You don't have to excuse yourself. You *never* have to excuse yourself. I should have handled it better. I shouldn't have let it get to my head and…"

"No," she shakes her head. "You defended me, and that's all that matters," she grabs my hand, bringing it over her heart. "You're my hero, Raf. Never think otherwise. You *always* save me," she gives me a tight smile. "No one's done that for me before. No one's ever cared to."

"Sweetheart, you never have to worry about that from now on," I tell her in a gentle tone. "I'll vanquish all your fears. Just say the word, and I'll do it."

"How are you real?" she whispers in reverence, her eyes on me as moisture gathers around the corners. My heart constricts in my chest, her words undeserved.

I'm a fucking bastard. I'm a fucking greedy sonofabitch who doesn't deserve her regard, yet I'm taking it anyway.

Her skin is warm against the rough pads of my fingers,

the feel of it driving me crazy. My breathing becomes harsher, my cock even harder in my pants.

What is it about her? What is it about her presence that has me so enthralled?

Slowly, she drags my hand lower so my entire palm covers her breast, her pebbled nipple poking through the material of her nightgown.

"I don't want you to go," she says, tugging me closer.

My knees hit the edge of the bed, and before I know what's happening, her tiny hands are working my belt.

"Noelle," I cover her hands with mine, stopping her briefly. "What are you doing?" I ask gently, not wanting her to do something out of some misguided sense of guilt.

Not when the fault rests entirely with me.

"I want to please you," she peers shyly at me through her lashes. "I want to make you feel as good as you made me feel. You're always…" she swallows, "touching me, but you never let me touch you."

"I don't want you to do it because you think you should, Noelle. I told you. We're going at your pace."

More than anything, I don't want to do something that would remind her of her past. In my inexperience, I can see myself blundering. She excites me too much for me to think logically, and with her hand on my dick…

"I'm ready for the next step," she adds, more confidently. "Unless you don't want me to," she whispers.

"I do," I groan. "Fuck, you have no idea how much I do…"

That's all the urging she needs to unbuckle my belt and slide my zipper down.

I'm so fucking hard I know I won't last long. Especially if she thinks to put her lips on me… The mere thought of those pouty lips wrapped around my cock makes me leak, pre-cum already leaking from the tip.

She bites her lip in concentration as she fumbles with my

pants, hooking her fingers over the band of my boxers and hastily pulling them down.

My dick springs free, slapping against the plane of my stomach. Her eyes go wide when she sees it, and her hands freeze on the band of my pants. She swallows hard, speechless for a moment.

"Noelle?" I ask, afraid something's wrong.

"Uhm," she clears her throat, raising her eyes to meet mine. She blinks in uncertainty as if she doesn't know what to say.

I bring my hand to her cheek, cupping it gently and swirling my thumb over her soft skin. All in an effort to make her more comfortable.

"I know how sex works," she starts, her voice quivering. Her gaze falls to my dick, her eyes widening ever so slightly as she sees it twitch in her direction. "But I don't know how *that* is going to work..." she trails off, blinking rapidly.

"What do you mean?" I frown.

"It's big," she says, pointing at my cock. "Is it supposed to be that big?" she suddenly asks, whipping her head up.

I stifle a laugh, especially as I realize she's in earnest.

"You're very good for a man's ego, pretty girl," I chuckle.

She scrunches up her nose, looking too freaking cute as she intently peruses my dick, as if she's trying to memorize all the angles.

"Can I touch it?" she eventually inquires, peering at me and batting her lashes like a born seductress.

There's something inherently sexy to her body language and the way she moves, her facial expressions always so mesmerizing it's no wonder I'm sporting a hard-on day and night.

"It's all yours."

Tentatively, she brings one hand up to take hold of my

length, her brows furrowing when she realizes she can't wrap her fingers around me.

My mouth parts on a silent groan when I feel her warm flesh against mine, but I let her explore at her leisure. She adds a second hand, holding them one on top of the other as she moves them over my shaft.

"Is this ok?"

"Anything you do to me is ok," I assure her, already biting back a moan.

Maybe she doesn't know what she's doing, but her touch alone is enough to drive me crazy. Jesus Christ, but I don't think I've known greater pleasure than having her hands on me.

"It's warm and soft," she notes, looking pensively for a moment before dipping her head and swiping her tongue over the head.

"Fuck," the sound escapes me, and she immediately looks up in question.

"It feels too good, pretty girl," I praise. "Too fucking good."

A satisfied smile appears on her face and before I know it, she does it again, this time slower and more at leisure, taking the time to move her tongue all over the head and under, licking me slowly yet thoroughly.

"God," I bark, my voice hoarse and out of control.

My eyes flutter closed for a moment, the feel of her wet tongue on my cock the heaven I never dared to dream about. I try to ground myself in the moment, focus on every single touch and sear it in my mind.

"It doesn't taste bad," she comments right before she opens her mouth to take me inside.

Fuuuuuuck!

If the feel of her tongue was enough to make me see stars,

her wet, warm mouth closing around me is more potent than dynamite.

She moves her hands over my shaft at the same time as she swallows me deeper into her mouth and I think I see stars.

No, correction.

I fucking *see* stars.

"Fuck," I curse out, my hand suddenly in her hair. "You're so fucking amazing, you know that? God," I mumble incoherently. "You're going to make me come in your lovely mouth, aren't you? You're going to let me blow my load in that sweet mouth of yours and you're going to swallow every drop of my cum."

Even with my dick in her mouth, she still manages to nod.

I look down to find those gorgeous eyes of hers on me, her pupils eclipsing her irises, and I know that my naughty girl is enjoying this—she's aroused by it.

"Do you like my cock in your mouth, pretty girl?" I ask, slowly caressing her cheek as she continues to suck me. She lavishes so much attention on the head—noticing it gets the most reaction out of me—that I need to make a conscious effort not to come too quickly.

"Yes," the sound is muffled, but the vibrations from her throat envelop my cock and I can't help the slight thrust of my hips.

She's surprised too, but doesn't complain. She merely opens her mouth wider, waiting for me to do it again.

I start thrusting in her mouth, shallow at first before slowly picking up the peace when I notice she's ok with it.

"Eyes on me," I order, my voice harsh. Her eyes snap open as she looks up at me, blinking in surprise.

"That's it, Noelle. Fuck, you're so hot with my cock in your mouth, pretty girl. That alone is enough to make me come," I rasp as I bring my other hand down her chest, tugging her gown down until one breast pops free.

I wrap my fingers around her nipple, playing with it and eliciting a moan from her. Every sound increases the vibrations around my cock, making it even harder for me not to blow up right here and now.

But if anything, I'm determined. This isn't just about me. It's a shared experience, and seeing her enjoy it as much as I do makes it a hundred times hotter.

"Tell me you love having my cock down your throat," I demand suddenly, pinching her nipple.

She pulls back, saliva dripping down her chin as she looks up at me.

"I love having your cock down my throat," she says with so much sincerity, my heart nearly jumps out of my chest. Her cheeks are flushed, and she blushes even more as she says the words.

But then she's back at work, peppering kisses all over my shaft.

"Because it's mine and mine alone," she adds with a languid smile on her lips.

"All yours," I agree. "Only yours."

Holding my length with her hands, she raises my cock up so she can have access to the underside. And parting her lips, she lays them right under the head, sucking and licking until my vision blurs.

No matter how much I'd like to delay this, I'm already far too gone.

"I'm coming," I warn, my breathing growing harsher. I expect her to pull away, and I wouldn't be mad if she decided not to swallow. But my pretty girl surprises me as she wraps her lips around the head, sucking her cheeks in, all the while jerking my shaft off with her hands.

My release is imminent, my cock twitching as cum shoots down her throat and coating her entire mouth.

The orgasm seems to go on forever, and as my entire body starts spasming, the aftershocks are almost as powerful.

"God," I breathe out in wonder.

Opening my eyes, I gaze down just in time to see my cock fall away from her lips, a trail of spit lingering behind.

She looks up at me, and before I know it, she opens her mouth, pushing her tongue out to show me my seed. White against pink, it slowly starts to dribble down her chin.

The sight of her like this is my undoing, and despite having just emptied my balls, I feel myself hardening again.

She swirls her tongue around before swallowing, looking at me expectantly.

"You're such a good girl, Noelle," I praise, gently caressing her face. "But where did you learn that?" I ask, since there's no way she would do that without having seen it somewhere.

She purses her lips, embarrassed.

"I watched a video," she whispers. "I wanted to please you," is all she says as she turns those big eyes of hers to me, looking like the teacher's pet waiting to be praised for acing her homework.

"You did. You pleased me immensely," I tell her, and her smile widens. "You always please me, Noelle," I commend her.

My hand on her nape, I lean down as I open my mouth over hers, licking her lips and thrusting my tongue in her mouth to taste myself on her. She meets me stroke for stroke, deepening the kiss until our mouths are almost one.

I only take a break to unbutton my shirt and throw it on the ground, my pants following suit. Then my lips are on hers again. She moans into the kiss, her hands around my neck as she holds on tight.

One hand around her waist, and I quickly maneuver us

around so I'm on my back on the bed while she's on top of me.

My dick is slowly recovering, blood already filling the shaft as my eyes feast on the goddess before me.

"You liked it?" She asks shyly, and a smirk pulls at my lips.

"I fucking loved it," I tell her, my hands on her waist as I tug her gown up. She raises her arms to help me, and soon it accompanies my clothes on the floor. Naked as the day she was born, she looks glorious sitting on top of me, her body the epitome of sinuous curves and sinful nights.

My hands on her ass, I bring her forward until her pussy rests on top of my cock.

"Oh," she whimpers, her hands suddenly on my pecs.

"What do you want?" I demand. "Tell me and it's yours."

"I don't know," she bites her lip, "this?" she asks as she moves up and down my shaft.

Her eyes snap shut, a low moan erupting from her throat.

"That's it. Use me," I tell her, holding on to her waist as I lean forward to wrap my mouth around a nipple. Sucking it in my mouth, I let her have full control as she positions my cock right between her pussy lips. She's fucking dripping, her arousal coating my flesh as she moves, slowly at first, before picking up speed.

Her lips part as her breath comes in short spurts, and I know she's building up towards her orgasm.

I bite down on her nipple, pinching the other with my hand as I feel her muscles tensing all around.

"I've never seen a more beautiful woman, Noelle," I rasp, blowing hot air over her breast. "You're so fucking hot, pretty girl. I could come from the sight of you like this alone."

"Raf," she whimpers, her hands on my cheeks as she brings me towards her for a kiss.

She keeps grinding over my cock, the friction so deliciously addictive, I know I'm never going to be whole again without her.

And to think I'm not even inside of her yet...

"You make me hot," she tells me. "You make me so hot," she moans, her mouth open as she lets me ravish it with mine. "I can't bear it if you leave me. Promise me you'll never leave me."

"Never," I promise just as she increases her speed.

I trail wet kisses all over her face and neck, sucking in on her skin and leaving my mark on her—wishing somehow it would be permanent.

"I'm yours, pretty girl. All yours."

"All mine," she repeats, her mouth forming an o as her eyes squeeze shut. "I'm yours too," she says as her breathing intensifies, her clit right on top of the head of my cock as she rubs herself on me. "So entirely yours," she gasps, stilling in my arms.

I feel her opening spasm on top of my shaft, more juices flowing out of her channel and drenching my cock in her cum.

She's absolutely breathtaking as she comes, her arms tightening around me, her tits squished against my chest. Her mouth opens on top of mine, our tongues wildly seeking one another. It's messy. It's anything but clean and orderly. We're both too frantic in our need for one another to care about anything else but being closer.

She grinds herself harder, riding her orgasm and driving me towards my own.

My balls tighten, the pressure too much and before I know it, my cock jerks against her pussy, cum shooting up all over my stomach.

Still, she doesn't stop. And I don't stop her.

She continues to move on top of me, our mouths fused to one another.

And in this moment we *are* one.

I may not be inside of her yet, but I fucking feel her to my very soul. And I know it's the same for her. Especially as she sucks my tongue in her mouth, biting on my lip before dragging her tongue across my cheek and towards my ear.

"I love you, Raf," she whispers.

I open my mouth to say the words back, but my throat clogs up, stopping them from being released into the world.

Laying her head on my chest, she's so worn out that she doesn't realize I haven't said them back.

And why haven't I?

I *do* feel deeply for her.

But why can't I say the words back?

CHAPTER EIGHTEEN
RAFAELO

I don't know how much time I spend staring at her. With her silken locks draped over my chest, her pert little nose in the air and her plump lips lightly parted, she looks too fucking sexy. Certainly too much for me to bear to leave the bed yet.

She told me she loves me.

God, but what did I do to deserve it?

I would have never imagined earning her love anytime soon. But now that I have it? A deep sense of satisfaction blooms in my chest, but with it, a wave of uneasiness hits me too.

I *do* return her feelings. Hell, I fucking adore her.

She's been the most unexpected gift that life has thrown my way, and I don't think I've ever been as happy as with her these past weeks. She's my very own ray of sunshine, and I'd vowed to myself that I would protect and cherish her at all costs.

Then why can't I open my damned mouth and tell her I love her, too?

The entire night, while my pretty girl's been sleeping

peacefully, I've been twisting and turning, battling with myself and unable to find a moment of peace.

I love her, yet what I feel for her is so much more than that, so I feel reluctant to say the words out loud knowing I've said them before...

As I laid awake and ruminated over everything, I came to the conclusion that because I've used the words with Lucero before, I couldn't use them again with Noelle. It wouldn't feel right. It also wouldn't quantify my feelings, and I know that what I felt for Lucero was different than what I feel for Noelle.

It's absurd.

Entirely ridiculous.

People love more than once in their lifetimes, so it's silly to even think that the word love cannot be used more than once.

Yet no matter how much I try to rationalize it, I can't.

There is this need inside of me to differentiate and compartmentalize my feelings for Noelle and Lucero—keep them separate from each other.

Noelle shifts in her sleep, interrupting me from my thoughts. One glance at her, though, and my smile widens.

She tips her head up to peer at me, a silly grin on her face.

"Morning," she whispers in my ear.

"Morning," I lay a gentle kiss on her nose. "How are you feeling?"

"Good," she nods. "Very good," she bats her lashes at me. "I was wondering..." She bites her lip as she traces a heart with her finger on my chest. "Would you like to shower together?"

Not one to miss an opportunity, I simply swoop her in my arms, the blanket falling from our bodies and leaving us naked. Taking her to the bathroom, I place her in the shower and proceed to spoil her, leisurely washing her body and her hair, making sure to be particularly attentive to that sweet spot between her legs.

She returns the favor, and we have a good laugh when she becomes a little shy as she gets to my lower region, her dainty hands exploring my hard cock.

"You're such a tease," I breathe out. She works her hand up and down, her touch so fucking maddening I have to rest my back against the stall for support as I feel myself coming.

"You secretly love it," she winks at me before dropping to her knees and cleaning me up.

After we're both done, I wrap her in a towel, drying her up and placing her on the bed so I can apply lotion to her legs.

On my knees, I run my fingers along the length of her calves, slowly massaging the moisture into her skin.

As I'm working on her body, she threads her hands through my hair, gently combing it.

"Can you forgive me for this?" One finger stills on the scar at the start of my hairline. She traces the ridge of it, her touch soft and healing.

"There's nothing to forgive," I raise my eyes to hers. "You did what you had to in order to survive. How can I blame you for that when you're here now? With me?"

It seems surreal that I'm able to let go of everything with those words. I'd spent so much time hating her—hating the glimpses I'd gotten of her at the *hacienda*—because in my mind, I'd built her up to be some type of unfeeling villain.

Retrospectively, though, I can recognize why I'd been so quick to condemn her. From the first moment I'd seen her, I'd thought her to be the most beautiful woman I'd ever laid my eyes on. And against everything inside of me telling me not to, I *had* been attracted to her.

There had been one decisive moment, before anything had happened, when our gazes had met. Maybe my memory is distorted, but in my mind that moment had stretched across time, her gaze on mine; mine on hers. Time had stood still as my soul had recognized something in her—something priceless.

But the spell had soon broken, and when she'd hurled the plate at me, her expression changing to one of smug satisfaction as she'd watched the blood pour down my face, she'd become dead to me. She'd become just like everyone else in my life—a tormentor.

My initial reaction to her had been so strong, it stands to reason that my subsequent hate would be even stronger.

"I may not remember what happened," she purses her lips, "but know that I *am* sorry, Raf," she says as she leans forward, placing her lips over the scar in the sweetest kiss. She lingers, and I find myself unable to break the spell.

"I love you," she says the words again and I freeze.

She doesn't notice as she continues to pepper kisses all over my face. Reaching my lips she draws back a little, her eyes on me.

Framing her face with my palms, I hold her still.

"I adore you, Noelle. You're my heart," I tell her sincerely. A look of pure pleasure appears on her face, and I know I've said the right words.

Better yet, they *feel* right.

After we dress up, Noelle goes to her music room to continue working on her piece while I head to Cisco's office, ready to get in contact with Carlos and the guys again.

To my great surprise, however, I bump into Cisco in the hallway.

"I didn't expect to see you here," I raise a brow at him.

"Good of you to make yourself at home," he adds drily as he takes his coat off, heading straight for the office.

"Right, and to what do I owe this pleasure?"

Yuyu is at the very end of her pregnancy, and it's unlike Cisco to leave her side even for one second.

"The concert is next week. We need to go over the details once more to make sure everything is perfect," Cisco says as he goes straight for his drink cabinet.

"Yeah, that's not going to happen," I remain in the doorway, crossing my arms over my chest. "I'm not going to put Noelle in danger, especially knowing how unhinged my brother is," I add confidently. "The plan is off."

Cisco's eyes flash at me, but he doesn't reply for a moment. He merely brings his glass to his lips, taking a sip.

"And I told you to keep your self-righteousness to yourself. The plan is moving forward." His tone is unyielding. "Now more than ever," he mutters.

"No," I state staunchly. "I'm not taking any risks with Noelle's safety. Now or *ever*," I look him straight in the eye so he can see I'm not going to budge on this issue.

"Raf, Raf," the corner of his mouth curls in derision. "Weren't you the one who came to me with the suggestion? Use my sister to stick it to your brother?" He smiles as he swirls the liquid amber in his glass.

"That was before. Things have changed."

"Let me tell you what's changed, Raf," he slams his glass on the table. "That little shit of your brother dared to go after my wife. I don't have many hard limits. But the moment *anyone* goes after my wife or my children, all bets are off."

The anger is palpable as it rolls off him, but I don't let it intimidate me. After all, we're all fighting for someone. He has his reasons that propel him forward, and I have mine.

One in particular.

"Surprised I'm not hearing anything about your sister. Or wait, she doesn't matter, does she?"

His nostrils flare, but he keeps himself in check.

"Of course my sister matters. To a certain extent. But the

plan is in motion, and she is the piece de resistance," he gives a fake smile. "You offered her up, now hold up your part of the bargain."

"And I'm saying no and that is final. I won't have Noelle anywhere near my brother. And I think it's high time I made a few things clear, Cisco. Maybe before she was under your guardianship, but now she is my wife. And that means you don't get a say in what she does, or doesn't."

His gaze holds mine for a moment before he chuckles.

"Don't tell me she got her claws in you."

"Your sister doesn't have any claws and you damn well know it. I don't think there's anyone more innocent or blameless than Noelle," I grit my teeth, his blasé attitude rubbing me the wrong way.

"Sure," he shakes his head, amused. "Whatever you say, lover boy. But the show will go on."

I take a deep breath, knowing I must approach this with a clear head. Though seeing Cisco care so little for his sister makes me so fucking mad I can barely control myself.

"Maybe we should reconsider our partnership," I raise my chin as I casually lean back against the wall.

"Wow. I have to say I didn't think you had it in you, Raf. So what, you're going to take my sister and you're going to live happily ever after chasing rainbows?" He laughs. "Might I remind you that you're nothing without my protection. The moment you leave this house you have a target on your back. Are you sure you want to risk my sister like that?" A smile threatens to overtake his face as he thinks he has me backed into a corner.

"I'll take the risk," I shrug. "I'll just trust myself to keep her safe."

After all, isn't it better for her to be away from her family of lunatics? My experience of my own family and now witnessing how things are done with DeVille don't give me much confidence about this family business, but I know that as long as Noelle and I are together we can surpass everything that comes our way.

"We'll go pack," I tell him in a stern tone so he realizes I'm not playing around.

Just at that moment, though, Noelle appears in the doorway, frowning as she looks between Cisco and me.

"Noelle, go pack, we're leaving."

"Noelle, what a surprise, do come in," Cisco calls her over.

Her eyes on me, she takes a tentative step inside.

"What's happening?" She asks, confused.

"Your husband thinks it's wise to leave the house and my protection," Cisco starts, a cunning smile playing at his lips.

"Why?"

"Noelle, let's go."

"Why don't we let her make her own mind, Raf? Weren't you preaching that until now?" he chuckles. "Your husband here had a marvelous idea to use you as bait to lure his brother out from hiding."

"It was before." I feel compelled to add. "Before I knew…"

She blinks, an unsettled look on her face as she asks Cisco to tell her more about the plan.

And as I listen to him list all of the things we'd planned—things we'd never talked to her about—I feel like the worst kind of scoundrel.

The best I can hope is that she won't hold it against me. That she will realize this was before my feelings for her changed—before everything.

"I see," is all she says as she nods thoughtfully.

"Noelle…"

"I'll do it," she declares.

My eyes widen in shock, while Cisco smiles in his glass.

"What did you say?"

"I'll do it," she turns to me. "This is your chance to get

your brother. Make him pay for everything that he did to you," she grabs my hand, holding it to her chest. "I know how important this is to you and if I can help with anything," she gives me a tight smile. "I want to help."

"No. Absolutely not, Noelle. I don't want you anywhere near that psychopath. He's dangerous—too dangerous. And I'm not going to risk you like that."

"But you'll be there," she argues. "You'll all be there," she nods to her brother. "I know you won't let anything happen to me just like I know how much you need to close that chapter from your life."

Then, turning to her brother, she proclaims loudly.

"I'm in, so tell me everything."

I look at her in wonder, unable to believe she'd do something like that for me—put herself in danger just so I can accomplish my stupid revenge.

"You matter more to me than getting my brother," I lean in to whisper, wanting her to reconsider her stance.

"And you matter so much to me, Raf, that I want you to accomplish your goal. Get your revenge. Please let me do this for you," her hand is on my face as she cups my cheek. "Together. Let's do this together."

The strength behind her gaze mesmerizes me, and in spite of all my reservations, I find myself nodding.

"I want you to bear one thing in mind, Noelle," I tell her later when Cisco's gone.

"If it comes down to choosing between you and my brother, I'll *always* choose you."

CHAPTER NINETEEN
MICHELE

"The explosion at the factory already has far-reaching effects. Customer trust has dropped in the brand, and the company's stock prices are going down as we speak. We have still had no statement from a spokesperson, but inside reports are saying the executives are scrambling to turn it around."

He tapped his foot impatiently, his eyes narrowed on the big screen as the news blared in the background.

"Down 200%," one of his employees yelled, followed by a couple others giving him a detailed summary of the market every passing second.

"Buy," he commanded, nodding at them.

The moments trickled by, and he waited anxiously for the verdict.

"Congratulations! You own fifty-two percent of the company now," Andreas slapped him on the back in a friendly gesture.

He gritted his teeth at the physical contact, but he allowed it for now. After all, this was a huge success, and he owed Andreas a lot of it for turning his vision into reality.

While Michele was the mastermind behind the plan, Andreas was in charge of the organization. Even he had to grimly agree that without his help he would have never made it this far.

"What about the other two?"

"Slowly getting there. They are still trying to salvage their reputations, and some are not willing to sell yet."

Michele grunted. It was to be expected.

"Good. We'll have something to present at the summit then," he nodded, going to the table by the window to pour himself a drink.

"They won't know what's coming for them," Andreas chuckled.

Michele nodded, but his mind was already far away. Images of success were swarming him, and he was getting increasingly jittery.

Soon.

Soon, he would be able to prove to everyone that he was capable, and that his leadership of the family would only usher it towards a new era—a brand new, gilded era.

His mouth curled up in a twisted smile as he could practically feel the breeze of the wind as it brushed against his skin from the top of the world.

It had been his dream since the moment he'd decided he was never going to be weak again. And how to ensure you were the strongest if not by having control over everything?

He had to give it to his father, though. The only good thing he'd ever done had been to force him to study economics and statistics in an attempt to steer him away from his artistic dreams. In the beginning, he'd acquiesced to his wishes, taking up numbers and leaving his pencils and colors behind. Soon, though, he'd realized he had a knack for them, and he'd used that to his advantage in laying the foundation for his takeover of the family.

At the end of the day, no one would have allowed him to get to where he was if they didn't see the potential in his leadership—the economic potential. And he'd rewarded everyone who supported him in kind, making them richer than they'd ever dreamed.

One of his favorite past times was manipulating the stock market through small, yet well-coordinated attacks that left the entire structure of a company reeling. He'd started out small, only going for specific companies that were sure to give him a good turn around.

But lately he'd gotten bolder.

He wasn't targeting specific corporate entities anymore. No, now his plans had extended to carefully planned terror-like attacks that left the entire world reeling—enough so he could make a fortune on their backs.

But this was neither here nor there, and his current target had nothing to do with getting rich. He already had enough money as it was, stashed all over the world.

No, his latest plan had to do with a few well-known construction companies from the D.C. area, all of which would be involved in the development bid of a new military center. And by Michele's calculations, if he got his hands on that, then his world would suddenly open up to new opportunities. Certainly, it would allow him to infiltrate the Washington elite and put his subsequent plan in motion.

"The boy is here," one of his men signaled him.

"Show him to my study," Michele said, taking the entire bottle with him as he walked across the hallway to his office.

Plopping himself in his chair, he lit a cigarette, the mix of nicotine and alcohol hitting him twice as hard and improving his mood.

Not a moment later, a lanky boy entered the room. He had a backpack clutched to his chest, trembling as he looked around the area.

His eyes stopped on Michele, and he swallowed hard.

"Here," he said, almost stuttering as he placed a key on the table.

"Good," he took a drag of his cigarette and released a cloud of smoke. Looking down, he merely gave a nod of approval before he turned his piercing stare towards the boy.

"You'll give me the pills?" He tried very hard to put on a strong front, but Michele knew he was one second away from wetting himself.

A bored expression on his face, he simply opened his drawer, taking out a small container and throwing it to the boy.

"This should keep her alive a while longer."

"B—but you said..."

"I said I would give it to you when I don't need you anymore," he rolled his eyes. "Which is not now. I still require your services, so take that before I forget my magnanimity and give you something to make her sicker," a lopsided smile appeared on his face, and he enjoyed taunting the boy.

"I-I..." he stammered, wildly looking around as if anyone would dare help him.

"You're not very bright, are you, Pancho?" Michele leaned forward, his eyes flashing at him. "You wanted to save your beloved, and I offered you the chance. If this is not a fair exchange then I don't know what is," he shrugged, barely stifling his amused smile at seeing the boy flounder.

"I can't do this anymore," he whispered, his arms tightening over his blue backpack.

"And what is that?" Michele merely raised a brow, waiting for the boy to go on his self-righteous tirade.

"I can't spy on my friends for you anymore," he gave a muffled cry, taking a step back as he saw the sudden change in Michele's eyes.

"Is that so?" Michele asked in a suave tone, getting up

from his seat and coming towards Pancho. He was a head taller than the boy, and as he leaned down, he set his unyielding gaze on him. He didn't move. He merely stared at him as one would an intriguing object. Lifting his hand to his mouth, he took a big drag of his cigarette, blowing the smoke in Pancho's face and waiting for him to devolve into a crying mess—they all usually did.

"Might I remind you what happens if you don't meet your side of your bargain?"

Pancho gave a small shake of his head, his features terrified as he glanced into Michele's unfeeling eyes.

"Anita dies. One," his lips pulled up a little. "Two," he continued, amused at the look of pure terror that was descending on Pancho's face. "*Dead*," he whispered, making a poof sound as he leaned back, bursting into laughter.

"I'm...sorry," he eventually apologized, his eyes on the ground.

"Good," Michele chuckled. "We still have the showdown, don't we? Now move along, will you? That dose will keep her alive exactly until next week. You do your thing, and I'll give you the rest. You don't... Well, you don't want to find out."

Pancho swallowed uncomfortably, but eventually nodded.

"You'll find that I'm not a man to cross, Pancho. I'm not my brother. I'm not...*good*," he smiled. "I'm the absence of good."

Pancho blinked, his entire body shaking.

Michele held his gaze for the longest time, instilling in the boy exactly what would happen if he dared betray him.

"Move along," he waved at him.

The door closed with a click, and Michele rolled his eyes at the short interaction. He would have cut his losses sooner, but Pancho had proved to be extremely useful to his plan.

Since Ortega's numerous attempts had all ended in failure, he'd realized he should have never tasked that idiot with something he should have done himself.

But at the time his mind had been on other things, and no matter how much he would have liked to see the downfall of his brother, he had more important issues to solve first.

Nonetheless, seeing the mess Ortega had made of his plans had been the last drop for him to finally get his head in the game and deal with this little pest problem himself.

There was only one issue—murder wasn't exactly Michele's style.

No, he lived for incendiary displays. He could never just commit murder—anonymous, inconsequential murder. No, no, no. That was for cowards and the weak. People had to know it was him, and him alone, who was behind everything.

And so he'd started scheming.

How could he end his brother, but also put on a show?

He'd managed to find cracks within Fenix, and with Pancho's—*unwilling*—help, he'd kept close tabs on his brother, feeding him misinformation and laughing at his poor attempts at tracking him.

The highlight had been when he'd ruined the DeVille gala and officially named both Cisco and Rafaelo as his enemies. Ah, but it had been so sweet to watch the recordings of the night and see how both men had reacted to his message.

His plan had worked wonderfully—more so, even.

Cisco had seen the danger that the secret identity of his wife being known in the wild posed, and he'd quickly acted, leaving Rafaelo alone and without any backing.

Ripe for the plucking.

And now the second part of his plan was in motion.

He smiled to himself. He was nothing if not patient.

Because he had to be in order to ensure that all the pieces would fit perfectly.

And that was his biggest advantage.

They didn't know who they were dealing with. They had no clue who Michele actually was and how his mind worked.

And they would be in for a surprise.

Scanning through a few more reports and assigning duties to his men, he watched the clock on the wall impatiently, waiting for it to strike midnight.

When it did, he pulled out his phone, finally making the call.

"Yes?" Her voice sent a shiver down his body, his eyes automatically closing as he barely stifled a groan.

For someone who'd identified on the ace spectrum his entire adult life, it was utterly disconcerting to realize that his dick, did, in fact, work.

Just for one person.

She was the only one who'd ever made him experience sexual attraction.

For the longest time, he'd thought he was broken. And if there was one thing Michele hated, more than his brother, it was failure—especially his *own* failure.

Though he'd initially gotten close to her because she fit his plans, he found himself increasingly more reluctant to part ways with her.

She made him normal.

Or as normal as someone with his past could be.

"How did the talk go with your family, pet?" He asked in that charming tone of his.

"Good," she answered. "They called the number you gave me and the teacher assured them it would be safe for me to go," she said with a breathless sigh. She was, no doubt, anticipating it as much as he was.

Knowing how strict her family was and that they were

monitoring her moves closely, he'd hired someone to pretend to be her teacher to convince them it was a legitimate school trip. He'd gone one step further as he'd organized one such trip at the train station, where her family would drop her off.

"Marvelous. I'll catch you at the train station in the morning, pet," he told her affectionately.

"Oh, I can't wait," she gushed.

He listened to her prattle about her day, asking a question here and there and giving her the security that he was interested in what she had to say. After all, that was how he'd roped her in. He'd given her the attention she craved when no one else had.

"You're such a good girl, pet," he praised when she told him about her latest achievement at school. She wasn't the smartest tool in the box, and her inane subjects would have long tired him if not for her exclusive brand of hero worship.

So abandoned by the world she'd been, that she'd found in Michele her very own idol, and he felt that worship to his soul—it *fed* his soul.

"Good night," he told her before he hung up, already envisioning the ways in which he'd take her over the weekend.

Two full days in which he'd have uninterrupted access to her body. If that wasn't heaven, he didn't know what was.

But sweet as that was, he also had another purpose for which he'd insisted on taking her with him.

After he'd struck up a friendship with the local elites of D.C. he'd noticed that more than one of his associates' daughters had started paying him too much attention.

He didn't like that one bit. In fact, he abhorred any type of sexual interest from *anyone*.

He'd already had a hard time fending off their advances the last time he'd been there. One in particular, Eloise, had gotten too handsy with him, and he'd barely been able to hide his disgust when she'd brushed her hand on top of his.

All in favor of keeping appearances, he'd kept a poker face while planning her death in minute detail in his mind.

The only downside of that was that he still needed his associates' influence, and as such, he couldn't go through with it—yet.

Chapter Twenty
Michele

Brushing his cheek against her shoulder, he lifted the zipper on her dress.

"You look extraordinary, pet," he murmured, watching how her expression brightened in the mirror.

They'd arrived at Liam Cooke's house late in the afternoon, and they'd been given a suite of their own. As guests of honor, they were among the few who were invited to spend the weekend with the Cooke family and deepen their connection. After all, this was to be an intimate affair with only a few worthy families attending.

His pet had been awe struck by the opulence, her eyes wide as she'd taken in the luxury of Cooke's home.

A stately mansion, it had been built sometime in the beginning of the nineteenth century, and had been in Cooke's family for generations. Situated at the outskirts of D.C. it was also one of the places that had hosted a slew of former presidents and forefathers of American Independence.

Though it had been largely remodeled after the War of 1812, the house still retained many of its original features, which included an impressive ballroom, a conservatory, and expansive grounds that housed a maze, and a singing fountain.

"Thank you," she blushed a deep red. "I'm not used to wearing something so fancy..." she trailed off, her eyes scouring her figure in the mirror.

She was dressed in a pale mauve gown that was molded to her body. Satin draped in crystals, she looked absolutely stunning, and Michele was glad he'd spent a small fortune on her dress. He knew that she'd never worn anything like this before, her usual wear consisting of loose hoodies and baggy jeans. Even for him, the sight of her like this threatened to make him lose the little control he had left.

Tucking her pendant in the neckline of her dress, she turned to him.

"We should head downstairs. Dinner is about to be served," he said in a thick voice, willing his eyes to stray from her tight little body. He quickly donned his leather gloves before offering her his arm.

She hooked her arm through his, letting him lead her down the stairs. Her walk was slightly off, but he attributed that to the fact that she'd worn heels—another novelty for her.

Her family still considered her too young to allow her to dress up or wear make-up, and he knew that this occasion was an extravagance for her. And while he couldn't help the sliver of pride that erupted within him at the sight of her exquisite beauty—especially on his arm—he found himself a little reluctant to share her with the world.

For once, he wouldn't be the first one to take note of the loveliness that hid within her—for she *was* lovely. More so than any other woman he'd ever seen.

And she was his.

His grip tightened on her as he noted the guests already

gathered at the bottom of the stairs, all turning their eyes to them as they reached the landing.

"Mr. Guerra," Liam Cooke approached him, his hand outstretched.

"Mr. Cooke," he grabbed it in a shake, masking his distaste and putting on his social persona.

He'd long learned how to play the game, and though he dreaded the contact with these people, it was necessary to advance his goals.

"And..." he trailed off as he redirected his attention towards his pet.

"This is my girlfriend," he introduced her, keeping it short in an unspoken warning—she was off limits.

"Wonderful. Why don't you head to the ballroom. Everyone should be there. We'll mingle a little before dinner is served," Liam smiled before he moved to greet the other guests.

His pet kept a small smile on her face as he led her towards the ballroom, and he was pleased to see she was listening to his instructions. The less she interacted with people the better. After all, she was here as a smokescreen first and foremost. Besides, he didn't exactly want her to open her mouth and make a fool of herself.

The moment they entered the ballroom, he could feel the feminine stares directed at him, as well as the envy that took root once they realized he was not alone.

"Why is everyone staring at me?" His pet whispered, a slight tremor going down her body.

He tucked her closer to him.

"They're jealous. They see you on my arm and they wish it was them instead," he told her blankly.

A few other men came his way, some looking for an introduction, others to deepen their connection. Michele was, after all, already famous for his business acumen and a lot of people were vying for his attention and maybe, his advice.

He made small talk with each and every one that came his way, remembering names, and cataloging important information for later use.

From the beginning, Michele had had one purpose in coming to Cooke's home—to increase his circle of political connections. He was aware that if he wanted to make D.C. his future home, he needed solid backing. Cooke was merely a stepping stone for his project.

"Michele, dear," Eloise's screeching voice made him want to draw his gun out and blow her brains up.

He refrained.

He forced his lips in a pleasant smile as he turned to her, his pet by his side.

"Eloise. I don't see your father around," he gritted out.

"I came on his behalf. He sends his regards," she batted her eyelashes at him.

His pet tensed by his side, and that's when Eloise decided to notice her.

"And who is this?" she pushed her chin up as she looked at his pet in distaste.

"My girlfriend," he said, loving the way the color drained from her face.

"You can call me Zia," his pet offered, extending her hand.

Michele didn't know whether to be shocked by the fact that his pet had spoken out of turn, or pleased by the scowl that marred Eloise's features as she was forced to shake her hand.

"I didn't realize you had a girlfriend," she tried her best to keep the venom out of her voice.

"She's my everything," he intoned, smiling down at his pet in an attempt to drive the point across. Eloise narrowed her eyes at the two of them before releasing a loud huff and stalking out of the ballroom.

If it wasn't enough, the same encounter was replicated a few more times as suddenly everyone took an interest in Michele's date and matrimonial status.

He made an effort to be cordial with the guests, exhaling in relief when dinner was finally announced.

To his great chagrin, though, they'd been seated across from Eloise and a few of the other girls from her posey, while to their right and left were two pompous asses who seemed too focused on his pet's cleavage to notice when the first course arrived.

Safe to say, his mood was black and only getting darker.

"And how did you two meet?" Eloise's voice rang out, her predatorial eyes set on him.

A few other men expressed their curiosity as well, and Michele barely refrained from telling them it was none of their business—but a little bloodier.

"It was fate," he forced a smile, noticing his pet was attempting the same. "I saw her and I knew I had to have her," he continued, a red tinge appearing on his pet's cheeks at the compliment.

"How old are you, Zia?" Eloise addressed her directly.

A twitch in his jaw, he was ready to commit murder as he looked into Eloise's smug expression while his pet was squirming in her seat.

"I don't see how that's any of your business," he ended up saying, but his pet chose that exact moment to issue a reply.

"Eighteen," she said, raising her chin.

Barely.

"Eighteen?" One of the girls shrilled. "Isn't that too young?"

More people shushed around them, some praising

Michele for scoring young pussy, while others seemed outraged at their age difference.

"Now it makes sense," Eloise's lips stretched in an evil smile. "She's young and ignorant. That's why she'd use the dessert spoon for soup," she chuckled.

His pet's hand stilled mid-air, slightly trembling before placing it back on the table and choosing another.

"That's the serving spoon," Eloise remarked again.

He set his eyes on her, the eerily light color of his irises almost translucent. In combination with his ire, it was a deadly combination.

"Here," he picked the right spoon and placed it in his pet's hand.

She gave a tremulous smile and a hushed thanks as she lowered her gaze to her plate.

From the corner of his eyes, he saw her place the spoon into her soup, gathering some before bringing it to her mouth.

All eyes were on her.

Her hand was shaking badly, and just as she was about to bring the spoon to her lips, some of the bisque spattered on her front.

Giggles and ill-intent laughter sounded across the table. A look of mortification crossed her pet's face as she quickly brought a napkin to her neckline, dabbing it to remove the stain.

"I'm sorry," she turned her innocent eyes towards him, tears burning at their corners.

He noticed.

Sharply, he turned towards the table, intent on ignoring the embarrassing episode and the way he'd like nothing better than to turn the entire table upside down, and stuff everyone's throats with their own feces so they would never laugh again.

The dinner continued

"Your girlfriend is very cute." Another man noted, his eyes sparkling with interest as he assessed her. "How much?" He asked blatantly.

Loud thuds started reverberating in his ears, his anger climbing to such a new height it was becoming increasingly harder to ignore it.

But ignore it he did. He had to.

To give in to the anger was akin to committing a massacre.

"She's not for sale," he maintained a pleasant smile as he replied.

"Come on," the man laughed. "I'll pay you a hundred thousand for a night," he continued.

He could feel the tension radiating from his pet. Her hands were two small fists in her lap as she tried her best to ignore the jibe.

"She's not for sale," he stated, his tone leaving no room for argument.

Disgruntled voices started arguing, and he could see Eloise looking at him with a satisfied look on her face.

"Your girlfriend doesn't go out much, does she?" she giggled, pointing to the mess in his pet's plate. "This must be her first function. If she doesn't even know how to eat..." she trailed off, the others laughing with her.

His jaw twitched. Not only did he take the affront personally, since his pet was his property, but criticizing her was akin to criticizing him.

And that he could not allow.

Though clearly hungry, his pet put her utensils down. He could see her gaze at the food longingly, but for the remaining of the dinner she did not take even one more bite.

A smile pulled at his lips, pride blooming in his chest at

her self-control and the fact that she did know how to behave in such a situation.

She may not know how to eat, but she did know how to stop bringing attention to herself.

"She doesn't have to go out," he murmured, "I keep her busy enough at home."

The innuendo was clear, and Eloise flushed with anger. His pet, too, blushed to the roots of her hair, once more situating her gaze on her plate to avoid the malicious stares.

The jibes continued, and while he did his best to deflect them, he knew that his pet wasn't unaffected. She'd stopped talking, and every time someone addressed her, she'd sneak her hand under the table to grab his, gazing up at him in question.

An hour later, everyone evacuated the dining room, once more heading towards the ballroom for socializing.

His pet trailed behind him, her arm on his for support.

"Why are they so mean?" she asked him when there was no chance of anyone else overhearing.

"This is the way of the world. You have to get used to it," he told her in a rather brusque manner.

She didn't reply, merely nodding as he led her to the ballroom.

If the humiliation from before had been bad, however, what awaited his pet in the ballroom was much worse.

Eloise seemed to have taken her role as ringleader seriously, and in an attempt to show how cultured she was, she insisted on a poetry session. Cook and his wife, both lovers of literature, immediately approved, praising it as an exquisite activity.

The staff brought chairs to the middle of the ballroom, and everyone formed a circle around. Since there were only about twenty people in total present, the arrangement felt both intimate and stifling. Michele almost cursed out loud when he realized everyone was going along with this ludicrous suggestion.

Bringing some collectible volumes from Cooke's illustrious library, Eloise handed them around, instructing everyone to pick a poem, read it out loud, and discuss it as a group thereafter.

Michele scoffed at the idea. He knew the game was targeted at his pet, all in an attempt to show everyone how ignorant she was. He was surprised Eloise didn't outrightly call her a peasant, since that's how she'd been looking at her the entire night, her little jibes painting the picture perfectly.

Her idea of an entertaining activity and everyone's approval revealed their elitist mindset, and aimed to put Eloise in a better light, showing her more worthy just by account of her superior education.

He saw right through her.

Oh, he saw very well, especially as she handed an Alexander Pope volume to his pet, smiling insidiously at her. He received a Shelly one—much easier to read and digest than the one his pet had gotten. But just as he was about to make a quiet exchange, Eloise spoke.

"Why don't we go around this way?" She pointed to their side of the room, her eyes landing on his pet.

Startled, she quickly glanced at him for assurance.

But he could only defend her so much. And he'd done so repeatedly. Maybe not as overtly as it would have pleased her, but enough to send a message to everyone.

A message Eloise chose to ignore.

He gave her a quick nod, after which she returned her attention to the book.

Opening it, she sifted through the pages. He noted her increasing panic, especially as she turned page after page without really skimming the contents.

"Let me help you," Eloise suddenly appeared in front of

her, opening the book to a poem and dropping it in his pet's lap.

Her sudden intake of breath alarmed him, and he frowned as he studied her better. She was pale, her muscles coiled tightly as she stared at the page in front of her.

He thought she was embarrassed about pronouncing the Old English Pope used in his verses, but as she started reading out loud, he realized the problem was totally different.

"Phr-y-phryne," she barely said the word when he groaned out loud. Of course Eloise would choose that poem.

"H-ad," she paused, scrunching her nose as she squinted at the page. "Ta-ta-lents," another pause as she read it softly before saying it out loud, "for man-mankind."

He frowned. That wasn't exactly hard to read. Sure, the meaning was obscene, but the verses themselves were not very difficult.

"Op-open," another pause as she blinked, "she was," a deep intake of breath and more concentration, "and un...unconfined."

Minutes stretched by as she barely finished the first verse. And as she stopped, glancing around, it was to find everyone staring at her. So focused she'd been on reading that she hadn't realized the meaning of the words.

Eloise was watching her like a hawk, her smile wide and malefic as she realized she'd hit a weak spot.

"I'm so sorry. I didn't realize you had trouble reading that," she said on a fake tone as she replaced the volume in his pet's hands with a different one.

She was nothing if not accommodating as she once more attempted to read. This time, the prose was even easier, yet the execution was the same. Choppy. She couldn't read normal words, and somehow he doubted it was stage fright.

By the time she finished her poem, she was all red and sweaty.

"You don't know how to read, do you?" Another girl turned to her, asking point blankly.

She turned to him, her mouth agape, panic all over her features.

"I'm sure it was the nerves, right, pet?" he inquired, his voice taut.

"I'm sorry," was all she said, looking away and barely holding back her tears.

"What eighteen year old doesn't know how to read?"

"Where did you find her, Michele? You should think twice before dating someone like that."

"I would be so embarrassed to be seen with her."

"Who knows what hole she crawled out of," someone said in a mean voice. "I wouldn't want to associate with those…"

The comments trickled in, everyone suddenly opining on his state of affairs and criticizing his pet—and by default him.

He gritted his teeth, forcing himself to bear it.

His pet, however, was so embarrassed, she barely dared to raise her gaze.

The activity continued, and while he tried to reassure her through small gestures, by the end of it she seemed inconsolable.

"Go back to the room. I have some business to discuss with Cooke and I'll find you later," he instructed her.

As was typical of these soirees, once the entertainment was over, it was time to talk business. And he knew he could not save face if he kept being confronted with the failures of his pet.

"I didn't mean to embarrass you," his pet whispered, coming closer and taking his hands in hers.

Usually, he was the one initiating any type of physical contact, his pet just following suit and abiding by his wishes.

It was striking to see her make the first move. And to his great surprise, he found he didn't mind it as much.

"I know, pet. But you did. I need you to go back to the room and sleep it off," he gentled his tone, her downtrodden and dejected appearance hitting a spot deep within him.

While his pet trudged her way up the stairs to their suite, he redirected his attention to the meeting at hand.

Cooke and the other men present gathered in his study to discuss the merits of the new military base, all giving their obsolete opinions.

Michele pretended he cared, immersing himself in the conversation. The men were all sufficiently influential in their social circles to sway public opinion, but other than that, they wouldn't prove to be much useful to his plans. Besides, the crooks currently present were but a handful of his new contacts in D.C.

As the minutes ticked by, he realized they would not be of much use to him.

Still, he continued to interact, as politeness dictated, while he thought of all the ways he would console his pet when he finally retired to his room. The most appealing way included, of course, her tears, and he was already salivating for a taste of them.

But as the topic of the new military base was quickly skipped over, the men started talking about other topics—money, drugs and women.

Not that Michele was surprised, considering those were the most prevalent topics in any circle. But seeing as he already had more money than he knew what to do with, drugs did not particularly interest him, and his woman was upstairs in his bed, he realized his time here had come to an end.

"If you'll excuse me, gentlemen." He engaged in momentary platitudes before he finally breathed out, relieved, as he left the room.

They were lucky they hadn't made another off handed comment about his pet, since now that their usefulness had considerably decreased, Michele wasn't so inclined to behave anymore.

His mind honed on his pet, and as he took two stairs at a time, his fingers were already on the buttons of his shirt, slowly unbuttoning them as he thought of all the ways he'd have fun with her.

Opening the door to the room, it was to find it bathed in darkness, the contour of a small form huddled under the sheets, the only thing visible.

A smirk pulled at his lips, and without lingering, he grabbed on to the edge of the sheet, flinging it off her.

"Have you been a good girl, pet?" he asked suavely, but as the sheet slid off the bed, revealing the body underneath, he was in for a surprise.

"What the fuck are you doing here?" He thundered, his gaze taking in Eloise's disgustingly naked body. "And where the hell is she?"

CHAPTER TWENTY-ONE
MICHELE

Eloise didn't seem to catch on the undertone of his voice, or if she did, she lacked self-preservation. Instead of feeling ashamed of being caught red-handedly, she undulated her body, seductively moving towards Michele.

"She realized she didn't fit in after all," she purred, the sound a cacophony to his ears as he stared at her unflinchingly. "Don't worry, whatever she did for you, I can do better," she had the shamelessness to add.

And as she extended her dirty hand towards him, he recoiled, as if burned.

His eyes were pure fire.

"I'll only ask this one more time," he enunciated each word. "Where is she?"

"Who knows? Maybe she found some entertainment somewhere else," she laughed. "Would someone like her refuse a hundred thousand dollars?"

The words did nothing to calm Michele down, especially as he knew how those old geezers had leered at her. And the thought of anyone other than him touching his pet was enough to make him mad.

His control snapped.

His gloved fingers curled around her neck, his hold so tight she whizzed, finally realizing the danger she was courting.

"Where is she?" He asked again, the words punctured. At the same time, he increased the pressure on her throat, squeezing so tight her neck almost broke.

And he would have killed her if his mind wasn't already conjuring up scenarios—all of them ending with his pet harmed. He flung her away from him, a loud thud resounding in the room as her body made contact with the wall. She yelped in pain, but he didn't linger to see the extent of her injuries.

He'd deal with her later.

After he found *her*.

He'd never known greater anger than when he realized he could *not* locate her.

He scoured the entire house, checking every single room. The more time he spent in his own head, thinking about the worst possible outcomes, the more chaotic and murderous his mood turned.

He neared the door of one bedroom, and hearing feminine moans and screams spurred him on, kicking the door open to find a couple fucking. But to his eternal relief, the woman was not his pet.

By the time he'd checked every room, he was becoming more unstable than ever, his hands itching for blood. Everyone was aware of the commotion and the ribald jokes didn't take long to start. Ready to combust, he exited the house, going towards the direction of the maze and hoping she'd gotten lost there.

Because otherwise…

He didn't need to step inside the maze though.

As soon as he was in the middle of the garden, he had a

clear view of the top of the house, and the glass conservatory built on the roof. The light from the moon reflected against the crystals of her dress, the beams sending him a direct signal.

He stalked back to the house, his steps heavy and determined. Though he was one of the youngest men in attendance, everyone gave him a wide berth as they saw him walk back inside the house.

It took him less than a couple of minutes to reach the roof, and opening the door, he made sure to lock it behind him lest someone bothered them.

Taking one step, he finally spotted her.

She was inside the conservatory, on her haunches as she gazed lovingly at a red rose.

"What are you doing here?" he barked the moment he was behind her.

Startled, she jumped to her feet, her eyes wide as she took in his disheveled appearance and the fact that his shirt was undone.

"I..." she stammered, her eyes roving wildly all over his body.

"I'm waiting," he tapped his foot impatiently at her.

"I thought you didn't need me tonight," she whispered, her eyes going to the floor.

Moving closer, he tipped her jaw, forcing her to look at him.

"You thought?" He asked with the arch of a brow. "And why would you think that?"

"She... She said you only brought me here to make her jealous," his pet said dejectedly and he noted the dampness of unshed tears on her lashes.

"And you believed her?"

"I don't belong here," she shook her head. "You saw..."

"What? That you don't know how to eat or talk? That you

223

can't read? Trust me, I saw," his harsh words made her blink rapidly, her eyes widening at him.

"Is that why you brought me here? To laugh at me?" She asked in a small voice, the first time she'd voiced something akin to an accusation.

"Why do you think?" He rolled his eyes at her. "I brought you here to fuck you. Was that not clear enough for you?" He gritted out, annoyed that his pet would challenge him so— that she would doubt him.

"Did you sleep with her?" her small fists were clenched by her side, her gaze on his naked chest.

"And if I did?" He countered in a lazy tone. He didn't like this line of questioning just as he didn't like her disobedience.

"I see," was all she said, her shoulders slumping down in disappointment. Yet she didn't argue with him. She didn't ask him to clarify.

Her indifference struck something inside of him. Something ugly and venomous, and he found himself wound so tight, the pressure was ready to explode. Before he could help himself, he shrugged his gloves off, carelessly throwing them to the ground. His hand found its way around her throat as he brought her to him, pushing her chin up so she would look him clearly in the eyes. Usually, he loved to see her bashful self and the way she would avoid his gaze. But now, it irked him. It bothered him on a level that he was not accustomed to, and he did not know how to react.

"Is that all you have to say?" He almost yelled at her.

Their breaths mingled, their lips one inch away from one another.

"You don't care if I fuck her, do you?" He drawled, his nostrils flaring.

He wanted a reaction, damn it. He wanted her fists and her accusations. For the first time, he *wanted* her rebellion.

"It's your decision," she responded, her eyes on him.

Suddenly, he saw something different there.

A clarity he'd never spotted before. Something that made him both angry and happy. Something...

"My decision," he laughed dryly. "Is that how you love me, pet? So much you'd let another woman touch me?"

Her eyes flashed at him, a sign this was affecting her. So he continued to twist the knife.

"You'd let another kiss me," he brushed his lips against hers. "Fuck me?"

She didn't answer, the emotion on her face increasingly more pronounced.

"Is that how much you love me? That you could imagine me sinking my cock into any pussy?"

His cruel words finally got a reaction out of her. Her lips drawn into a determined line, she brought her palm to his cheek, the sound reverberating in the night. He felt the pain —the sweet yet biting sting of the slap.

His head to the side, he brought his thumb to his lip, noting a hint of blood.

His pet might have claws after all, and he didn't know why the realization made him harder than he'd ever been.

"I hate you," she raged at him. "I hate you but I love you," she cried out, struggling in his arms.

She brought her fists against his chest, banging them against his skin—touching him in a way that he hadn't allowed anyone to touch him. Yet he didn't feel repulsed. Oddly enough, he felt anything but the usual revulsion.

"Really?" He continued to provoke her. "Is that why you're so calm thinking I fucked another woman?"

"I'm not calm, damn it! Do you think I like this?" she screamed, her hands wrapped around the material of his shirt. "Do you think I like knowing you can replace me at any moment? That I'm nothing but an embarrassment?" She

VERONICA LANCET

shook her head, her entire body trembling from the power of her emotions.

Michele swore.

A rush of power and lust unlike any other hit him, his cock hardening, not from her tears, but from her destructive emotions.

He wanted to consume them.

He wanted to consume *her*.

Never before had something like this happened to him, and he didn't know what it meant—only that he needed more.

Addictive.

It was more addictive than anything he'd ever known.

"I love you," she declared passionately—more so than she'd ever done before.

Gone was the meek little girl. Instead, he was staring at a wild cat—a savagery he'd always known she possessed suddenly peeking through the surface. And while she'd reined it in until now, he found that he didn't want that.

He wanted to push her—get her to the brink.

Fuck.

He was done for. This was it, something that was so potent it made his blood boil.

"Prove it," he dared her. "Prove that you love me."

She stilled, her eyes wide.

"How can I believe you when you'd so easily give me away?" he murmured softly, using his charm on her. "I didn't fuck her. I didn't fucking touch her," he continued, noting the quickening of her pulse. "But do you even care?" He shook his head, suddenly entering a new role—all in an effort to see how far he could push her.

"Of course I care!" she exclaimed. "Do you think it's easy for me to know you're always surrounded by women who

226

are better, smarter, and more beautiful than me? Do you think I want that?"

"Prove it," he uttered again, watching every play of emotion on her face as one would watch a gripping movie. He was scandalized. He was entranced. He was fucking gone.

"Prove to me that you love me," he continued. "That you love me above all."

"But I do," she immediately burst out. "You know I love you more than life itself," she shouted her confession, and his heart sang in his chest.

Finally!

They were getting somewhere.

"Prove it, my sweetness," he cooed, his palms suddenly on her cheeks as he held her tenderly to him. "Show me you love me more than life itself," he turned her words against her.

She didn't react. Her stare unyielding, her emotions were visibly raging inside of her.

In her eyes, he saw everything he'd ever wanted. Everything that had always been within reach but forever out of grasp.

"How?" She asked the magic word, and he almost sighed at the pleasure of that one sound.

"Would you die for me?" he asked, his tone serious.

To prove a point, he let go of her, his hands back at his side as he stepped away.

She reeled back, confusion swathing her features as she looked bereft without his touch.

"Die... for you?" she repeated the words, her voice barely a whisper.

"You know I'd die for you, pet," he told her, his voice holding such a mesmerizing quality to it she was instantly hypnotized by his words. "But would you die for me too?"

He stepped back. Slowly moving away until his back hit the edge of the roof, the implication clear.

She lifted her eyes to his, and as he gazed at her, he thought she'd never looked quite like this—so majestic and so enthralling.

He was the one playing her, but suddenly he felt played. Because she was awakening things inside of him he'd never thought possible.

He wasn't...broken.

And it was all because of her.

"Would you?" he asked again.

A look of determination crossed her face. Pushing her chin up, she took a step towards him.

"Yes," she said, conviction dripping from that one word. "I'd walk through fire for you. You know that," she continued, but he wasn't satisfied.

Would he ever be?

She saw the doubt that stained his features, and before he could utter another challenge, she surprised him by taking off her heels and throwing them to the side.

"I would *die* for you," she emphasized, placing her hands on the cold concrete as she pulled herself up on the edge of the roof.

He watched, entranced, as she bravely faced him.

She was on the edge of the precipice, looking at him for confirmation.

So he did what he'd been wanting to do from the beginning.

"But would you die if I told you to?" his voice was low, a hint of anguish hidden in his tone.

She blinked at him, but she didn't seem surprised. If anything, she seemed even more resolute.

He stared at her.

Him, on the ground.

Her, on the edge.

His breathing was harsh. Hers was equally so.

Their eyes met, something passing between them.

He took half a step towards her. She spread her wings.

And jumped.

Time stood still as she braced herself for the fall. His words echoed in the air, her name on his lips a call for a divinity he'd disavowed.

But skin met skin.

He furled his hand over her arm, catching her just in time. And with one pull, they both fell down.

His back hit the cement. Her breasts hit his chest.

All the while, their eyes never broke their connection. He looked at her and she looked back, a spark coming to life from the abyss.

"I died," she said.

"You died," he repeated, half in wonder, half in satisfaction.

"You saved me," she stated confidently.

"I saved you," he nodded.

"I knew you would," she added with unwavering conviction.

In that moment, the world opened up before him like never before.

"You're a devious little thing, aren't you?" he brought his hand to her face, a soft caress against her cheek before his fingers curled around her throat, his grip tight.

There was no fear in her eyes as she looked at him—none at all. She waited, and he could swear she'd welcome anything he would give her.

Soon.

A slow smile pulled at his lips. The more he looked at her, the more he found himself yearning for something…more.

"Let's go," he helped her to her feet, tugging her to his

side. Her chest was flush against his as he snaked his hand around her waist. "I have a reward for you," he whispered against her hair, inhaling her sweet scent.

There was something different. He couldn't pinpoint what, but something had fundamentally changed.

Trailing his mouth along her jaw, he found that the action was no longer a necessary evil, it was *necessary*.

Her lips parted, her breath was coming in short spurts, anticipation building inside of her. He teased her flesh with his lips, moving forward before retreating. The mere feel of her soft skin gained a new meaning—one that he'd have time to explore more in depth later.

Now, he wanted to feel.

He licked the seam of her lips with his tongue, and with a punctured sigh, she opened up, allowing him to kiss her like he'd never done before—like he'd never thought himself capable.

He kissed her because he wanted to, not because he had to. He took his time, leisurely exploring the depths of her mouth as if it was the first time he was tasting her. And as he leaned back, her pupils two huge black circles that had eclipsed her irises, he knew he had her at his mercy.

Just a little longer...

"Come," he commanded in a hoarse voice, the kiss having an unexpected effect on him. He took her hand, leading her down the stairs until they both reached the landing.

There was a commotion in the hallway, some already deep in their cups as they were talking loudly about the recent events—about his pet.

If before his rage had been monstrous, now it knew no bounds.

Something hadn't just shifted in the way he regarded his pet. No, something had shifted his entire reality and how he perceived everyone else in relation to his pet.

As he saw that everyone had gathered on the ground floor, a smile pulled at his lips.

It was showtime.

"There she is," one of the men laughed. "It seems no one stole her after all," he joked, and the others joined in.

His grip tightened on his pet's hand, but he didn't let it interfere with his plans.

More started adding their useless two cents, making fun of his pet and asking why Michele was so pussy whipped with someone who was clearly beneath him in every area.

His pet stiffened at some of the insults, but she didn't say a word, letting him guide her.

"Gentlemen," his voice rang out. "I have a special announcement. If you could all follow me to the ballroom."

Hushed voices started arguing, but eventually everyone acquiesced and headed for the ballroom.

He scanned the crowd, counting the heads and making sure everyone would be present for his pronouncement. In particular, he was looking for one person. And then he spotted her. She'd gotten dressed, and going by the ugly scowl on her face, she wasn't at all pleased by the developments.

Entering the ballroom, he lowered his mouth to his pet's ear, whispering something. Her eyes widened at his words, but she nodded, moving to the side.

Michele took the time to close the doors to the ballroom, making sure they were sealed. He did the same with the windows and the double doors that led to the garden.

Instead of presuming something nefarious would take place, everyone was amused. They continued to look at his pet and make jokes on her account, some suggesting he was going to teach her a lesson in front of everyone.

He let them believe that. In fact, his slow movements were deliberate, letting a sense of false security seep into them, making their hell that much sweeter when it descended upon them.

He sneaked a glance at his pet. By the sidelines, her hands were in front of her as she fidgeted, her eyes watching his every move.

He stopped.

She looked so beautiful, her hair flowing down her back, wild and untamed—just like her. That part of her that he wanted to reach.

Now that he'd witnessed its existence and what it did to him, he knew he could no longer ignore it.

He gave her a reassuring smile.

Without any warning, his hand shot out, his fingers in Eloise's scalp as he wrenched her towards him. She gave a yelp, falling to her knees. Bringing her hands to her hair, she tried to get out of his hold.

But Michele didn't react.

He merely dragged her towards the center of the room, right in front of his pet.

Everyone watched raptly, and to a certain degree, amused.

They thought it was all a joke—a game. They would be in for a rude awakening.

He tightened his hold on her hair.

"What did she say to you, pet?" He asked, his eyes on his pet. "Tell me everything."

For a moment, he didn't think his pet had it in her to participate. He already had the next bit planned out, but he wanted to give her the opportunity to dole out her own punishment.

His pet stepped forward, her gaze on Eloise.

If before she'd looked shy and timid, her eyes often down-turned, now it was the opposite. There was a spark in her gaze, her back straight with confidence as she took another step.

"She told me I was trash. That you would never willingly associate with trash, and that you only brought me here to make her jealous."

"Is that so?" He asked Eloise, leaning down, his breath on her cheek.

She was trembling in his arms, but the bitch did not yet know terror. Oh, that would come.

"No...I..."

"She said I must have come from the gutter, because there's no way someone like me would step foot in this house. She kicked me out of the bedroom and told me to find the man who offered to pay for me for the night," his pet continued, and his ire increased.

"You kicked her out of my room, and told her to go sell herself?" He asked in an angry voice, forcefully tugging on her hair until tears were flowing down her face.

"I'm sorry," she whispered, finally realizing the severity of the situation.

"Her. You apologize to *her*," he pointed at his pet.

"I'm sorry..." Eloise cried out.

His pet nodded, taking a step back.

He could hear shushed voices all around him, and he knew those bastards were enjoying the show. After all, they were friendly with each other out of necessity and to fulfill social obligations. They didn't care if something happened to one of them.

Bringing his heel to his hand, Michele removed a four inch retractable blade, swinging the sharp part around until it made contact with Eloise's face.

She stilled.

Everyone stilled.

He wondered if they thought he was bluffing.

A sick smile formed on his face as he looked around, enjoying the fear that was seeping into their features.

"You insulted my pet. *Mine*. That means you insulted *me*," he told Eloise in a cruel tone. And before she could voice out any objection, he brought the blade to her temple, cutting into her skin.

He held her scalp tightly in his fist, bringing the blade around her forehead and circling her head.

Her screams were echoing in the room, and everyone was watching flabbergasted how he was scalping the woman— yet none dared intervene.

He spared a glance to his pet, and realized that she was watching the procedure not scandalized, but entranced.

A chuckle escaped him. She wasn't lost to him—she would *never* be.

Once the edges were off, the real work started. He brought his blade against the scalp, hitting between the skin and bone. Slowly, it started to become detached.

The screams, too, abated, her voice losing its volume.

The more he tortured her by prolonging her pain, the more her voice was losing strength, until it was nothing more than a wheeze.

One last hit, and the scalp came detached off her skull. Lifting it by the hair, he threw it to his pet's feet.

"It's yours," he told her with a smirk. "Your justice."

Eloise had fallen to the floor, her eyes red from sobbing, her throat working up and down in an effort to produce more sounds. What to any other person would have seemed like a painful sight, to Michele it signified victory.

The crowd was quietly watching from a corner, none daring to intervene.

He briefly wondered if any of them knew of his family's history. But seeing that they were still not running around screaming, he guessed not.

"You didn't do your homework, gentlemen." He winked at them before gripping Eloise's neck and turning her to face them.

She was still sobbing, her voice barely a whisper as she pled with the others to help her.

"No one will," he told her matter of factly, holding tightly as he brought the blade to her neck.

From ear to ear, a gash slowly appeared, blood gushing out and flooding the floor. Her mouth remained open, frozen in a perpetual silent scream.

But the sight of the blood finally prompted all of the others to start panicking, some running for the doors, others for the windows.

His pet was still sitting by the side, observing. But she wasn't devolving into a crying mess like he'd expected and that warmed his heart.

He gave his victims just a few seconds to warm up, then he gave chase.

One after another, he caught them and tore through their jugular, draining them of blood.

He went for the inconsequential people first. The ones he didn't give a damn about. Still, they had laughed at his pet, and that required a punishment.

For last, however, he kept those that needed to be taught a lesson—those who had been directly cruel to her.

And as corpse after corpse fell, he was left with four men.

Four that had dared to mock his pet and offer money for her.

Four that would not meet an easy end.

The pudgy old fucks were barely a match for him, and with a couple of fists to their midsection, he fell them all.

They groaned in pain, and they could barely move as he grabbed on to them. The entire floor was a puddle of blood, and as he dragged their bodies towards his pet, they smeared even more of it around.

"What did you say? A hundred thousand?" He addressed the one who'd dared to insinuate his pet was for sale. "How about a hundred thousand cuts?" he smiled, and before the man knew what was happening, Michele was on him with his knife, slashing and cutting indiscriminately.

The man tried to defend himself, but it was all in vain.

Michele cut an ear, then the next. He took his nose, before digging the knife deep into his eye socket and popping the eye out like it was child's play.

And it was.

Because in his manic state, that was just the beginning.

"What do you say, pet? His dick stays or goes?" he asked her.

She was trembling slightly, her face pale, but she didn't glance away. If anything, she forced herself to look at him— truly look at him.

"G-goes," she whispered. Still, it was loud enough for Michele to hear it.

"Your wish is my command," his lips pulled in a twisted smile.

The blade cut through the man's pants, and soon his genitals were out in the open.

The screams were deafening, his attempts to free himself from Michele's grasp useless. His foot on top of the man's chest, he merely stooped down to grab the fat man's penis. He didn't cut it. He just pulled.

And with enough strength, the organ gave way.

Blood stuck to his palm, more oozing out of the man's body.

Michele flung the dick aside, giving his pet a charming smile as he stuck his knife in the man's heart.

"Three more," he intoned in a singsong voice.

The others moaned in pain, unable to move away from him. The entire massacre happened just as Michele had pictured it, and as one after another the other three gave their last breaths, he finally felt like himself again.

"Marvelous!" he exclaimed, screaming at the top of his lungs and waiting for the sound to echo back.

He was full of blood.

His naked chest was painted red, his blood pendant swinging from side to side as he strode towards her. Splatters of scarlet marred his face, his sick smile showing his true nature and his lost humanity—if he ever had any.

And as he approached his pet, he was suddenly curious about her reaction.

She'd been a good sport so far, standing unmoving in the same spot, watching him kill indiscriminately without making a sound.

He prowled towards her, each step carefully measured to provide the perfect momentum for his arrival. His eyes were on her neck, that lovely column that housed her pulse point and that told him exactly what was brewing inside of her.

He was a few steps away. She swallowed hard.

Their eyes met.

His gaze was twisted and depraved. Hers was alert yet full of longing.

He held her stare as he put one foot in front of the other until he reached her side.

She stopped breathing, blinking rapidly as she took in his ragged appearance and the blood that kept trickling down his skin.

CHAPTER TWENTY-TWO
MICHELE

"**Y**ou killed them," she finally said, remarking on the obvious. It was rather amusing, and Michele didn't know whether to laugh or cry at the statement.

"I killed them," he repeated, giving her a lopsided smile.

"For me," she whispered in awe, and her gaze slid past him to the mass of corpses lying on the expensive ballroom floor.

Blood oozed from all directions, and the opulence of the room had been turned into a house for the mad—where he was king, and she, his future queen.

"They insulted you, pet. And when they insult you, they insult me," he murmured, leaning in until they were mere breaths apart.

"You're not afraid," he noted wryly.

She shook her head, though he could see hints of trepidation.

"Why?"

"Because it was for me," she spoke softly, and in her eyes he saw once more the food his wretched soul was starving for—pure worship.

TILTING his head to the side, he studied her.

She looked exquisite. Like a doll worthy of display, he wanted nothing more than to put her on a pedestal and stare at her when the need arose.

"You're so beautiful, pet," he whispered, almost in awe.

Sometimes, like the moment at hand, he forgot she was just a means to an end. That she wasn't his to keep, merely his to defile. He forgot that this was all temporary, and when the time came, he'd have to use her for his last hit.

But he couldn't bring himself to remember that. Not when she was standing before him like an offering for an errant god.

Her limbs were trembling, he could see that.

For all her outer bravado and her reassuring words, she *was* afraid.

He supposed that was normal. Who in their right minds would react positively to murder? Even he had, once upon a time, been sensitive to it.

That time had passed, warping him and shaping him into what he was today. He looked like a human, moved like a human and spoke like one. But he'd ceased to be one after years of abuse and watching the world turn its back on him.

Instead, he'd simply turned *his* back on it, shedding the last of his humanity.

As he looked at her, though, he had the vague feeling there were still remnants of his old self inside of him. Because she made him want to behave in spite of himself.

He regarded her with a melancholic expression. He wished for that too.

But it was too late.

He'd sold his soul.

He'd sold everything that was of value for his revenge.

And soon, he'd sell her out too.

"Take your clothes off," he commanded, taking a step back.

The walls were painted red, the entire room holding tightly onto the cloying smell of death.

Her eyes widened and she instinctively took a step back.

"Now?" She asked, biting her lip as her eyes zeroed in on the mess of mangled flesh behind him.

"Now," his voice boomed, his expression serious.

She took a moment before she brought her hands to her back, lowering the zipper on her expensive dress and slowly shimming out of it. Flinging it aside, she stood only in her bra and underwear, her arms going to her midriff in an effort to cover herself.

"All of it," he raised a brow in a quiet dare.

She obeyed, taking everything off and baring herself to him.

She straightened her back, her tits bouncing up. His gaze was immediately drawn to her nipples, those dusty pink peaks that he'd never given much attention before. Suddenly, they intrigued him, making her look more luscious—more appealing than ever.

His eyes trailed down to her slim waist and her shapely hips before settling on the small patch of hair between her legs.

Unnerved by his perusal, she squeezed her thighs together.

"Don't," he rasped, and in two steps he was in front of her. He brought his hand up, trailing the back of it down her neck and between the valley of her breasts.

He didn't miss the way she swallowed, the tension between them growing thicker as her fear increased. There was always a certain trepidation within her the moment the clothes came off, and he'd never managed to figure out why.

The pendant with their mixed blood lay heavy against her skin, and the sight of it only made him harder, the idea of their mixed blood getting his cock to swell painfully in his pants.

He'd stopped reacting to death and gore a long time ago. Blood was always the sign of a life lost.

Not *this* blood.

This was the sign of a life gained. Because he knew he had her in the palm of his hands.

"Why are you afraid, pet?" He barked the question.

Odd how she'd barely batted an eye when he'd slaughtered the entire room for her, but now he could see the sheen of sweat on her pale skin, her lower lip trembling with unease.

"I'm not," she shook her head. "I'm not afraid of you," she whispered, raising her eyes to his.

Such a lovely shade of honey mixed with a hint of green. Had he ever truly stopped to admire the color of her eyes?

"You are," his low voice sent a shiver down her back, her skin pebbling under his touch. "Are you afraid of what I'll do to you?" He leaned down to murmur in her ear.

"No," she whispered.

His lips pulled into a wide smile as he leaned back.

"On your knees," he ordered her.

Her knees buckled, his words a holy sound that could only be obeyed.

"Good pet," he praised as her hands went directly to his belt, unbuckling it with ease and taking his hard cock out.

Ah, but he didn't think he'd ever tire of the sight of her like this—obedient, meek, *docile.*

She wet her lips, the tip of her tongue coming into contact with the head of his cock and making him groan out loud. She opened wider, lathering him in her spit as she took his cock inside her wet, warm mouth.

She worked his cock like she usually did, every movement rehearsed as he'd taught her. Knowing his distaste for surprises, she'd never strayed from her routine.

Yet this time he found that he didn't want the same old thing. He didn't want her on her knees, quietly sucking his cock like a trained hooker. He didn't want her to be obedient and he certainly didn't want her quiet.

Screams.

He wanted her screams.

Blood.

Mayhem.

Disorder.

For the first time, he considered breaking the routine.

He'd gotten one taste of her destructive emotions, and he realized he couldn't go on anymore pretending they didn't exist. Not when they had fascinated him for the first time in his life—truly enthralled him..

Looking down at her servicing him like a robot, his lip turned up in distaste.

He didn't want her apathy, or her controlled façade.

"Stop," he gritted out, his hand already on her jaw as he kept it locked in place.

She looked up at him, her eyes wide and innocent—still innocent.

Not for long.

"I love you, pet," he caressed her cheek, his voice lower and more emotive than before.

A smile of pure satisfaction appeared on her face.

"I love you too," she replied, batting her lashes at him.

"Go lay there," he stepped away, motioning to the pile of dead bodies in the middle of the floor.

He wanted to break her. He was startled by the realization, since that's what he'd wanted from the beginning. But this time, he wanted to *break* her. Not for some stupid revenge, or to appease a wounded ego. No, this was for his own selfish reason. He wanted to see her break by his hand, for him and with him.

He wanted to be her salvation and her damnation—her Messiah and her destroyer.

"But…" she argued, but one look at his taut features and she didn't finish her words.

She started to get up, but he had other ideas.

"Crawl," his voice echoed.

He knew his pet wanted to rebel—she wanted to argue. He could see it in the way she pursed her lips, her muscles wound tight with tension. Still, she didn't. Because she knew he wouldn't like that.

How long would it take for her to snap out of it? To finally show her real self?

He guessed he was about to find out.

On her hands and knees, she moved slowly towards the pile of dead bodies, the blood on the floor sticking to her skin and painting her all red.

While she was crawling to the center, he took the time to remove the last of his clothes, standing as naked as she was, and just as red.

She reached the mass of corpses, and for a moment she paused, looking back at him. Whatever she saw in his expression made her continue until she was seated on top of the dead flesh—a queen of the dead.

She leaned her back against a corpse, opening herself to him and waiting.

He stalked towards her, ready and anticipating every second of it.

"Are you ready for my cock, pet?" he asked as he fisted his length, dropping to his knees in front of her.

Blood splattered all around, and his eyes were on her features, looking for any sign of distress—of rebellion.

Still nothing.

"Yes," she nodded, spreading her thighs to accommodate him.

Wrapping his fingers around her ankles, he suddenly pulled her forward, the blood helping her slide towards him.

"Beg me," he murmured as he placed his palm in the blood before bringing it to her chest, smearing it over her pale skin. "Beg me," he repeated, waiting for her words.

"Please fuck me," she whispered in a sweet voice—not at all the urgency he wanted to hear.

A wave of anger hit him in the chest, somehow dissatisfied with every little thing she was doing. Digging his fingers into her thighs, he brought her closer to him, impaling her on his cock in one smooth thrust.

Her mouth opened on a ragged moan—one not of pleasure but of pain. He hadn't tried to make it easier for her, that thought had never crossed his mind. He'd known that she'd be dry as fuck and as he forced his full length inside of her, he could feel her tear around him in an attempt to accommodate his size.

Still, she didn't scream.

Did she ever?

It wasn't the first time he'd taken her like this—he'd never bothered with her readiness or with her pleasure before. But it was certainly the first time he wanted a reaction out of her.

The fact that she flattened her lips in a thin line, stifling her cries of pain instead of giving them to him enraged him.

"Do you like this, pet?" he asked, retreating all the way before slamming inside her again. "Do you like the way my cock is tearing your cunt apart?"

A fake moan escaped her as she pretended to enjoy it, though the corner of her eyes were filled with unshed tears.

At some point, her tears would have aroused him to no

end. They would have made him want to make her cry buckets just so he could get some sick satisfaction out of it.

Not now.

He didn't want her like this. He *hated* her like this.

And to prove it, he continued to fuck her like he'd never done it before—viciously and out of control.

His hands were digging painfully into her flesh as he slammed her small body down the full length of his cock. Again and again until he could feel his shaft getting chafed from the dryness of her cunt. As he continued to thrust, the tip of his dick hit her cervix in what he knew would be painful for her.

Still, she pretended.

Her hands by her side, she didn't attempt to touch him—just like she knew she shouldn't.

Blood and death were everywhere. Still, she didn't make a sound.

Something broke inside of him.

He didn't want a lifeless fuck doll. He didn't want *just* a hole to stick his dick in. He wanted *her*—her wildness and her savagery.

He wanted her to bite and scratch him, to yell and curse at him.

Only when he saw pain reflected on her face and in her voice would he be pleased.

Releasing a ragged breath, he stopped, withdrawing from her. Looking between their bodies, he saw the blood at the entrance of her pussy—the same blood that stained his cock.

He'd fucked her so raw, he almost bled her dry.

Yet she didn't make a sound.

Not. One. Fucking. Sound.

"Tell me you love me," he demanded. "Tell me how much you love me, pet."

"I love you," she wheezed, the mounting pressure inside

of her released as she spoke. She was breathing hard, her chest rising and falling as she looked at him. "I love you more than anything," she repeated.

The words should have appeased him, but they didn't.

Bringing his hand to her pussy, he teased her lips, watching her arch her back as he lightly brushed his fingers against her slit. But he didn't linger. Instead, he tested her entrance.

She was probably sore and hurting, yet she would never admit that to him.

He pushed two fingers inside, carefully studying her expression.

Biting her lip, she held it all in. Especially as he pushed more inside, adding another finger, and then another, until his entire fist was inside of her.

She gasped, her eyes going wide as she fought to calm herself.

"Does this feel good?" He cooed, though he knew it must hurt like a bitch.

"Yes," she gave a strained answer.

His nostrils flared as he watched her face—the way she kept trying to pretend everything was alright.

Suddenly, he withdrew. More blood stained his hand, and as he brought it to his mouth for a taste, he held her gaze.

There was something there—something he needed to bring to the surface.

He wanted to see her on the brink, truly on the brink. Just like she'd been on the roof, all fists and violence. He wanted to taste the bitterness of her cries, her fear coupled with her anger. He wanted it *all*.

But she wasn't giving it to him.

Holding on to her hips, he had her on her stomach in a smooth move. She gave a startled yelp as she found herself face to face with the unblinking eyes of one of the dead men.

"I'm going to make you feel even better," he leaned over her, his breath on her neck as he trailed his lips on her pristine skin.

She tasted sweet—a sweetness that he wanted to spoil.

Spreading her legs, he pushed his cock inside of her again, this time the blood helping with the friction and easing his way in.

He held tightly on to her small body, one arm snaked across her stomach, the other to her front and across her breasts. He laid his cheek to her back as he slammed his hips forward, the thrust so vicious, it finally made her gasp in pain.

"Just like this pet," he murmured. "Feel the way I'm destroying you from the inside. The way my cock is ripping through your pussy."

Her breathing picked up, and for the first time, she started struggling in his arms. He increased the speed of his thrusts, holding her to him as he pushed his thick length all the way inside of her.

"Aghh," she finally gave a pained cry as he hit a spot deep within her.

Still, she didn't ask him to stop. She didn't fight. She merely accepted the pain.

More. He needed more.

Slipping out of her completely, he brought his palms to her ass, spreading her cheeks apart and spitting in her hole.

"What..." her voice was barely audible. "What... What are you doing?" she asked, looking over her shoulder, a nervous expression on her face.

"You're all mine, aren't you, pet?" he asked in a charming voice. "You're all mine to do as I please," he continued as he brought his thumb to her tight hole, swirling it around the surface before pushing inside.

She jerked in his arms, trying to get away.

"Shh, this is mine too," he told her, working his thumb in and out of her ass.

"Michele, please don't," she uttered the words in such a soft voice, he couldn't help but gaze up.

She was pale, dark circles under her eyes as she regarded him with fear in her eyes.

Finally!

"You'd dare deny me this?" his voice boomed, and she jumped, startled. She shook her head, her lips mouthing an inaudible no.

"Good. Because I own all of you, pet. *All.* Your mouth is mine, your pussy is mine, and now your ass is mine."

Removing his thumb, he didn't give her time to move as he brought the broad head of his cock against her tight ring of muscles, forcefully pushing it in.

Only then did her mouth open on a shrilling scream.

"It hurts," she breathed out, trying to get away from him. Twisting, she brought her fists against his torso in an effort to extricate herself from his grip.

"Does it?" he asked, his voice a fake pretense.

Holding tightly on to her hip bones, he didn't let her move away from him as he forced his dick inside her, inch by inch.

Fuck, but her ass was tight. Tighter than her pussy and he didn't know how he was going to stop himself from coming. Just the thought of her tight little ass filled with his seed excited him more than ever before.

He continued to push inside of her until his balls slapped against her pussy, his entire length buried in her ass.

She screamed.

A deafening sound that echoed in the great hall. Her arms flailing around, she tried to push him away from her body.

"That's it, my sweeting," he groaned. "Fuck," he swore as

he closed his eyes, enjoying the feel of her ass—the last of which he hadn't claimed from her. Now, it was his.

"Please stop," she cried out, banging her fists against the floor. All in an attempt to get his attention.

What she didn't realize was that *this* was what he'd been searching for all along. The high of hearing her scream in pain and fear, and the combination was his new kryptonite.

"Fight me, pet," he told her. "Hit me, bite me. Fucking fight me," he yelled at her.

Her eyes were wide as she shook her head, unable to comprehend what was happening.

But as he retreated and surged once more, the pain increased tenfold. His palm against her ass cheek, he slapped her, leaving his mark on her—again and again.

This time, she wasn't subdued.

She started fighting in earnest, moving her legs and twisting around so she could push him off her.

He inhaled deeply, feeling himself complete in a way he never had.

But it still wasn't enough.

No, he doubted it would *ever* be enough.

He pulled out, releasing his hold on her. Immediately, she scrambled from him, her eyes wild as she tried to back away.

Unfortunately, there was nowhere to run.

A manic smile on his face, he just watched, wanting to see her next move. And as she rose to her feet and started to dash, he went after her, giving chase.

He allowed her a few steps before he jumped her, tackling her to the ground and knocking the wind out of her.

She was so soft under his hard body, her belly cushioning his erection as he ground it against her. Bringing her small fists against his shoulders, she tried to punch him.

"Please stop," she pleaded with him, her voice cracking.

"You're hurting me, Michele," she whispered, tears at the corners of her eyes.

"I can't stop, pet," he told her, easily restraining her. "You make me so fucking hot, fuck," he cursed as he secured her hips once more, lifting her ass and spreading her cheeks to receive his cock again. Just as tight as before, he couldn't help the moan that escaped him as he pushed into her,

She yelled. She screamed. She cried.

All music to his ears.

Especially as she started to hit his face.

His cock buried so deep inside of her, he took all she had to give him. He felt his skin give way from her nails, blood reaching the surface and flowing down his face. The bitter taste invaded his mouth and he could barely keep himself from coming.

"That's it, pet. Fuck, yes! Hit me," he riled her up. "Fucking hit me!" he yelled.

She brought her small hands to his face, slapping him, clawing him, doing everything in her power to get him to stop. But she didn't realize that was what he wanted—her violence, not her submission.

He wanted to feel her savagery alive, her aggression directed at him as she hurt him just as he hurt her.

Holding tightly onto her hips, he started thrusting, working his own demons into her and wanting her to mirror him and give back as good as she got.

And by God, she didn't disappoint.

She put all her strength in her punches, kicking against his sternum until he could feel his lungs constricting, his breathing growing labored. Bringing her nails down his chest, she lodged them so deep into his flesh, he thought he saw stars. And as she brought them down, taking skin and flesh with them, he finally felt himself coming.

His balls drew up, his cock swelling in size inside her

tight little hole. He quickly withdrew, straddling her waist and fisting his length until he painted her entire face in his seed.

She went still, her eyes wide as she regarded him. Not a few seconds later, her body was racked by tremors, followed by loud, earth-shattering sobs.

There was blood all over her body—both from the others and from her own wounds.

Exhausted, he fell on his back next to her, trying to catch his breath. Looking up at the ceiling, he found an eerie comfort for the first time in his life.

Her sobs continued to echo in the room, before a small word escaped her lips.

"Why?"

"Because you're mine," he answered her. "And because you love me," he continued, turning his head to look at her.

They were both lying on their backs in the middle of the massacre. Two naked bodies among twenty corpses.

Her face was red, blood mixed with tears and cum streaking her cheeks and making her look like an apparition —a stunning apparition.

"You love me, don't you?" He asked, waiting for the confirmation.

She released a resigned hiccup as she continued to look at him, her eyes roving all over his face and down his body—to the wounds she'd inflicted on his chest and the blood she'd personally drawn.

"I love you," she said. "But I also hate you."

The corner of his mouth pulled up. His hand searched hers, threading her fingers through his and holding tightly.

"You're not the only one," he told her with a rueful smile.

CHAPTER TWENTY-THREE
MICHELE

He strode out of the building, his arms around her frail body as he headed straight for the garage. Opening the door to his car, he deposited her in the passenger seat, buckling her up and stilling for a moment as he took in her crusted hair, stained face and dirty body.

He'd done that to her.

A foreign feeling pulled at his senses as he watched her delicate features and her soft appearance.

He'd spoiled her.

From the beginning he'd known he would.

He'd set out to do just that.

Why was it that now, faced with the result of his actions, he couldn't muster any of the necessary satisfaction?

She gave a small whimper in her sleep, curling up and hugging her knees to her chest the best she could.

The reminder that he'd worn her out to the point of exhaustion—that he'd used her so thoroughly she'd had no other recourse but to close her eyes and hide from the world —made him seethe quietly. At her, or himself, he didn't know.

He realized his resolve was slightly shaken—as a result of what, he could not say. Still, he recognized the precarious situation he found himself in. As such, he needed to pull himself together.

Popping a cigarette in his mouth, he rounded the car, getting behind the wheel and starting the engine.

And the moment they were out of the estate's gates, he pulled his phone, dialing Andreas.

"Burn everything to the ground. A faulty electrical outlet. Make sure the bodies are crisp," he inhaled the cigarette smoke, coldly staring at the road before him. "If anyone asks questions, bribe or get rid of them," he added.

"Yes, sir," the answer was immediate. He could always count on Andreas to be efficient and *never* ask more than Michele was willing to share. That and his staunch loyalty made him the best soldier. The *only* one Michele trusted, to a certain extent.

"Good," he grunted. "Erase all traces of me from that party, too."

"I'll have the technical team deal with that."

The moment he had his confirmation, he hung up, throwing his phone in the backseat.

He brought the cigarette to his lips, taking a deep drag, his attention on the road as he headed to the apartment he kept in the city.

Andreas would deal with the mess he left behind, as he always did. Since Michele had gotten his first taste for blood, realizing there *was* a way out of the continuous torment in which he lived, he'd never stopped. He'd developed his own routine, using the exercise as a form of catharsis—exorcizing his demons and *himself* at the same time.

But as much as murder might be a fun pastime when the chance availed itself, he also knew it was a precarious one.

Though he was as erratic as expected, giving himself to

the euphoria of blood, losing himself in the throes of the moment, he knew there was a fine line between madness and justice. And though he might be walking the very fine line between, he always managed to pull himself back up—back where he knew he belonged, though the whole world thought differently.

This time, though, he'd given in. He'd forgotten all about black and white, right or wrong, fair or unfair. He'd only felt the moment. And he'd given into the *madness*—that rush of freedom that was as unexpected as it was sweet. Liberating and extreme…

A glance at the sleeping form next to him and he swore under his breath.

He'd long ceased to be a *fair* person. Even so, he steered clear of those who owed him *nothing*. He might rejoice in bloodbaths, but they were all a price to be paid—a debt owed.

His justice.

What he'd done at Cooke's house had neither been for his benefit nor *his* justice.

It had been for *her.*

He scowled as he realized the slight deviation from his plans.

Though he'd long eschewed proper etiquette, behaving strictly as he felt, he realized this was extreme—even for him.

One man here, one there, and no one would bat an eye.

Yet this time, he'd gone beyond that, killing indiscriminately until he filled the entire house with blood.

Because they had insulted *her.*

He told himself that by extension they had insulted him. But deep down, he knew the truth…

His hands tightened on the steering wheel, the direction of his thoughts startling him and making him madder than he'd already been.

She was *his* possession. Whatever happened to her concerned him by default. There was nothing more to it. And as instrumental as she was in his plan, he needed to ascertain she was well at all times. Only then would his revenge serve its designated purpose.

She meant nothing.

Not now, not ever.

He nodded to himself as he finally found a more comfortable train of thought. To attribute to those events more importance than they had was ludicrous. And if Michele had learned anything in his twenty-six years on this earth, it was that you were *always* on your own. The moment you gave someone else even a modicum of importance was the moment it all ended.

Didn't he know that all too well?

All the suffering he'd endured had been because he'd held on. He'd tightly grasped on to those people he'd thought closest to him, and when they had abandoned him, he'd been left alone.

Bleeding and alone.

And *that* had been the moment he'd stopped feeling. He'd simply stopped caring. And so he'd put himself first—or, better said, his revenge.

Nothing else mattered.

Just the blood and tears his enemies would shed.

That was the only thing keeping him going.

Nothing else…

The journey to his apartment took longer than usual. Michele avoided all the open roads, choosing instead the less popular ones in an attempt to keep a low profile.

He wasn't concerned about CCTV cameras picking up his traces, since that was easily solved with the push of a few buttons. Rather, he was worried he'd come across a patrol car doing its rounds. With both their appearances, a stop and search was unavoidable.

Not when he was still full of blood, the red liquid splattered all over his body, face and hair. His pet was in a similar state, if not worse. Anyone who would see them like that would reach the worst, though rightful, conclusions.

Eventually, he reached the neighborhood, and parking his car, he took his pet in his arms, heading to the private elevator that would ensure their abysmal appearance was kept hidden.

She stirred, but barely.

Her head was in the crook of his shoulder, and as she released a pained moan, she trailed her face over his skin.

A slight brush of skin against skin, but it was enough to get a reaction out of Michele, his body stiffening, his breathing growing labored. For someone who'd eschewed human touch for so long, tolerating it only when it was necessary to his plans, this was the equivalent to a bullet to the chest.

Yet the more she moved, the more the pain abated.

He blinked in surprise, slowly recognizing that the initial touch had activated his own expectations of pain and disgust. Gradually, though, they molded into a peaceful calm —something that hadn't happened before.

She tightened her arms around his neck, reinforcing the skin contact. Yet he wasn't...disgusted.

"Michele," she whimpered low in her throat, struggling to open her eyes.

Michele was frozen to the spot, unable to react to her continued proximity. He was stunned at his reaction and every subsequent one as she continued to move against him, touching him in more places—all at once.

"Where are we?" she asked, a hint of unease in her tone as the elevator doors opened to his apartment.

He stepped inside, ignoring her question. Instead, he walked straight to the master bedroom, unceremoniously dumping her on the bed.

"Wha—what?" she blinked, surprised.

Her big eyes were on him, watching, assessing.

"We're at my place, pet," he told her in a thick voice.

There was still residual adrenaline from his previous outburst, and now that she was awake, he tried to keep his distance lest he get more ideas—dangerous, dangerous ideas.

She continued to regard him with that innocence of hers, and sick laughter bubbled in his throat at the sight.

He'd defiled her—debased her in the worst manner possible. He'd hurt her worse than he thought himself capable of hurting someone, and she still looked at him as if he could pluck the moon and hand it to her on a platter.

He took a step forward.

She flinched.

Or...not.

"Go clean yourself," he barked the order, somehow unable to face the consequence of his actions.

She was huddled in the center of the bed, her arms bent to her chest as she tried to protect herself. At least subconsciously she knew she needed to be afraid.

Something inside her was aware of the danger he posed to her. Too bad she wasn't smart enough to heed the warning.

"But..." her lip trembled as her lashes fluttered.

"Pet," he snarled, his fingers suddenly on her jaw. Her eyes flared with fear and he cursed. Taking a deep breath, he managed to get his tone under control as he continued. "You're covered in blood from head to toe. You need to wash that off."

She stared at him, unblinking.

Slowly, she brought her chin down in a subtle nod.

It was all the confirmation he needed to take his hand off

her, turning to his side on the bed as he watched her tentatively get off the bed. She put one step in front of the other, wobbling to the bathroom door.

It was then that he realized the gravity of her injuries.

She limped slightly, and there were gashes all over her body leaking blood. He couldn't be sure it was all coming from her, but remembering the way he'd taken her, he wagered a good deal was.

She finally closed the door to the bathroom and it wasn't long after that he heard the water running.

Only then did he let out a relieved breath—why, he couldn't tell. There was something inside of him, a tightness in his chest that he could not explain away with words. He only *felt*, something he hadn't done in too long.

And he wasn't sure he liked it.

Suffocating like a man deprived of air, he lifted a fist to his injured chest, banging over the open wounds and feeling the pain suffuse his being. It was sharp and immediate, effectively taking over anything else his mind might have honed on.

He relied on it, relished it.

It was the only way he knew he was still human, though shunning the *feelings* that should have made him human.

Time passed, his pain increased. His pet *didn't* return.

That's when he heard it.

Something more than just the sound of water running.

He blinked, surprised to find himself off the bed and nearing the bathroom door, his ear on the hard wood as he listened to the muffled cries and the blanketed sobs—all somewhat muted by the jet of water as it poured down into the bath.

Before he could help himself, he pushed the door open.

She was in the middle of the sizable bathtub, her knees to her chest as she rocked slightly—side to side, in rhythm with her sobs. The water reached her waist, already a muddy pink from the blood that had poured off her body.

His feet took him further, to the edge of the tub as he simply watched her.

There it was again.

Another tightening in his chest. He wondered if all that adrenaline had prompted a premature heart attack.

"Pet," his voice boomed in the room.

She whipped her head back, tears streaking her perfectly sculpted cheeks as she looked at him like he was the worst bounder in the entire world.

The expression was there—clear as the day. Yet soon, it was clouded, shifting until nothing else remained on her face but pure lethargy.

It was at that moment that Michele fully understood one thing.

He wasn't the only one with a poker face.

"What are you doing?' he demanded sharply.

She brought the back of her hand to wipe her eyes. Still, she didn't answer him.

He was getting more and more impatient, and bringing his hands to the shirt he'd haphazardly put on before leaving the manor, he ripped at the buttons, flinging it around before affording the same treatment to his pants.

Fully naked, he motioned her to scoot over as he entered the tub, joining her.

Immediately, he felt the hot water on his skin—it was scalding hot.

"Damn it," he cursed under his breath as he barely made himself comfortable.

He had to wonder how she managed to sit in the water if it was that hot. But just as he was about to voice that question, he spotted her unguarded expression.

Hurt.

So much hurt.

Hurt he'd caused.

Hurt he'd purposefully inflicted.

She blinked newly formed tears away, attempting a feeble smile for his benefit.

Did he want it?

The answer came with a resounding force.

No.

Since he'd gotten a taste of the real her—the damaged, out of control her—he didn't know how to get used to the old her again.

He wanted her raw... He wanted *her*, damn it. Not some second-hand version created only for his benefit.

And the more he got to know her, the more he *studied* her, he realized she might be just as crafty as he was, if not more. The only difference was that she had a masochistic streak.

"What are you doing?" she asked softly, almost as if she could not believe he was in front of her.

"What does it look like I'm doing?" he raised a brow, smirking at her. Anything to cover the growing storm raging inside of him.

Taking a sponge from the rack behind, he wet it, and lathering it with soap, he motioned two fingers at her to come closer.

"What..." she blinked in surprise.

"Come," he gruffed out.

Hesitantly, she obeyed, coming closer until she was within the cradle of his thighs.

His eyes fluttered closed as her scent hit him. Even with so many layers of dirt, blood and bodily fluids, there was something about *her*. Something addictive he'd never encountered before.

"Thank you," she murmured shyly as he brought the

sponge on her neck, lowering it between the valley of her breasts, and lower.

Any other moment and this would have marked the beginning of his arousal. Yet in that moment he couldn't muster it. Not when his foremost purpose was to get her to the initial state—the one where she didn't fear him any longer.

He didn't know why it was imperative to do so, but it was the only thing he could come up with as he racked his brain for an answer to his current actions.

His touch was brisk and efficient as he cleaned her thoroughly. First her torso, then her legs. All the while he had the vague impression she was holding herself back. She was barely breathing, barely moving, barely...

"Pet," he addressed her, one finger to her cheek as he turned it so she could face him. "How are you feeling?"

"I'm fine," she strained.

He tilted his head, studying her. The words sounded fake to his ears. But he didn't dwell on that—he couldn't afford to do so. Instead, he brought the sponge to her flushed cheeks, washing her gently, carefully.

The same feeling as before overtook him, his heart squeezing in his chest in a foreign manner, one he didn't dare question.

She looked at him with her big, luminous eyes, and he found he couldn't utter another word. So, silently, he urged her to turn, settle with her back between his legs—touching but not really.

It wasn't sexual. Though in his mind, he told himself this couldn't be anything *but* sexual. Still, his desire wasn't aroused. He didn't feel his blood boil with a need to claim her —not as he usually did, anyway.

He only felt that same tension in his chest, almost as if someone had tightened his skin over his ribcage, pulling and pulling until it was strained over bone, no freedom of movement—nothing.

At first, he sponged her back, barely keeping a controlled expression as he noted the various injuries his pet had sustained. There were scratches, some smaller, some bigger.

All caused by him.

He soaped the surface of her skin, gently brushing his fingertips over her shoulder blades. And before he could catch himself, he lowered his lips, skimming them over the softness of her skin. It was the barest of touches, yet she startled all the same.

"Does it hurt, pet?" he asked her in a low voice, doing his best to hide the lump that clogged his throat.

"Not...now," she answered cryptically. But the tone of her voice was enough to tell him everything he needed to know.

She was in pain.

And he wasn't gloating.

Carefully, he proceeded to tend to every area, making sure it was nice and clean by the time he was done with his ministrations. Then, he shifted his attention to her hair—her lovely, lovely hair.

It was crusted with blood and semen, strands lumped together, harsh to the touch.

Using the same care as before, he lowered her to the water, getting the entire mass of tresses wet before he applied shampoo.

His touch was gentle—a first.

But it was more than that. It was borne from a foreign need he couldn't fully understand. And it was as strange to him as it was to her.

Nothing made sense anymore.

Yet in spite of that, in spite of knowing this was out of the ordinary, that the entire situation was so antithetic to everything he stood for, he found he couldn't stop.

He could only watch himself continue, almost as if it was an out of body experience. It was him, but it wasn't... Because how could *this* be him? How could he behave in such a manner when he'd never experienced it himself?

His fingers in her hair, he lightly massaged her scalp, the sigh that escaped her lips all the payment he required.

And when he was done, he quickly cleaned himself too, before getting out.

His pet was watching him with apprehension as he donned on a robe before taking a big towel and swathing her in it. He swooped her up in his arms, and finally, he took her to bed.

She still didn't speak, just watching, observing.

And before he lost whatever impetus had been guiding him until then, he went back to the bathroom to pick up a medical kit.

"You don't have to..." she whispered as the bed dipped under his weight.

"I do," he grunted, opening her towel and baring her to him—baring the evidence of what he'd done.

The injuries were worse than he'd imagined, but he didn't let the image of them bother him. He put everything in the back of his mind as he settled on the same mechanical response as before—though it wasn't, not really. It was merely his way of dealing with which was foreign to him; that which he had no experience and neither the imagination to picture. He let himself be driven by a long forgotten instinct, or maybe one that just now was rearing its head to the surface.

His pet was confused.

No more than him.

And because he couldn't deal with what she made him feel, he simply put some disinfectant on a small piece of gauze, dabbing it at her injuries, wincing when she winced, shuddering when she did.

"Why?" her hand came to rest on his, stopping his advancement.

His brows went up in question.

"Why are you doing this?" she asked on a whisper, almost as if she didn't want to give away the vulnerability in her voice.

"I break you, I put you back together," he answered in a cold voice, continuing to tend to her wounds.

"Why break me at all?" her hand once more found his, holding on to his wrist and not allowing him to do his job. Yet this time, he sensed something different in her question. More so in her tone, an uneven sound escaping her before she could mask him.

He lifted his gaze to find hers.

Tears were streaming down her face, this time unbidden.

She was crying.

Sniffling, she continued to glance at him with that wounded pup look, her eyes damp and getting damper. And he suddenly felt at a loss.

Her small hands clenched into fists and out of some misplaced reflex, one skimmed the right side of his jaw.

The misplaced *reflex* was about to happen again when he caught her wrist, holding tightly as he tugged her to him.

He expected aggression. Destruction. A glimpse of the explosive outburst he'd seen on the roof.

He got none.

She was staring at him through wet lashes, her entire face red as she continued to bawl in his hold.

"Why?" she cried out. "Why?"

"Why, what, pet?" he ground his teeth, narrowing his eyes at her.

The energy was similar, the violence simmering in the air.

But this was different. Too different than what he wanted—needed and craved. This was the polar opposite of that.

"Why do you enjoy hurting me so much?" she asked, her voice breaking with emotion.

He reeled back, the question taking him wholly by surprise.

He could only stare at her. At her beautiful, beautiful face and the fact that she could move him when he thought himself unmovable.

"Because I enjoy hurting myself," the words were out of his mouth before he could help himself.

His eyes widened.

Hers did too.

Silence enveloped them. The type of silence that could make the dead weep. The type of silence that said more than a thousand words.

Her lower lip trembled as she tried to get herself under control, absorbing the fullness of what he'd just said. Yet she couldn't. No matter how much she tried, she couldn't stop the shrilling sobs that took over her body, the way her emotions spilled forth with that outburst.

He continued to look at her, envious at the ease with which she could unload herself; anger at himself for closing that part of his heart long ago.

When was the last time he'd cried?

He couldn't remember... He did not *want* to remember.

Chapter Twenty-Four
Michele

He brought one hand to her face, wiping away some of the moisture as he let her cry her heart out. His thumb brushed at her cheek, a soothing gesture that didn't go unnoticed, her eyes flaring with shock.

Michele wanted to say something—anything. But as he opened his mouth to utter fake platitudes, or even a dumb response, no sound came out.

Instead, he merely brought her closer to his chest, holding her tightly, so tightly her breath hitched in surprise.

Not speaking, he simply held her.

She cried. She cried and cried and was unable to stop.

And he didn't stop her either.

For a man prone to anger at the smallest inconvenience, he held on to her, bearing down her sadness and her sorrow, her pain and her hurt. He took everything on to himself, not only as the cause, but also as the cure.

And only when she was so spent from crying and her sobs abated did he let go, noting her even breaths and her sleepy sighs, did he gently lower her to bed.

His actions were against himself, but for a brief moment

he considered himself out of his body, out of his mind, out of what made him *him*. And so for a moment he let himself do what he'd wanted from the beginning—touch her. Not in anger, not in revenge, and not in deviousness. It was simply the touch of a man starved for touch, but one who was afraid to take that leap.

He settled her head on the pillow, brushing her hair from her face as he placed her in a comfortable position. Grabbing the edge of the blanket, he pulled it on top of her, covering her and swathing her in a small cocoon of warmth.

He moved slowly, as if he knew the precariousness of the moment—the fact that any errant movement could take him out of it, make him lose it forever. His gaze still on her, he stepped away, slowly, carefully.

He backed away until he found himself in the kitchen, his cabinet fully stocked with his favorite whiskey.

He didn't want to miss that period in time, yet he needed to get away—he needed to become detached. Because in that instant, he'd had a flash of himself in another life, in another time where he hadn't lost himself or his capacity for empathizing with another human being. Where he was still the old him—the one who'd taken life in stride with shining optimism in his eyes.

But he wasn't that person anymore.

He didn't know *how* to be that person anymore.

And he was afraid that for her... For her he might wish to be again.

He poured himself a generous glass of whiskey, emptying it in one go and wincing at the bitterness of the liquid as it washed down his throat.

"Damn it," he swore, bringing the glass down on the counter with a resounding thud. The force was so great that it instantly broke, shards of it snapping all around, with the largest one embedding in his skin.

He opened his mouth on a moan of pain, but instead of cursing the discomfort, he welcomed it.

For a moment, his gaze was arrested by the red of the blood as it poured from his wound and on to the marble counter, the white inundated by that substance of *life.* Yet in his mind's eye, it was the substance of death, of everything that was wrong and foul and awful on this earth. Of everything he'd suffered with no reprieve or hope for salvation—for everything he was still wont to suffer.

He'd tried to end it once. Unsuccessfully.

And since then, he'd resigned himself to seeing this all to the end—to leave his mark in a way that everyone expected but that no one saw coming.

Wasn't he, like any monster, the product of his environment?

It was in times like this, when his mind was in continuous turmoil that he once more debated whether he'd been a monster by birth, or one by making. Because even in the darkest times of his life, there had still been a glimmer of hope... Something to tell him that not everything was bad—that he wasn't *all* bad.

Now...he didn't know anymore.

He took the bottle of alcohol, drinking greedily, the liquid pouring down his chin just as tears stabbed at his eyes, longing for the same treatment.

Step by step, he was heading down the road of no return—perhaps he'd already done so.

And as he glanced longingly towards the bedroom door, he knew he was embarking on the worst torment yet.

He just couldn't acknowledge it.

Deep down, he was well aware.

But up, where his conscience lived, he was still confident in his plan, in his revenge and everything that would follow.

The demons weren't quieted though. If anything, they

were more restless, and impatient, crowding his mind and sending him on a winding spiral—one that had no beginning and no end.

His forehead creased as he screwed his face in pain—this time of the mental variety.

Dropping the bottle to the ground, he stepped back, bringing his bleeding hand to his temple as he sought to assuage the pain.

He just wanted relief.

For one second, he wished for relief.

He wanted out of his head, out of his mind that was full of the most atrocious thoughts that would not let him be. Past, present, and potential future mingled again in his eyes, and he saw the possibilities—the countless possibilities.

But he also saw more.

He saw the disappointment and the devastation if he should hope for something only for it to turn to dust.

From the moment he'd put his plans into motion, he'd been one with his demons. And because he'd chosen to embark on that journey, he knew there was nothing else to be done.

Nothing but see it to the end.

He swiveled, his grave gaze on the tentative form hiding behind a pillar.

It was *her*.

His pet.

The one who'd hate him the most. But also the one who'd cut him the most.

"You're hurt," she whispered, her eyes landing on his hand. Without a thought about her own safety, she dashed towards him, the intention on her face clear.

But just as she stepped into his space, he suddenly swooped her up, her feet not touching the hazardous ground. Gently, he deposited her on the other side of the counter, the clean one where no glass lay. And for a second, his touch lingered on her, almost as if he tried to commit it all to memory.

She grabbed his arm, raising it to her assessing gaze.

"Why weren't you more careful?" she asked in a soft, caring voice, her fingers trailing over his cut. And damn if that gesture didn't take away all his hurt...

"Didn't I tell you, pet?" his lip curled up in a sad smile. "I like to hurt myself."

She frowned, regarding him with confusion.

"Don't," the sound escaped her, the soft order cloying the air.

Her eyes widened as she realized her faux pas, but she didn't retract it.

She merely continued to regard him, her courage rising by the second.

"Don't hurt yourself anymore," she continued, taking his hand in her two small ones and bringing his open palm to her mouth for a soothing kiss. "Please..." she whispered against his skin, the hotness of her breath penetrating his open skin, traveling up his veins and making its home in his body.

The moment grew tense as he didn't speak. He didn't reply, for he did not know what to say. A tremulous smile appeared on her face as she didn't quite know how to continue.

And though he sensed her growing discomfort, he didn't move, or say anything. He wanted to know what *she* would do.

He was letting *her* call the shots, curious to see what her next step would be.

From the beginning of their relationship, he'd been the one ordering her around and dictating how every moment in each other's company would go. He would command and she would follow. For that was her purpose, wasn't it? A lowly distraction, but one with which he could advance his revenge. She fit his plans, and so he continued to indulge her.

Yet at some moment, something must have switched. Something incredibly minuscule that neither of them realized.

Because as it stood, Michele should have thrown her away months ago. He should have broken her, then discarded her without a second thought.

Maybe it was comfort, he told himself as he continued to watch her directly, yet furtively.

He'd become so used to her presence, her company, that he found it hard to give it up even as his mind was screaming at him to put an end to everything—focus on his end goal.

"When you hurt, you hurt me too," she finally said, searching his gaze with her insistent one. Her expression was one of worry, of *caring*, or *real* love, not the make-believe kind he'd used as his shield from the beginning.

He perused her features, from her heart-shaped face to her chiseled cheekbones and pouty lips. Everything was sexy about her—everything but her eyes.

Big and doe-like, they reeked of innocence and kindness, the type he'd never been familiar with, especially with him as the main target.

A flash of rage entered his mind at that thought, a poisonous need to dispel any illusions she might have had about them, crush all the remaining innocence in one last blow. But no matter how much he readied himself for it; how much he tried to muster the strength to do it, he found he could not—at least not yet.

One last time…

He let himself be led by her dainty hand as she took over, beckoning him to the bedroom where she seated him on the plush mattress of his bed. He let her order him to stay still as she brought the same medical kit he'd used before, tending to his injury with such care, he didn't know whether this was his reality, or just a fantasy—one he'd had before, in the deepest recesses of his mind.

"I know you don't like to talk about yourself much," his pet started, startling him with her words. "But I understand," she gave him a shy smile, all the while working to patch his hand back together, dabbing disinfectant and cleaning the wound of any residue glass before carefully wrapping it with bandage.

"What do you understand?" he asked hoarsely.

As if he'd been bespelled, he looked upon her like one would a mirage—one half of him hoping it was real, one half hoping it would dispel faster, so the disappointment wouldn't be so dire at the end.

"Your pain," she answered. "Here," she lifted two fingers, brushing them against his naked chest right over his heart— or what should have been his heart. "You're alone. Like me," her face strained in a sad smile.

"What do you know of alone, pet," he didn't recognize his voice as he spoke, the words seemingly stuck in his throat.

She shifted in front of him, coming closer. Slowly. She was slow, almost as if she sensed he was like a wounded animal about to bolt at the slightest brusque movement.

Raising herself on her knees, she leaned in, her hand on his face before he could voice any objection.

It was so gentle, so foreign, so…

He blinked.

"I know of alone, but I know even more of loneliness," her cheeks tightened as she tried to imbue her words with a smile. "Of wanting to belong, but never knowing *where*. Of longing for that one connection…"

"You're wrong," he told her harshly, his breathing out of control. Yet he didn't swat her hand away. "I don't want to belong anywhere," he added with extreme certainty. After all, he'd exorcized those particular demons a long time ago.

She didn't argue with him.

She merely smiled, though at what, he did not know.

"What if *I* want to belong?" she fluttered her lashes slightly. She had no idea of her own appeal and the fact that one bat of those pretty lashes of hers could have such an effect on him.

But it did. Oh, but it did.

He felt the surface of his skin heat up, his pulse accelerating.

"Where?" he asked, not taking his eyes off hers.

She shook her head.

"Not where," she corrected, her hand continuing to stroke his cheek, going down to his chin and brushing her thumb over his lips. "To whom."

The words were an echo in the room and in his own brain. Sounding and resounding, until he looked at her and could only see one thing.

His.

She was his. Wholly his, unlike anyone had ever been before. Unlike anyone would be after.

She was *his.*

"You're mine," he declared, the statement heavy, but encompassing all those foreign feelings she awoke within him.

"I *am* yours," she nodded, as if she'd been waiting an eternity for him to reach that conclusion.

His hands covered hers, squeezing tightly before moving and cupping the sides of her face. He had no idea that every little touch, of his own volition, was a prized possession for his pet. He had no idea that she saw more than he wanted her to see.

That she wasn't *just* the cute, adoring and loyal pet he assumed her to be.

But for his benefit, she was.

"Zia," he groaned, her name burning on his lips, hurting, but also purifying. "My Zia..." He closed his eyes, lest she see the anguish in them, but it wasn't before he, himself, saw the unguarded reaction on her face.

Shock. Wonder. Love.

So much love, he didn't know what to do with it.

And as he blinked anew, it was to watch her move closer, leaning in until her face was inches away from his, her breath already on him.

"Take me," she whimpered, the urgency in her tone as foreign as the moment itself. She'd never once taken the initiative for anything. Yet there she was, waiting. Never the other way around.

He shook his head slightly.

"You're sore," he whispered, regarding her through hooded eyes as the storm inside of him raged and raged. He wanted her. He wanted her too damn much. And for once, the first and maybe the last, he wasn't going to take. He wasn't going to...

"No," she denied vehemently, lying to his face though he knew the truth. "I'm not. Please, Michele..." she wet her lips, her vulnerability shining through in every uncertain breath and the tentative smile she put on.

He lowered his hands to her shoulders, dismayed to find her trembling against him. And as he saw the powerful need inside of her, as powerful as the one that had been building in him, he couldn't tell her no. He couldn't deny what was freely given.

Michele bent his head, his lips brushing against hers—a light caress. He felt her shuddering against him, giving into him as she'd never done before.

"Take me," she repeated, a cry for something...

He thrust all rational thought out of his mind as he maneuvered her around the bed. On her back, he loomed over her as he tore at her towel, leaving her naked and bared to his sight.

For a second, the numerous cuts on her body made him pause. But her honeyed voice was enough to make him forget about anything and everything, the moment at hand the only one that mattered.

His own robe was wide open, and he shrugged it off his shoulders, throwing it next to the bed. Fully naked, his arousal was evident, his cock rigid against the plane of his stomach. Yet this time she wasn't afraid. She was looking at him straight in the eye, urging him on, *needing* him.

"You're so beautiful," he rasped as he took hold of her thighs, parting them so he could settle between them.

He was in no hurry—not as usual.

His hands were on the swell of her hips, and he tenderly moved them up, caressing her and memorizing her features.

She responded beautifully, her skin immediately shivering under his touch, her little noises of encouragement making his chest swell with the same foreign feeling as before.

"And all mine," he said in awe, as if he could barely believe it.

She nodded fervently, reaching out for him, her arms around his neck as she drew him to her.

His lips were on hers, probing, tasting, consuming. And it was all instinct. No longer was he concerned with restraint, or keeping himself aloof—or God forbid, have her touch him. In that moment, none of that mattered.

His skin was on top of her skin.

And it didn't burn.

It didn't hurt. Far from it.

It made him feel powerful—overflowing with *power*.

She wrapped her legs around him, drawing him in. And reaching between their bodies, he adjusted the tip of his erection to her center, stroking her lightly before pushing inside of her.

Her mouth opened on a gasp, but he swallowed it, keeping her with him rooted in the moment as he joined his body to hers, slowly, passionately.

"Does it hurt?" he leaned back to ask, only to find her eyes shimmering with tears.

He frowned in confusion.

She just shook her head, her fingers peppering small, ghost-like touches over his face as she looked at him like she'd never seen him before.

"It doesn't hurt."

She smiled then. A smile so blinding, it took him a moment to catch himself. A moment to wonder what the hell he was doing.

But then she tilted her hips, moving with him.

He groaned.

She moaned deep in her throat.

"Zia," he found himself calling out her name as he established a rhythm for both of them.

A slow, rocking motion that had nothing to do with fucking, though that's all he knew, and barely. It was so much more that neither could properly define it.

He continued to move within her, thrusting and withdrawing, his eyes on her face as he tracked every small reaction. The way her mouth parted ever so slightly as he was wholly inside her, or how her breathing accelerated in anticipation as he moved back.

"Kiss me," she whispered, and he did.

He didn't think he could deny her anything at that moment.

He kissed her, moments on end.

Even as he spilled himself inside of her, he didn't stop kissing her.

It was sometime later when, spooning her from behind, his arms wrapped tightly around her slight body, that he finally spoke.

"Did you," he cleared his voice, swallowing hard as a lump formed in his throat, uncertainty eating at him. "Did you like it?"

He'd never asked her that before—had never cared if she did or not. Yet now it was imperative he knew.

She turned, shifting in the cradle of his arms as she brought her front to his, brushing her nipples over the hard plane of his chest.

She nodded, a deep pink coloring her cheeks.

His lips stretched in a smile as he simply took her in—her sweetness and her unusual beauty.

Bringing a finger to her face, he brushed it over her cheek, tugging a stray strand of hair behind her ear.

"You're all mine," he found himself repeating, wanting that sentence to be the culmination of everything. Regardless of what tomorrow brought, and regardless of where his fate would take him. He wanted her to be *his* forever—beginning to the end.

She caught his hand, fitting his palm to her cheek as she burrowed deeper, an expression of pure satisfaction descending on her features.

"Mhm," the sound vibrated in her throat, enthralling him further. "Are you mine, too?" she asked in a soft tone, her big eyes on him as she regarded him with trepidation.

Was he hers?

He didn't have an answer to that question. He didn't know what it was like to be anyone's. And so he answered the only way he knew how.

"I'm not *not* yours."

She frowned in confusion. But it wasn't for long as her lips worked in silence, repeating those words just as a smile spread over her face.

"You're not *not* mine," she chuckled lightly, taking his hand and laying a gentle kiss in the middle of his palm. "I hope you'll always be not *not* mine."

She understood.

That was the first thought that crossed his mind.

She *got* him. She…

"Michele…" she called his name in that lovely voice of hers.

"Huh?" he raised his brows, regarding her indulgently as two dots of pink appeared in her cheeks.

"Why do you love me?"

He blinked, wholly taken aback by the direction of her questioning.

"Why do *you* love me," he countered, uncomfortable being the first to answer such a loaded question.

Instead of feeling slighted, or put on the spot; instead of finding outrage on her pretty face, he only found a smile.

"Because we're the same," she said, and he narrowed his eyes at her. "There's a void inside here," she took his hand and placed it over her heart, "that only you can fill. Just like there's a void inside here," she placed her other palm on *his* heart, "that only I can fill."

He blinked, awareness slowly seeping in. A few words, and it had been enough to realize his error of judgment, and the fact that he *may* be prone to bouts of insanity, in spite of his previous convictions. Otherwise, he couldn't explain the madness he'd just committed.

She seemed so pleased with herself, so happy at the prospect of being the same as he.

What did she know of him, or of his void?

What did she know?

The ugly voice inside his mind asked, awoken and ready to wage war.

"We're not the same," his chilly voice resounded in the room. "We're nothing alike, pet," he said coldly, his eyes already blank as he stared in the distance.

So lost was he in his own head that he didn't notice the stiffening of her body, or the way her eyes became dead at the sound of that one word.

Pet.

She was his pet once more.

CHAPTER TWENTY-FIVE
NOELLE

"You don't have to ask, Raf. Of course we'll help," Catalina gives us a warm smile, while Marcello nods by her side.

"We'll be on standby too. We're not exactly Michele's biggest fans," Sisi mutters dryly.

"I offered to kill him for you, hell girl, but you refused my offer," Vlad, her husband, pouts.

"It's odd to think about killing him personally." She turns, adding thoughtfully. "We do share DNA after all."

"And *that* is a pity," he shakes his head, amused, but his hand finds his way around her waist, dragging her closer to him—if that's possible. "No offense, but your brother," he looks between Raf and Sisi, "is a pest."

"Tell me about it," Sisi rolls her eyes. "I've only met him a handful of times but it was enough to make me want to puke," she makes a funny expression.

"Michele has the ability to awaken those feelings in people," Raf chuckles.

It soon becomes clear that Michele is hated by everyone in the room, and why.

A few years back he assaulted Catalina, and was subsequently discovered to be involved in a decade-long organ trafficking ring that involved children.

The more I hear about him, though, the more I realize that monsters are *everywhere* and under different disguises. Sergio's vile character had been reflected by his appearance. But with Michele, you wouldn't be able to tell that so much depravity could hide under such a beautiful face. I've seen pictures of him, and he looks like a fallen angel with his dark curly hair and pale skin, all emphasized by the lightest eyes I've ever seen—eyes that he shares with Sisi.

"We can't underestimate him. I don't think we've seen everything he's capable of yet," Raf adds grimly.

With the piano recital fast approaching, Raf had reached out to everyone he could think of to ask for backup, telling me he would *never* risk my safety to save some misplaced pride. His proclamation had warmed my heart, especially as I'd seen him work day and night to make sure there were no loopholes in the plan.

"I'll always put you first, Noelle," he'd told me at one point, and I'd *almost* swooned. For someone who'd been relegated to last place my entire life, his words had warmed my heart in a way that nothing else could.

Marcello and Catalina had been more than receptive to the idea, and Sisi and Vlad had jumped in right away.

It had taken a while for Vlad and Raf to work out their differences, but once Vlad was convinced that Raf had no interest in making a play for his wife, he'd become more tolerant. He'd still imposed a no touching rule, as evidenced by his tight grip on Sisi at the moment.

We've met a few times already, but it's always the same. What starts with them sitting like normal people usually ends up with Sisi on his lap by the end of the meeting. At this point, I have to wonder if they're joined at the hip, since they don't seem to be apart for one second.

Curious, one time I'd even asked Sisi if they are *ever* apart and she'd given me a guilty smile while recounting that both of them have separation anxiety, and they are rarely apart for more than five minutes.

I was shocked.

Sneaking a glance to Raf, I can't help but compare. Vlad doesn't care that people see how over the top he behaves with his wife. Raf, on the other hand, always follows etiquette.

We're always together in private, but in public he maintains a polite distance. And I can't help but wonder why...

"Oh, great, the tea is here," Catalina interjects, and a member of her staff brings over a tray of tea and a selection of cakes.

"You have no idea how happy I am to see Raf settled," she continues as she serves the tea. "For a while we were very worried about him," she sneaks a glance at her husband.

From what Raf had told me, not many are aware of what had happened to him while he'd been missing.

"I don't think I told you, but I'm sorry about your parents," Marcello says. "I know you never wanted to step in your father's shoes."

"It wouldn't have been my choice, no," he agrees, "but I've learned some valuable lessons along the way. One being that the things that are truly worth it are never easily acquired," he murmurs as he looks at me.

A blush envelops my features, only to deepen when I feel his hand on top of mine, squeezing it.

"My, my, but don't you look all lovey-dovey?" Vlad drawls, amused.

"As if you're one to talk," Raf shoots back, but Vlad merely shrugs.

"It is what it is. I don't think I'd manage a moment without my hell girl," he winks at her.

The discussion turns to playful banter as everyone becomes more at ease, the previous morose subjects promptly forgotten.

Both Catalina and Sisi do their best to draw me out of my shell and include me in the conversation, which slowly makes me more comfortable. And as I note the jokes being passed around and the air of levity around the room, I can't help but feel surprised.

I've never had that.

Growing up, I'd been a necessary evil to my parents. Already in their mid-forties and fifties, and tired of rearing children, they'd had certain expectations of me—all of which included behaving *not* like a child.

I was not allowed to make loud noises, throw tantrums, or play the silly games children play. Learning to play the piano was the only acceptable thing, since it was a classical endeavor.

Instead of annoying them, I strove to make them proud with my achievements. At the same time, that meant I grew up in an entirely sterile environment. My parents were disinterested in me and my siblings were too old to bother with someone over a decade younger.

That made me seek refuge in whatever I could—my piano, and sometimes my computer.

As I watch Sisi's interactions with her brother, I can't help but feel a little jealous that I'd never shared such a bond with *any* of my brothers. Yet somehow, I can't see Cisco smiling tenderly at me like Marcello does with his sister.

"Are you ok?" Raf whispers in my ear, snaking his arm around my shoulders and drawing me closer to him. Instantly, the heat of his body transfers into mine, enveloping me in a protective cocoon.

"Yes," I give him a small smile. "I like this," I tell him, and his expression turns soft.

"I'm glad," he leans in to kiss my cheek. "I want you to make friends and do whatever pleases you," he whispers. "I hate that Cisco isolated you from everyone, but I vow to you that as soon as the danger is over things are going to change."

Late at night, as we lay in each other's arms, we talk about everything and anything. And as we've both opened up about our childhoods, Raf knows very well that mine wasn't the most stellar one. In comparison, his sounded like heaven. He's been transparent about his parents' faults from the beginning, but he's also shared that they truly loved and cared for him—most of the time to the detriment of his brother.

It's one of his biggest regrets, that he did not react in time to stop the abuse that was going on with his brother, and to a certain degree, I think he blames himself.

Still, the more we talked about our pasts, the more he vowed to me that our family would not turn out like that.

I'd listened to his assurances with a smile on my face, but inside he'd opened up a storm of feelings and doubts. If I won't be able to have children, then what family could we possibly have?

And just as that thought surfaces, a wail permeates the air —a baby's wail.

A young woman rushes into the room, a baby in her arms as she tries unsuccessfully to calm her down.

"We were just playing and she started crying," the girl explains, a downcast expression on her face.

She hands the baby to Catalina, who is quick to coo sweet words in her ears, swaying her gently in her arms before the baby suddenly stops crying. Her big eyes are open wide as she looks around the room, blinking rapidly and curiously at everyone present.

"This is Mirabella, our six month old daughter," Catalina introduces her, and Sisi wastes no time in taking her in her arms, raising her in the air and playing with her until she's laughing—a sweet sound that touches my heart.

"Raf, you remember Venezia, right?" She asks as she points to the young woman who'd brought Mirabella down.

"Of course!" he exclaims with a wide smile. "Nice to see you again, Venezia. You've grown so much."

He quickly introduces us, and I find out that she's Marcello's youngest sister.

"Pleased to meet you," I offer my hand in a small shake.

She has a timid smile on her face as she takes a seat across from us. Dressed in a long gray gown that covers her from head to toe, there's still no denying that she's extremely beautiful.

"They finally relented and let her go to public school," Sisi mentions, giving her brother a dry stare.

"And she's been doing amazing," Marcello replies, ignoring his sister's jibe. "I've been in contact with her teachers and she's been making great progress," he states, looking at Venezia with a proud expression on his face.

The conversation flows, and I glean that Venezia is severely dyslexic, and since her education had been neglected for a long time, she'd had to put in extra effort to catch up.

"Have some cake, Venezia," Sisi grabs the tongs off the table and adds a selection of cakes to a small plate, handing it to Venezia.

She accepts it with a trembling hand, her smile a little strained as she looks at the assortment.

"She still doesn't know what she wants to do and her graduation is right around the corner," Catalina continues, talking about different career options Venezia's been exploring.

Though being the subject of the conversation, Venezia doesn't interject a lot, merely letting her family do the talking. In fact, the more I look at her, the more I realize she is unusually withdrawn—somehow reminding me of myself.

"We're not that far off in age," I tell her as I strike up a conversation. "But I've never been to school. It must be so fun," I exhale dreamily.

She doesn't realize how lucky she is. I don't know any other don who'd let his young sister attend public school so easily. Certainly, my family would have *never* allowed it. I'm happy I'd gotten at least *some* education, since I know a lot of girls in our situation don't even get that.

"It is," she smiles. "I've made a lot of friends," she explains, and her features start to relax as she tells me about her school life and her favorite subjects.

More than anything, she's lucky her brother is allowing her to think about a career instead of marrying her off.

Bringing a piece of cake to her lips, she seems reluctant to bite into it. Her hand trembles a little, and out of nowhere, she puts it back, placing the plate on the table and rising up.

"Excuse me..." She barely gets the words out as one hand flies to her mouth, the other to her midriff as she dashes out of the room.

"Oh no!" Catalina stands up. "She might have caught that bug from Claudia." She purses her lips in worry. "I'll go check on her," she excuses herself, following after Venezia

Sisi is still playing with Mirabella, and I can't help my eyes being drawn to the two of them. Sisi notices this too, and she stands up, moving closer to me—to Vlad's chagrin.

"Do you want to hold her?" She asks in a kind tone.

I keep staring at the baby, unsure whether I want to hold her or not. But before I can reply, Mirabella is already placed in my lap.

I blink.

"How... How do I hold her?" I ask in wonder, staring at the little human in my arms.

"Like this," Sisi shows me, placing my hands under her arms. "Just follow her cues. She'll let you know if she's uncomfortable."

Mirabella is looking at me curiously, and Raf chuckles as he leans in to get a better view.

"She's so cute," I breathe out, amazed. Sparkling green eyes and a small tuft of blonde hair, she's such a pretty child —will most likely grow up to be a beautiful woman.

I don't know what I'm doing, though. We just sit like that, staring at each other. Suddenly her mouth widens in a silly grin, and my own mouth tugs up in response, her giggles infectious.

She waves her hands at me, grabbing a fistful of my hair as she tugs on it, somehow fascinated by it.

More happy sounds escape her lips and she starts to jump up and down in my lap while playing with my hair.

"She likes you," Raf comments, extending his finger for her to grasp on to. She turns her head towards him, her mouth opening in a wide smile as she waves his hand.

"I think she likes *you*," I add, amused.

His body is molded to me as he leans in to make funny faces at Mirabella, his heat enveloping me and giving me *hope*.

This is what it would look like if we had our own family...

But just as that thought surfaces, so does the unyielding reality and the fact that might *never* happen.

My breath hitches as pain clogs my throat, but I do my best to keep my smile on as I continue to play with Mirabella.

This time, however, as I try to focus on her, my mind starts playing tricks on me. I look at her, but she's no longer in my arms, not *her*.

The image is distorted, but I can tell something is wrong.

The baby in my arms isn't moving or making *any* sounds. It's just...there.

I frown, squinting to get a better view. But, God, how I wish I hadn't...

"Take her from me," my voice sounds broken to my own ears as I thrust Mirabella aside, my skin itching, my entire body on the verge of a meltdown.

Sisi is quick to act though, and as soon as Mirabella is out of my hands, I'm up and dashing out the door, going to the first vacant room I can find.

I barely close the door behind me when I slide to the floor, trembling uncontrollably, my entire mind both a blank and a whirlpool of images—things I wouldn't wish on my worst enemy.

"Noelle," Raf's voice resounds from behind the door, followed by a loud bang. "Open the door," he demands, but I find that I can't do anything.

I can barely move, and as I slowly crawl away from the door, I see it burst open, a mad looking Raf entering inside.

"I'm sorry," I start chanting, tears running down my cheeks. "I'm so sorry. It's all my fault," I cry out as I bring my legs to my chest, rocking from side to side. "I'm so, *so* sorry."

Like a broken record, I can't say anything *but* sorry.

The images keep replaying in my mind.

"Pretty girl, what's wrong?" Strong arms envelop me.

"I'm sorry. So sorry," I sob, laying my head on his chest.

Deep within the recesses of my mind, I know what I've done deserves no forgiveness, that I've committed the ultimate sin and I don't deserve *anything*.

But for the life of me I can't figure out why.

There's only *that* image. That haunting image that breaks my heart and makes me want to scream in pain.

"Shhh, you're safe, Noelle. I'm here," Raf's calming voice gets to me—just barely.

He holds me tightly, murmuring soft words in my ear until whatever's sunk its claws into me lets go.

"I saw it," I whisper brokenly, nestling closer to him—my only source of comfort.

"What? What did you see?"

I shake my head, unable to utter the words.

"Noelle, my heart, I'm here. No one's going to harm you, I promise," he continues to speak softly, stroking my hair and holding on to me as if the entire world depended on it.

Reaching for him, I wrap my arms around him, returning his embrace.

"The baby," I whisper, squeezing my eyes shut in an attempt to exorcize the image from my mind.

"Mirabella?"

"No, no," I shake my head.

My mouth opens and closes, my throat dry.

"My baby," I say in a small voice, feeling the pain to my soul. "I saw my baby."

"Noelle..." he leans back, his palms to my cheeks as he searches for my eyes.

Worry is etched all over his features, and for the first time I'm confronted with the fact that there is someone out there who cares about me—who loves me.

"He was dead, Raf," I tell him as I bring my hands to his, squeezing lightly. "He was dead in my arms and..."

My breath catches in my throat, the image I'd seen too much to bear—too much for anyone to bear.

"You don't have to tell me. Fuck, Noelle. I didn't realize..."

"No," I shake my head, meeting his eyes. "It's not your fault. It's mine. It's my fault. All my fault," I ramble like crazy, though I don't know why I'm saying that.

"Pretty girl," he purses his lips, the gentlest look on his face as he calls out to me.

"He was unrecognizable, Raf," I tell him, the words

pouring from my mouth. "His face... It looked like someone had smashed..." a sob escapes me, and I barely manage to recount to him what I'd seen—what no one should ever see.

"Fucking hell, Noelle," he rasps, his lips on my forehead as he peppers kisses all over. "I wish I'd been there for you. I wish..."

"You're here now," I breathe out. "And sometimes you're the only thing that keeps me going," I confess, almost ashamed.

"Fuck," he curses out, and for a moment I think he's going to get mad at me. After all, who wants to have that much responsibility on their shoulders? Who wants to be fully responsible for someone else's happiness?

But he surprises me again as he brings me flush against him. Our lips are a mere breath apart, the tips of our noses already touching in the sweetest way possible.

His eyes are on mine. Caring. Determined. So full of love.

"Then use me. Use me as your tether," his deep voice caresses my senses, his words latching themselves deep inside my soul. "Anytime you feel like falling, I'll be there to catch you. Let go and know I have you."

I stare at him unblinking for a second before I launch myself at him, wrapping my arms around his neck and letting everything pour out of me.

Sobbing like crazy, I let myself go.

Because for the first time, I realize something. Love isn't just about being strong together. It's also about being weak, and trusting the other with your worst.

CHAPTER TWENTY-SIX
NOELLE

"The perimeter is secure," I hear someone tell my brother. "We have eyes and ears on every side of the building."

"Good. Make sure everyone is on standby," he says, dismissing the man with a pat on the back.

I'd had to come earlier to familiarize myself with the building and all exit routes. Raf had insisted on having every base covered. Everyone had volunteered some of their best men to pretend to be part of the audience today, and while no one recognizable would be in the main stage area, they would be monitoring the situation closely.

They'd apprised me of everything, and the plan looks solid—in theory. In practice, nothing is certain. Which is why Raf's been a little unbearable today, coming to check on me every five seconds, asking me to reconsider doing this.

I understand his stance, and it warms my heart to know he is worried about me. But if I can help him fulfill his goal of getting revenge on his brother, then I *will* do it. I want nothing more than to see him happy, and I know that once Michele is a thing of the past, we'll be able to focus more on

293

our lives. We'll certainly be able to breathe more relieved knowing we won't have to hide, or go out with a hundred guards every single time.

Looking down at my schedule, I read the times once more to make sure I have everything memorized. Although I will be the main act of the evening, there are still a couple pianists before me.

"Are you nervous?" Cisco asks as he reaches my side.

I've been huddled inside the backstage area for hours now, going over my music sheets and trying to put a stop to my growing anxiety.

"A little," I give him a strained smile. "But I know everyone is monitoring the situation, so I'm not worried about being in danger."

I'd gotten to know Raf's acquaintances, and I've been made aware of some of their *infamous* reputations in the underground world. That alone had put me more at ease.

If I'm honest, it's not Michele's appearance that has me on a bed of nails. Rather, it's the fact that I have to perform for an audience—and not *just* anything, but my own compositions.

Playing someone else's pieces is completely different than playing my own. Although with the former I do add my own spin to the performance, for the latter it feels like I'm baring my soul to the world. It's even more embarrassing considering that every piece I'm playing tonight is about *one* person —my husband.

It's unavoidable when he's awakened within me so many emotions—from hate, to anger, to passion, to love, he's given me the full spectrum. And for the first time in years, I found myself, pen in hand, scribbling down notes and musical arrangements.

The inspiration had taken me by surprise, and sometimes I would spend hours blocked on a piece, toiling on it until it was perfect.

He's made me cry, and he's made me laugh. More than anything, he's made me want to live. And I've channeled that *joie de vivre* into my work as I'd filled my repertoire with more upbeat pieces than morose ones—a first for me.

My notes no longer depicted a carnival of death, but a celebration of life.

Our life.

"Don't be. Raf won't let anything happen to you," Cisco says, pausing for a moment as an odd expression crosses his face. But just as it appears, it's gone, and he's quick to head to the exit.

"Cisco," I call out, rising from my chair.

He stops, turning so only his profile is visible.

"Why?" I ask the question, calmly for the first time.

Because as I'd reflected more on our relationship, I'd realized I couldn't remember the last conversation we'd had that hadn't ended in an argument—usually with me throwing a tantrum.

"Why?" He raises a brow, leaning against the door as he regards me.

"Why did you agree to my marriage to Raf?"

It's a question I've asked myself multiple times but one that I haven't been able to answer. While he may have a personal vendetta against Michele *now*, that wasn't the case before, when he'd encouraged Raf to marry me.

"Why indeed," his lips spread in a wide smile—genuine, or not, I'm not sure. Just like I can never be sure of anything my brother says or does.

"Have you seen how the man looks at you?" He takes a few steps towards me.

I blink, confused by what he means. When we'd first gotten married, Raf's feelings for me had been decidedly *not* positive.

"Contrary to what you may think of me, Noelle, I do care

about you. And I am sorry for what happened with Sergio," his lips stretch in a thin line, his gaze distant.

"But Raf..." I shake my head. "He hated me."

"He hated what he thought he knew of you," he corrects. "But he never really hated you, did he?" His hands come to rest on my shoulders, spinning my chair and turning it towards the mirror on the wall.

Raising my gaze to the reflation, I note the striking simi-larities between us—proof of our shared heritage. But I also see a world of difference.

"I pride myself on being a good reader of people," he continues, gazing into the mirror. "And your marriage wasn't to punish you. It was to reward you."

"Reward me?" I frown, almost scandalized at his conde-scending tone.

"The first time he saw you, he couldn't take his eyes off you. And it wasn't in a *I want to kill this woman* type of way, though I'm sure he convinced himself of that," he chuckles. "It was in an *I can't bear the thought of not touching this woman* type of way. Trust me, I know that look. Yuyu can attest to it."

"So you thought he wanted me?" I scoff.

"No, Noelle. I didn't think he *merely* wanted you. I knew he'd give his right hand to have you, and I was right," he smirks. "Raf is a good man. He's a much better man than I'll ever be, and I know he will make you happy."

In an unprecedented gesture of kindness, he leans forward to lay a kiss on my forehead.

"After this is over, I won't interfere again in your life," he promises. And with that he's gone. He doesn't linger for an answer—does he, ever? He just dictated what's going to happen.

I'm left staring in the mirror at my own reflection and mulling over his words.

In his mind, he must have convinced himself that because

Raf and I have feelings for each other he's done the right thing in matching us up. But he doesn't realize the core of the issue—he might be too self-centered to ever get that.

It had all started from a hunch. A gamble.

He gave me away—again—on the off chance that Raf might desire me.

A dry laugh escapes me as I realize that no matter how good my brother's intentions may seem, they're always mercenary. It's just that he's convinced himself that they aren't—or has he, really?

Throwing the rather unpleasant meeting out of my mind, I take off my robe, putting on the black dress I'd chosen for today's event. I'll need to reserve some time to add wires and other devices the guys had decided on.

Just as I'm about to put up my garter, a knock on the door startles me. I don't get to respond, though, as the door opens and Raf strides in.

He's dressed casually—or as casual as I've come to expect from him. A pair of black khakis and a black shirt, he looks sleek and entirely too handsome.

"One more hour," he says as he comes behind me, his mouth on my naked shoulder. Parting his lips over my skin, he lays small kisses, making his way up my neck until he reaches my cheek.

"You're so beautiful," he breathes in my ear. "So delectable I'd like nothing better than to eat you," he groans.

"You're getting ahead of yourself," I chuckle.

"Already counting down the minutes until everything will be over. Then I'll have you…" he trails off suggestively.

My cheeks redden at the innuendo, images of us naked and in bed already flooding my brain—and other parts of me.

His arms come around me as he stoops down, laying his head on my shoulder.

"Promise me you'll be careful," he says in a serious tone.

"You know I will be. I won't deviate from the plan and ruin things."

"That's not what I meant," his hands tighten over my body. "I don't give a shit about the plan as long as you're safe. I told you, and I will continue to tell you. I don't care if the plan is successful as long as nothing happens to you."

"Raf…"

"Please," his anguished tone startles me. "Promise me you won't do anything to put yourself in danger. That you won't act outside what we planned. *Not* even if you see me in danger."

"What are you talking about," I push him off me, suddenly turning. "Why would you be in danger?"

"Just promise me," he continues, not answering my question.

"Raf, I don't think you understand something," I cup his jaw. "I could *never* leave you like that. You think you're the only one worried? I couldn't live if anything happened to you," I tell him sincerely.

At this point, I'm too far gone. I've tasted happiness, and I've tasted love. How could I ever turn my back to those two things when they are the only things keeping me alive?

"Fuck, Noelle," he rasps. "You don't understand what you mean to me, pretty girl," he starts and my insides turn to mush. For as long as I live, I don't think I'll ever tire of him calling me that or telling me how much he cares about me. "You're my heart. Do you think I could live without my heart?"

"Then we're at an impasse," I raise a brow.

"We're not. Because it's my duty to take care of you and to protect you. *You* come first."

He's breathing harshly, his eyes fixed on me.

Out of nowhere he's on me, backing me against the vanity table, one hand on my nape, the other on my leg.

"This is the one thing I'm not willing to make allowances about, Noelle," his mouth brushes against my earlobe, his hold on me tightening. "I need you safe and well," he says as his hand moves further up my thigh, taking my dress with it and raising it over my hip.

"Raf," my breath hitches when I realize what he's doing.

"I used to have nightmares about my time in captivity." His raw voice sends a shiver down my back, the emotion I find in it making me reel. "I used to dream of being held down by Armand, of having my free will stripped from me," he continues, right as he slips his fingers under the band of my panties, tugging them down. "But now, my true nightmare is having *you* taken from me, pretty girl."

His words make me draw back, searching for his eyes.

We've talked about our past and our trauma, but Armand has always been a sore subject for him. I've never pushed for more information than he's been willing to give me. But to hear *that* comparison when I know how hard it must have been for him? For this strong and proud man to find himself at the mercy of another yet unable to fight back...

That's what I love about him—the hints of vulnerability that peek through his carefully built façade. He exudes raw masculinity, his domineering presence making me want to relinquish all control and let him *own* me.

But there's another side of him—the soft, vulnerable one. The one he doesn't share with the world, yet I've had the privilege of witnessing.

How he can be the most manly man I've ever met but also the sweetest one is beside me. I may have initially been drawn to him by sheer physical attraction but it was the hints of his beautiful soul that have touched me deep within. The fact that we're so alike, yet so different in a way that makes me strive to become *more*.

He's been through hell—through things that no one

should ever go through. Yet instead of wallowing in self-pity, he challenged himself and grew stronger. He's the opposite of me, and that only makes me want to do better—to attempt to be like him and move forward not because of my past, but in spite of it.

He once told me my music touched his soul. But it was the reverse. His words have been the music my soul has been searching for. The guided melody drawing me back to safety, beckoning me and helping me moor myself into one place.

His gorgeous blue eyes sparkle as he gazes at me, so much emotion hidden in those depths. And as I bring my hand to cup his cheek, it's to wish I could immortalize this moment—the way he makes me feel like I'm the only thing that matters for him.

So lost I am in his gaze, I barely realize as my panties slide down my ankles, or the fact that my dress is bunched up around my hips, his hand already between my legs. But as brushes his finger against my clit, my lips part on a silent moan.

"You're my little piece of heaven, Noelle. And I won't let *anyone* take you from me. If I have to take on the fucking world," he pauses, taking a deep breath, almost as if seeking to calm himself. "I'll do it. I'll fucking do it."

He slides his finger between my folds, my arousal immediately coating his digit.

"How are you so good to me?" I barely manage to ask as he lifts me on the table, his hand exploring my pussy before pushing two thick fingers inside me. There are calluses on his hands from the hard labor he'd been subjected to, but those harsh ridges only serve to tantalize me further as he strokes my flesh.

Stabilizing myself against him, I keep my hands to his shoulders, never once taking my eyes off him. He starts working his fingers in and out of me, the friction so deliciously addicting, I don't know how I'll keep myself from screaming out.

"That's it," he murmurs, coming closer as his thumb presses against my clit, circling it and making me buck in his arms. "Give me everything you have, pretty girl. I want your moans, your cries, your screams," his teeth scrape against the side of my face. "*Everything.*"

Skimming his lips over my jaw, he suddenly brushes them against my mouth in a slow seduction.

"Please," the word falls out of my mouth as I bring myself forward, grinding on his fingers and seeking my release.

"Fuck," he curses. "You're so wet and ready for me."

His voice alone would be enough to make me climax, that rough, deep rumble sending electric sparks to my clit even when he's not touching it.

"Yes," I gasp when I feel his fingers hitting a spot deep within me before retreating and surging again. "Always."

"You're mine," he says as he brings his teeth over my lower lip, biting on it before swiping his tongue into my mouth.

"Only mine, pretty girl," he groans. "Only ever mine."

"Only yours. Only ever yours," I repeat, those words the ultimate truth. I couldn't imagine belonging to someone else —not when his embrace feels so right. Like two pieces torn from a whole, we just fit.

His mouth is on mine, his lips parted, his tongue seeking entrance. Wrapping my arms around his neck, I bring him closer, the multitude of sensations wreaking havoc on my body. He keeps pumping his fingers into me, his mouth devouring me with such ferocity, it's not long before low tremors erupt all over my body, my pussy clamping down on his fingers with the power of my release.

"Give it to me," he rasps against my mouth. "Give me your pleasure, Noelle," he demands, not letting me catch my breath before wringing another orgasm from me. "Give me everything."

I'm a trembling mess as he leans back, my lids heavy, my breath out of control.

His hands are on his belt, and with an urgency that's uncharacteristic of him, he rips through his zipper as he takes his cock out, the daunting length slapping against my inner thigh. Before I know it, he has me turned around, my ass to him, my hands braced on the counter. The euphoric haze slowly dispels, and I feel him there—hard, long and throbbing.

"I won't fuck you," he tells me when he hears my sudden intake of breath. "Not now. But I need you, pretty girl. I need to know you're mine. That you're here, that... Fuck," he mutters as he takes hold of my hips, sliding his cock between my legs.

I give a low whimper when I feel the head right at my opening.

"Shh," he whispers in my hair, bringing me closer to him. "I need your heat. Your arousal. I need you to drench my cock in your cum, so I can carry you with me just like you'll carry me with you."

He starts moving, thrusting not inside me, but against me. His shaft slides against my pussy lips, the head bumping against my clit and eliciting a moan from me.

"Right there," his voice is tense, as if he's barely in control.

And I realize why too, because just as he pushes forward, the head bumps against my entrance, stilling for a moment before moving past it.

He's trying to control himself to *not* fuck me, even if it kills him.

"Raf," I bring my hand behind, cupping the base of his shaft and squeezing. He continues to thrust his hips against me, his movements wild and uncoordinated. "You're killing me," I breathe out, the temptation to get him inside of me too much.

"Goddamn it, Noelle," he growls as his palm spreads over my breast, kneading the flesh and making me whimper as he pinches my nipples through my dress.

My entire body is a jumbled mess of sensations, but it's the feel of *him* there that threatens to undo me. He's hard yet soft, the warmth from his skin seeping into mine, and God, I wish for nothing more than to feel him slide inside of me, stretching me and fucking me into oblivion.

"I can feel your greedy pussy begging for my cock, Noelle," he purrs in my ear. "I can feel your tight little hole spasming. Tell me, do you feel empty?"

I give a jerky nod, unable to form the words.

"Do you want to be filled? Have my cum so deep in your pussy you won't ever be rid of me? Do you want that?"

"Yes, please," I cry out when I feel his cock at my entrance, rolling my hips in an attempt to draw him inside.

"Just the tip," he says on a groan. "Just the fucking tip, pretty girl. Enough so I can come inside of you. Will you let me do that?"

"Please," I'm close to pleading with him, the allure of the unknown too much to bear.

Holding my hips with one hand, he aligns his cock to my entrance. The thick head is suddenly there, pushing forward. There's a slight burning sensation as he makes it past my ring of muscles.

But then he stops.

"Damn it all to hell, Noelle. Fuck!" He groans, his body wound so tight, the tension is radiating from him. "I swear to God this is the tightest place I've ever been. My God," he breathes out, his chest falling and rising.

"No," he grits out when I try to wiggle. "Don't move.

Don't you dare move, or I'm going to forget about everything and fuck you until you can't walk anymore."

"Is that a threat?" I ask softly, the feel of him inside of me unparalleled. Still, it's not enough. I want more—I want everything.

"It *is* a fucking threat. And I'm going to spank that little ass of yours if you don't stop. Jesus Christ, this is pure torture," he brings his forehead to my nape. "It's the best and worst idea I've ever had," he chuckles.

There's the tiniest bit of movement as he brings his fist over his length, moving it up and down until his cock jerks inside of me, hot liquid filling me.

For the longest time, he doesn't let go. Bent over me, he keeps me in place, his cheek on my back as he tries to regain his breath.

"You're wrecking me," he shakes his head, slowly pulling away.

His cock slips out of me, the sudden emptiness hitting me hard.

Still, I feel his cum inside, pooling low and slowly dripping out of me.

"Let me see," he says harshly, turning me to face him, and maneuvering me until I'm bared on the table for him.

His hands are on my pussy, spreading my lips as he studies me.

A blush envelops me at the perusal, but any feeling of embarrassment I might have felt is soon gone as I note his entranced look, and the way he can't seem to wrench his eyes from me.

"You're such a good girl, Noelle," he praises, one finger dipping inside of me as he pushes his seed back inside. "The very best," he continues, his eyes almost black from the size of his expanded pupils.

"Goddamn it," he swears, shaking his head. "Look how

my cum is feeding your pretty pussy," he says reverently, splaying the sticky substance around my pussy. "This is how I want you. Marked. Stained. *Owned.*"

Swirling our mixed juices around one finger, he brings it up to me, pushing it between my parted lips and making me taste *us.*

I suck it in my mouth, and he releases a ragged breath, his eyes on my lips. As he takes his finger out of my mouth, he brings it to his own lips, licking it clean.

"You're mine, pretty girl. And that means *I* take care of you. *I* make sure you're clothed, fed and fucked. *I* keep you safe, is that clear?"

I can't help but nod, especially as his tone is completely different from before, the lust almost gone from his voice, replaced with a frightening severity.

"That also means you *never* put yourself in danger for me. I only accepted this because you'll have minimal contact with what happens once Michele arrives. But that doesn't mean you can jump in the crossfire for me."

"But…"

"No buts," he says, his palm making contact with the side of my ass and making me yelp in surprise. "I told you I'd spank you until you saw reason," he smirks. "You do everything according to the plan and we won't have an issue."

"If I don't…?" I don't know what prompts me to ask the question, especially as I see how tense he is.

"If you don't, I'll make your ass red, and after that I'll fuck you so hard you won't ever think to disobey me."

I flutter my lashes rapidly.

Does he think that sounds unappealing? Because to my ears, that sounds like heaven.

"I can see where your mind is taking you," his mouth tugs up. "But trust me, pretty girl, I'll keep you forever chained to my bed until you learn to listen."

Taking a step back, he puts himself back together, giving me a wicked grin.

Jumping off the table, it's to feel more cum slip out of me. Looking around, I grab a napkin to clean myself.

But just as I'm about to wipe the inside of my thigh, his hand is on my wrist, stopping me.

"This stays in," he says in a commanding tone, swiping the small trickle and pushing it back inside me. "Think of me while you play," he kisses my cheek before leaving me to put myself together.

The show doesn't start in another hour, so I have time to redo my makeup and to ensure everything is in order. I also douse myself in perfume, because no matter what Raf says, I don't think it's appropriate for me to smell of sex as I go on the stage.

Fifteen minutes before I'm supposed to start, Raf comes by once more, assessing me from head to toe while ensuring my wires work.

"This is just a last recourse thing." He assures me as he stuffs the tiny microphone in my bra. "I need to know you're ok at all times."

He goes on to tell me that he'll be on the sidelines, with men on standby at every emergency exit. Whatever happens, Michele *will* be cornered once he makes it inside the room.

When the last guest pianist is done, my turn is up.

"You're going to be amazing," Raf tells me, ushering me on stage and giving me an air kiss.

My husband's words work wonders on making my confidence soar. He has a way of always complimenting and praising me, showing me I *am* capable of excelling. And he's been saying the words to me so often, I've slowly started to believe them.

My resolve fortifies as I know he will be listening, so I straighten my back and walk on the stage.

The audience claps when I make my entrance, but as I scan the crowd I don't notice Michele *anywhere*. Thinking he might show up later, I simply take my seat, running my fingers over the keys and getting into a comfortable position.

Since I am performing from memory, I have no page turner by my side—a huge relief if I'm being honest.

I'm already sweating just thinking about baring such an intimate part of myself to the entire world, but at least since there's a distance between stage and audience, I'll be able to put a mental distance too.

After all, I'm playing just for one person today.

My lips pull in a smile as my determination soars. I shift my focus to the piano instead of the audience, thrusting even the idea of Michele out of my mind, knowing that Raf and the others have it under control.

Instead, I bring my attention to my keys, my fingers settling on the white surface as the first note permeates the air.

Closing my eyes, I let myself be led by the music, forgetting to even breathe as I fall deeper and deeper into a hole of my own making—my own abyss.

Chronologically, every piece signifies an encounter with Raf, each note the sonorous manifestation of my feelings.

And it's only fitting that the first piece's central theme is confusing attraction. Just like that night when I'd been playing the piano and he had intruded into my space and the confusion he'd wrecked on my mind. More than anything, it's the nascent attraction that I'd felt for him despite the thick fog that had suffused my mind.

The intensity only grows, each act propelling me deeper into our history and our exchanges.

The music pours from my fingers, and for a moment I forget I *am*. Because like this, I'm only music, nothing else.

It takes someone gently shaking me to realize that the

intermission is here and that I've already finished the first part of the concert.

On shaky legs, I release a deep breath, almost as if I'd run a marathon.

"Pretty girl," I hear the sound in my earpiece, the voice reverent and breathy. "That was the most amazing thing I've ever heard," Raf tells me, and I can't help but blush at his words.

I had hoped he would like it, since it's all for him.

"Michele's still not here, and I don't know if he will come. But we'll continue as planned. You did so well," he can't stop praising me.

"I'll go freshen up for my break, and then I have another surprise for you," I tell him cheekily.

I'd only covered the first half of our tumultuous acquaintance—the half that had been filled with hate, fights and mistrust. I still have to reach the good one—the half that shows just how deep my feelings for him run.

The break is only fifteen minutes, but it's enough to relax a little and plan for the next pieces. I also have a new outfit planned that I can't wait to change into.

Opening the door to the backstage room, I step inside, my hands immediately going to my zipper to slide it down.

But as I turn on the light, it's to come face to face with *him*.

"Well, hullo there," he winks, as he twirls on my revolving seat. He has a manic smile on his face, his eyes such an odd color it's like they're transparent.

CHAPTER TWENTY-SEVEN
NOELLE

S crambling back, I don't get to take a step before he's on me. The door closes with a thud, my back making contact with the wood. Before I can think to evade him, he has me caged.

"No, no," he chuckles. "Did no one tell you it's bad manners to not greet your brother-in-law?" He's so close I can smell him. His breath is on my face, so I turn my head to the side to avoid his touch.

Fumbling with my microphone, I know the best course of action is to alert Raf, but before I can do anything, a knife cuts through my dress.

My eyes widen, my hands moving to stop him, but it's in vain as he quickly secures them above my head.

"It's not personal, darling," he drawls as he rips my dress to shreds, pulling stripes of it and flinging them to the ground. "But I can't have my brother here," he says as he cuts the wire twirled around my bra, throwing the small device to the ground and smashing it with his foot. "At least not *yet*."

He smiles as he takes a step back, a twisted grin that makes me sick to my stomach.

"Don't try anything," he waves at the door with his knife, "I have perfect aim," he winks as he retakes his seat.

"What are you doing?" My arms come around my midriff as I hug myself, my skin already erupting in goosebumps from the cold.

I would have thought that being semi-naked in front of a stranger would make me break in a sweat, but somehow, I don't detect any nefarious interest in my bare skin. If anything, he hasn't glanced at me once.

His perusal had been clinical as he'd pulled the wires from me, but aside from that, he's kept his eyes to my face.

"I wanted us to have a chat. You have fifteen minutes before you're going to be missed. I'd say that's plenty of time to get acquainted," he jokes, leaning back in the chair and watching me with a relaxed expression on his face.

My eyes search the entire room for the camera, since I know Raf's monitoring the entire building, but Michele picks up on it immediately.

Lifting one finger in the air, he waves it in front of me.

"Have you heard of a loop?" He asks and I frown, shaking my head.

"My brother is currently watching footage of you reading your music sheet, on a loop. He won't know anything's wrong," he smiles wolfishly.

"You planned this…"

Which means he knew about Raf and Cisco's plan.

"I did. Not as much as Rafaelo did, but then, he was always very thorough," his eyes grow icy under my gaze. Almost as if uttering Raf's name has the power to give him frostbite.

"Why do you hate him? What has he ever done to you to be so…vile?" I shake my head in disgust.

"Cover yourself," he takes my robe from the chair, throwing it at me. "And we'll talk."

I quickly pull the robe around my body, the material offering some comfort.

"Are you going to kill me?" I ask, almost on a whisper. My eyes take in the room, and the fact that there's something written in red lipstick on the mirror.

He had this all planned.

"Hmm, am I?" He pins me down with his eyes. "Maybe," he shrugs. "I haven't decided just yet," his lips widen in a malicious smile.

My legs are shaky as I follow his directions and take a seat across from him, all the while thinking of ways to get away.

But he's not going to make it easy—not with the way his eyes keep tracking my every move.

We sit for what feels like forever, his unnerving gaze sending chills down my back. But it's very clear that's the intent.

He's a bully. And that's how bullies act—through intimidation.

"What are you going to do with me?"

Not only am I out of my depth here, but I also have a hard time grasping his goal. If he knew the entire event was a trap, why show up at all? He must have known Raf and my brother would have troops stationed everywhere. Even if he came prepared, how is he going to manage to leave the building unscathed?

Nothing makes sense.

"Call it a curiosity. I wanted to know the woman my brother married. But then again, he only married you to get your brother's backing, didn't he?" he smirks, thinking he stroke a chord in me.

"Maybe," I shrug. "I do what I'm told," I lie.

This will go better as long as he doesn't believe that I mean anything to Raf, because then he won't have anything to use as leverage.

"Such a good girl," he drawls, but his appellation rubs me all kinds of wrong. Whereas with Raf I yearn for that praise, in this instance it takes everything I have not to be ill on the floor.

I force a smile.

"Liar, liar, liar," he chuckles, taking out a tablet from under the vanity and laying it on the table, the screen facing me. With just a few touches, the scene from earlier plays on the screen.

My cheeks are on fire as I see Raf taking me from behind. Though I know we didn't actually fuck, in the video, it looks like we did.

"Stop it," I whisper when it gets to the next part, where I'm on the table, spread out with Raf between my legs.

"At least he's getting his money's worth," Michele mocks, pausing the video.

"I find it hard to believe you only came here to humiliate me. *Or* to show me you're a peeping Tom," I raise a brow, doing my best to remain calm.

From what I'd learned about Michele, he's unpredictable, and that means I don't know how he will react to a more direct confrontation.

"Hardly," he laughs. "I'm not interested in who my brother fucks," he chuckles. "But *you* may be interested in who fucks *him*," he says with a satisfied smile on his face. The smile that only widens as he sees my sudden discomfort.

"What are you talking about?" The words are out of my mouth before I can help myself.

"And there it is, the jealousy," his tongue peeks between his teeth, his lips pulled in a broad smile. "We'll get to that too."

My fists clench in my lap as I realize what he's trying to do—sow distrust between us.

"I trust Raf. He would never be unfaithful to me," I

declare staunchly, without realizing that those words reveal major insight into our relationship.

He doesn't reply, merely looking at me expectantly, a jocular expression on his face, as if he's waiting for the end of the joke so he can laugh.

"Hmm," he hums. "How well do you know my brother?" He suddenly asks, bringing his hand to his chin as he regards me curiously.

"Well enough," I shrug.

"Is that so..." he narrows his eyes at me. "Did he tell you about his childhood? About his reputation as *the* retard?" he chuckles, but I don't reply.

I don't want to play his game when it's clear that all he wants is to undermine Raf's position.

"I wonder... Would you still see him in the same light then?" Michele muses before he clicks on another video.

It's a house party of sorts, and the video is filled with a lot of background noise. But as the image starts focusing, there's no mistaking Raf's blonde hair and blue eyes. Everything else, though...

I blink, unable to believe it's the same person. He is still tall, but his clothes hang loosely on his lanky frame. But that's not what Michele wanted me to witness. No, it's what happens next.

As someone approaches him, he hunches his shoulders, avoiding direct eye contact, his entire body shaking.

"I d-don't k-know," he answers to a muffled question.

"What do you think of your husband?" He asks with a satisfied smile on his face.

The video continues, and Raf seems to be in a heated argument with someone, his pale face growing redder by the second, his stutter becoming increasingly more pronounced. That's when the front of his pants becomes wet.

My eyes widen, while Michele can't stop himself from chuckling.

"He told me about that part of his life," I get my bearings together as I address Michele.

"Really?" He raises a brow.

"Of course. He told me it was all a disguise. And if I'm not mistaken, it was for *your* benefit. So that his father would discount him as his heir."

His lip starts twitching in distaste as I bring up their father—or rather, Raf's father.

"Did he also tell you *why* he did that?"

I tilt my head, frowning.

"I see he didn't. Then maybe the next video will help," he says as he swipes the video on the tablet.

The background is black and the sounds are muffled, but I think I hear harsh breathing.

Suddenly, though, the image shifts. Someone is in control of the camera, and as it begins to stabilize, I inhale deeply, barely able to control myself.

It's Raf—my Raf—yet it's not.

He's pinned to a table, a man's hand on his nape as he holds him down. He's naked, his back marred with fresh and old scars. The camera moves lower, and I bring my hand to my mouth, stifling a sob at what I'm witnessing.

The camera focuses on his ass, a man's dick sliding in and out of him, grunting as he rapes a barely conscious Raf. One hand is holding the camera, the other is kneading his ass as he thrusts into him.

"Stop it," I whisper, unable to keep on watching.

"Why?" Michele laughs. "How does it feel to see someone else fucking your husband? And I hear he fucked him good, too. He was his favorite."

"You're sick," I shake my head, suddenly standing up.

My stomach is churning, and I barely make it to the trash

can before puking. On my knees, I continue to heave just as the images keep replaying themselves in my mind.

"So sensitive? What is it that did it? The sight of your husband fucking another? Or was it the fact that it's a man?"

"You mean raping him?" I turn to him so he can see the disgust in my eyes. But it's not disgust with Raf—it could never be with him. It's with the man in front of me—the lousy excuse of a human that seems to derive pleasure from others' misfortune.

"Raping, fucking," he shrugs. "Semantics," he says with a grin on his face.

"You're a degenerate," I spit at him.

"Maybe. Not all of us can be such paragons of virtue like Rafaelo."

"I don't understand. Why are you doing this? What did he ever do to you to be so...evil?"

He looks at me with a serious expression for a moment before he bursts out laughing.

"Evil," he brings his arm around his midriff, holding on to it as he laughs. "I quite like that," he winks. But suddenly his countenance changes again.

From hilarity to seriousness, it's like he has a control switch.

"It's all a matter of perspective. You say it's evil, I call it justice." He rises from the chair, stooping on his haunches in front of me.

"But in your world, justice only encompasses the good, doesn't it?" He asks as he grips my jaw with his fingers, looking at me with a strange expression on his face. "I'm used to being the bad guy. I've *only* ever been that. But can Rafaelo say the same thing?" His mouth tugs up in a dry smile as he shoves me aside.

"What are you talking about?"

"Your *Raf* is so used to being the *good* guy, he doesn't

know what it's like to be on the other side. Or," he pauses, "he merely doesn't want to admit it."

"I don't..."

"You don't understand, of course," he interrupts. "You, like everyone else, are probably convinced that poor old *Raf* has been tortured his entire life by me. That I'm the monster who's persecuted him and made him suffer, isn't that right?" A strange expression washes over his face.

"You mean sending your brother to be raped and killed isn't persecution? It isn't a torment? What the hell is wrong with you?" I ask, shocked at his gall.

His delivery is flawless, and it's clear that he strongly believes in whatever delusions he has.

"What the hell is wrong with me?" he grits out, his tone changed.

Suddenly, his hand is in my hair, his fingers buried deep in my scalp and a yelp escapes me.

His features are drawn up in cruelty. His physical beauty might be uniquely appealing, but it's the pure malice reflected in his expression that makes him the ugliest man I've ever seen.

"You can only have good if you have bad, Noelle," he addresses me by my name for the first time. "I was branded bad, so Raf became good by default," he says, his hold tightening. "You want to know how good your husband is? You asked me why I sent him to be raped and killed. Because he did the same to me," he states with unwavering conviction.

"What..." My eyes widen, unable to believe my ears. "You're lying."

"I'm not. You can ask him, if you survive that is," he gives a dry laugh. "But I merely gave back what he deserved. I engineered his entire sojourn so that he can experience everything on his own."

"The *hacienda*..."

"Ah, Sergio's heaven. Yes, indeed," he smiles. "Although I expected him to waste away there, not to escape. I'm still not clear how that happened," his pupils become two slits as he gazes down at me in disgust.

Flinging me away from him, I fall on my ass. I'm breathing hard, adrenaline kicking in my veins.

But what can I do?

There are five more minutes until the next part of the show is supposed to start. If I don't go on the stage, Raf will definitely wonder what happened to me and will likely come to check.

"Get up," Michele orders me, this time, removing a gun from his waist and aiming it at me.

"Wha—what …" I slowly rise to my feet, afraid of making the wrong move and enraging him. Considering the many mood changes I noticed in such a short amount of time, it's safe to say he's *too* unpredictable.

Putting my hands up, I say a small prayer in my mind, wishing I would have had more time with Raf. Because if this is the end…

"We're going for a walk," he intones, swinging the gun around as he ushers me towards the hallway.

"Don't worry. No one will notice us. The loop is playing on all screens. They will only come when *I* call," he tells me in a satisfied voice.

"So that's it? You're going to kill us both?"

"You're an awfully curious woman, Noelle. Don't you know what happened to the cat?" He's close behind me as he pushes the butt of the gun in my back. I feel his breath on my nape, and that fact alone has the power to make me hyperventilate. I guess it's a small mercy that he hasn't already raped me, or hurt me in any way.

But as he leads me out of the backstage room and towards

a row of stairs, I'm suddenly afraid he's just biding his time, taking me somewhere else to do the deed.

Instinctively, I tighten my robe around my body.

Instead of ushering me down the stairs, though, he motions me up, towards the roof.

And just as he kicks open the door to the roof, pushing me forward, I feel a blow to my head.

A quick intake of breath, and my eyes flutter closed, darkness claiming me.

I may die after all.

CHAPTER TWENTY-EIGHT
RAFAELO

"You're tense," Cisco mentions, bringing a cigarette to his lips in that relaxed manner of his.

"Of course I'm fucking tense, Cisco. Noelle is out in the open where anything could happen to her, and Michele isn't even here," I grit out as I pace around the small office we'd enclosed ourselves in.

The entire building is bugged, and we have access to all live feeds.

Still, even having eyes on Noelle at all times has me worried.

"You're exaggerating," Cisco waves his hand towards the screens in front of us. "Your man's on it." He motions towards Panchito who is hard at work keeping track of everything.

"She's going in," Panchito tells me, slowly sipping from his soda.

Turning to one of the screens, I see Noelle slowly walk on the stage, seating herself at the piano and preparing herself to start.

"See, nothing to worry about. Nothing will happen with her with so many people around," Cisco continues, as if it's not his sister there. "Now chill, and let's listen to the performance."

"Michele isn't here," I state the obvious.

"Maybe he is late. Or he decided not to come."

"Why would he not come?"

We'd had reports of his scouts coming to check the building, so I assume he's taken all precautions to attend the events. There's also the fact that he has a rather obsessive personality. If he decides on something, he sticks with it until the end.

It had been milder in our childhood, but it seems that it's become more severe with age.

"You won't solve anything by being so anxious. Take a seat and let's wait," Cisco rolls his eyes.

Easy for him to say when there are no stakes for him other than getting Michele or not. His wife isn't currently bait out in the open.

"How's the screening for snipers going?" I ask, still unable to sit still.

"Nothing," Panchito answers, pointing to his screen. "Aside from your men, it's clear."

"Good. That's good," I nod, finally taking a seat.

I may have underestimated Michele in the past, but I've seen how he managed the famiglia while I was gone. There is something more to him than meets the eye.

At the end of the day I might not have been the only one wearing a mask.

Noelle starts, and her music has the ability to finally make me ground myself and concentrate on her.

She'd told me she had a surprise for me, and as she jumps straight in the first piece, I realize what she meant.

A burst of flavor explodes in my mouth as I close my eyes, letting my senses lead me as I listen to the music.

What starts as a confusing piece, the notes erratic soon

increases in intensity, all making me swallow hard, the flavor sweet and bitter at the same time, almost like marzipan. But as she continues to play, I realize why she'd told me it was a surprise for me. Like a journal, each note serves as a word that spells out our disastrous first meeting and the progression of our relationship.

Everyone is enjoying the music but no one realizes its depth.

Only me.

Her pieces speak of the volatility of our relationship in its incipient stages, followed by the fact that we'd both hated and wanted each other, the feelings more confusing than ever.

The more the plays, the more she immerses herself in the sound, drawing me in and making me forget about the purpose of today—or even reality. With her taste on my tongue, I could starve to death and I'd still be happy.

As I watch her so absorbed in what she's doing, my heart swells in my chest, pride overflowing for her achievements.

I sneak a glance at Cisco, and I note that he, too, is not unaffected by her skill.

"Your sister is one of a kind," I tell him.

He grunts, drumming his fingers on the surface of the desk, his eyes glued to the monitor.

"She's talented," he concedes.

"I want her to pursue a career in it," I add boldly.

I know Cisco's stance when it comes to his family and what they can and cannot do. Holding a public position or one of fame is simply out of the question as it would draw too much attention to the family and its business.

He turns, his mismatched eyes narrowing at me.

"You've certainly embraced your role as doting husband," he remarks drily, the disapproval obvious.

"I want her to be happy," I shrug. "And free. Something she's never been in her life."

"She's still married to you," he raises a brow. "How is that freedom when I basically coerced her into the marriage?"

"She loves me."

"Hmm, I wonder. Will she think the same in five years? When she's out in the world and realizes there are other opportunities, other people..." he trails off, a smirk on his lips.

"That's not going to happen."

"We'll see," he chuckles.

"Why are you so sure? Did that happen to you? Or to your wife?" I suddenly ask, knowing I'm courting danger by the mere fact that I'm mentioning Yuyu. "Did you find that there are greener pastures?"

"My wife and I are different," his voice goes up a notch. "We were never forced to marry. If anything, we had to force the world to *accept* us. But to answer your question, no. There are *no* greener pastures because I can only survive on *one* type of grass," he smirks. "Same goes for my wife. Any other type would be...poisonous."

I raise a brow at him, surprised by the admission. But if there's anything I've learned about Cisco is that his wife is the *most* important thing for him. She's where he draws the line —*always*.

"Then we're on the same page. Noelle and I may have started on the wrong foot, but this isn't something temporary. Not on her part, nor on mine," I state confidently. "And I'm not so insecure as to isolate her for fear she might find someone better. Because, simply put," I give him a smile, "she won't find anyone else."

"You're rather secure in your relationship," he notes curiously.

"Precisely. And I wasn't asking for your permission

regarding her career. I merely informed you what's going to happen."

He doesn't reply for a moment, merely looking at me—almost intrigued.

"I think I made the right decision in giving her to you," he eventually says. "After this is all done, I promised her I wouldn't interfere in her life again and I will keep that promise. If you decide she can pursue a career, then I have no say in that," he shrugs.

"I'm glad we're in agreement."

"Ditto," he chuckles.

Sometimes I think that Cisco argues just for the sake of argument—the need to be the Devil's advocate all the time. In fact, it's rare that I know what his stance on certain issues is. He's crafted his rhetoric so well, he will circle you around the issue until you arrive at your own conclusion, but you never get a glimpse into his side of the argument.

It's admirable, but it's also problematic.

The first part of Noelle's performance done, I contact her through her ear comm to tell her how proud I am before letting her have some time to freshen up.

Although she loves what she does, I know it's not easy to play for such a large audience, especially since she hasn't done it in so long.

I barely stop myself from heading to her dressing room and pinning her to the wall for a short session. She needs her time, and I need to respect that.

Instead, I focus once more on the screens, watching closely in case Michele might show up.

"What if he doesn't come?" Panchito inquires.

He looks a little red—probably from being cooped up inside for so long.

"Then we try again until he does come."

"Maybe he knows about your wife?" he offers, but I shake my head.

"We made sure there would be no traces of her. You erased all pictures of her from the internet. And with Cisco's secrecy? There's no way he could recognize her."

We'd been extremely thorough in ensuring that everything went according to plan. And since my brother has isolated himself—at least within the New York community—there would be no way for him to get any information on DeVille.

"He's not coming," Cisco mentions, disappointed. "Might as well enjoy the show, I guess," he says right as the curtains open again.

There's just one problem. There's no Noelle.

"What the…" I jump up, reaching for my comm as I try to connect with her. "She's not answering," I turn towards both Cisco and Panchito. "Pull up the feed," I tell Panchito, bracing my arms on the table and watching the screens like a hawk.

"She's there," Panchito frowns as he points to the video of her backstage in which she's studying her music sheet.

"That can't be right," I frown. "She wouldn't miss the start. Hell, someone would have called her." I shake my head. "I'm going in," I declare, not waiting around for their reply as I wrench the door open, heading straight for the dressing room.

But as I kick the door open, it's to find it empty, a message written all across the mirror in red lipstick.

As above, so below.

"Damn it," I curse out, my fist making contact with the mirror, shattering it.

"What are you…" Cisco drifts off when he realizes that there's no one in the dressing room.

"Where is she?" he asks, his eyes alert as he takes in everything around.

"How the fuck could this have happened? We had eyes everywhere!"

"The monitors," he notes. "The network must have been compromised."

"But how? Panchito was on it at all times. And I doubt anyone could get past him."

"Unless…"

My eyes widen at his suggestion.

"We don't have time to make guesses. Not now. We need to find her first."

"But where?"

He frowns when I point towards the broken mirror. Blood is already pooling down my hand, but I can't even feel the pain anymore. My adrenaline is at an all-time high, my vision tunneled on only finding her.

"He's playing with us," I tell him as I read the phrase out loud.

"The roof or the underground parking lot," he immediately says.

"The roof. It's the roof." I nod grimly. "It's symbolic."

"What do you mean?"

"We used to meet on the roof."

That time seems like an eternity ago. When we'd been just two kids trying to avoid our parents' wrath. And since they had both hated Michele, they had discouraged any type of relationship between the two of us. Still, we'd found ways around that. Once upon a time…

Cisco barks some commands to his soldiers, but I don't waste any time in taking a few stairs at a time, rushing to the roof.

If anything happened to Noelle… I don't think I could ever forgive myself for it.

"Reinforcements are coming," Cisco notes from behind.

"He's caught. There's nowhere to run if he's on the roof..." He continues to talk, but I tune him out.

The door to the roof opens with a bang, and that's when I finally stop.

My brother is on the edge of the roof, gun in hand and aimed towards an unconscious Noelle. My blood starts to boil as I take her in. She's on the ground, barely clothed, and my mind immediately goes to the worst.

"And the guests of honor have arrived," he laughs, brandishing his gun in the air.

Both Cisco and I stop dead in our tracks, afraid he's going to pull the trigger on Noelle.

"I must say. It took you slightly longer than I expected."

"What are you doing, Michele?" I grit out.

"What does it seem like I'm doing, brother?" He tilts his head to the side, studying me.

For the first time in almost three years, we are face to face once more.

He hasn't changed much. Still as slender as before, he's wearing an all-black outfit topped with a leather jacket—his signature.

But I look at him, though his appearance hasn't changed, there is something different.

His expression.

It's cold—colder than before. As I find his gaze with mine, it's to be met with the chilling realization that he's gone.

The brother I knew—the one I once cared about—is all but gone.

Maybe until now it hadn't quite sunk in that we're two worlds apart. Two worlds that, it seems, cannot cohabitate.

There's a brief moment where all our past flashes before my eyes—the good and the bad. But all I can think is...how?

How did we get here?

I can still remember those precious moments when we'd

had each other's backs. But that had shifted in the span of a second.

"Let her go. This is between the two of us," I shout at him, not daring to go closer in case he might go rogue and press the trigger.

"The snipers will be in position soon," Cisco whispers from behind me. "We have everyone positioned at eight o'clock and three o'clock. They will wait for the signal."

I give him a nod.

"And what would you do for me to let her go?" He raises a brow.

"What do you want?" I ask, taking a tentative step towards him.

"Hmm," he regards me with an amused expression on his face.

Once more, I'm forced to admit that our operation must have been compromised from the inside. Otherwise Michele wouldn't be standing there, looking so smug as he's facing danger from all sides.

"See there, Rafaelo," he smiles. "If I were any other man, I might have been charmed into an exchange. But I am here because I have nothing to lose. Nothing but killing you that is."

"It doesn't have to be like this, Michele. We don't have to be at each other's throats," I add and his countenance immediately morphs—if before he'd been relaxed, now he looks on the verge of combusting.

"It doesn't have to be like this," he repeats, laughing derisively. "Let's take a walk down memory lane. Shall we?"

"What are you talking about?"

"You know exactly what I'm talking about," he grits out, waving his gun more. My eyes are fixed on it, afraid he might accidentally shoot Noelle.

And with her out...

"You *ruined* me," he accuses.

"It was a mistake," I explain. "We were both so young... Do you think I knew what effect it would have?"

"You saw..." he shakes his head, his features strained. "You stood there and watched and you didn't do anything. You didn't do a goddamn thing," he shouts.

"Michele..."

"You watched how I was shunned by everyone. You stood there and let it all happen when you could have very well prevented it. You *betrayed* me!"

"And I'm sorry for that. But how many times do I have to apologize for something I did out of immature idiocy?"

"That something *wrecked* me, Rafaelo."

"And didn't you return the favor? I spent my entire life trying to make up for what I did. Trying to go under the radar so father would reconsider and name you as the rightful heir. I spent a fucking decade trying to apologize," I say in frustration.

This confrontation is not just three years in the making—it's a lifetime.

"Didn't you sell me to Armand just for that? To live everything on my own skin? Because congratulations, you achieved your goal."

A shadow passes over his face—an unknown emotion that is gone in a flash.

"It wasn't enough. It will never be enough," he shakes his head, his nostrils flaring. "You should have stayed away, Rafaelo. You should have stayed gone, and maybe I would have forgotten about you."

He stares at me, his face marred by an echo of pain—one that squeezes at my heart because I *know* my failings, just as I know he was entitled to his revenge. But how much is too much? When does justice become cruelty?

I open my mouth to say something—another apology?

But not two seconds pass before his lips spread into a smile, his entire countenance changing.

"Now that you're here, I should tell you something," his lips tip up in an arrogant smirk as he nods at Noelle, "I had quite the one-on-one with your wife."

My muscles tense. Fuck apologizing. Noelle is where I draw the line—regardless of my guilt.

"What are you talking about?" I ask, my syllables measured as I attempt to control myself. If he laid one finger on her...

"What can I say?" He smirks, using the barrel of his gun to undo the knot on Noelle's robe, her entire front exposed as the material falls away. "Your wife is now intimately acquainted with Armand's dick in your ass," he chuckles. "And with my cock. Isn't that the best punishment? Fucking your wife while she watches you being fucked by another man?" He starts laughing maniacally, holding to his midriff as he continues to wave his gun around with another hand.

Chapter Twenty-Nine
Rafaelo

"He's insane," Cisco utters behind me. "Don't listen to him."

My hand tightens on my own gun, and as much as I'd like nothing more than to draw it and shoot him right between the eyes, I can't. He's baiting me. I'm sure of it.

I scan Noelle's figure, looking for anything amiss, or a sign that what Michele is saying might be true. Because I refuse to believe it.

If anything happened to my pretty girl because of me...

I don't care if she saw me with Armand. I don't care if she's disgusted with me. And I certainly don't care if she never wants me to touch her again.

Anything as long as she's safe and untouched.

If this motherfucker dared to defile her...

"I can see your brain working, Rafaelo. Are you trying to see if I'm lying or not?" He challenges. "Not to worry, I can do another demonstration."

Before I can even blink, his palm makes contact with Noelle's cheek. The slap is hard enough to move her head to the side, but also to wake her up. She startles, her eyes going wide as she blinks repeatedly. Looking around, her gaze settles on me, her mouth parting in an o.

"Look who's here, sleeping beauty. Your husband's ready for the showdown," he says as he tugs her forcibly to her feet.

"Don't you dare Michele. I get it. I'm guilty of whatever sins you've convicted me of. But she's innocent. Please... Just let her go," my voice breaks as I implore him, especially as my eyes meet Noelle's terrified ones.

Fucking hell. What did he do to her?

That alone is enough to make me want to explode.

I should have protected her. I should have fucking protected her.

I failed her...

"Hmm, what are you willing to do if I let her go?" He asks with a raised brow, his gun still trailing over Noelle's skin,

"Anything," I take a step forward, my arms spread open in a gesture of surrender. "Just let her go," I tell him in a gentler tone.

"Keep him talking," Cisco whispers, "It will buy the snipers time to get a good angle."

I give him a small nod, hoping they will act in time. If not...

Michele has a wicked smile on his face as he ponders what to ask of me. Although I already know what he will demand, I wait for his words.

"Kill yourself," he drawls. "Kill yourself. Right here, in front of me. And I'll let her go."

I swallow hard, bobbing my head up and down in acquiesce. Didn't I know he would go for the most extreme punishment? It would be only fitting after he's made me suffer for years.

I put one foot in front of another, my gaze flittering to

Noelle. Her features anguished, she keeps shaking her head, willing me to reconsider.

But I can't.

How can I, when I would do anything to see her safe?

My life ceased being my own the moment I realized the depth of my feelings for her. She's had me in the palm of her hands since then. And maybe this way, I can atone for some of the things I've done to her.

"Forgive me," I whisper the words, knowing she can't hear me.

"No," Noelle yells, wildly moving her limbs around and trying to run towards me. Michele is quick to stop her, pulling her back. A yelp escapes her as he handles her roughly, his touch bruising. That is enough to make my blood boil.

"The snipers don't have a clear shot without getting my sister," Cisco tells me, and my lips flatten in a thin line.

"Two choices, my dear brother. You either put a bullet through your brain right here and now, or you watch me fuck your wife while I put a bullet through her head. How about that?" His lips spread in an arrogant smile, his grip on Noelle tightening.

Leaning closer to her, he whispers something, and I note the tears falling down her cheeks as she nods, her eyes still on me.

My entire body is wound so tightly, the tension is ready to blow up. More than anything, there's the fear and anxiety at something happening to Noelle.

Just as I get ready to meet his demands—hoping somehow that Cisco's men will end this in a timely manner—Noelle moves.

Her robe is wide open, her bra and panties visible. Through a mass of sobs, I watch flabbergasted as she pulls down on her panties, sliding them down her legs and throwing them to the ground. She's trembling, her legs visibly shaking, and my heart hurts to see her like this.

The intent is clear, and without even thinking, I drop to my knees.

"Don't!" I shout. "Don't you dare, Noelle," I tell her.

I can hazard a guess as to what he told her, and I won't let her do that. I won't ever let her do that for me. I'd rather die a thousand deaths before allowing her to whore herself for me.

"I'll do it!" I say as I raise my gun to my forehead.

"Raf," Noelle's cry resounds through the air, but I try to ignore it.

"Damn, brother. I could say I'm shocked to see you so gone for pussy, but I'm not," he chuckles. "Not really," he shrugs, his gun still aimed at Noelle. "Of course you'd be the most likely to end up pussy-whipped," he laughs derisively. "Now let's end this once and for all," he nods towards me.

I pull the safety off the gun, meeting Noelle's terrified gaze one last time.

There are so many things I never had the chance to tell her. Most of all, I want her to know how much I love her. My lips part as I mouth the words, but there's no recognition on her face. She keeps shaking her head at me, begging me with her eyes to stop.

But I can't. Not when it would be either me or her.

Next to her, my brother has a smug look on his face, already anticipating my brains staining the concrete.

I squeeze my eyes shut, a prayer for the time I'll never get with the woman I love.

But as I bring my finger to the trigger, a loud cry permeates the air. My eyes snap open, horror overtaking me at the sight. Noelle dashes towards me, her robe tearing as she pivots forward, half of the material remaining in my brother's grasp, the other half still on her back.

"No!" I yell. "No, no, no," I keep chanting. "Stop!"

A few steps forward and a gun goes off, followed by a few more shots.

I act faster than ever, lurching forward to catch her. But as I bring her to my chest, it's to see my brother's gun drop to the ground, two bullet holes in his chest as he teeters towards the edge of the roof. His eyes are unblinking as he looks at me, surprise, shock and regret written all over.

Our eyes meet, and for a second, the connection is there.

It doesn't last though, not as he trips on the ledge before dropping over the edge.

I blink, my eyes widening at the realization. But I don't let myself dwell on that. Not when I have my pretty girl in my arms.

"Noelle," I shake her, quickly shedding my shirt to cover her with it.

"You're alive," she sighs, relieved.

"What did you do, pretty girl?" I ask softly. I can't muster the strength to tell her off. Not when seeing her so close to death took off years of my own life.

"I couldn't let you," she shakes her head. "I couldn't, Raf. I would have done anything to avoid that," she says as she looks at me with those big eyes of hers.

"Damn it, Noelle. Don't go there," I breathe out. "Don't tell me you would have..." My voice breaks and I can't even bring myself to say the words.

"I would have," she confirms, tears falling down her cheeks. "I would do anything for you. Anything. You don't know how strong my love is for you," she licks her lips, taking in a deep breath to prevent the sobs from taking over.

"Not that, Noelle," I shake my head, feeling myself near tears too. "Never that."

"You don't understand, do you?" her voice is low and anguished. "There's nothing left if you're not there."

I want to shake her. Take her in my arms and shake her so

she can see reason. So she can understand that I'm not worth defiling herself for. That there's nothing more precious than her.

As I bring one hand to her shoulder, though, it's find it damp and stained with red.

"Pretty girl?" My voice trembles as I quickly pull away what's left of her robe until I'm able to see her injury.

"I don't feel so well, Raf," she murmurs, her eyes straining to stay awake.

"Noelle, stay with me," I order her.

"Sleepy," she whispers, before she slumps down in my arms.

For a moment, panic overtakes me. I feel my heart in my throat as I lift my hand to her cheek, caressing the bruised flesh and trying to get her to react. But as I bring one finger under her nose, it's to realize her breathing is even.

Not in danger.

I release a relieved breath.

If something had happened to her... Not going there.

Forcing myself to stay in the present, I use the remaining material of her robe, ripping it in long stripes, tying them around her shoulder to keep the bleeding to a minimum.

"How's she?" Cisco asks as he crouches by my side.

"She got hit," I say, my eyes on her shoulder. "I don't think it went through, but we need to get her to a doctor."

From my initial inspection, the bullet only grazed her shoulder. I'm more concerned about her fainting, but that could be attributed to shock. God knows, she's had enough of that today.

"Good," he grunts. And as I rise with her in my arms, he helps me by placing my shirt over her naked body.

"He's dead," he says as I take a step towards the door.

"Is he?" I stop briefly, the news hitting me harder than I'd thought.

"My men are down as we speak. He fell off the roof. Dead on impact, if he didn't already die from the bullets."

"At least you got what you wanted," I reply dryly.

His hand comes to rest on my shoulder, his expression grim.

"We both got what we wanted. All things considered, I'd say this day is a success."

"A success," I laugh. "A success?" I swivel towards him, my features tense. "It's not a fucking success when my wife got injured. *Your* sister."

"She'll be fine," he shrugs.

"Right," I nod, pursing my lips. "She'll be fine..." I add sarcastically, barely resisting the urge to fucking punch Cisco in the face.

But my pretty girl is all that matters now.

"Keep everyone with access to the servers on retainer. We need to see who the mole was."

"Already on it."

His words are almost an echo as I walk away, only one purpose in mind. Getting into the car, I place Noelle on my lap, holding her tightly to my chest and murmuring loving words to her.

"I'll take care of you, little one. I promise," I whisper as I place one kiss on her forehead.

But even as I feel relief at everything being over, I can't help the hurt in my heart.

He'd been my brother. Once upon a time.

We'd been close.

I'd...loved him.

As fucked up as that sounds, maybe I still did.

And as one lone tear made it down my cheek, I decide to remember the good rather than the bad.

The time we were still brothers...

"YOU CAN'T BE SERIOUS," Carlos comments as I close the door to Noelle's room.

"We're still checking, but we can't discount anything right now."

"Panchito's been with us for a long time. He would never do something like that."

"If not him then someone else. How would Michele have control over the video feed if not? He knew about the plan and targeted our weak spots," I add grimly.

We'd borrowed extra people from Marcello and Vlad. We'd had the best of the best in charge of the operation. From the outside, the plan was solid—more than solid. The only explanation for this abysmal result is an inside job.

"He wouldn't do that to you," he shakes his head.

"That's what I hope too. Because it's not *me* he hurt, it's Noelle. And goddamn…" I bring my hands to my face as I release a big breath. "That must have been the most nerve-wracking experience I've ever had."

Carlos grunts.

"What about Michele? How do you feel about his death?"

"I don't know yet…" I trail off.

I'd brought Noelle home to be seen by the family doctor, and luckily her injury had been superficial. He'd administered some antibiotics to stave off an infection, but had told me not to worry moving forward.

While she'd slept, though, I'd gone to the morgue where my brother's body had been taken.

It had been…awful. Downright awful.

He'd collided face-down with the ground, and there hadn't been much of him left to recognize.

I'd stayed for a minute by his side, willing myself to forgive him, at least in death. Considering we'd stopped being close a decade ago, I'd felt his absence deep in my soul. Like a rift opening in my heart, I mourned his loss.

Regardless of what happened between us. Regardless of whether we share blood or not. We *were* brothers.

And that pains me the most. The memory of those long departed times, and the fact that I'll never get the opportunity to mend fences with him.

"You need to give yourself some time," Carlos says, startling me from my thoughts. "He was still your brother."

"I know. It just doesn't feel real. I've thought about all the ways I would kill him once I escaped the *hacienda*, and now he's really dead. And not even by my hand."

"Does that bother you? The fact that you didn't kill him yourself?"

"I can't say for sure," I give him a sad smile. "If anything, I wonder if I would have been able to do it..."

"He *would* have killed you," he counters.

"*I* would have killed myself," I chuckle. "He knew how to play me."

Carlos is quiet as he regards me thoughtfully.

"I think that's the difference between me and my brother. I planned and planned yet he won..."

"What do you mean?" He frowns. "How did he win?"

"He would have pulled the trigger. Me?" My lips stretch into a tight smile. "I guess we'll never find out."

Cisco, ever the enterprising man that he is, has already started the chain of succession to ensure that I get my rights as the new Guerra head as soon as possible.

As fucked up as it sounds, I don't care. At this point all it matters is that Noelle is safe and we won't have to hide anymore.

That means the first thing on the list is to get rid of the bounty on my head.

I spend the rest of the day solving the logistical issues

arising from Michele's death, including dealing with his body and subsequent funeral. And as the next of kin, I can ensure that both him and my parents are buried in a family mausoleum.

"She's awake," Greta announces over the phone.

"Thank you. I'll be there soon," I tell her.

Quickly wrapping up the business of the day, I head home to Noelle.

As I open the door to the room, I find Noelle seated against the railing of the bed, a book in her hand.

"You're back," her lips tug up in a blinding smile.

My heart thuds in my chest, an immediate reaction to seeing her well and healthy. My initial assessment of her injury had been right. The bullet had only grazed her flesh— a lucky occurrence considering the mayhem of the day. The shock had been more powerful than the injury though, likely a result of her past trauma too. I know she's not overly fond of guns and fists.

The biggest relief, though, had come from knowing that Michele hadn't done anything to her—his words had been empty threats meant to rile me up. In a moment of brief awareness, she'd told me that he hadn't touched her.

Fuck, but I'd like nothing more than take her in my arms and kiss every inch of her body. Yet I can't. Not when she needs to understand that what she did was *not* ok.

Whether we want it or not, we are confined to this life, and this won't be the last dangerous situation we'll be faced with. It's unavoidable. And I can't have her putting herself in danger to save me.

"How are you?" I ask as I take a seat on the bed next to her.

"Much better," she wets her lips as she bats her lashes at me.

She knows she's in trouble.

"I heard what happened to your brother," she continues when she sees I'm not continuing the conversation. "I'm sorry. I know that despite your enmity, you cared about him."

"Thank you," I murmur. "I'll miss him," I admit. "Well, the memory of him."

"That's right," she places her hand on top of mine, the touch searing. "But no one can take your memories away," she gives a tremulous smile.

I don't have the heart to move her hand away, so I stay still.

"You know what's the funniest thing," I shake my head, amused. "Growing up, he always wanted to become a super-hero. He had this idea that he would save the world," I swallow hard, the memories painful.

"Ironic that he ended up becoming the villain."

"Was he?" I purse my lips. "I doubt that's how he saw himself."

"You're right," she nods thoughtfully. "He claimed it was justice for what had happened to him."

"Maybe in his mind it was. Who knows," I sigh.

"What did he mean by what you did to him? He said he was only paying you back…"

"It doesn't matter," I cut her off. "It's all in the past," I give her a tight smile as I get up.

I can't help myself, though, as I lean down to lay a kiss on her forehead.

"Rest. I'll be in the other room," I say as I go.

Confusion swirls in my head as I make my way to the other room. I hadn't meant to shut Noelle out like that. But some things… Some things are not easy to talk about.

Although I've shared more with her than I've ever shared with another human, some memories are too painful to bring up—and some too shameful.

Michele's descent into pure madness and his subsequent

actions might have been extreme, but they were never *not* unwarranted.

Even as it pains my heart to admit, I am partially guilty of the way he turned out. Because what I'd done to him had hurt more than what *anyone* else had done to him.

He'd trusted me, and in a moment of weakness, I'd betrayed him.

I threw him to the wolves, and it's *my* fault he ended up more feral than them.

Shame eats at me, just as much as regret.

I wish I could let Noelle in—tell her everything that happened.

Everything.

But she would never see me in the same light if she knew.

"Fuck," I curse as I bring my fingers to my forehead.

Maybe Michele was right.

We've both been chasing our own justice from the beginning, forgetting how that would be seen by other people.

Me? I'd caused Michele to lose faith in humanity—shed the last bit of it he had. I'd acted like a coward and then behaved like a victim.

And then there's Noelle. My brand of justice had brought her more suffering than I can ever atone for.

In the end, am I any better?

Unscrewing the lid of a bottle of scotch, I pour myself a glass, bringing it to my lips and reveling in the burning sensation as it travels down my throat.

"Cheers, brother," I bring my glass up, toasting to the moving shadows on the wall. "May you rest in peace now," I whisper.

Because I certainly won't.

CHAPTER THIRTY
NOELLE

"Congratulations," I lean in to kiss Yuyu's cheeks. What were the odds that she'd go into labor so soon?

She's lying in bed, her pale cheeks ruddy from effort, but there's a radiance to her that makes her look so beautiful.

"Thank you, Noelle," she gives me a smile.

My brother hasn't left her side the entire time she's been in labor, holding her hand throughout the entire ordeal. Raf had told me all about it, since I'd preferred to stay away for that period, afraid it would trigger bad memories.

"He's precious," I tell her, my eyes softening as I take in her newborn son.

I don't offer to hold him, or get a better look. Not when I know it could have an adverse effect on my psyche.

"Thank you so much for coming here. I know it hasn't been easy with you guys," she takes my hand in hers, giving it a quick squeeze.

My lips tug up in a tight smile, and I assure her it's my pleasure.

God knows, though, it really hasn't been easy. Something changed since that time on the roof.

Raf changed.

I don't know if it's the death of his brother, or if his issue is with me, but he's been more distant than ever.

He comes to bed at dawn, getting only a couple of hours of sleep before he's up again, leaving the house to conduct whatever business he has pending.

In a way, I wonder if he's doing all this to avoid me. We haven't exchanged more than a couple of words here and there since Michele's death. Sometimes he gazes at me as if he'd like to say something, but ultimately never does.

I wish he'd yell at me. Blame me for what happened. Anything but this silent treatment that's slowly killing me. Yet, even if he did bring it up, I would remain staunch in my reply. I don't regret what I did. I'm not sorry I disregarded my promise, and most of all, I'm not sorry I saved him.

My arm is getting better and it no longer pains me as much. I'm aware that I'd been lucky—all things considered— to only get away with just a scratch. I'd been lucky that I hadn't been killed by Michele's errant bullet. But in that case, death would have been more than welcome. And *that* is what Raf doesn't seem to get.

How am I to continue living without him?

He was about to put a bullet through his brain to save me. How is *that* acceptable, yet my sacrifice is not? He fails to understand that my love for him is not any less than his. And just because I'm a woman, that doesn't mean I can't protect him as well.

While Yuyu is busy breastfeeding her baby, I take a step back, ready to leave the room. The moment I am about to go out the door, though, I reel back, my entire brain jolted from inside out. I reach with my hand, placing it on the wooden frame of the door as I seek to stabilize myself.

Squeezing my eyes shut, I try to take deep breaths, hoping it's just the beginning of a migraine.

But as images flash inside my mind, I know it's not.

"What are you going to name him?" Lucero asks, her hand on my baby bump.

"You can't know it's a boy," I reply, a small frown on my face.

Oh, how I'd love for it to be a boy. Because if it's not… No, I can't think about that.

I couldn't bear to do that again just to give Sergio an heir. I'd rather die.

"It will be a boy. Trust me, you have all the signs," she sighs. "If only he'd get a doctor here. Or at least a midwife."

Since my pregnancy had become evident, Sergio had locked me in the west wing of the house, with only a couple of people allowed to see me. It had been his punishment for what I'd done, but also his way of ensuring that I wouldn't do anything to harm the baby—as if I'd ever try something like that.

"It's ok, Lucero," I give her a tight smile. "We're going to be fine," I tell her as I gently caress my stomach, sending all my love to my baby.

Regardless of the circumstances of his conception, he is loved.

"Mali," I whisper after a brief pause. "His name will be Mali," I repeat, absentmindedly bringing my fingers to my neck.

"Noelle, are you ok?" I hear someone's voice in my ear, but I can only muster a small nod. "Let me call Raf. He'll come get you," I turn to see my brother looking at me with worry in his eyes.

"You don't have to bother him. I'm sure he's busy," I mutter, feeling a little weak in the knees.

"Nonsense," he shakes his head, whipping his phone and dialing Raf.

"Take a seat," he guides me to a chair while he talks to my husband on the phone.

Mali

I bring my hand to my chest, a searing pain bursting inside of me. Spreading my palm above my breasts, I breathe slowly—in and out. I feel the absence of something. What, I couldn't say. But my soul yearns for something ineffable. I just know I'm missing a crucial part of myself.

The more I dwell on it, the more inconsolable I become.

Mali.

"Noelle," I feel arms shaking me.

Blinking repeatedly, I focus on the person in front of me.

"Raf," I utter his name, startled.

When did he come?

"Let's go home, pretty girl," he says gently as he swoops me in his arms, tucking me to his chest.

"But Cisco and Yuyu…"

"They won't care if we're here or not. They have their new baby to care for," he tells me.

His hot breath is on my cheek, his scent invading my nostrils as he holds me tight.

"I didn't realize how bad this would be for you or I would not have suggested the trip."

Opening the car door, he deposits me in the passenger seat, buckling my seatbelt for me. He pauses for a moment, looking at me with a strange expression on his face before shaking his head and getting in the driver's seat.

The drive home takes a while, and with Raf barely talking with me, the silence becomes awkward. Since Cisco had decided to relocate with Yuyu to another place at least until the baby is a few months old, we have the brownstone all to ourselves.

And that means even *more* awkward silence.

"It feels so good not to have so many cars following us around," I add after a while, trying to lighten the mood.

Raf had managed to get the bounty off his head removed,

and as the new Guerra head, he is no longer in danger from random attacks.

"It does, doesn't it?" He attempts a smile, but he doesn't glance at me, his eyes on the road.

My face falls, but instead on dwelling on it, I turn my attention to the moving landscape. He might be mad at me, but he's bound to get over it at some point, right?

It's a little disconcerting, though, that he's been shutting me out like this. I've gotten so used to him being part of my daily routine—an extension of myself—that this rift between us is making my heart hurt.

From the outside everything looks perfect. He's still the doting husband and the worried lover. But it's when we're alone that he becomes aloof, seemingly seeking to be as far away from me as he can.

I miss our talks. I miss the intimacies. I miss *him*.

Since the incident on the roof, he hasn't touched me. He claims he was worried about my injury, but I wonder if it's not something else.

"Mali," he suddenly says, and I whip my head around, my eyes widening. "What did you mean by that?" he asks, and I realized that in my stupor, I'd said the name out loud.

"Nothing," I murmur, doing my best to keep my expression neutral.

"Are you sure? Did you remember something more from the past? You were really pale."

"No, just tired," I force a smile on my lips.

He turns to me, his eyes narrowing at me as if he's trying to decipher something from my features—as if he's sure I'm lying.

"You'd tell me if it was, wouldn't you?" His words are measured, yet I don't miss the implication.

"Of course. You know I tell you everything."

"I'm here," his hand finds my thigh as he gives it a tight squeeze. "I'm always here for you, Noelle."

I don't respond, ashamed of my little lie. But I'm worried that if I keep freaking out on him about my past, one day he's going to have enough.

The last thing I want is for him to finally see how screwed up I am and realize I'm not worth the effort.

Given his new position, he needs someone strong by his side. Someone who can help him trudge his way through the New York society and get back what was taken from him. He doesn't need a fumbling fool who is afraid of her own shadow.

The long and tedious journey gives me enough time to reflect on myself—on my strengths and my weaknesses.

And so I come to a startling realization.

I need to change. I have to show him that I'm not a dead weight. That I'm not a slave to my mental issues. More than anything I need to bring something to the table so that I become indispensable to him.

That way, he'll *never* tire of me.

CHAPTER THIRTY-ONE
NOELLE

I bang my fingers on the keys, the dissonant sound echoing in the room. Pouring all my aggression into my notes, I play like never before.

A few pieces I'd composed in the spur of the moment, they are better fitted to an organ than a piano, the intensity more discernible in the way the bass resounds in the room, permeating every atom of its surroundings.

That's exactly what I want—what I envision. The waves produced from my music undulating in the air and hitting every surface, shifting the very fabric of reality as it makes it congruent with my feelings.

I become immersed in my playing, forgetting about everything but the sound of the piano keys.

And as I hit the last note, I stop. Letting my fingers rest on the keys, I release a deep breath, the tension slowly seeping out of me.

Opening my eyes, I look up, startled to see I'm not alone in the room.

Like the first time I'd seen him, Raf is leaning against the wall, his hooded eyes regarding me intently. He's wearing his office work, a pair of dress pants and a white shirt cuffed at the wrists. A few buttons are popped at the neck, hints of skin peeking through.

Bringing my tongue over my lips, I lick them as I take his imposing figure in.

I wonder if his effect on me will ever lessen. Every time I see him, it's like the first, my body reacting to his in a primal way that has me clenching my thighs together as desire clouds my mind.

He tilts his head to the side, studying me.

"You're pissed," he simply states.

I frown, but he doesn't wait for me to reply as he takes a step forward. And another. Until he's in front of me, placing his arm on the piano and raising a brow at me.

"You're pissed at me, aren't you?"

"I don't know what you're talking about."

"Cut the crap, Noelle. You think I don't feel it? You think I can't taste the frenzy of your music on my tongue? If you're trying to be secretive about it, then you're doing a very poor job."

"I'm not pissed at you," I shrug as I get up. "I was just experimenting with sound. You don't have to read too much into it."

I make to move past him.

"I don't have to read too much into it?" He repeats my words, his voice chilling. "Your music *is* you, Noelle. So let's put our cards on the table. What's happening? Is it from yesterday? From what happened at your brother's place?"

"No. Nothing's wrong, Raf. I mean it," I force a smile. "This was just a musical experiment. Nothing more."

"I don't believe you," he says, his hand on my upper arm as he tugs me towards him.

"What's wrong, pretty girl? Tell me so I can fix it," he says gently, his fingers coming up to brush my hair out of my face.

I still in his arms, my eyes on his.

Slowly, I move my head from side to side, though my body starts trembling.

"Noelle, what…"

"Why don't you touch me anymore?" the words tumble on a whisper. "What happened to us, Raf?"

"I don't understand," he looks at me perplexed.

"Something happened to us that night. Something…" I shake my head, biting my lip as I look at him. "You've been avoiding me, and I've tried to give you space but I don't know what else to do."

"Noelle…"

"You're shutting me out and I don't like it," I admit, my eyes moist.

"Sweetheart," his arm snakes around my waist, bringing me flush against his chest.

His lips skim the surface of my cheek, moving towards my temple before he stops, drawing in a deep breath.

"Shit. I've been dealing with this all wrong," he mutters. "It wasn't my intention to shut you out. Far from it but…" he pauses and I hear an intake of breath.

My hands are on his back, my fingers wrapped in his shirt as I hold on for dear life, not wanting him to let go. I breathe in his familiar scent, assuring myself that this is not a dream. That he's by my side.

"Shh, it's all my fault," he coos, one hand gently caressing my back. "It's been a hard few days. And the fact that you were hurt…" I feel him shake his head against me. "It nearly broke me. Yeah, I mourned my brother's loss and I feel incredibly sad for his death. But it's not his face I see when I go to bed at night. It's not the thought of him that doesn't let me close my eyes. It's you."

I draw back so I can look at him, my eyes searching his. But as our gazes meet, it's to be struck by something else. His lashes are heavy with tears, the blue of his irises even more intense as he looks at me with so much emotion, my entire heart threatens to burst in my chest.

"All that time on the roof, I could only think about your safety. I was going mad with thoughts of him hurting you. Of him defiling you…"

"You know he didn't do anything," I bring my palms to his cheeks, molding his face in my hands and looking up at him. Due to his height, I have to raise myself on my tiptoes so I can reach his face to lay a chaste kiss on his chin. "He didn't touch me, Raf. He just threatened to do it to get a rise out of you. If anything, he didn't even look at me."

He blinks and I can detect the worry in his features, but most of all, there's weariness.

"You took your panties off, Noelle," he rasps out, the sound throaty and anguished. "You would have fucked him to save me, wouldn't you?" The tone isn't accusatory, it's just desolate, so inconsolable it squeezes at my chest.

"I would have," I admit, unashamed. "I told you I would do anything for you, Raf. That means *anything*."

I don't know how I could stand another man's hands on me. I don't know how I could stand anyone else's hands on me. Yet I would have done it. I would have closed my eyes, and I would have borne it all. It might have broken me. It might have destroyed me. But at least I'd have *him* by my side.

"Noelle," my name on his lips is like a punch to the gut, the emotion so strong it makes me reel. There's no reproach, but there is disappointment—or something akin to it.

I continue to look in his eyes—those eyes I've come to love more than anything in this world—and I find that I don't waver in my answer. Because I would do *anything* to preserve them.

"Tell me you wouldn't do the same for me," I challenge

softly. "Because what you were about to do was worse, Raf. Much, much worse."

"You don't understand, pretty girl," he sighs, a tear rolling down his cheek. "I can't bear it if you're hurt. There might be something wrong with me, but the thought of *anything* happening to you burns my insides like acid. It's *my* job to protect you, and I failed," he takes a deep breath. "I failed."

"You didn't," I shake my head. "You didn't fail. You offered your life in exchange for mine, Raf. Do you think anyone else would have done that?"

No one else would have. My brother would have likely taken the shot with me in the way, regardless of the potential danger to me.

That's what Raf doesn't seem to get.

All my life, I've always been an afterthought. No one's put *me* first—ever. He's the first to put my safety above others—above his own. He's the first one to show me I matter.

And he matters to me just as much.

"I haven't been able to sleep," he suddenly confesses. "All sorts of scenarios have been going through my mind—the what-ifs…"

"But nothing happened. I'm alive and well and so are you."

"You're my heart, Noelle. And the heart *always* rules. When the heart is bruised, the rest of the body follows suit."

"Where does that leave us?" I ask on a whisper. "Because my love for you is not any less than yours."

For a moment, we just stare at each other, unmoving.

He blinks back tears. I let mine fall.

There's a closeness that has nothing to do with the fact that our bodies are touching.

I just look in his eyes and I *know*.

We connect on a physical plane, but also on a spiritual one, our souls touching, caressing, grasping.

He's mine and I am his.

And I *would* do anything to preserve this.

"I know," he answers, closing his eyes. "I know, pretty girl," he says as he brings his forehead to mine. "We can only strive *not* to put ourselves in those situations—where it's one or the other."

"Because I'll always save you."

"And I'll always save *you*."

And that's the true quandary. We'll always be at a standstill.

"Please don't shut me out again. You have no idea how hard it was thinking you hated me—hated the thought of touching me again…"

"Never," he doesn't even let me finish as he utters the word. "It's my fault for being an idiot. But every time I looked at your arm, I blamed myself for failing you. I tried so hard to keep you out of this. To make sure you were safe. And ultimately…"

"It doesn't matter. Please," I wet my lips. "We can't keep doing this to ourselves. And we can't live in the what-ifs, Raf. I'm fine. It was *just* a scratch. *We* are fine. That's all that matters."

"You're right," he nods. "I'm sorry. I'll do better," he immediately says, taking me by surprise.

"You…will?" I blink.

"I'm still learning how to do this marriage thing, so I might mess up a time or two. But please bear with me," he whispers and the sincerity in his voice threatens to undo me.

How did I get so lucky?

"That you're willing to try means everything to me, Raf. I'm not perfect either. I don't know what I'm doing most of the time, but I think we've done well so far," a small chuckle escapes me. "We're learning together."

"Together," his lips draw up in a smile.

He moves his forehead on top of mine, the tips of our noses touching.

"We're free now," I breathe out, closing my eyes and reveling in his proximity.

"We are," he repeats, taking a step forward and backing me against the piano.

I brace my hands on the shiny surface, bearing almost all his weight on top of me.

His eyes on mine, he looks like he'd like nothing better than to devour me.

His nose nuzzles my face as he moves slowly, caressing my flesh and trailing his lips all over my cheeks before reaching my mouth.

He doesn't close in for a kiss. He hovers his lips over mine, his breath transferring to me.

I inhale deeply, wishing I could absorb his essence.

"I want you," he rasps. "I want you, Noelle. So very much."

His hands go down my body, tracing my curves over the silky gown I'm wearing.

"I want to bury myself so deep in your body you'll never question me or my loyalty," he says harshly. "I want to kiss you, taste you, fuck you until you're a quivering mess. Until you forget where you begin and I end," his lips trail down my earlobe, the skin so sensitive goosebumps erupt all over the surface. "I want all of it, Noelle. *All of it*," he states, his deep rumble making me shiver. "But I need you to want that too."

I know what he's asking. He wants to know if I'm ready for the next step—for the final step. We've been dancing around it for too long. From the beginning it had been an inevitability. Not a question of *if* but of *when*.

He's done everything in his power to make me comfortable as we've explored each other's bodies. Every little thing, he's made sure to ask for my full consent before proceeding, afraid something would trigger a bad memory.

It seems surreal to think how much care he's taken with me, how patient he's been when I know others in his position would have simply taken.

Not him. Never him.

It's another reason why my love for him knows no bounds. He respects me and my choices, and he always makes sure I have one.

Maybe it's because of his trauma and the fact that he's had his choices taken from him too many times. Maybe it's just who he is—a good man, a *worthy* man.

"Yes, I do," I reply. "I want you just as much, Raf. Make me yours," I tell him, cupping his cheek with my hand.

Laying a kiss to the center of my palm, he trails his fingers down my body until he reaches the hem of my gown. Pulling on it, he tugs it up and over my head.

"That's it, pretty girl. Let me see my treasure," he says, his eyes roving over my naked body.

I'm still wearing my panties, but he's quick to slide them down my legs, leaving me completely bare for his sight.

"I'll never tire of watching you like this, Noelle. You're the most beautiful thing I've ever seen in my life," he whispers reverently, taking a step back so he can study me at leisure.

With a boldness I haven't felt in a long time, I pull myself on the piano, settling in the middle of it and slowly parting my thighs.

"That's it," he rasps, his breathing harsh. "Show me my pussy, Noelle. Show me that sweet spot between your legs that's mine and only mine."

I nod fervently.

"It's yours," I tell him, my hands on my knees as I part my legs. "I'm all yours."

His eyes immediately go to my core, his heated gaze making me blush from head to toe.

"Fuck, you're already glistening," he curses, coming closer.

His fingers wrapped around my ankles, he pulls me towards him, hitching my legs over his shoulders as he positions his head between my legs. Startled, I push my arms back, resting on my elbows as I wait for him to make his next move.

He doesn't do anything, though. He merely watches.

"This," he brings one finger between my folds, tracing the contour of my pussy. "Such a pretty little flower you have here, Noelle. A flower that yearns to give me its honey."

I feel the rough pad of his finger against my sensitive flesh, the touch minimal, but enough to make me whimper.

He's fully focused on my pussy, his breath fanning over my wetness and increasing the stimulation. Bringing one finger to my clit, he flicks it over the small nub, and my muscles immediately twitch in response. A smile appears on his face at my reaction.

"And this is my tiny pleasure button," he brings his lips forward in a brief kiss.

"Mine," I correct.

"No," he pinches it, "it's mine," he looks up, raising a brow as he dares me to argue.

My lips tug up, and I can only nod at him, needing to know what he's going to do next. Already, my arousal is at its peak, my pussy gushing even more liquid with every second of his perusal.

I expect him to finally put me out of my misery and give me what I need. But he doesn't.

Instead, he swipes his finger lower, brushing it over my lips before settling at my entrance.

"And this tight little hole is going to take all of me inside, isn't it, pretty girl? It's going to swallow my cock so fucking deep you'll feel me everywhere."

"Yes," I breathe out, my voice coming out thick and throaty.

"Fuck," he curses, as his head whips up, his gaze on mine as he undoubtedly sees my hooded eyes and the way I'm slowly melting with every small touch.

His mouth curves in a satisfied smile.

"And I'm going to give it to you, pretty girl. I'm going to fill you until you can't take it anymore, and then I'm going to do it some more," his finger probes at my entrance, my muscles spasming at the contact. "Again and again until you're ripe with my cum. Until you're so fucking full everyone will know who you belong to."

"Raf," my mouth opens on a moan. "Please just... do something," I ask with an uncharacteristic urgency in my voice.

He's barely touched me, merely toying with me, yet I already feel on the edge.

"What do you want me to do, Noelle? Tell me. Ask me. Command me," he adds suavely.

"Your mouth. I want your mouth on me," I blush as I say the words.

"This?" he asks as he tugs me closer to him. His hands on my ass, he brings my pussy to his face for an open-mouthed kiss.

My hips shoot off the table, a mewling sound escaping my lips at the contact.

"Is this what you want?"

"Yes, please."

"Ask me. Ask me to eat your pussy, Noelle," he says with a roguish grin. "Ask me to lap at your juices and make you come all over my face."

I draw an intake of breath at his words. But my shame is

already out the window. This is Raf—the man I love. The man who would lay down his life for me.

"Please, eat my pussy, Raf," I give him the words.

"Your wish is my command, pretty girl," he winks right before diving in.

His mouth opens over my lips, his tongue making contact with my entrance as he drags it up—slowly and tantalizingly. He laps at my arousal, eating me up like I'm the best meal he's ever had.

Leaning back on my elbows, my eyes snap closed, my mind honing in on the sensation—the pleasure he's racking from me.

He brings the flat of his tongue over my clit, licking it before wrapping his lips around it, sucking it deep in his mouth.

"That… Right there," I moan, one hand in his hair as I guide him.

My clit pulses with unreleased pressure, my lower belly filled with knots of tension.

He continues to suck on my clit, hitting one particular spot that makes me lift my hips off the table in pursuit of my climax.

His hands move from my ass higher, gliding over my waist until his fingers pinch my nipples, his thumbs flattening over the raised peaks as he caresses them gently.

The combined stimulation is almost too much.

"Raf, please," my voice doesn't sound my own anymore—not that it did before. But I'm so gone, I don't care.

"Right there, pretty girl. Come on my face," he orders, his voice holding an edge to it. Right as he says the words, though, he bites on my clit.

"Raf," I scream, my back hitting the shiny surface of the piano as my body starts spasming. My legs are wrapped around his neck, and I hold tight—so fucking tight. The release is so powerful, it feels like my soul has left my body.

I breathe harshly, unable to come back down from the high.

"Fuck, Noelle. More, give me more," he rasps against my pussy, his tongue suddenly at my opening, pushing inside until he's fucking me with it.

Apparently one near death orgasm is not enough for Raf as he pulls another from my body until I'm barely able to talk coherently.

CHAPTER THIRTY-TWO
NOELLE

"You're magnificent," he says as he comes up for air. "I love making you come. The taste of you on my tongue. The feel of your body against mine. You're all that's gentle, soft, and lovely. And you're all mine."

His hands moving down to my hips, he pulls me closer towards him just as he advances, his mouth laying a kiss at the top of my mound before going higher.

He lays small kisses all over my belly until he reaches the valley of my breasts. Wrapping his lips around a nipple, he sucks it into his mouth.

"You drive me so fucking crazy," he rasps as he moves to the other nipple, giving it the same attention.

Soon, I'm back on the edge of the piano, his body wedged between my legs.

"You, too. God, I don't think you realize what you do to me, Raf," I tell him as I wrap my legs around his hips, the hard ridge of him nestled right where I want him to. "You make me lose my mind, and you're still wearing too many clothes," I tell him with a smile.

He smirks at me, leaning down to swipe his tongue over

my lips before seeking entrance to my mouth. His hand on my nape, he brings me wholly into him as he devours my mouth and makes me lose my senses.

How is it possible for two bodies to act so in sync? For two distinct people to feel so distinctly one? How is it possible to feel him so deeply in my soul when he isn't even inside of me.

Our tongues tangle together in a frantic dance, our mouths fused together and working at a pace that awakens the butterflies in my stomach once more. There's an imperative need to feel closer to him, to merge with him and become one.

Taking his lip between my teeth, I pull it back, taking the chance to look into his eyes as my hands work on the buttons of his shirt.

His eyes are glazed with arousal—his pupils large and overshadowing his irises. And that's how I know he's mine—when the blue of his eyes becomes the darkness of my desire.

With hurried movements, I get frustrated when his buttons don't give way. Instead, I tug at them until they fly on the floor, scattering around.

He has an amused expression on his face, but he doesn't stop me.

I quickly push the shirt off him, taking a moment to run my hands over his hard chest.

Releasing a satisfied sigh, I can't help but admire his physique, his muscles coiling under my fingertips.

Going lower, I hover over the hard plane of his stomach, the ridges that speak of hours of training and hard labor—how hard he'd worked to get where he is.

I briefly remember the Raf I'd seen in the video Michele had shown me. He'd been so thin back then, a mountain of difference to the man he is now.

"You're so strong," I murmur, skimming my lips over his

chin before going lower, to his neck and pecs. "There's so much strength radiating from you, Raf... You make me feel so safe."

"Always," he replies, watching me intently as I pepper kisses all over his body.

Hopping off the piano, I switch our positions, backing him against the edge as I start exploring his body.

I haven't had the opportunity to do it so leisurely before, and I find myself getting addicted to his hard and unyielding edges.

He's easily twice my size, both height and weight wise, yet he doesn't scare me—not even close. He makes me feel secure, and confident in a way I'd never felt before.

Dragging my lips down his chest, I reach his nipples, wrapping my lips around them in an effort to show him what he does to my body—to give him the same pleasure.

"Ah, pretty girl," he says in a hoarse voice, his eyes fluttering closed.

"I love your body," I tell him, licking downwards until I reach his abdominals. "I love every scar on your body," I say as I lavish attention on every faded mark and every indentation.

His body, not unlike my own, is a canvas that speaks of the past. Every little scar bears witness to suffering and perseverance. There are gunshot wounds, lash marks and knife cuts, all telling me just how much this man has suffered before.

He's here.

And that's all that matters.

Dropping to my knees, I look up at him to find him watching me with so much love my heart nearly bursts in my chest.

I bring my hands to his pants, unzipping them and

tugging them down. His length immediately springs free, almost slapping my face in the process.

I give a small chuckle that he returns as he threads his fingers through my hair.

"You're going to be the death of me," I joke, wrapping my hand around his cock.

"Is that so?" He raises a brow. "I must say, death by my dick doesn't sound so bad, does it?"

"I'll take what I can get," I shrug, amused, fisting both hands over his length and moving them up and down.

He hisses at the contact, especially as I bring my tongue to swipe at the head.

"I love the taste of you," I confess, licking the precum off the tip. It's salty, and musky, but the moment the taste hits my tongue, my pussy contracts in anticipation.

"And I love your mouth on me. God," his breath hitches. "I fucking love anything you do to me," he says, and I gain even more confidence to explore him. "You can do no wrong," he assures me.

Opening my mouth wide, I take the tip inside, swirling my tongue all around it and sucking it into my mouth. His groans are my guides, and I do my best to drive him crazy— just like he did with me.

He's so thick and long, I only manage to get half of him inside before I start gagging.

"Fuck, Noelle. Just like that," he brings his hand to my check as he caresses me. "Drench me in your spit," he instructs, and I do. I gather all my spit and lather it around his cock, using my hands to jerk him up and down while I suck on the tip.

"Let me feel your throat," his deep voice demands, and I can only comply as I let him push his length into my mouth until I feel the head against the back of my throat.

I try to relax my throat as he slowly thrusts into my mouth.

"God, Noelle," he rasps, his voice needy and full of arousal.

I revel in my power and the fact that I can make him lose his control like this. And as his moves become more and more uncoordinated, I know I must be doing something right.

I'd looked up all sort of tricks to make sure I please him as much as he pleases me, but I'd never thought I would enjoy going down on him as much as I do. It's such an intimate act, but more than anything, I love the way he opens up for me, every emotion on his face for me to see.

There's the vulnerability, and the want—all mine.

"Enough," he breathes harshly as he stops me. Replacing his cock with his thumb, he tips my chin up to look at him. "I need to come inside of you."

I nod my agreement.

At this point, no matter what he told me to do, I would do it. I'm so far gone that every word he utters is like an automatic command for my brain.

Please.

That's what I want the most. To please him and give him as much pleasure as he's given me.

Swooping me up, he places once more on the piano, and taking a step back, he proceeds to remove the last pieces of clothing from his body until he's as naked as I am.

Unwittingly my eyes are drawn to his hard cock as it strains against his stomach. He's big, and growing even bigger under my gaze. Instinctively, I clench my thighs together, both in anticipation and trepidation. Because even through the haze of desire currently residing over my mind, there's still the fear of the unknown—that it might hurt.

His hands are on my knees as he spreads my thighs apart,

coming to rest between my legs. I feel the tip of his cock against my pussy, but he doesn't move.

Sensing my slight apprehension, he dips his head, capturing my lips with his, one arm snaking across my waist as he brings me closer.

"We can stop if you want," he whispers as he breaks the kiss. "We don't need to…"

Lifting my finger to his lips, I shush him.

"I want you, Raf. I want *all* of you."

A smile spreads over his lips.

"And you'll have me. All of me."

He grabs the base of his cock, guiding the tip to my center. Still, he doesn't push in. Gliding the head between my lips, he coats it in my arousal all the while circling my clit with it.

"You're so fucking wet, pretty girl," he rasps, his eyes on mine as he brings the tip to my entrance. "This is mine, now, Noelle," he adds with a decadent intensity. "Once I'm inside you, my cock is the only one you'll *ever* know. I don't do half measures. If anyone else thinks to come near you, I'll put a fucking bullet through their brains. Understood?"

Wetting my lips, I nod.

"I would never want someone who is *not* you. You already own me, Raf. So take me," I urge him softly.

A triumphant smile spreads across his lips. Slowly, ever so slowly, he pushes into me.

My mouth opens on a silent moan. Lost in his eyes, I can only look at him as I feel the head of his cock breaching me.

"Ok?" He asks before advancing forward. "Tell me if it hurts," he says gently.

I nod, and he pushes inside even more. There's a slight burning sensation as he slowly fills me, stretching me to accommodate his girth. The more he advances, the more my discomfort disappears.

"Fuck, Noelle. You feel so good. Like you were made for me. For me and me alone."

He's only halfway in at this point, but already, I feel something build inside of me. Raising my hips, I wiggle a little in signal that he can go all the way inside. Grabbing my hips, he leans in to kiss me.

In one smooth slide, he thrusts into me.

I draw a breath in.

The world stills.

My hands cling to his shoulders as I hold on to him, my heart exploding in my chest as a multitude of sensations take over my body.

Shock.

Lust.

Love.

Predestination.

My walls close around him like a fine glove. He fits inside me like we were molded from one whole, separated only to be reunited like this.

And as I part my lips over his mouth, dragging them lower to his chin and neck, his salty and spicy taste hitting my tongue, he tastes like mine.

Like he's been mine all along.

"Noelle," he calls my name, his voice harsh, his breathing even harsher. "You're killing me, pretty girl. I swear I've never known heaven until this… Fuck…" he mumbles incoherently. "Your sweet pussy is fucking milking my cock. Shit… I don't know how I'm going to last."

"Whatever you do to me, Raf, I'm yours," I tell him.

"Sweet Jesus," he shakes his head, his forehead on top of mine as he takes a deep breath. "You're strangling my cock, pretty girl. That tight pussy of yours is trying to kill me," he rasps through gritted teeth, as if barely keeping himself under control.

"Tell me I can move. Please," an anguished sound escapes him, and I urge him on, wrapping my legs around him as he draws back, his shaft caressing me on the inside before he surges forth once more, hitting a spot so deep within me I gasp.

"Again," I tell him.

He pulls back until only the tip is still inside before slamming back in, his thrust making me reel.

"I'm not going to last, baby. But I promise I'll make it up to you," he vows, and a few thrusts later I feel him come inside of me.

His mouth on my shoulder, he bites my skin with the power of his release.

My arms and legs are wrapped around him, trapping him within me. But he has no intention of moving. And as he regains his breath, he tells me right so.

"I'll make it better," he promises. "You're just so fucking hot and... God..." he shakes his head. "I have no control when it comes to you."

"I like having you inside of me," I tell him as I caress his cheek, taking him in.

He's so handsome, the hard planes of his face and angular features complemented by the softness of his piercing eyes and the fullness of his kissable mouth.

"I swear I'll make it up to you," he continues, his mouth on my neck as he nibbles at my skin, sucking it in and leaving his mark on me.

"I know you will. You can't do anything wrong to me, Raf. I'll love everything you do," I tell him gently. It's not only my first time, but it's his as well, and we're figuring this out as we go. Just being with him is enough for me.

He continues to pepper kisses all over my skin, and I feel his cock twitch inside of me.

"You're so beautiful," he breathes, but the truth is that *he* makes me feel beautiful. "So entirely mine," just as he says the word, he pulls back.

I try to protest, but he slams his hard length back inside of me, making me gasp.

"I'm going to fuck you now, pretty girl. Any objections?"

I shake my head, a languid smile on my lips.

"Good," he purrs, grabbing my hips and thrusting hard into me. Our mixed juices help him slide easier inside of me.

The sound of flesh slapping against flesh resounds in the air, drowned out only by our joint breaths and moans.

"Raf..." I open my mouth to say something, but I forget the words, his cock doing wonders to me as he moves.

"That's it, Noelle. I want to feel you come on my cock," he commands as he continues to slide in and out of me, increasing the speed until I feel myself on the edge of a precipice.

"I... I think I'm close," I tell him, my nails digging in his back as I attempt to bring him closer to me.

"Fuck," he swears, sneaking his hand between our bodies to touch my clit.

A zap of electricity goes through my body as he continues to flick it. Soon, my entire body goes limp as my orgasm tears through me, my walls clutching at him.

His mouth finds my shoulder again as he bites my flesh, pain and pleasure mingling together and making me lose my mind.

In that moment there's nothing else but him and I—not two, just one.

"My God, Noelle," he groans.

His hands cup my ass as he lifts me in the air. Our size difference makes it easy for him to hold my entire weight while he slides me up and down his cock.

He surprises me, though, as he continues to thrust into

me while moving, exiting the piano room and going to our bedroom.

"I'm just getting started, pretty girl. I've dreamed of fucking you for too long," he rasps. "I'm not letting you go. I'm going to fucking imprint myself in you."

"Oh, Raf. You already have," I sigh in pleasure.

He imprinted himself on me from the very first moment. And now that I know him intimately, I can only confirm what I've known all along. There's *only* him for me.

I belong to him in a way I'd never thought possible.

Suddenly, he throws me in the middle of the bed, my back making contact with the clean sheets. My pussy clenches, already feeling his absence.

But as I look at him, standing naked at the edge of the bed, his hand working his cock as his eyes are glued between my legs, I find myself growing even more aroused—is that possible?

"Fucking hell, pretty girl," he swears. "My cum's leaking out of your pussy and fuck if it's not the hottest thing I've ever seen in my life," he says, his teeth raking over his bottom lip.

The respite is brief, however, as he drags me towards him before flipping me on my belly.

I gasp at the sudden switch in positions, but I don't protest as I feel him spread my ass cheeks, dragging his cock along my folds and splaying our mixed juices around.

"You're mine. Your perfect little body is mine," he says, pushing the head into me before taking it out, only to do it all over again, teasing me to no end. "Your beautiful heart is mine," he rasps thickly. "Every inch of you is mine," he states.

"Yours," I reply enthusiastically, thrusting my ass towards him.

While every orgasm he'd ever given me had felt like heaven, there's something different about coming with his dick inside of me. Something that ties us together in a unique way.

Just as I think I can't take it any longer, he's inside me, surging in at full speed and filling me to the brim.

"Fuck," he groans at the same time as a loud moan escapes me. "That's it, pretty girl. Scream my name. Tell me how much you love having my cock wreck your tight little body," his voice makes me tremble, his thick length stretching me as it thrusts into me, only to retreat and make me whimper at the loss.

"Raf," I cry out. "Please… More…"

"What do you want? Give me the words," he challenges.

"Fuck me harder, please," I plead.

"My pleasure," he leans over my body, kissing my shoulder as he snakes his arm around, his fingers wrapping around my neck as his hips start pistoning in and out of me.

The pressure keeps building, his hold on my throat only making me wetter.

He increases his speed until he's fucking me so hard I'm seeing stars.

My eyes close, and I no longer have any notion of existing, or of being. I'm just a mess of sensations at his mercy. He's destroying me and putting me back together just to do it all over again.

"You're my heart, Noelle. My fucking everything. You have no idea how much you mean to me," he speaks in my ear, his voice rough.

Tears burn at the corner of my eyes, and my cries intensify the more he thrusts into me. Like a savage, his grip is almost bruising, but in the most delicious type of way. And before I know it, my climax is upon me, my entire body combusting as I start trembling uncontrollably.

He continues to fuck me until he shouts his own release, his cock jerking inside of me as more cum floods my insides.

Pulling out of me, he turns me to my side, cradling me to his chest as he murmurs sweet words to me.

"I love you, Raf," I murmur, depleted of my strength.

"I adore you," he replies, kissing the tip of my nose.

A while later, I languidly stretch on the bed, sated and content. Sneaking a peek at Raf, it's to find him watching me intently.

He's on his stomach, and I swallow hard as I take in the shape of his body, from his broad shoulders to his shapely ass —everything is perfect.

And he's mine.

How did I ever get so lucky?

"What are you thinking about?" I whisper, peering at him.

His mouth spreads in a satisfied smile.

"That our marriage is officially consummated. You can't get rid of me now."

"As if I wanted to," I snort playfully.

"Still, you're chained to me now. Forever."

"I quite like the notion of that," I bat my lashes at him.

Moving closer to him, I drape my leg over his body, placing my cheek on his skin as I trace the hard ridges on his back.

I can tell he's been caned and lashed, long and narrow indentures spreading across his skin in what must have been debilitating pain at some point.

"You know," he starts, and with my ear on his back, I hear his vibrations as he speaks, the sounds so intimate and unique. "There's a reason I didn't have sex until now."

"Hmm?" I steel myself, not wanting to hear about his loyalty to Lucero or how he thought she'd be his forever.

"I've never told this to anyone before," I feel him smile, his voice a little hesitant. "But I was waiting."

"You were waiting?" I repeat, surprised.

"Yeah. I was waiting for it to mean something. I was waiting to *feel* something."

I blink, taken aback by his confession. Slowly, a smile forms on my lips.

"So you waited for marriage," I tease gently.

"You could say that," he chuckles. "From when I was old enough to understand what love was, and from seeing my own parents in love, I knew I could never do it without feelings."

Moving back, I tilt my head to look him in the eye. His expression is shrouded in tranquility as he looks at me languidly, his lips tipped up.

"I could never *just* fuck someone, pretty girl," he tells me softly.

"You fucked me," I raise a brow in challenge, amusement playing at my lips.

"I did," he rumbles. "But even when I fuck you, I'm making love to you, Noelle. Never doubt that. No matter how hard or dirty or out of control I take you, I'm still making love to you."

A blush climbs up my cheeks, a sudden shyness over-taking me.

"I like that," I confess. "I like that I'm the only one who knows this side of you. And more than anything, I'm honored that you waited for *me*," I say, wetting my lips as I flutter my lashes at him, waiting for his reply. Maybe it's bold of me to say he'd waited for me specifically, but that's how I want to imagine it.

His hand finds mine as he gives me a quick squeeze.

"I *was* waiting for you. For this. For everything you make me feel. *This* feels right."

"It does."

He gives me a quick tug, bringing me flush against his

body as he nuzzles his face against my throat, slowly kissing his way up.

His lips are gentle, his touch feather-like and all the feelings he was talking about are suddenly translated in his gestures—the way he tends to me like I'm a precious thing. And when he kisses my lips, I'm once again reminded that I've been waiting for this too—this once in a lifetime feeling of being complete, of feeling so whole I'm about to burst with happiness.

I kiss him back, showing him with my lips that he's my *something more* too. And suddenly, I understand why I'd never so much felt anything for another man, why no one had ever even entered my radar.

From the beginning, I was waiting for him, too.

We kiss and kiss, enjoying the simple act of intimacy that has the power to convey so much. And in every brush of his lips, I feel *everything*—the spoken and the unspoken.

Rafaelo Guerra is mine. Truly mine.

A while later, wrapped in each other's arms, I feel him tensing as his gaze flies far away.

"Did Michele lie, or did he show you the video of..." he trails off.

"Of you and Armand?"

He has a worried expression on his face as he nods.

"He did," I admit, knowing we would need to have this conversation at some point. Now, more than ever, my heart bleeds for him and what was so brutally taken from him.

He doesn't answer for a moment. Closing his eyes, he releases a deep breath.

"What was in the video?" He eventually asks.

"It doesn't matter," I try to assure him, but as he insists, I tell him.

His features draw back in pain as he listens.

"I never wanted you to see that part of my life, Noelle," he says as he turns to his side, his hand coming up to cup my cheek. "I never wanted you to see and...look at me differently."

"I could never look at you differently, Raf. How could I when it wasn't your fault? When that video only showed your suffering?"

"Pretty girl..."

"Armand was disgusting for raping you and your brother was even more disgusting for deriving satisfaction from it. He was a sick bastard and I'm glad he's dead," I add vehemently.

He purses his lips, swirling his thumb across my cheek.

"You're not disgusted with me?"

My eyes widen when I realize he's in earnest.

Dragging myself to a sitting position, I move closer to him, placing my hand on his chest.

"I care about what's here. I love the man inside."

"But you saw," his anguished voice startles me. "You saw him *fucking* me." Pain is written all over his face and my soul hurts for him.

"He was *raping* you. There's a difference, Raf," I pause as I gather my thoughts. "I didn't tell you before, but for me to get pregnant, there was only one possible explanation," I confess.

His eyes meet mine as realization slowly seeps in.

"You mean..."

"Yes. I know it deep in my heart that I would have *never* willingly slept with someone. Yet do you revile me for it?" My brows crease as I regard him. "Are you disgusted with me because of that?"

"Of course not," he immediately replies, his hand covering my own. "Never," he shakes his head.

"That's exactly how I feel about you, Raf. I don't think any less of you. If anything, I *hurt* for the things you were subjected to. My soul weeps for everything you went through."

"Noelle, God," he groans, burying his head in my lap. "How is it that you can offer me so much peace when I've known nothing but clamoring noise for the last three years?"

"It goes both ways. You're my safe haven," I whisper as I caress his forehead, threading my fingers through his hair.

He settles comfortably in my lap, and the words start pouring out of him as he tells me about his time with Armand. I listen attentively, my eyes red, my cheeks wet as tears fall unbidden. He tells me of the horrors he endured at Armand's hands and how he only managed to survive by thrusting it all to a deep corner of his mind, creating a box for the unwanted memories. Yet for everything he's recounting, I can't help but feel I'm only getting a censored snapshot of it. And *that* pains me more.

"We're not that different. Your brain acted on your behalf, creating a self-defense mechanism and prompting you to forget all the horrors that happened to you. Mine," he chuckles drily, "left it up to me, to push everything aside and deal with it one step at a time."

"Your version sounds a little healthier," I joke. "Because I don't want to imagine what would happen if all my memories came back at once."

They would end me. Plain and simple. They would wreck my sanity and *really* turn me into the crazy woman everyone thinks I am.

It's one of the reasons I've taken my therapy so seriously. I've realized that what happened to me was worse than I'd previously thought, and as such, I need to be prepared for when all hell breaks loose.

And it will.

My brain is a damned time bomb waiting to go off.

CHAPTER THIRTY-THREE
NOELLE

W e're the only two people here among hundreds of dead.

As he'd set out to do, Raf had bought a mausoleum for his parents where he'd had them interred together with Michele's body.

Today is a milestone for him though. It's the first time he's visited his parents' graves since he arrived back in New York.

Over time, he's opened up about them, and I'd found out that for all the issues in their family, he'd had a good childhood, and his parents had loved him. His mother, one might say, had loved him a little too much—to the detriment of Michele and Gianna.

The mausoleum door is open, but he doesn't go in yet. He's just staring longingly at the edifice.

"What sort of a son am I, when I'm only now paying my respects to my parents?" He shakes his head, pursing his lips in self-castigation.

"They would have understood," I tell him, slipping my hand through his and offering him my silent support.

"The last I saw of my father was after Sisi disappeared,"

he starts, his gaze distant. "I expected him to chastise me. To tell me off for the failed wedding. Instead, he just patted me on the back and told me he was sorry."

I squeeze his hand in comfort.

"My father wasn't an emotive man. Yet in that moment he showed more emotion than I'd ever seen from him. I felt his love—for the first time."

"Do you think he knew about Michele? That he wasn't his son?"

"I think he always suspected. Otherwise he wouldn't have been so adamant about me succeeding him when tradition dictates that the eldest should be the heir."

"Why didn't he say anything, then?"

"Because it would have shamed him. To have an unfaithful wife who saddled him with a bastard son would have been extremely shameful. The entire family name would have suffered for it."

"Instead, it was your brother who suffered, and he never knew why."

He nods, a pained expression on his face.

"My father was mostly absent in our lives since he was always chasing one financial high after another, mostly ending up unsuccessful," he chuckles. "But my mother was always there for me. For every step of the way," he takes a deep breath, moving forward as he places his palm on the door of the mausoleum.

"I always felt bad about deceiving her with my handicap. Because even though she thought me useless, even though she saw me as nothing but a burden, she still cared for me as if nothing happened. Sometimes I wonder if she convinced herself of that..." A sad smile plays at his lips.

"It sounds like your mother loved you a lot."

"She did. I know she was awful to Michele and to Gianna. But to me she was the best mother I could have asked for. She loved me even when she thought I was defective, and in essence," he looks down at me, "I think that's the definition of love."

"She taught you a wonderful thing, then, Raf. Because not everyone knows how to love," I tell him gently. "Not everyone knows how to be a decent human being."

His lips spread in a tight smile.

"She certainly wasn't practicing what she was preaching," he chuckles. "She was only a decent human being with me, and I'll always have those fond memories..." he trails off and I can sense the conflict within him—the fact that the mother he'd loved had been awful to everyone else.

"She may have been an enemy to your sister and brother, but she was still your mother. Just because she was a bad person doesn't erase the fact that she was, in fact, a good mother to you."

"Thank you," he murmurs. "I needed to hear that. Sometimes I find myself hating her, even though I still love her," he confesses.

"You miss her," I state, and he nods numbly, his eyes misted with tears.

"It's ok to mourn her, Raf. You've held back until now, haven't you?" I ask tentatively, because until this point he hasn't really let himself face the reality that his parents were dead.

"I don't know how to feel about them," he says brokenly. "I'm sad they're gone, but I also know that, objectively, they weren't good people."

"Raf..."

"I miss them. Does that make me a bad person too?" he asks quietly.

I pull at his arm, tugging him towards me. His brows go up in question, but as I bring my hands to his face, cradling his head and bringing it to my shoulder, he doesn't object.

I gently caress his face, feeling his suffering as my own.

"It doesn't make you a bad person," I whisper. "It makes you human. So grieve, my love. Let yourself feel the pain. Because they *were* your parents. And no one can take that from you."

I hold on to him as he sobs quietly.

This giant of a man is leaning on me—both literally and figuratively—trusting me with his vulnerability.

"Thank you," he whispers in my hair after some time.

His arms come around me as he molds me to his body, his heat transferring to me.

"Humans are never black and white. You may care for me now, but before, you saw me as the enemy," I murmur as I caress his cheek, my eyes meeting his. "We're always going to be the bad guy in someone's life."

"Indeed," he nods.

"That doesn't mean we should stop celebrating the good, does it?" I give him a small smile. "We have no control over how people perceive us, whether purposefully or not."

"You're right," his lips tug up in a smile in spite of his sadness. "You're so wise for one so small," he pats my head, ruffling my hair.

"Hey," I pout, "I'm not *that* small."

"You're small enough for me to do this," he says, immediately scooping me up and taking me in his arms—or rather, one arm—and proving to me that I am, indeed, *that* small.

"Raf," I choke on a giggle, "you're going to drop me, put me down."

"Not going to drop you," he lays a loud smooch on my temple, and with me in his arms, he takes a step inside the mausoleum, finally making the courage to face his parents.

The three tombs are all laid side by side.

"There's no place for another one," I add, thinking he'd want to be buried with his family at some point.

"There's no need for another," he shrugs.

"But…"

"I have a new family," he cuts me off. "*You*'re my new family. And that's where I'll spend my eternity. With you by my side."

I blink at him, his words taking me by surprise.

"Raf," I whisper.

"I'm not willing to part with you. Not even in death," he tells me, the light hitting his piercing eyes at an angle and making them even more intense.

"You're so sweet," I blink back tears. "So very sweet," I bring my cheek to nuzzle his.

He lowers me gently to the floor, and taking my hand in his, he points towards his mother's tomb.

"Hello, mamma," he clears his voice. "I'm sorry I haven't been here until now," he pauses, taking a deep breath. "I love you and I will remember you fondly as the best mother I could have hoped for."

Bringing his other hand up, he wipes at the moisture in his eyes.

"I wanted you to meet someone," he tugs me closer to him. "This is Noelle, my wife, and she is my heart," he says with so much sincerity, my own feelings threaten to overwhelm me. "I wish you could have met her. She's the strongest woman I've ever known, and against all odds, she's charmed her way into my heart."

I swallow hard, listening to his words and realizing once more how much I love this man, and how much he loves me back.

"You would have liked her. She has such a kind and gentle soul…" he stifles a sob. "She brought light into my life when I thought everything was doomed. She's a pianist, like you, and God, if you heard her play… She has the ability to hypnotize people when her fingers hit the keys. She's so talented... You would have *really* loved her."

"Thank you for your son, Mrs. Guerra," I add when he pauses. Surprised, he turns to me, but I just continue. "You've raised a gentleman. He is the best man I know, and he truly makes me happy. I've never met someone as sweet and loyal as your son. He makes me feel safe when my own shadow scares me. He's there for me when the entire world is against me. I have no words to describe how much I love him and how much I'll continue to love him. Please know I will take care of him," I say as my hand brushes against the cold stone.

"Noelle..." Raf groans.

"I love your mother, just for the simple fact that she gave me *you*."

"Pretty girl, you're killing me," he whispers, taking both my hands in his and bringing them to his lips.

"It's the truth. Nothing but the truth."

"Sometimes I have a feeling that ours was meant to be," he says as he peppers kisses on insides my wrists "That everything I went through, every little thing that seemed insurmountable at the time, brought me one step closer to you. That all that suffering was the price I had to pay to find *you*."

"You're making me cry," I turn my head to the side, blushing profusely.

"Against all odds we found each other, Noelle. And I wouldn't trade it for anything in the world."

"Me neither," I whisper. "Never."

"I adore you, my little piece of heaven," he murmurs, bringing his lips on mine for the sweetest kiss.

"I love you, Raf. Forever and ever," I speak against his lips.

"Forever and ever," his words linger in my ears.

CHAPTER THIRTY-FOUR
MICHELE

"You're a crazy bastard," Andreas muttered as he stared at Michele's shirtless form.

The bullets had left their mark on his skin even though he'd worn a bulletproof vest. And he'd seen in the last days how hard it had been for his boss to move around.

Michele shrugged a shirt on, raising a brow at Andreas.

"Lighter," he said as he popped a cigarette in his mouth.

Andreas complied, getting the lighter from his pocket and lighting his cigarette.

"You're not thinking about going out, are you?" Andreas asked, blinking in surprise.

Michele rolled his eyes at his Andreas' tone, merely taking a deep drag of his cigarette as he regarded him lazily.

"Of course I am."

"B—but… You haven't gone through all this trouble just to reveal yourself…"

"Andreas," he turned sharply. "No one will notice. For one to see, one must first look."

"You're crazy…" he muttered, shaking his head in disbelief.

"So we've ascertained," Michele added mockingly.

"I don't understand. Truly, sir. Why did you go to such great lengths to fake your death when you could have ended your brother right then and there."

At Andreas' tone, Michele tilted his head, listening.

"You could have gotten rid of your issue once and for all. I don't get why you'd take a detour when you *had* him," Andreas blinked at him, confused.

A slow smile spread over Michele's face. He'd expected this line of questioning, since his decision may seem aberrant to most.

"Andreas, have you read the Art of War?" He asked his trusted man as he took a seat on the leather sofa by the window.

His gaze was on the endless skyscrapers, the smoke from his cigarette hitting the hard pane of the window before refracting into the room.

"No," he answered, coming closer and regarding him with a confused look on his face.

"You should," he half turned and winked. "It will show you that no action is random in time of war."

"I don't understand, sir," he frowned.

"*All warfare is based on deception,*" Michele quoted, before adding, "*simulated disorder postulates perfect discipline and simulated weakness postulates strength.* War is never about pure strength Andreas. And it is *never* decided in just one battle."

"Yes, but..."

"He wins who knows himself and his enemy. It's a matter of a series of principles coming to play. You could say I was lucky enough to find out about the trap beforehand. But you've seen the blueprint of the place yourself. With the soldiers he had stationed, and the planning my brother put into it, it would have been suicide to go there on the offensive."

His mouth parted, Andreas frowned as he tried to make sense of his words.

"Let me put this differently. No matter how I approached the situation, I *would* have walked into a trap. One, might I add, that would have proven deadly. Instead, I played on their expectations. I pulled the trigger before they could."

"I see," he nodded tentatively.

"I gave them a show because that's what they expected. But my purpose was different. It was not losing or winning. It was learning."

"Learning?"

"Know the enemy," Michele stated. "And not only did I get to meet my dearest brother, but I also got to know his greatest weakness—his wife."

"Ohh," Andreas' face lightened with a new understanding. "You wanted to test him."

"In a manner of speaking," he smiles cunningly. "I played on his expectations while gleaning information about him and his new brother-in-law. Did you know the man didn't even bat an eye at the sight of his sister in danger? This, while my brother was willing to put a bullet through his brain for her. All quite enlightening, wouldn't you say?"

Andreas nodded.

"You get the best read of people when you put them in extreme situations. How do they react? Is it selfishly, or not? In self-preservation or something else?" Michele mused, almost to himself.

After reviewing the information from Pancho, Michele had realized that he couldn't take his brother head-on. At least not when he had an army worth of people all gunning for him. He knew Rafaelo had reached out to others for help too—others who *hated* him as much as he did. And so he'd realized that the safest course of action was to take control of the narrative. Even if that ended with his *death*.

The plan had been rather simple. He had his own men infiltrate Raf's snipers, all positioned around the roof. And when he'd given the signal, one of his men had been the first to fire, hitting him with two rounds in the chest, in designated areas covered by a bulletproof vest.

But that was not the highlight of the plan.

He'd scouted the area days before, mapping out strategic points that he could use, and he'd planned everything accordingly.

The roof had been planned. The spot he'd taken Rafaelo's wife had been planned. Just like the spot right below, where Andreas was waiting with a body double. The moment Michele had been shot, he'd taken a step back, given the signal, and jumped from the roof.

A few cords attached to the edge of the building had smoothed his fall to the floor below. Quickly getting rid of the evidence, they'd thrown the body double face down, ensuring there would be no way to really ID him.

After that, he'd merely watched the fruits of his hard work—all of which included the funeral and Rafaelo's subsequent ascension as the family head. All while sporting an amused smile.

Over the years, he'd prepared so meticulously, he had several back-up identities with full background checks as well as a multitude of off-shore accounts that ensured he would not have to worry about money for the rest of his life —regardless of his name.

"What now then?" Andreas asked, coming to him and offering him a glass of whiskey.

"Now we wait. We let them become comfortable in this false security and then...poof," he chuckled. "You don't hit someone when they are at their strongest. You hit them at their weakest."

"Wow. I'm impressed, sir," Andreas breathed in awe as he looked at him.

Bringing the glass to his lips, Michele took a large gulp.

Everything would come together. Soon.

He was prepared to give the last blow to his sire's killer—had been for some time now. Yet he found himself stalling.

A scowl marred his features as his thoughts turned to that particular subject.

He wasn't *stalling*. He was merely enjoying himself and dragging the anticipation. For then, the pleasure would be far more potent, and he would be able to pat himself on the back and congratulate himself for the amount of patience and foresight he'd exhibited.

Finishing his cigarette and finding himself buzzed to a pleasant state, he finally buttoned up his shirt, wincing as his fingers brushed along the bruises he'd gotten from the bullets.

"What about the girl?" Andreas asked as Michele was about to leave the room. His shoulders tensed at the question, and slowly, he turned to face his most trusted man.

Andreas knew about his pet, just as he knew not to inquire too much into her. Sure, she was a pivotal part of the plan. But she was also something else.

His.

And he did *not* like it when other men gazed upon her, much less uttered her name.

She was off-limits. At least for as long as she was the source of his amusement.

"Inconsequential," he replied, his voice thick.

He didn't like to discuss his pet with anyone, because that meant sharing about her with another being and he could *not* accept that.

No. She was only his. *For now.*

Andreas nodded, understanding the quiet rebuke.

"I'll see you later then, sir," he said in an *almost* tremulous voice.

Andreas was a competent employee and a trusted man— or as much as Michele could trust anyone. He knew what his boss was capable of, and tried to keep to his lane, rarely speaking out of turn. Michele appreciated that, since there was always a shortage of men with Andreas' qualifications on which he could count. He'd proved himself useful from the first, and slowly, he'd earned Michele's trust enough that he'd made him his direct liaison with the *famiglia*.

Throwing *a little* caution to the wind, he exited his building, jumping in his car and driving midtown.

He knew that Andreas' words weren't unfounded. He was risking a lot by going out in the open, but he couldn't help himself. He counted on the fact that his *death* had been so convincing that everyone was currently celebrating his funeral. And by his last update, his brother had left the city with Noelle, while DeVille had relocated to a secluded location with his wife—all in fear of being tracked down by people wanting revenge on the Black Monarch.

By all accounts, he had nothing to worry about.

Still, he *was* courting danger. For all his careful and meticulous planning, he was being reckless. Yet how could he resist an opportunity when it was being handed to him?

Reaching his destination, he strode confidently through the museum's doors, going straight to the source of his frustration. His men had informed him of her latest position, and that's how he found her—enthralled by an ancient stone block.

He approached quietly, not wanting to attract attention to his presence just yet. Instead, he took the time to study her.

Her chin was tipped up, the light hitting her chiseled cheekbones and making her look like one of the marble statues dedicated to Venus. She was wearing a long dress—

unusual for her—and her beauty was out there for everyone to see.

His fists tightened in anger, and the more he watched her —the more he saw *others* watching her—the more he felt himself slipping.

She had a look of contemplation on her face as she studied the designs of the ancient temple. A notebook in her hand, she scribbled down some notes for her assignment.

When he'd been informed of a class trip to the Met, all of which meant his pet would be in public, with men to leer at her, he'd immediately reacted.

She always made him react.

She took no notice of anything around her. So focused she was on her tasked, she saw nothing but the pile of stones in front of her. And as he advanced forward, he could see what she was working on—a sketch.

"The angle isn't right," he added as he took his position by her side. His deep, rumbly voice startled her, and as she raised her gaze to him, her mouth parted in surprise.

He looked down at her, a disinterested look on his face that belied the turmoil inside. His hands to his back, to the regular onlooker, his position spoke of casual boredom. To Michele, it was the only way he could stop himself from reaching out.

"What are you doing here?" She asked, peering at him through her lashes.

His gaze was affixed to her plump, rosy lips, and for a moment he found himself unable to respond.

"I happen to have an annual membership to the museum," he quickly recovered.

It wasn't a lie. He did own annual memberships to a few other museums in the city, and he'd donated a few paintings and artifacts in his time—anonymously, of course. He was also one of the most generous patrons, and his contributions helped fund a few scholarships as well as organize charity events that raised awareness for the art community—all off the books, of course. No one knew that side of him, and no one would.

"You do?" she squeaked in surprise, regarding him with wide eyes.

He grunted, not offering an explanation.

She wet her lips, and he could see the wheels turning in her head, her eyes sparkling with new adoration.

A smile pulled at his lips. *That* was more like it.

"And which wing do you like the most?" She asked, her voice holding a new type of warmth. One that flooded his insides and settled deep within, feeding him with renewed energy.

He cleared his voice, feeling himself redden at the innocent question. But it wasn't every day that he could boast about his vast array of knowledge when it came to art and history—certainly, it wasn't every day that he could elicit even more adoration from his pet.

"I'm rather fond of the Greek and Roman section," he waved to the back, to the great hall of statues. "But I've always had a sweet spot for 19th century Romanticism and Symbolism," he told her, his tone more enthusiastic than it had ever been.

She blinked, her eyes settling on him and seeing him as if for the first time.

"I like ancient art," she said, a blush high on her cheeks as she brought her gaze down. But the smile that tugged at her lips was unmistakable.

"Then let us head there," he motioned to the entrance.

She nodded, and together, they started walking.

Side by side, they weren't touching.

But the tension radiating from the proximity marred by the slightest distance couldn't be ignored by anyone around.

Like a thread of electricity that coiled under great pressure, the air was thick with an intoxicating allure.

She gazed up at him, adoringly. He gazed down at her, indulgently.

Hands behind his back, he was relaxed for what felt like the first time in his life.

Reaching the great hall of Greek and Roman art, marble statues and works of pristine art took over their field of view.

Michele closed his eyes, breathing in the history and for a moment, he felt himself separate into two. He was both his ruthless self, but he was also the *other*—the side of him he'd repressed.

They stopped in front of a statue of a goddess pertaining to the Classical period. His pet studied its form, her mouth parted in awe.

"I can't imagine how hard it must have been to sculpt something like this," she said, absentmindedly.

"Like any form of art, this took time to perfect," he remarked, pointing towards the smoothed ridges and the flawless human form. "From the Classical to the Hellenistic era, the Greeks committed to depicting humanoid forms in art form as faithfully as possible," he explained, going into depth about the artistic differences.

His pet listened attentively, engrossed in his words, and his chest exploded with pride.

They moved slowly, stopping at every statue and admiring the mastery with which it had been sculpted while Michele explained the historic context that led to certain details.

As they left the hall, his pet was hanging onto every word he said, regarding him with such awe and reverence his ego soared.

"What is your assignment, pet?" He asked as they returned to the ancient temple she'd been studying before.

The Egyptian temple had been built around 10 B.C. during the Roman Period.

"I need to sketch this, but I can't seem to manage to do it right," she sighed. "I'm not very good at drawing," she admitted with a desolate expression on her face.

"Let me see what you've got." He extended his hand to receive her notebook, his brows shooting up in surprise as he took in her design.

While technically abysmal, she'd captured the meaning perfectly.

From base to top, she'd depicted the Egyptian landscape as perceived from the bas-relief, starting from sea and vegetation and ending with the sky and its constellations, including their divine counterparts.

"I don't think you need any help, pet," he told her.

She frowned at him, looking from her drawing to the actual construction and pointing out the obvious differences.

"I doubt your teacher wanted you to depict it faithfully. I can help you with that," he paused as she wrinkled her nose in confusion. "But what you did here is far better than I could add," he admitted, for the first time proud of something that wasn't his *own* achievement. Because his pet had observed that which was not visible to the naked eye. She'd taken the time to study it in so much depth she'd actually deciphered the meaning behind it.

"Really?" She fluttered her lashes, obviously flattered at his words.

"Why did you focus on the bas-relief and not the structure?"

Usually, with a task like this, one would go the easy route and copy the structure of the building, maybe adding minimal shading to turn it into a three dimensional object. But she'd focused her efforts on meaning *not* functionality.

She shrugged, almost embarrassed. But with a little coaxing, she finally opened up.

"Ancient Egyptians put meaning to everything. A temple wasn't *just* a building. It was the culmination of their beliefs and how they saw the world around them. I can't draw the building, but I can doodle some of the shapes that make out the temple."

He looked at her—truly looked at her.

"You're right," he nodded.

He kept to himself the fact that she had impressed him with her short yet insightful analysis. For the first time, he was faced with a conundrum.

His pet might not be as simple as he thought.

"Your teacher will appreciate your interpretation more than if you sketched the temple perfectly."

"I'm glad you think so." She smiled to herself.

"Let's move, then, shall we?" he steered her towards the second floor, to the European Art exhibit.

A foreign feeling tugged at his chest as he sneaked a glance to her. Keeping up with his long strides, she wore her heart on her sleeve as she marveled at every little thing they came across.

Inexplicably, he felt drawn to the innocence he found in her gaze—the fact that she could find so much enjoyment in the world around her.

When was the last time he'd felt like that—had he ever?

He'd always enjoyed art, always striven to learn more about it and advance his knowledge. But had he ever reveled in it? Had he let himself go and just enjoyed its existence?

His pet reacted to every novel thing as if it was the most astounding thing she'd ever seen.

Her facial expressions were addictive. Everything about her consumed him on a level he wasn't sure he understood.

And as he realized that there might be more to her—more

depths he had yet not explored—he felt his heart swell in his chest, a foreign anticipation building inside of him.

For as long as he could remember, revenge had been foremost in his mind.

First against his family, then for the untimely death of his real sire and everyone he'd cared about—all in preparation for the final showdown. Since then, he'd never stopped to live, even for a moment.

Yet her unguarded expressions and her intoxicating happiness were drawing him out of the bubble he'd locked himself in.

In his single mindedness, he'd isolated himself from the world, content to watch from afar as it burned.

But there she was.

Unexpected.

Unwelcome.

Uninvited.

He still wanted to watch the world burn. But a small voice inside his head wanted her to join him—take her seat beside him as they reveled in the flames that engulfed every wretched being that had ever stood in his way.

But that was the dilemma. That was the source of his frustration and the cause of his recent unhappiness.

She *was* part of that wretched whole.

She was nothing but a means to an end.

Then what was he doing here?

"Can you take a picture of me?" Her voice startled him from his thoughts. He blinked, focusing on her figure.

She had a shaky smile on her face as she waited for his answer. Her hand extended towards him, she held her phone for him to use.

He disregarded it, however, taking his own phone out to snap a picture.

"Go on," he drawled, waiting for her to get into position.

In the middle of the gallery, she twirled around, choosing a painting at the far end and darting towards it before signaling him to take the photo. He aligned the phone and captured a few photos of her, belatedly realizing how fitting her choice had been.

"Done?" She asked cheerfully, running to him to check the picture. "Oh, I like this," she said as she scrolled through the pictures he'd taken. "And this," she marked the ones she liked, asking him to send them to her.

Michele dazedly agreed.

"Let's take one together," she suggested, and before he could give his assent, she grabbed the phone from his hands, asking a passerby to snap a picture of them.

With a boldness uncharacteristic of her, she grabbed his arm, pulling him next to the painting to pose with her.

Ready to tell her off, he looked down at her. But as he opened his mouth, the words would not come. Not when she sported the most ethereal look on her face.

Beautiful.

The thought came unbidden in his mind, and he could only stare at the mass of mahogany curls that flowed down her back, her porcelain skin and the most beautiful pair of eyes he'd ever seen in his life. And as her lips widened into a radiant smile, he found that his own followed suit.

Madness.

There was no other explanation for what was happening. He thirsted like he'd never know thirst before—but he didn't know for what.

He was caught in a web of confusion unlike he'd ever experienced, and as she took the phone back to show him the pictures, he had to begrudgingly agree that he looked entranced.

In every single photo, he gazed upon her like she was a blessed oasis and him a parched desert traveler.

Shaking himself from his reverie, he clenched his fists in annoyance.

How was it that this little slip of a woman could make him forget himself?

"I sent them to myself," she declared proudly as she flipped through the pictures.

"Why?" he asked, his voice rough and almost unrecognizable.

"Hm?" her brows went up in question.

"Why this painting?" He cleared his throat as he signaled to the painting in front of them.

Clouds of smoke and rivulets of magma drew the eye to the center of the canvas, the picture depicting an eruption of Mount Vesuvius—a vision of the world burning just as he'd imagined.

She tilted her head to the side, deep in thought. Her eyes on the painting, she mulled over his question thoughtfully before giving him her answer.

"Because that's how you make me feel," she told him, vulnerability meeting stark sincerity in her tone.

"That's how I make you feel?" he repeated, shocked by her answer. Of all the things she could have told him, this was the last he would have guessed. "How so?" he inquired, his blood pounding, his thirst increasing.

"Like I could combust at any moment," she confessed, her eyes clear and sincere. "Like you could *end* me at any moment," she continued in a whisper.

He swallowed hard, his throat dry. He *could* end her any moment. Unwittingly, through her words, she was feeding him water on an arid day.

He didn't reply, lazily swinging his gaze to the painting and pointing towards the small dots right on the edge of the volcano.

"That's us," he told her. "Watching the world *end.*"

It wasn't a denial, but it wasn't a confirmation either. Because he might end her—no, he *would* end her.

Eventually.

They stood together in front of the apocalyptic painting, admiring the work of the artist, but more than anything admiring the *end*. Two lonesome figures watching the flames engulf the world.

Their joint breathing was the only sound that permeated the air, swirling around and engulfing them in an intimate cocoon.

Inhale. Exhale.

Cheeks flushed, heart pounding, she kept herself still by his side. Yet, inching closer, she brought one finger against his own, a touch that should have revolted him.

It didn't.

Her small pinky grasped on to his much bigger one in a tender gesture.

Unmoving, their hands linked, they stood together.

He immersed himself in the moment, committing the artwork to memory just as he was committing her—her appearance, her moves, her *innocence*.

Carefully, he was storing every bit of information in his brain—details that went beyond a mere picture in front of an explosive volcano.

But ultimately, he couldn't help the ironic grin that spread across his lips. She didn't understand—couldn't understand. She'd chosen the epitome of destruction, and she'd situated herself right in its path of ruin.

She hadn't just chosen a grim picture. She'd chosen her own fate.

The end *was* coming.

Chapter Thirty-Five
Michele

"You're rather quiet today," he told her as the waiter brought the wine, filling his glass.

"School's been busy." She gave him a tight smile.

He knew she was about to graduate soon, and that meant his time was also running out. But he thrust the thought from his mind. It was neither the time nor the place to think about that.

He'd taken her to one of his favorite Italian restaurants in the area where he always had a semi-private table booked.

It was the first time he'd done so, but he found himself in a magnanimous mood that day. Spending time at the museum always made his spirits rise.

"You'll soon be done, right?"

She nodded, picking at her food. At least she wasn't eating with the wrong fork—again. He was thankful their position avoided them too much attention.

"What are your plans after?" He attempted to make pleasant conversation.

"I haven't decided yet. I was accepted to a few colleges, but I'm still undecided."

"You don't have anything you like?"

She shrugged.

"I like a little bit of everything. But not everything likes me back."

He blinked. Then he burst out into laughter.

"I didn't realize you had a hidden humorous side to you, pet," he chuckled.

"It's the truth," she muttered as she brought her chin down.

"Nonsense. I can tell you something you're very good at." His lips pulled into a dangerous smile.

She fluttered her lashes as she looked at him in confusion before awareness sunk in.

Two fingers up, he waved her towards him.

"Now?" Biting her lip, she looked around, worried someone might see her. "I'm not sure…" she mumbled.

"Come," his voice was rougher, more tense. "I want you to sit on my cock, pet," he told her as he leaned back, his eyes hooded as he waited for her next move.

"But…"

"Now," he commanded.

Like the good pet she was, she rose from her seat and came to his side.

Her lip between her teeth, she assessed him quietly for a second before she seated herself on his lap. The skirt of her dress was long, but she managed to arrange it on either side of him. He could feel her warmth through his pants, but he didn't move a muscle. He waited for her to do everything —*wanted* her to do everything.

Legs forward, she brought her hands to her ass as she slowly shimmied her underwear down her legs, letting them drop under the table.

Then she paused.

"What are you waiting for?" He asked, his breath on her nape as he moved his mouth alongside the delicious curve of her neck.

She smelled delectably—a mix of jasmine and sandalwood. Fresh with hint of floral and so thoroughly *her*, the scent made him lose his mind, his cock hardening in his pants.

"I want you to warm my cock while we eat, pet," he whispered in her ear. "Because that's something you're *very* good at," he murmured in a charming voice, and soon her inhibitions melted.

She gave a brisk nod as her small hands reached back to unzip his pants, cupping inside and taking his dick out. Flushed and breathing hard, she fumbled around as she raised her ass, positioning the tip of his cock at her entrance and lowering herself on it.

His eyes snapped closed. Groaning, he felt her wet channel engulf him, and she *was* wet—a surprise.

Wiggling on his cock until he was all the way inside her, she gasped. Her pouty lips parted, and a moan escaped her as she sought some relief against him.

"Don't," he warned. "Don't move," his front met her back as his arm snaked around her waist, holding her in place. "You're not fucking yourself on my cock, pet. You're just warming it. Understand?" He asked in a biting tone.

Her muscles were tense, but she nodded.

He liked her like this—squirming and uncomfortable. He knew she wanted to move. She wanted him to both fuck her and let her go.

Even now, while she enjoyed the feel of him inside her, mortification burned at her cheeks as she peered around.

But the world was oblivious to what was happening. To everyone else they were just a doting couple unable to keep their hands off each other, not at all a depraved spectacle waiting to be unleashed.

Soon, the server came around to bring them the main courses. True to his training, he didn't bat an eye at the change in positions.

His pet kept her head down, embarrassed to be seen like that.

A plate was placed in front of them and he brought his hands around her, cutting into the steak and bringing a piece to her lips. He watched her closely, his intuition telling him something was wrong with her.

With trembling lips, she parted her mouth to take the piece of meat inside, chewing slowly, and swallowing even slower.

The next piece he brought to his own lips, giving her a small reprieve.

He kept alternating, one bite for her, one for him, all the while studying her and her reactions.

Every time she took a mouthful of steak, her walls clenched around him tighter. While he wasn't moving inside her, he could feel every contraction and every slight pulsation in her womb. In a manner of speaking, he felt closer to her like this than he'd ever had.

"You don't like it?" He asked after a while, noticing how hard it was for her to swallow.

After every bite, she took a sip of water, almost as if the meat got stuck in her throat and she needed to chase it down with some liquid.

"I do," she answered softly, tucking a strand of hair behind her ear as she gave him a bashful smile.

Momentarily struck by the beauty of her profile, he felt his cock twitch, small spasms at the tip and moving down his shaft to his balls. He knew he wouldn't last much longer, and the thought of filling her with his cum—sending her home with his cum dripping from her cunt—had never appealed more.

"What's wrong, pet? Why aren't you eating properly then?" he eventually asked, unable to believe the fact that he cared about her *that* way. Still, it unnerved him that she was suffering—or something akin to suffering—in silence. She was his, and as such it was his task to deal with everything that happened to her, good or bad.

He heard her swallow hard before taking a deep breath of air.

"Speak," he said more forcefully. Based on her body language, he *knew* there was something wrong with her.

"I think I'm pregnant," she said, the words low and full of trepidation.

"What?" He asked again, afraid he hadn't heard her right.

"I… I think I'm pregnant," she reiterated, turning slightly to gauge his reaction.

"And why would you think that?" He raised a brow.

"My period hasn't come in a couple of months and…" She gulped down. "I've been feeling very tired and nauseous…" she trailed off when she heard him swear under his breath.

The moment the news sunk in, however, his cock jerked inside her, cum shooting from the tip and into her already fertilized womb.

"Motherfucker," he groaned, his arms coming around her and squeezing her tight as he breathed through his climax.

"M—Michele?" She asked in a worried whisper.

Positioning his hands on her ass, he moved her slightly, the added friction delicious as his cock spasmed inside her to completion.

"We can't be sure until you take a test," he told her on a ragged breath. "Then I'm taking you for a consultation," he added grimly as he got his bearings together.

He knew he needed to plan thoroughly in case she *was* in fact pregnant.

He'd never taken precautions with her—had never wanted to. Deep down, he'd known about this potential outcome, but he'd pushed it down and hoped for the best. Knowing he'd been her first, and with a clean history himself, he hadn't wanted anything between them. More than anything, he couldn't imagine sinking into her sweet pussy with a barrier separating him from *feeling* her.

But now, he was forced to reexamine his plans.

He could have forced her to take birth control. He could have done *anything* to ensure there would be no consequences. But he hadn't.

As he looked into the terrified face of his pet, there was a side of him—one that needed to be squashed down—that wanted to take her in his arms and tell her everything would be ok. In an alternate dimension, he saw himself rejoicing at the news, leaning down to kiss her lids as he whispered sweet words in her ears.

Nevertheless, *this* was the reality he found himself in—the grim, bleak one he'd been forced into.

And so he told her the only thing he could bring himself to.

"Go clean yourself."

An hour later, back at his penthouse, he was leaning back against the cold bathroom wall, watching his pet fumble with the pregnancy test in her hands.

"Faster," he barked the command, rolling his eyes at her.

He had a few more hours until she was due back at her house. And in that time, he intended to ascertain if she was or not pregnant. Because if she was... He needed to plan accordingly.

"Can you..." she stammered, looking between him and the toilet, "wait outside?"

"There's nothing I haven't seen, pet. Go on, I'm waiting," he told her flippantly, staring at her through narrowed eyes.

Nearly overcome with shyness, she was slow in getting the test out of its box before taking a seat on the toilet.

Her head down, she fumbled with her dress as she stuck the stick between her legs. Soon, he could hear her peeing on it.

"Done," she told him after she flushed and washed her hands, placing the test on the sink to wait for the allocated time.

"Good," he nodded at her, waiting.

"What will we do if I am pregnant?" She asked as she bit on her lip.

He wanted to tell her there was no *we*, but he refrained. He would see to that later. His pet, though, had other plans as she went on.

"We can get married before my family finds out, and I'm sure there won't be any issue. I know they frown upon unmarried women having children, but…"

"Is that what you think?" He snapped, his eyes coldly assessing her. "That I'll marry you?"

She blinked, shocked by his sudden outburst.

"Well, yes," she said in a shaky voice. "We love each other, don't we," she added in an unsure tone, her gaze skittering from him to the test.

"We do," he tried to dial down on his anger. "But you know I'm not the marrying type, pet," he told her in a gentler tone.

"But," she started, only to stop as the timer went off on her phone.

The time to find out the verdict had come.

With hesitant movements, she picked the test up, sliding the plastic down to look at the result.

"Well?" He tapped his foot impatiently, waiting her answer.

But her expression should have told him everything.

She went white, her pallor changing before his eyes.

"Pregnant," she whispered.

"Fuck," he cursed, bringing a hand to his forehead to massage his temples.

"We can't know for sure, though, right? These things aren't one hundred percent reliable," she tried to comfort him.

"Don't move," he told her as he whipped out his phone, dialing one of his contacts.

He spoke fast, a barrage of orders coming out of his mouth as he made call after call until he managed to find what he was looking for.

"Put your jacket on," he spared her a glance. "We're going for a consultation."

He didn't tell her, though, that he'd managed to secure a consult in a seedy part of Brooklyn, since if she *was* pregnant, he wouldn't miss taking care of the issue on the spot.

Michele could never let a child born to him to exist. *Never.* That would open a can of worms he didn't think he could ever deal with—not with how unstable he already was. He was on the precipice. He knew it. As such, he had to tread carefully. Before he screwed everything up. Before he let years of planning go to waste...

His expression grim, he drove them to the underground cabinet, where a *female* doctor would see his pet. He might have nefarious intentions, but he wasn't about to allow another male to defile his property—not while she was still *his.*

"I'm sure it will be fine, right?" his pet asked as he led her towards the decrepit building that housed a state-of-the-art clinic.

"Of course," he lied. "We will take care of it."

Dr. Ryan worked at one of his private hospitals and she answered directly to him. He knew she would deal with everything efficiently and without much fuss.

They walked inside, passing by a few offices as they headed to the basement.

"This isn't a normal hospital, is it?" she asked, moving closer to him as her hand went to his arm, holding for support.

"No. But it is secure," he told her in a bored tone.

Since he'd heard the news that she might be pregnant, something had shifted inside of him. His reactions were erratic and he couldn't trust himself anymore.

At random moments, he found himself pleasantly surprised by the news as he conjured scenarios of his pet with a baby in her arms. The image, he found, wasn't as horrible as he would have thought. In fact, one might say it even made him warm…

But there was also his default setting, and he saw the situation for what it truly was—a disaster. And he couldn't allow it to continue.

Knocking on the door of the cabinet, he ushered his pet inside.

Relatively clean compared to the rest of the building, the cabinet was fully equipped to deal with every issue.

"This is Dr. Ryan." He waved towards the middle aged woman currently assessing his pet curiously.

"Pleased to meet you," his pet extended a hand.

"How old is she?" the woman asked in a harsh tone.

"Eighteen," she answered, her voice tentative as she took in the woman's unyielding features.

Dr. Ryan grunted, instructing his pet to change into a medical gown before lying on the bed. Dragging a heavy machine towards her, she uncovered her smooth stomach, layering it with some type of gel.

She didn't look pregnant. She looked just as slim as she always did, and he was intimately acquainted with every inch of her body.

Maybe it *was* a false positive and he wouldn't have to do anything.

That's what he convinced himself as his pet beckoned him closer, taking his hand in hers and giving him a small smile— one that hit him straight to the chest, nonetheless.

She was beautiful. She'd always been beautiful, but today, in *that* moment, he found her most beautiful. He didn't know what it was about her *now* that made him regard her so. And for a moment, his gaze on hers, hers on his, time stood still. He could see every small mark on her face, the defining mole on the tip of her nose, the flecks of green in her brown eyes.

"It will be ok," he found himself saying in an effort to comfort her.

She nodded, her spirits lifted by his words, and suddenly, she brought his hand to her mouth, laying a kiss to his knuckles.

Michele went still, shock coursing through his veins at the action. It was just one peck, but there was so much gentleness and emotion in that action that he felt himself reeling. He felt his *entire* world shift.

"I love you," she told him, the adoration in her eyes reaching new heights as she placed all her trust in him, her words of affirmation more potent than ever.

Whereas before he'd been satisfied at hearing the word love from her mouth, now it was different. He *felt* it. Which in itself was wrong, since he never felt.

"I love you too," he returned the words, and her smile grew bigger under his eyes. Belatedly, he realized the lie didn't burn on his tongue any longer. It didn't...

"Let's see what we have," Dr. Ryan interrupted, bringing

the machine to his pet's side and gliding a stick on her stomach.

A few seconds passed before an image appeared on the monitor.

And a heartbeat.

His eyes widened.

His pet was shocked.

"Yes, we have a heartbeat. And judging by the size," the Dr. went on, pointing to various things on the screen, "I'd say she is about ten weeks pregnant. You'll soon start showing," she told his pet.

His pet barely nodded, her eyes glued to the screen and the tiny dot on it.

Their baby.

He couldn't believe it. He looked and looked, yet he couldn't help the shudder that went down his body.

Unable to deal, he disentangled himself from her as he lit a cigarette, his foot tapping against the floor in anxious impatience. Taking a deep drag, he felt the initial burn down his throat, the specific lightheadedness as his entire body went numb. Still, he couldn't shake the foreign feeling that overcame him.

"It's our baby, Michele," she told him gently, and as he swung his gaze to her, it was to find a wholly different expression on her face than he'd ever expected—than he'd ever seen. There were tears at the corners of her eyes—not of sorrow, but of happiness.

The more she looked at the screen, the more her face changed under his eyes. A happiness he hadn't known her capable of suffused her features. A *love* he hadn't dared hope for was evident in her visage.

And he didn't know how to deal.

He tapped his foot with increased urgency as he

continued to smoke his cigarette, his mind working around different scenarios and finding he did not like any.

"I can't believe this. We're going to be parents..." she breathed in awe.

They weren't going to be anything. *She* wasn't going to be anything.

He couldn't allow it—now more than ever.

The thought of *that* child—of *his* child—coming into this vile world terrified him. He would be defenseless against the dangers out there, and if Michele couldn't protect him—protect them—then...

The possibilities were endless. And in that split second he saw it all. He saw the potential happiness. But he also saw the never-ending anguish. The pain that would truly end him.

He couldn't trust his mind anymore. Not when it was going into overdrive with all the things he wanted to do. He had brief moments when he saw the walls of the cabinet painted red, blood dripping from the ceiling as he pulled that little creature from her womb with his own two hands.

His body was shaking, his head pounding.

"Get rid of it," he ordered flippantly, his eyes on Dr. Ryan.

Always the professional, she just nodded.

"Get... rid..." his pet repeated, pulling herself in a sitting position and grabbing at his sleeves. "What do you mean?" She asked in such a soft voice, he almost didn't hear her.

"You can't be pregnant, pet," he turned to her, regarding her with a blank expression. "You're going to get that little shit out of your body and we can continue as we were."

She shook her head, her eyes wide with horror.

"No," the word escaped her lips as she scrambled back. "You can't do this. It's our child, Michele. Our baby," she kept on blabbering, but it didn't have any effect on him. Not when he shut himself so thoroughly, any humanity he might have possessed locked so tightly away, he could barely recognize his own self.

"So?" He raised a brow. "I don't need a child. You don't need one either, pet," he tried to reason with her. "You're eighteen. What are you going to do with a child? I sure as fuck am not marrying you, so you'll have everyone shame you for being an unwed mother, just like you said," he continued.

She flinched, looking as if he'd just slapped her.

In the meantime, Dr. Ryan was sitting by the sidelines, watching the interaction unfold.

"Please don't do this," his pet whispered, getting off the table with hurried movements and tripping in the process.

To her knees, she dragged herself to his feet, her hands going to his shirt.

"Please don't do this," she repeated, tears coursing down her face.

He looked at her and found himself split in two. There was the unfeeling side of him that couldn't care less about the display, but there was also another side of him. One that he didn't want to dwell on because it made his chest hurt. The unfeeling one won as he slapped her hands aside.

Falling on her ass, she looked numbly at him.

"He's going, pet. End of discussion," he said, shrugging and keeping on his mask of indifference.

"No," she shook her head. "You can't do this, Michele. It's *our* child," she cried out.

"So you want it?" he asked skeptically.

She immediately nodded.

"You want to have a child that even his father won't recognize? You want to be called a whore by everyone around because you were dumb enough to let someone come inside you without protection? Is that what you want, pet?" His voice was stable as he set his icy glare on her.

411

She froze at his questions, slowly raising her head to look at him.

"Is that… Is that what you think of me?" she whispered, her voice soft and hopeless.

He nodded dispassionately.

"And it's what everyone will think too. You think they won't badmouth you? Talk about what a slut you are? The world isn't a kind place, pet."

"We can… We can get married. Then no one would talk, right?" she asked the question, though she knew the answer.

"You know I won't marry you," he told her.

"But you love me," she said numbly.

"Not enough to marry you, pet," his voice was cold, his words cruel. "I just love to fuck you," he told her squarely. "But you're not good for that either, are you? You had to get pregnant and ruin everything."

"Ruin everything?" She frowned, confused.

"We can still go back to how we were. You just need to get rid of that shit inside of you, you get me?"

She blinked, her eyes on him.

One second. Two seconds.

"I see," she finally said.

A smile probed at his lips. He knew his pet would see reason.

"Good. Dr. Ryan can perform the procedure right away and then you can go home. Just like nothing happened."

"Just like nothing happened," she nodded like a broken machine.

His brows pinched in concentration as he studied her. Something wasn't quite right, but he couldn't understand what.

"You can proceed," he told Dr. Ryan as he leaned back against the wall and popped another cigarette in his mouth.

"I don't want you here," his pet said in an icy voice, slowly turning to him. "You've made your choice. At least let me bear this in peace."

Surprise enveloped him at her tone. She'd never spoken to him like that before.

But just as he was about to reply, Dr. Ryan interjected.

"You should wait outside," she pursed her lips. "We need a sterile environment, and you're clearly *not* helping," she told him as she practically ushered out of the room.

CHAPTER THIRTY-SIX
MICHELE

On his way out, he didn't dare look at his pet again. She didn't attempt to look back either. He simply exited the room and waited for the procedure to be done.

Alone in the darkened corridor, his mind was still reeling from what he'd seen and heard. He could tell he was softening, his conviction swaying—even if it was for a minuscule fraction.

He recognized the part of himself he'd long buried trying to claw its way back to the surface—trying to tell him he was doing this all wrong.

That tiny voice he'd long thought extinguished whispered things, dangerous, dangerous things.

Give up your revenge for her.

Treat her like the treasure she is.

Keep her...

Michele's hands were balled into fists as he squeezed his eyes shut, breathing harshly as he focused on the past—on everything that had made him the person he was today.

This wasn't just *his* revenge. This was for everyone who'd been taken from him, those whose deaths, just like their previous existences, were imprinted on his very soul—or what was left of it.

To give everything up would be to make a mockery of everything he'd held dear.

No, he couldn't do that. He could never allow himself to be swayed.

Fishing his phone out of his pocket, he called his house staff, instructing them to prepare something that was bound to give him the desired effect. Something that would cut his ties to his pet forever.

An hour went by, and then two. When his pet was finally led out of the room in a wheelchair, he felt a heaviness settle in his chest like never before.

It was done.

Dr. Ryan came out with her, handing him a small medicine pouch.

"She needs to take antibiotics to prevent an infection."

He nodded, sparing his pet a glance and feeling his ribcage tighten with an elusive emotion. Fear? Anticipation? He couldn't tell.

Addressing the doctor, he exchanged a few words with her, making his voice purposefully loud so his pet would hear his words, priming her for what was to come.

He emphasized the term *evidence*, sneaking a glance at her from the corner of his eye. Yet she didn't react. She never did. She was merely staring blankly in front of her.

And as he led her to the car, he was truly surprised at the deafening silence. She wasn't talking—barely even breathing.

"How are you feeling, pet?" he asked as he helped her in the passenger seat.

She shrugged, her eyes set forward. She wasn't looking at him.

"We have one more hour before you're due at home. Let's

get you some food," he told her in an affectionate tone, hoping it would snap her out of her stupor.

She nodded. Yet she didn't say anything more.

For the entire duration of the journey to his place, she didn't look at him. She didn't talk to him. She just ignored him.

He felt his ire mounting, and it exploded when he tried to help her to the elevator, only to have her flinch at his touch.

"What the hell is wrong with you?" he snapped, glaring at her.

She barely moved. But slowly, she raised her chin, gazing at him for the first time since he'd left her in that consultation room.

There was no trace of warmth on her face.

Nothing.

It was like his pet was no longer—no longer his.

The more he stared at her, the more he saw the differences. Her face was sallow. Her eyes, which usually glowed with happiness and the power of her worship, were now bleak.

Bleak.

"Nothing," she replied, her voice devoid of any feeling.

She looked at him as if he didn't exist. As if he was *nothing* to her.

"It was for the best, pet," he told her, for her benefit or his own, he wasn't sure. "You love me, don't you?" he felt compelled to ask—needed to hear her say the words.

He yearned for those three words more than anything in the world, and for a brief second as she paused at his question, he felt his heart in his throat as he waited.

"Of course I love you," she murmured, yet the words were mechanical—nothing like they'd once been. "But I hate you more," she raised her eyes to his. Her gaze was unflinching, and for the first time, he truly saw it.

The hate eclipsed the love.

He'd done that. He'd killed it. He'd finally killed her love.

Sick laughter bubbled inside his throat at the realization, and as he put a hand around his midriff, he started laughing mechanically—maniacally.

Even as the doors to his penthouse opened, he could not stop laughing.

He laughed until his belly hurt and his heart ached.

He'd done it. He'd fucking done that with his own hands.

And he didn't know whether to be mad or proud.

Taking a step inside his house, he was struck by something extraordinary. The world wasn't just bleak—it was colorless.

He blinked, looking around from side to side. Yet he couldn't see color. He couldn't see anything but black and white, with shades of gray nestled in between.

His gaze found her, and right before his eyes, he could see her colors shifting. Her hair wasn't a lively mahogany color anymore, slowly losing all its luster as it became gray and tepid. Color was trickling out of her face, and even the eyes he'd once thought the most beautiful in the world were now a muddy nondescript color.

He froze.

What the fuck was happening?

He was going crazy. The thought briefly crossed his mind. But it wasn't *him* that was losing it. It couldn't be him.

It was her.

Her with her icy stare and colorless countenance. Her with the lack of smiles and twinkling eyes. Her with the words of hate instead of love.

At that moment, he hated her too. He hated her more than anything in the world.

Because she was shutting him out when he wanted

nothing else but take her in his arms and hear her eternal avowals of love.

Yet she wasn't giving him any. She was quietly sitting by the side, staring into empty space as if he wasn't there. As if he didn't exist, or he wasn't worthy of her notice.

By God, he hated her.

He hated her but he wanted her.

He hated that she was depriving him of her smiles. He hated that she was ignoring him. But most of all, he hated the extinguished light in her eyes. She no longer looked at him like he could give her the sun and the moon. There was no more worship to be found in her eyes.

None.

And for that, he wanted to hurt her.

Something insidious took shape inside of him. A demon that would not be satisfied until it tasted blood.

Blood and tears.

"Let's go," he told her, his expression tight. And as he led her to the dining room, motioning her to take a seat, he could do nothing else but observe her.

His pet was gone.

In one last attempt to salvage things, he uttered a challenge.

"I'll marry you," he told her, watching her closely. He expected to see her joy. Her light returning to her features at knowing that *now* he would have her. He wanted to see her *adoration* again.

He wanted her love, not her hate.

Yet the realization came too late.

For the first time in his life, Michele admitted to himself that he'd been wrong.

He'd pushed and pushed, but it wasn't her who'd fallen. It was *him.*

Her lashes fluttered, but it wasn't in her usual lovable way. She merely shrugged.

"If you want," she said, her gaze snapping back to the table as she proceeded to ignore him again.

His fists clenched, he studied her and could not believe this was the same person who'd been ready to die for him. Where was that loyalty? Where was that love?

If she could shrug it off so easily, then it must have never existed in the first place.

The more he dwelled on the issue, the angrier he became, a need to hurt her eating at him. He wanted to make her bleed as much as he was.

Maybe his wounds were not visible, but he could feel the blood trickling on the inside. He could feel the ache deep within him, and for that, she needed to pay.

They stood in silence, her ignoring him, and him seething quietly at her.

A while later, one of his men came with a tray, placing a lidded plate in front of her, and one in front of him.

He could have dropped his plan—that monstrous *show* he'd concocted. He already had her where he wanted, didn't he? He had her hate, the *ultimate* indifference.

But *that* was the problem.

She might be gone, but he wasn't. No, he was still there, his weakness glaring in the open for everyone to see—for everyone to take advantage of.

That emotion he'd purposefully instilled in her bothered him on an atomic level. As self-awareness crept in, he realized something—something that made him push through with his plan and become the ultimate bastard in her eyes.

She wasn't the problem.

He was.

He hated her hate. Just as he felt something else for her. Something…

"Eat, pet. Then I'll take you home," he gritted his teeth, wanting to see her gone, but wanting to see her stay at the same time.

Taking the lid off her plate, she wrinkled her nose as she assessed the contents.

"What is it?" She asked, swirling the spoon around the liquid.

"It's a coveted delicacy, or so I'm told," he gave her one of his dazzling smiles.

He wanted to see her squirm and hurt. He *needed* her to suffer, for she deserved nothing less for making him feel this way—for touching that one part of himself he'd thought untouchable. And he deserved nothing more for failing at his revenge as he had.

Frowning, she brought the spoon to her lips, taking a sip.

He watched intently, his eyes boring into her.

"How is it?" he inquired.

"Good," she shrugged. He knew she wasn't fussy about food, eating everything and anything. But this was different. It wasn't for her to enjoy.

With a strained smile, he added, "Is that so?"

"What is…" She was about to repeat her question, but the words died on her lips as she took a closer look at her plate.

Her eyes widened. Her mouth parted in horror.

Lifting her spoon, she fished a small, barely developed leg out of the soup, regarding it for a second before flinging the utensil aside.

"Tell me it's not," she whispered, her features pained.

"Oh, but it is. I wanted you to still have it, pet. See, I only think about your wellbeing," he drawled, leaning back and watching the spectacle.

Even for him this was extreme, and he couldn't help the distaste that assailed him. But he masked it with amused indifference.

Her hands trembled as she pushed her chair back, stumbling to the ground.

Tears on her face, she finally turned to him.

"How could you?" she asked in a small voice.

He felt a pang in his heart. But it wasn't enough to stop it. Everything had been set in motion, and he knew this was the last time he'd ever enjoy his pet.

"How could I?" he repeated the question as he got to his feet, towering over her and regarding her with a mocking smile. "Simple, pet," he said as his fingers wrapped around her throat, bringing her into him until their lips were mere inches apart, their breaths mingling. Hers labored from fear, his excited from *her* fear. "You hate me already, so what's another push? Detest me. *Abhor* me," he ordered, his voice biting.

"You're a monster," she uttered the words, ending him forever.

"Monster," he laughed. "Yes. I'm a monster. I've always been a monster," he sneered at her. "Good on you to finally notice."

"Let go of me," she whimpered.

"Why? What's wrong, pet? Until a few hours ago you loved my hands on you. You loved my cock inside of you."

She shook her head, her lips trembling as she sought to get away from her.

"I can't do this," she whispered. "I hate you. I hate you. I *hate* you," she uttered continuously, not even deigning to look him in the eye.

The words burned him, and without even realizing, he flung her away from him.

"Get the fuck out," he bit out. "Get out and don't let me ever see you again!"

She raised her head to look at him. Her face was pale, her

eyes lost. He thought he spotted a glimmer of something before harshness took over her features.

Getting to her feet, she smoothed down her skirt with quiet dignity before straightening her back in a gesture of rebellion. And giving him one last look, she was gone.

At that moment, his pet ceased to be *his*.

––––––

HE WAS NEVER DRUNK.

From the first time he'd imbibed alcohol, Michele had known his limit and he'd never crossed it. After all, his worst nightmare was not having any control over his body.

Yet what was he doing now?

Staring at the blinding city lights, his mind was slipping from him, his control waning.

One glance to the side revealed an almost empty bottle of whiskey and two empty packs of cigarettes.

Still, he opened the third, popping one into his mouth and waiting for the deadly combo of nicotine and alcohol to kick in.

Numb.

He wanted to be numb.

Yet no matter how much shit he poured into his body, nothing helped.

"You called, sir?" Andreas spoke from behind him.

Slowly, he advanced until he reached his side, gazing down at him with worry in his eyes.

If only…

But she was gone. His pet was gone.

He knew it was for the best. He'd finally severed the only ties that were holding him back, and he was about to reap the benefits from that.

"Is it done?" he slurred his words as he blinked some clarity in his eyes.

"It is. It's already on the news."

"Play it for me," he motioned lazily towards the huge TV hanging on the wall.

"As you wish, sir," Andreas nodded, grabbing the remote control and turning the TV to the local news station.

"The head of one of the most influential New York families was arrested today at noon on sexual assault charges. Marcello Lastra, formerly known as Marcel Lester, was a close colleague of the D.A. and worked as a public attorney for over ten years. The entire legal community is aghast at the charges brought against him. Though he has refused to comment on the issue, sources say that the police received incriminating video material from over a decade ago that depicts Mr. Lastra as a perpetuator of rape…"

Closing his eyes, he breathed in the air of victory.

"What about the business?"

"Three of his shell companies have already been hit. The other two are scrambling. Their assets should diminish slowly until they will be in the red. Until they will owe you everything."

"Good," he nodded, stumbling to his alcohol cabinet and grabbing another bottle.

His sire had been a conniving bastard, and he'd kept incriminating material on *everyone* in his circle. It hadn't been hard to find out what he had on Lastra, more so considering it was a brutal rape perpetuated against his own wife.

Laughter bubbled in Michele's throat at the irony. He wondered how his wife could have stayed with someone like that.

But it wasn't his business.

On all accounts, his job was almost done.

"What about the other bit?"

"The video is circulating on the internet as we speak. Already, people have identified her and shared it further. There are a lot of malicious comments though..."

"You can go," Michele burst out, not wanting to hear more.

"Of course," Andreas nodded.

And as he got out, Michele slumped on his couch, bottle in one hand, remote control in the other as he played the video.

She was on her knees, her head bobbing back and forth as she choked on his cock until tears stabbed at the corner of her eyes.

He'd thrust the camera in her face, recording every bit of humiliation he could, knowing at some point he would have use for it.

She was still gazing at him with love back then.

And as he looked at her adoring eyes, and the way she sought to please him even in the most extreme ways, he felt his chest constrict.

His dick was painfully hard, as it always was when he looked at her. And for the first time, he took himself in hand.

Eyes set on the TV as he followed the way her lips wrapped around his cock, he attempted to replicate it with his hand. Led by the sounds of her sloppy blowjob, he spit in his hand as he gripped his length harder.

If he closed his eyes, he could almost imagine it was her.

Alas, it wasn't.

His mind knew it. His hand knew it. His fucking cock knew it, and in no time he lost his erection.

"Damn it," he cursed out loud, zipping himself back up.

It wasn't working.

Nothing was working.

And it was all her fault.

If before she'd been a social pariah, he imagined now

she'd be the butt of jokes. He'd made sure of that when he'd released all the videos he'd filmed of her on her knees, sucking him off like a trained hooker.

He wanted her to suffer, yet deep down he also wanted to save her.

Scowling, he thrust all thoughts of her out of his mind. This wasn't him—this was *nothing* like him—and he needed to remember that.

To aid his detachment, he withdrew his worn wallet, perusing the precious picture nestled within. From the beginning, he'd had a purpose—a promise to those he'd loved and lost. It was high time he remembered *why* he was doing everything.

Michele Guerra was dead—had died a long time ago. A dead man could not have feelings, wants, or needs. No, a dead man was dead and bringing only death.

Now, only vengeance steeped in blood remained.

And this was just the first step.

Marcello Lastra would remain with nothing.

No family. No money. No dignity.

Nothing.

Then the road would be clear for phase two—the *mass* destruction.

CHAPTER THIRTY-SEVEN
RAFAELO

"You've really given this a lot of thought, haven't you?" Noelle smiles.

"Of course," I reply, getting the luggage out of the car. "This was one of our favorite properties growing up. I have a lot of fond memories inside," my lips tug up as I take in the edifice.

Built in a neoclassical style but retaining some local features, the house sports three floors and nine bedrooms. Dating to the Gilded Age, the mansion is full of history and ostentatious displays. It was an extravagance my mother had insisted on even when we'd encountered financial difficulties.

"Shall we?"

She nods enthusiastically.

After the succession matter had been tended to, I'd wanted to surprise Noelle with a small getaway to Newport, at our beach house.

I'd racked my brain to compile a thorough list and give her the honeymoon she deserved—certainly *not* the one she got.

When the lawyer had handed me a list of the family's properties, I'd immediately known I wanted to take her here.

"When was the last time someone's been inside?" She asks as we creep into the house.

"I asked someone to come clean. The ground and first floors are operational, so you have nothing to worry about," I wink at her.

"Wow, this is so beautiful," she exclaims when she gets a peek of the main hall. Darting inside, she twirls in the middle, her infectious laughter echoing through the entire structure.

"Where are you going?" I chuckle as I watch how entranced she is by the house.

"Come," she grabs my hand, making me drop our luggage as she ushers me towards the day room, where the musical instruments are situated. Almost the size of a mini football field, the room is spacious, and absolutely perfect for the dancing she has in mind.

"You know," she starts, catching her breath as she pushes me towards the center of the room. "My favorite fairytale growing up was Cinderella," she mentions just as I lift her arm up, leading her into a twirl.

"Really? Why?"

"Hmm, many reasons," she smiles. "It tells the story of a regular girl who gets the prince and who wouldn't want that?"

Amused, I raise a brow at her.

"But most of all, because it's sprinkled with magic. And I think everyone, at one point or another in their lives, wished for a little magic," her words are soft but full of meaning.

"When did you wish for magic?" I ask, unable to help myself.

Her smile is tight as she continues to sway in my arms.

There's no audible music, but we're moving according to a

shared internal melody and I find the dance even more glorious because of it.

"Many times. When I was younger, I just wanted someone to notice me—to show me that they cared," she says with a melancholic expression on her face. "I thought that if I had just a little magic, I would be less ordinary and I would make them *see* me."

From what I'd gleaned from Noelle, her birth had been so unexpected, no one had cared about raising another child by that point. Even now, though her mother still lives, she ignores her, preferring to live with her circle of fancy friends than with her own daughter.

"But then, as I grew," she takes a deep breath. "I wished for magic so it wouldn't hurt anymore…" she trails off, afraid she's revealed too much.

"Pretty girl… You know you can talk to me," I tell her gently.

Though we've talked at length about our pasts, her time with Sergio has always been a sore subject, one she'd preferred not to get into details.

"The first time he beat me was on our wedding night. I was in so much pain I couldn't even move," she confesses. "After that it became a regular occurrence. If he was mad, or I happened to be around when he was in a bad mood, he'd use his fists on me."

"Noelle… Only a coward uses violence against a woman. He wasn't a man. He was a coward."

"I know," she attempts a smile. "In public he was always a gentleman beyond reproach. No one knew the animal he was in private."

"I'm sorry you had to go through that," I lean in to kiss her nose. "I promise I'll try to sprinkle some magic in your life from now on," my lips spread into a sheepish grin.

Throwing back her head, she laughs, the sound so

melodic it's making my mouth water. I can decidedly say that her happiness is my biggest turn on, my entire body vibrating in tandem with hers.

"You already have," her lips spread into a blinding smile.

Lost in her gaze, I continue to twirl her around the floor, our bodies in sync as we move to the soundless music.

"Oh, I'm sorry," a voice interrupts us, and as I look to the entrance, I see one of the staff I'd hired. "I didn't know you had already arrived, sir," an elderly woman says before going in depth about everything she and her team had done.

"On your request, we've also stocked the fridge with food and drinks, so you shouldn't want for anything. There are shops close by too, and I've left a mini guide to the area since I know it can be confusing for some."

"Thank you," I say as I lead her out, tipping her generously for her work.

"This house is absolutely dreamy, Raf," Noelle exclaims when she sees the first floor. "Can we live here?"

"I reckon we could. At least for a few months of the year."

The master bedroom is one of the highlights of the house. Spread over half the floor, it comes with a sitting room, an enclosed closet and a huge ensuite bathroom.

As soon as Noelle opens the door to the master suite, her eyes go wide at the size of the bed.

With no warning, she dashes towards it, jumping on top and giggling as the mattress bounces with her.

"You're having too much fun, aren't you?" I comment as I shrug off my blazer, rolling my sleeves and joining her.

Sprawled on the bed, her skirt is ruffled around her thighs, her top riding up ever so slightly and revealing delectable inches of flesh.

"Yupp," she answers impishly, "I can feel the freedom in the air. Freedom and happiness." She spreads her arms, tipping her head back and closing her eyes as she inhales deeply.

Though not an open invitation, I can't pass up on the opportunity, and I slip between her arms, hugging her at the waist and drawing her into my embrace.

A giggle escapes her as she pushes me on the mattress.

Tumbling together on the soft cushion, she lands on top of me, nestling closer. We sit like that for what feels like forever, lost in the contentment of the moment.

"Do you find it weird that this is where your parents used to stay?" she asks in a quiet voice.

Resting on my chest, she places her hands under her chin as she gazes at me.

"Not really. At least not in that way. There's a melancholic quality to seeing the house again, especially knowing how much it meant to my mother."

"She had good taste," she smiles as she points towards the furniture.

The interior had been decorated in a Louis fourteenth style, with gilded and ornate accessories everywhere to complement the ostentatious ceiling.

"She did," I smile fondly.

Her hand reaches out as she strokes my cheek, an affectionate look at her face.

"You're such a sweetheart, Raf," she whispers in awe, her eyes sparkling with so much love I feel my own chest swell with the feeling. "I feel incredibly lucky to be your wife," she says as she leans towards me to lay her lips on mine.

"It's me who's the lucky one, pretty girl," I cup her face with my hands, bringing her closer. "Because you forgave me when I didn't deserve it," I confess.

Though our relationship has improved considerably over time and I can feel her love in every pore of my body, I still can't find it within me to forgive *myself* for everything I've caused her—for the known and the unknown.

Maybe I should just be glad she only sees the good in me. Yet how can I, when I know the extent of what I've done?

She keeps seeing me as the good guy, and maybe in time, I'll learn to see myself through her eyes. But until then, I know the truth.

I'm a farce.

I'm nothing but a charlatan.

Michele's words ring in my head. How many times had he called me out for it? That my being branded as *good* had nothing to do with me, it was all relative to *him?*

In reality, I'm so far removed from good, it would be laughable to refer to me as such.

"It was based on a misunderstanding," she says, frowning. "How could I *not* forgive you when you've admitted your mistake and have continuously tried to correct it? When you've dedicated yourself to show me how much you care about me? How could I not, Raf, when I've never in my life felt as cherished as I do now?" There's a poignancy to her words that reaches deep within me, affecting me when little else does these days.

But isn't that the core of the issue?

She sees me through the prism of her experiences. She's only known heartache and pain, so how is she *not* to react when someone extends a hand of kindness?

But how would she react when she realizes the man she's gotten to love isn't what he seems?

The doubts continue to plague me.

It's quite ironic. Now that the danger is gone, I should rejoice at my good fortune and at this precious moment of peace. Yet I find myself unable to do that when my insides are on fire, the lies burning on my tongue even as I tell them to myself.

It had been easy to ignore that side of me until now. It had been easy to pretend.

But that one encounter with my brother has made me face my inner demons in a way nothing else could. It had put a mirror in front of me and it had ordered *look*.

And I looked.

I fucking looked, and I hated what I saw.

I'm the *good* guy. Yet how come this *good* guy succeeded in hurting both his brother and his beloved?

"Don't leave me," the words are out of my mouth before I can help it. "Don't ever leave me," I plead with an uncharacteristic urgency.

"Never," she whispers before her lips are on mine again.

At first, it's the tiniest brush—a tentative contact that makes my heart summersault in my chest. But soon, her lips gain more courage as she parts them, her tongue reaching out to mine as they embark on a slow yet sensuous dance.

My hands on her waist, I keep her to me—close to my body so she can't ever escape. But even this nearness isn't enough.

Will it ever be enough?

The kiss becomes increasingly heated, but we don't go further. We kiss and kiss until kissing is all I know.

Me. Her. Kissing.

Her lips are my solace and my escape, and I revel in the intimacy of the moment. Her presence calms me and draws me in until I'm drunk on her, her touch my imperative to live.

For the longest time, we just stay like this—lost in a never ending embrace.

And one thing is clear.

I would do *anything* to keep this. Anything to protect the love I see in her eyes. Anything to make sure she never finds out.

Because then…

I'll truly lose everything.

———

"YOU'RE SURE IT'S DONE?" I place my phone between my ear and my shoulder as I try to flip the meat in the pan.

"Everything has been filed. I'll send you pictures of documents," Carlos tells me, the sound of cars honking in the background making it hard to hear.

"Good. I'm glad we got that out of the way. It's one less stress for me," I breathe relieved.

"Does she know about it?"

"No. I haven't told her yet," I purse my lips as I speak.

Knowing how precarious Noelle's situation is within her family, I'd been liaising with a lawyer and her doctor to find ways for her to inherit everything in my name and *not* have to depend on a guardian, thereby dissolving the conservatorship Cisco had enacted over her.

For that, though, she'll have to undergo a thorough psychiatric exam and get Gianna's signature that she's good to go.

I'd had some talks with my sister on the matter, and though she'd preferred not to disclose any details from her meetings with Noelle, she'd told me she was doing much better. In fact, she'd attributed her change in spirits to our relationship and the fact that she'd become more optimistic towards the future instead of being hung up on the past.

From the beginning I'd known that in order to be on equal footing I'd have to do this. Otherwise, how am I to prove to her that I've changed if I still hold the keys to her future in my hands? If I'm still a potential executioner?

Briefly, my previous plan about having her committed flashes through my mind and I feel ashamed of everything I'd schemed.

She doesn't know.

Another item on the list of things I'm keeping from her.

This, though, might be something she'd forgive me for. I can practically see her as she'd look at me with that forgiving expression on her face while telling me it was all because of a misunderstanding.

She can think it was a misunderstanding as much as she wants, but at the end of the day I know what it is—taking ownership from me for something *I* did, and excusing the inexcusable.

It wasn't a misunderstanding so much as it was my stubbornness and my pride—the fact that I was so sure in my version of justice I was ready to crucify her for it.

Who the fuck did I think I was?

The more I think about my initial behavior towards her, the more I hate myself and my fucking self-righteousness.

For as long as I live I don't think I'm going to make up for all the hurt I've caused her. But I sure as hell can try.

"What about the other thing I asked you?" I change the topic.

"I'm monitoring him closely. I haven't told anyone else that we're suspecting Panchito of the leak, so I'm flying solo on this," Carlos grunts.

He doesn't like this any more than I do.

Panchito has been family over the last couple of years. And family doesn't stab family in the back—mine excluded.

I wish this was nothing more than a hunch, but as I'd gone over every variable of that day, there had been only one answer. Panchito had been the only person that knew *all* the details of the operation and with access to the network to be able to mess with the footage.

"Good. Keep me posted."

I've been relying a lot on Carlos lately, relinquishing to him all the control over our new venture into the weapons black market. Truthfully, he's more invested anyway, since his main objective is to get to Ortega and reclaim his legacy. I was only involved because it was a direct link to my brother. With that issue out of the way, it's not my business anymore. Especially since the bounty on my head expired with Michele's death. After all, there wouldn't be anyone else to pay the money.

Now, I'm content to manage the family enterprise, carefully skirting the line of legality as I build a future for me and my wife. More than anything, I don't want to get wrapped up in another dangerous situation and put *her* at risk.

"How long are you staying there?"

"I don't know. A while. Noelle deserves a vacation after everything that's happened."

"You deserve one too, Raf," Carlos chuckles. "I'm happy for you, man. Truly. Now go to your girl. I'll talk to you later."

Hanging up, I throw the phone somewhere on the counter before I check the temperature of the chicken.

Good thing that the kitchen is fully stocked, because after reading so many articles and recipes, I've realized that cooking isn't only about having all the ingredients in one place. Oh, no. You need so many tools, pans, and utensils that even thinking about it has me on the brink of a headache.

That's not to say I will give up.

Satisfied with the temperature of the chicken, I place a piece on each plate as I start working on the side dishes.

While I put the rice on the stove, I start chopping vegetables. In the back of my mind, though, I keep thinking I'm doing something wrong.

"Something smells good," her voice startles me, and my knife goes straight through half an onion instead of a section. *Damn.*

"I'm making lunch," I pull my lips into a smile as I turn

around, using my hand to push the badly cut onion to the side.

"You are?" her brows shoot up in surprise. "Wow, I was *not* expecting that," she exclaims as she comes around the table, peering at the plates.

For a moment, as I take her in, I forget about cooking.

I forget to fucking breathe.

She's wearing a pair of shorts that are *too* short, her ass cheeks visible as she makes a quick twirl. There's only a *tiny* bandeau top covering her tits, her nipples already two pointy tips angled in *my* direction.

That's a lot of naked flesh and it's only noon. How am I supposed to last until tonight?

My throat goes dry as I try to swallow.

"What can I do to help?" She smiles at me, her eyes twinkling with warmth.

"Absolutely nothing!" I declare loudly. "You will take a seat while I finish things up, and then we will eat together."

She tilts her head to the side as she studies me in amusement.

"If you say so," she shrugs, taking a seat.

Repeating the recipe steps to myself, I make sure everything is right before throwing the vegetables in the pan.

I'm almost sweating looking at the messy counter and the fact that the vegetables look as if they'd been cut with an ax.

Damn it, but why did she have to come here earlier?

Now, instead of seeing the perfect end result, she's going to witness me scrambling about the kitchen like I've never been in one before—which, admittedly, is true.

"What's the occasion?" She inquiries, amused, and as I turn to her it's to see her eyes rove over the counter top, no doubt cataloging all my mistakes.

I gulp down as I close my eyes. Then, taking a deep breath, I simply put on my best smile.

"Can't I surprise my wife with a home cooked meal?"

"You don't know how to cook, Raf," she rolls her eyes at me. "So spill. What did you do?"

I frown.

"What do you mean?"

"Did you do something wrong? Is that why you're trying to make me lunch? If you tell me about it I promise I won't be mad," she nods, her lips tugging up in a pleasant smile.

I swivel, my gaze intent on hers.

"I didn't do anything, *my dear wife*," I tell her proudly. "I do aim, however, to become a more *domestic* husband," I add, internally cringing at my word choice. "We're all alone here, so I won't expect you to cook all our meals," I hurry to explain. "Besides, can't I do something nice for you?"

"Really?" She leans back, still looking at me unconvinced. "I'm surprised you didn't use your hunting knife," she chuckles. "Or wait," she puts her palm up as she jumps out of her seat and comes to my side. "You did, didn't you?" She asks as she points at the wedges I'd cut.

"I didn't," I grumble under my breath, realizing it's futile to argue now.

And this is exactly why I didn't want her to see the food before I got to cook it. I'm sure once the vegetables steamed, they wouldn't look like uneven blocks anymore.

"Hmm," she hums as she looks around, inspecting everything I'm doing. "I look forward to having a *domestic* husband then," she raises herself on her tiptoes to kiss my cheek, twirling and going back to the table before I can react.

One touch of her lips and my body is already heated.

"Damn it," I mutter as I do my best to focus on the task at hand.

Having her here is nothing but distracting, and I find myself sneaking peeks at her when I should be watching the food.

"Raf!"

I blink suddenly, my confused gaze clashing with her scandalized one.

"What?" I sputter, jumping up as the smoke starts assailing my senses.

"Move aside," she says as she pushes me out of the way.

Smoke is coming from the food, and I assume that means it's no longer good to eat.

"I did that, didn't I?" I sigh, looking at the desolate sight with disappointment.

"You could have prevented this, you know," she adds, amused—not at all annoyed as I would have expected. "If you had answered me the first five times I called your name."

Taking the pan, she dumps the already darkened contents in a trashcan. Then, she proceeds to cut another batch.

"You... did?" I ask tentatively, my eyes following her movements as I try to memorize the right way of chopping vegetables.

"Sure did. But you seemed rather transfixed by something else," she tilts her head, daring me to defend myself.

"I did," I nod, thoroughly chastised. "But it's *not* my fault," I'm quick to add. "How can it be my fault when you're a walking hazard?"

"A walking hazard? Me?"

"Indeed. Who told you to wear that?" I point towards her flimsy top. "I was doing mighty fine before you walked into the room." I cross my arms over my chest.

"So now it's *my* fault?"

"Of course. How can I focus on preparing food when you're dangling dessert in front of me?" I ask in indignation.

"Dessert, huh?"

A playful smile spreads on her lips as she bats her lashes at me. At the same time, she thrusts her ass backwards, the curve so tantalizing I can't help my eyes roving over her shape.

"Eyes here, my darling *domestic* husband. You were cooking, weren't you?" She whispers, her husky voice going straight to my cock.

To hell with cooking. To hell with food. Fuck, to hell with everything else that isn't her...

"Right," I clear my throat, pushing my primitive thoughts aside. Grabbing the pan from her, I put it on the stove, throwing some oil and the vegetables inside while taking a spatula and stirring them around.

This time, she doesn't leave my side, watching everything I do and making sure I don't set the house on fire.

"Let me add some seasoning," she browses the selection before sprinkling a few types on top of the stir fry.

"Is it done?" I ask after a while, unable to tell.

She nods.

"Great," I release a relieved breath. "Let's eat then." I gently steer her back to the table.

When the meat is already cooked, I quickly portion the rice and vegetables, taking a seat when everything is done.

"This isn't half bad," she notes as she takes a bite of the meat. "There might be hope for you after all."

"I'll become the best cook ever," I declare, puffing my chest. "Just you wait and see."

"If you say so..." she trails off, but her tone tells me she's laughing at me.

"Give me your top five favorite foods. By the end of the week, I'll be able to make them all," I burst out, belatedly realizing I'm biting more than I can chew—ironic as it sounds.

"Raf," she laughs, "this isn't a competition. If you really want to learn, I'll be happy to eat whatever you cook," she says with a gentle smile.

"So?"

"I'm not a fussy eater, although I prefer food on the spicier side. Chicken is good. I also like seafood so you could try that next time, especially since we're close to the ocean."

"That's right. We can go to the market and see if they have any fresh stuff."

"That sounds lovely."

She continues eating, and while I should do the same, I find myself just staring at her—again.

Fuck, I'm such a lucky bastard.

CHAPTER THIRTY-EIGHT
RAFAELO

The rest of the day passes in a flurry as we do some work around the house to make it more hospitable. For all my mother's love of expensive materials, the house looks more like a museum than someone's home.

It's particularly heartwarming to see Noelle put her own soft touch to our room, all without changing the original décor too much.

And as the sky starts darkening, I take two plates of pasta —cooked without setting the kitchen on fire—and I join Noelle in the day room.

She's sitting by the piano as she scrunches her nose in concentration while scribbling down some notes on a sheet of paper. She's wearing different clothes from earlier in the day, mostly because I couldn't stop staring at her and thus was not able to get any work done. Instead, she put on a long, light skirt and a top that this time covers her delectable midriff.

I won't obsess over her.

I keep reciting the mantra as I walk towards her. At this point it's become a necessity so I remind myself that not everything is about hugging her to my chest and keeping her tied to me, preferably with my cock buried deep in her pussy.

I need to get a hang of myself.

It's just the honeymoon phase...

Except it's *not*.

The honeymoon phase is long gone, yet I can't help myself. My eyes are always glued to where she is, and when she's not by my side I get insanely paranoid that something might happen.

There's this need inside of me to safeguard her and envelop her in a protective cocoon, one so thick she'd never be able to leave it.

And we'd stay there, together. Just the two of us as we'd share our deepest thoughts and desires.

Sometimes I feel like I'm going insane.

Maybe it's a side effect of seeing her at Michele's mercy— at knowing anything could have happened to her.

More than anything, it's the fact that she'd so easily admitted she would let herself be raped by a madman in order to save me.

In order to save my worthless ass.

I'd rather die a thousand deaths than let *anyone* lay a hand on her. The moment anyone tries to put even the tip of one finger on my pretty girl, all bets are off.

When it comes to her, I know I'm capable of the impossible.

The last few years have been nothing short of a journey of self-discovery.

I'd learned that I can survive even if pushed to the most extreme limits, and that in spite of anything I can move on and even *thrive*. But since meeting Noelle, I've also found another part of myself that lay dormant until her—that I'm a possessive bastard.

Growing up and used to my circumstances, women have

always been the furthest thing from my mind. I'd always hoped that I would eventually find someone to settle down with, but I'd *never* imagined this type of emotion.

All-consuming.

Maddening.

Addictive.

There's nothing normal about how I feel about Noelle. *Nothing.*

She has me tied up in knots the moment she walks into the room, and the thought of anyone else getting near her sends me into an irrational rage.

Multiple times, I've had to ask myself—who am I? Who is this person that behaves like a fucking savage? Because I don't recognize it.

I don't recognize myself.

There's a part of me that *knows* that she's mine and only mine, that she belongs to me in a way that cannot be explained by natural phenomena—and believe me, I've tried.

During my captivity, I'd thought that what I felt for Lucero was intense. But at times, I have to ask myself, how much of it was true and how much was it the effect of the drugs? I'd been so doped up, that even my realest memories could be nothing more than hallucinations. I don't know for sure if what happened was *real*, or just my own perception of real. I might never find out.

And that's fine.

For the first time I'm not living in the shadow of the past anymore. I'm not looking forward to tomorrow just so I can wreak revenge on someone who's wronged me.

For the first time I'm free.

Free to love her.

Shaking myself from my musings, I put a pleasant smile on as I walk towards her.

"What are you up to, pretty girl?"

I take a seat by her side, handing her a plate and utensils.

"It's a secret," she smiles sheepishly as she places her hand on top of the paper. When she sees my curiosity piqued as I strain to make out the contents, she goes one step further and flips it on the other side.

"You made dinner," she changes the subject, thrusting the sheet away from my field of view.

"I think this one is a success," I tell her, though the antici-pation is killing me as I wait for her to dig in.

"Ohh," she licks her lips as she takes a bite. "This is wonderful, Raf. I stand corrected. You might actually become a great cook," she laughs.

"I'm committed to the task of becoming a *domestic* husband," I joke.

After we finish eating, I take the plates back to the kitchen before returning to pester her about showing me her surprise.

I know she's been working on a new piece, but she's been tight-lipped about it.

"Nope," she shakes her head, popping the *p* in a way that is both cute and sexy at the same time. "It wouldn't be a surprise anymore." She slaps my hand as I try to pluck the sheet of paper from her side.

"But I'm curious," I feign a pout, batting my lashes like she usually does when she tries to get her way.

Amused, she looks at me for a moment before waving a finger in front of me.

"You might be cute, but I'm still not showing you."

"Please," I say as I shift closer to her on the bench.

"Still a no," she pushes her chin in the air, pretending to ignore me.

Not one to give up easily, I snake my arms around her waist, lifting her up and depositing her in my lap. She's so small, it's entirely too easy to maneuver her around. And as she starts squirming, I do just that, holding her still while her arms flail around.

"Raf, what are you doing?" she laughs, moving her body as she tries to get away from me.

"Hmm, I wonder if you're ticklish... What about here?" I slowly graze my fingers up her ribcage before tickling her right under her arms until she's crying out for mercy.

"I give up, I give up," she shouts, barely able to squeeze the words amid her fit of laughter.

"What was that? I didn't hear you."

"I give up," she whizzes, just as I turn her around, her legs on the outside of my thighs as she sits on my lap.

"So, will you tell me now?" I whisper as I bring her face closer to mine.

She blinks, startled at the sudden proximity. Hot air fans my face and I can feel every little hitch in her breath as she squirms around my lap, getting herself in the *perfect* position. The proximity makes my heart skip a beat—another thing that's become the norm.

"You're not playing fair," she whispers, licking her lips as she raises her eyes to mine.

"There are no rules, pretty girl. That means," I pause as I wrap one arm around the small of her back, pushing her closer to me, "there is *no* fair."

"I'm still not showing you," she tries to put on a strong front even as she grinds her pussy against me.

"You will. Everyone cracks under duress."

"I won't," she says confidently.

"Oh, you will," I smirk. "And I know just the way to get you to talk."

"Really?" She raises a brow. "I'm waiting," she adds with a knowing smile.

The little witch.

"What if I were to brush my fingers up your leg?" I drawl

out the words just as I bring my hand to her ankle, slowly skimming the surface of her flesh and dragging the dress upwards in my advance.

She swallows, her eyes still on mine.

"I wouldn't tell," she whispers.

"Hmm. What about this then?" I ask just as I spread my palm over the curve of her ass. "What if I rest my hand here and *not* move it?" the corner of my mouth tips up in an amused smile.

She shakes her head, though I can tell her breathing is getting increasingly labored. Fuck, but I bet she's already soaking wet, and the thought only makes me react stronger— the need to touch her almost my undoing.

"What if I promised to pet your pretty pussy? Would you tell me then?" my own voice is becoming huskier the more I think about the wonder that nestles between her thighs, that sweet little pussy that owns me.

"Maybe," she replies saucily. "Why don't we give it a try. Who knows," she shrugs. "I might talk after all," she winks at me.

"Damn," I whistle, "I better get started with my interrogation then."

No sooner are the words out of my mouth than my fingers dip between her ass cheeks.

She's wearing a flimsy material that barely covers her pussy. I easily tug it to the side as I glide my finger between her folds.

"Soaked. You're truly soaked, pretty girl."

"Uhm," she hums, rocking slightly against my fingers. "You want to know why?" she leans forward, her lips brushing against my ear.

A shiver of anticipation goes down my back.

"Why?" I demand on a ragged tone.

"Because I saw you when you walked in," her lips smack together right before I feel her tongue on my earlobe.

At the same time, I bring the rough pads of my fingers against her clit, petting the sensitive flesh and eliciting a moan from her.

"You saw me and..."

"You were already hard," she blurts out, moving against my hand. "I could see the outline of your cock. God, and I kept thinking," she gasps as I slide one finger into her tiny opening.

"You kept thinking?" I repeat, amused every time she loses her train of thought.

"I kept thinking there was a different type of food I would prefer."

"Is that so?" I chuckle in her hair.

Her scent envelops me, and I inhale deeply, letting it wash over me. My cock is painfully hard, but I want her pleasure first. I *need* to feel her release coating my fingers, her moans in my ears.

"You make me think dirty thoughts when I shouldn't," she adds on a whimper as I work my fingers in and out of her pussy.

Her hands grip my shoulders as she brings her mouth to my neck, biting to stop herself from screaming out loud as she comes.

"Tell me," I ask roughly, "tell me those dirty thoughts, pretty girl. I promise I'll turn each and every one of them into reality."

Bringing my fingers to my mouth, I suck in her essence, all the while staring into her eyes and showing her the depth of my desire for her.

"I..." She flutters her lashes, taking a deep breath and barely getting herself together after her orgasm. "If you want

449

to know what is on that sheet, then you'll have to fuck it out of me. Fuck me while I play it for you."

For a moment I can only stare at her—at my pretty girl who just asked me to turn one of my own fantasies to reality.

"Fuck, Noelle," I swear, overwhelmed by too much emotion and excitement. Closing my eyes, I groan as I bring my other hand to my head, threading my fingers through my hair. "You're killing me, pretty girl."

"You...don't want that?" she asks tentatively, her lip between her teeth as she looks at me in worry.

"Want that? Fuck, I don't think I've wanted something more. You have no idea... God," I exhale. "From the first time I saw you behind that piano, playing as if you were one with the music, all I could think about was how you'd play with my cock filling your cunt. Jesus... does that scare you, pretty girl? Does it scare you to know what a sick fuck I am? That all I could think was your music on my tongue, your pussy milking my cock and bringing me closer to nirvana than I could ever hope..." I trail off as I realize how much I've revealed.

"No," she breathes out, her hands suddenly wrapped in my shirt as she tugs me closer until our faces are mere inches apart. "Because that's been on replay in my mind from the beginning. Raf..." She rakes her teeth over her bottom lip. "You make me hot in a way I never thought possible. Sometimes I feel like I'm no longer in control of my body, because all it wants is to be near you, on top of you, *mating* with you. I feel *empty* without you," she confesses with unparalleled poignancy and an urgency that has me about to rip the clothes off her in an attempt to get that close.

"Sweet Jesus, Noelle. Keep talking in that sexy voice of yours and I'm going to burst in my pants."

"And we wouldn't want that, would we?" she bats her lashes as her fingers fumble with the zipper on my pants.

The moment it gives way, her hand is inside, wrapped around my cock and squeezing tight.

"Fuck," I curse, my muscles tensing.

She has a mischievous expression on her face as she brings her thumb over the head, swiping every bit of moisture before using it to lubricate her movements.

"You can't come," she says in a resolute tone. "You can't come until you're inside me. I need you to fill me, Raf—fuck me so hard until I see stars."

My mouth agape, I can only stare at her. Until now, every time we've made love, she's been quiet, letting me do most of the talking. The fact that she's issuing commands of her own has me harder than I've ever been. And fuck me if I can't wait to give her just *that*.

And anything else she asks.

"I would never," I shake my head vigorously. "Every bit of my cum is reserved for your sweet pussy, Noelle. Because she's hungry, isn't she?" I ask as I brush her hair from her neck so I can lay kisses all over her tender skin. "She's starving for my cum."

She nods, her pupils taking over her irises, her desire clearly written in her features.

"And I'm going to give it to you, pretty girl," I coo in her ear just as I grab her waist, turning her around so that she's sitting on my lap while facing the piano.

"Now," I bring my mouth to her ear, swiping my tongue up the column of her neck as I go and feeling her shiver in my arms. "I want you to put me inside of you. Wrap your hand around my cock and guide me into your tight heat," I tell her in a soft voice, yet the command is unmistakable.

She doesn't argue. Raising herself slightly, she reaches back to grab my cock, positioning the head at her entrance. Slowly, she pushes herself down on my erection.

My chest rumbles with pleasure, her pussy walls closing

in around me and enveloping me in pure heat. Wiggling down, she struggles to take me to the hilt, so I grab her hips, thrusting into her in one smooth slide.

We both moan at the sensation.

"Raf," her velvety voice caresses my senses. Leaning back, she tilts her head and brings her lips to mine. Opening her mouth, her tongue darts out to lick my lips as she urges me to return her kiss.

And I do. Fuck, but I do.

I part my lips, bringing my tongue against hers and kissing her like I'm suffocating and she's the last bit of oxygen left in the world.

My cock twitches inside of her, needing to move yet at the same time relishing the way I feel her walls pulsating around me.

We are one—like we were always meant to be.

"Play for me," I rasp against her lips. "Play for me while I fuck you, pretty girl. I'll fuck you just the way you want me to as long as you give me your music. Your goddamn essence. Guide me to fucking heaven, Noelle," I demand harshly, my words marked by an unusual urgency.

She gives me a languid nod, her eyes still closed as she struggles to get her breathing under control. Straightening her back, she leans closer to the keys, the sudden movement making her bounce on my cock.

"Fuck," I curse out, knowing it will be a torture to keep still.

"I know it's your birthday soon," she whispers, "and I composed you a little something," she says in a throaty voice.

I don't get to reply though as her fingers connect with the keys, the first sound reverberating in the air. At the same time, I bring my hands to her hips, holding her in place and moving her up and down my cock as I follow the rhythm of the melody.

My eyes snap closed as sweetness bursts on my tongue at hearing her play—each note unveiling more about the piece as a whole and the message underneath. I feel the love in the base melody just as I feel the passion as the piece climbs into a dramatic crescendo. There's a sensory overload as I feel her *everywhere*, the sound only accentuating my pleasure.

Her fingers skillfully trace the keyboard, her music impeccable even as I pump in and out of her. My hands on her waist, I place my head on her back, pounding into her like a man consumed by love, desire, and something else that eludes me.

Something that makes my fucking heart sing in tandem with hers,

"This is for you, Raf," she whimpers. "All for you, my love."

She bangs her hands on the keyboard just as a moan escapes her lips, the entire room echoing with her pleasure.

I'm not too far behind either, and as she slumps against me, her piece done, I quickly turn her around until her chest is flush against mine.

My cock briefly slips out of her at the sudden movement, but I'm quick to rectify that as I thrust into her, keeping her so close to me it's like we *are* one.

She wounds her arms around my neck as her mouth seeks mine, and for the longest time, we just lose ourselves in this feeling of completion.

"I'm coming," she moans, increasing her speed as she rides me, her pussy clamping down on my dick and squeezing so hard, my own release is impending.

"Fuck," I mumble incoherently, my cock jerking inside of her as cum fills her to the brim—just as she demanded.

Still, I don't let go. I keep her wrapped in my arms, flesh against flesh,

Leaning back, she looks at me dazedly, an odd look crossing her face.

"You're my heart, pretty girl," I tell her, caressing her cheek and laying a soft kiss to her nose.

She blinks, almost confused, looking at me as if I were a stranger.

"Noelle?"

For a moment she doesn't reply, as if she's lost inside her head.

"Noelle," I repeat, cupping both her cheeks as I force her to look at me. "Are you ok? Did I hurt you?" I ask, immediately fearing the worst.

She squeezes her eyes shut before a slow smile appears on her face.

"I'm fine," she shakes her head as she lies. "I love you too, Raf. Too much," she whispers in a sad tone, her eyes sparkling with unshed tears.

I want to ask what's going on—to get a clarification of what happened.

But she quickly brushes it off as she lays her cheek against mine, murmuring sweet words of love.

CHAPTER THIRTY-NINE
RAFAELO

"You can't catch me," she squeals as she dashes down the beach, chasing the advancing and retreating waves of the ocean.

"Are you sure you want to play that?" I chuckle.

Turning back, she makes a funny expression, daring me to chase her as she starts running at full speed.

And since what Noelle wants, she gets, I go after her.

To say that the last two weeks have been a miracle is an understatement. We've taken the meaning of vacation literally and we've done nothing but lounge around all day—playing, talking, and making love.

Not keeping any staff on retainer had been the best idea, since it's only the two of us in the house and we can truly let loose.

More than anything, we've gotten to know each other thoroughly. I know how she spreads butter on her toast and how she takes her coffee every morning. I know she prefers her food spicy and that she's a Diet Coke addict, or that she loves to be surprised with chocolate whenever she least expects, or in *ways* she least expects.

We've had spa days together where she'd coaxed me into trying face masks—which, admittedly, had been quite nice. We've done everything from giving each other massages, to frolicking in the jacuzzi and exercising together.

A while back, we celebrated my birthday together, and it was hands down the most amazing birthday I've ever had.

While I'd slept, my pretty girl had spent the entire night baking me a cake and decorating the ground floor. And when I woke up, she handed me a card that said *free pass* which meant I could do anything I wanted to her for twenty-four hours.

"Are you sure you're up to this?" I'd asked, already planning all the nefarious things I could do to her.

"Of course. It's *your* day. As such, I am fully yours," she'd batted her lashes at me before muttering under her breath, "not that I'm usually not."

Her idea had been brilliant, though, and not one to waste an opportunity, I'd used it to pamper *her*. If there's one thing that makes me happy, it's *her* happiness. And seeing a smile on her face, or hearing her laugh—the sweetest sound in the world—is worth everything.

I would have thought that the more a couple spends time together, the more they start to annoy each other. But it's been the opposite with me and Noelle.

No matter how much time I spend with her, I still crave more. Not even knowing that she's in the next room helps sometimes, and she's started joking that I've caught the separation anxiety bug—which I most definitely did.

Something inside of me tells me to grasp at every moment with her, a feeling of ephemerality threatening to drown me. I want to be *present* in the present so I can store every bit of information about her as I can—every memory and every feature.

And so I've done my best to be by her side, but also *not*

suffocate her with my insatiability for her or my ever-growing obsession with having her all for myself.

A few days ago though, she got her period, and with it came the pain. Although it was manageable with pills, she'd spent most of her time in bed, unable to move much.

That's how my role as a domestic husband had gone from part-time to full-time. I learned how to make desserts for her to brighten her mood, and I started reading her stories to keep the boredom at bay. For the latter, the idea had come to me when she'd told me how much she loved my voice, and that the first time she'd heard me speak her heart had skipped a beat.

I'd also spent an exorbitant amount of time on the internet in search of something to keep her mind off the pain, and I'd found the perfect thing—a pet shelter. Contacting them, I was able to set a visiting day in which they would bring some of their pets to the house and let us spend a day with them.

Noelle had been thrilled.

She has a naturally warm personality and animals take to her immediately. When the dogs had started running about the house, somehow all of them had ended up in her direction, overwhelming her with attention and love.

She'd laughed and played as much as she could, given her condition, but she forgot all about the pain.

As the pets had been taken back to the shelter, she'd begged me to get her one, and I'd promised I would consider it. What she doesn't know is that I'm already in contact with the shelter to finalize the adoption papers for one of the dogs she's fallen in love with.

A small, black Pomeranian with a bad leg, he'd immediately won her over as he'd limped gracefully to lick her hand. Even I'd been a little thrown off by how cute and adorable the dog was.

And as the hours trickle by, I can't wait to see her reaction when it's time to pick him up.

"Raf, what are you doing?" She shouts at me from a few hundred yards ahead, waving her hands in the air.

"Admiring the view," I reply, my voice booming across the rather empty beach.

"You were supposed to chase me, remember?" She asks playfully as she gets into position once more, dashing forward.

I know she resents how debilitating her periods are and how useless they make her feel, which is why she's decided to go crazy the moment it stopped—as in *now*.

A small smile plays at my lips as I shake my head at her.

She's just so full of life—so fucking beautiful and cheerful —that it pains me to think about anyone hurting her.

"I'm coming," I call out as I pick up speed.

Her giggle is infectious as she keeps looking back at me while she runs, all the while taunting me that I can't catch her.

Letting her take the lead for a while, I linger behind, simply enjoying the sight of her like this—so happy and carefree.

I commit every second to memory. The way her dress sways with the wind, or how the warm breeze kisses her skin, cheeks flushed, hair disheveled. Then there's her beaming smile—the way she gets my heart pounding and my blood pumping like there's no tomorrow.

Running towards her at full speed, I quickly catch up with her, tacking her to the ground. My back hits the fine sand as I bring her on top of me to break her fall.

"Who said I can't catch you?" I raise a brow.

She's laughing hard, her hands wrapped in my shirt as she's trying to catch her breath.

"Let's do it again," she suddenly says, her tone serious. "This time you *won't* be able to catch me."

"Noelle," I smile at her. "Your legs are almost half the size of mine. Statistically speaking you're never going to outrun me."

"Maybe," she shrugs, settling on my chest as she places her hands under her chin. "Maybe I *really* enjoy the chase," she winks at me.

My lips tug up in amusement.

"I know you do. And because of that, I'll chase you every time you want. Because I *know* that I'll always catch you."

She peers at me from beneath her lashes, her cheeks tinged with red as she blushes furiously.

"I know you will," she wets her lips. "I trust you with my life."

"Pretty girl," I groan. "That's the best thing you could ever say to me. Because that's who I want to be. Your protector, your best friend, your lover. Your *family*."

A smile plays at her lips and she makes herself more comfortable, laying her cheek over my heart.

"I used to think the world was such an ugly place," she sighs. "I don't think I knew happiness before you, Raf. It pains me to admit it, because *no one* should experience that... I really thought the world was a bleak place. That everyone was evil and only looking out for themselves to the detriment of others."

I bring my hand over her hair, caressing her lightly as I listen to her speak.

"I admit I felt an attraction to you from the beginning. But do you know when my heart started yearning for you?" Her voice is barely above a whisper as she asks the question.

"When?"

"We were still at each other's throats, and I guess that

made it even worse at the time, but..." she gives a sad laugh. "When you saved me at that dinner..." she trails off.

"Baby," I wrap my arms around her tighter.

"The dark room incident was still fresh in my mind. That type of fear..." I feel her shake her head. "It doesn't go away as easy. Yet you slipped past that wall of defenses I'd built, and slowly wormed your way into my heart. I asked myself countless times if maybe I was sick. If I was a masochist because even though you kept hurting me, I still yearned for you."

Emotions clog in my throat at her words and I can't even find the strength to apologize.

I don't deserve any forgiveness.

"You saved me when no one had done so before, Raf," she continues. "You hated me, but you still saved me. Who does that?" she asks, more to herself.

"Then," she chuckles, "there was the time you brought me chocolate when I was in pain. You kept surprising me and at some point, I think I started believing there might be something more out there. Something other than pain."

I blink back tears, cursing myself once more for everything I put her through. I don't think I'll ever understand how she found it in herself to forgive me.

"You're so amazing," I gently caress her cheek, my voice full of awe.

"What about you," she suddenly whips her head up, looking at me expectantly.

"What about me?"

"When did your feelings for me shift?"

"They didn't shift," I reply, amused at her little frown. "They were always there. But somehow, I doubted every interaction that would put you in a good light. My heart was miles ahead of my head in this instance," I chuckle.

What I don't say is that I'd fallen for her the moment I'd

seen her play the piano. Her music is the door to her heart, and unwittingly, she'd welcomed me right in.

I may have convinced myself she was the worst person on the earth, but even then I would have laid down my life to protect her.

"There's something about you, about *us* that isn't mere happenstance. I know it deep in my gut, Noelle. Nothing worked in our favor, yet we still found our way to each other."

"We did," she smiles before dipping her head to brush her lips against mine. "And you've taught me so many things," I feel her smile against me.

"Like what?"

"Like…kissing," she whispers as her teeth tug at my lower lip. "I've found that I love kissing."

"Just kissing?" I ask in an indignant tone.

"And more. Everything," she says as she peppers kisses all over my face. "I love it when you hug me. When you whisper sweet things to me and tell me I'm the most beautiful woman in the world. And I love when you worship my body, making love to me like we aren't two bodies, just one."

"We are one," I state resolutely as I frame her face in my hands, bringing her for a kiss.

But just as things become increasingly heated, a loud cry permeates the air.

We both turn, startled.

A toddler runs at full speed towards us, his cheeks ruddy and tear-streaked.

"What?" I blink, but we quickly jump to our feet, ready to offer help.

There's no one else in sight but the little one running towards us.

"Shh, it's ok," Noelle hurries to his side, dropping to her knees to be on eye level with him.

I take a step closer just as she tries to pacify him, caressing his cheeks and asking questions in a gentle tone.

For some reason, that sight alone is enough to make my heart ache in my chest.

"Raf, get me my bag, please," she turns to me.

I hand her the bag, watching in awe as she pulls a small pouch, quickly emptying the contents.

"It's going to be ok, sweetheart. It's just a tiny scratch," she says as she cleans the sand from the wound before applying a layer of tincture. She tops it with a mini band aid, giving the child a smile.

"What's your name?"

"T-T-Trevor," he manages to say between hiccups. He's all red from crying, but as he looks at Noelle's sweet expression, he becomes less timid.

"Where are your parents, Trevor?" she asks as she brushes a strand of hair from his forehead.

"I don't know," he says before he starts crying again.

"Don't worry. We'll find them for you, isn't that right, Raf?" She turns to me for confirmation.

"Of course. Why don't we head towards the more populated area?" I suggest, and just as I'm about to take little Trevor in my arms, Noelle beats me to it.

For a moment, I can't move.

I look at her as she hugs his little body to her chest, all the while whispering comforting words, and I bring my hand to my chest, banging against my heart to alleviate the pressure forming inside.

She looks… I'm not sure there are words to describe how she looks.

"Raf, are you coming?"

"Yes, of course," I shake myself.

Sticking by her side, I watch her closely, worried the child might bring back bad memories.

She's just so sweet to Trevor, an inherent calmness and gentleness oozing from her as she gets him to stop crying. In fact, now he's listening attentively to every word she says.

"Trevor!" someone yells in the distance.

A couple run towards us, both with frantic expressions as they spot Trevor.

"Oh my God, he's safe," the man exhales in relief, while the mother takes little Trevor from Noelle's arms.

"Thank you so much for bringing him back. He ran off from our side and we couldn't find him. Good Lord, the scare I got..."

"It's ok," Noelle smiles. "He has a minor scratch on his knee, but I cleaned it for now so he should be fine."

"Thank you, really. Thank you so much," the woman keeps repeating.

We make a little small talk with the couple after which they leave, taking little Trevor away with them.

Noelle, though, is rooted to the spot as she stares after them in the distance.

"So that's what it feels like to be a mother," she whispers.

"Pretty girl," I wound my arm around her shoulder as I bring her to my chest. "Don't go there."

"He didn't trigger any flashbacks," she says, almost mechanically. "Just a deep, deep ache in my heart."

"I'm so sorry."

"I need to do something about my condition. I'll do that surgery or whatever the doctor recommended," she takes a deep breath. "I don't want us to be childless..."

"Anything," I hurry to say. "Anything you want and I'll be there for you. We can try anything."

"Thank you," she whispers after a brief pause.

"It warmed my heart too, you know... Seeing you with him. I kept imagining how you'd look with *our* child and..." I swallow hard. "We'll try everything."

"You're so good to me Raf," she sighs as she leans into me.

"Not yet," I brush my lips against hers. "I have a surprise for you," I tell her, hoping the puppy news would help offset her disappointment.

"Amaze me," she chuckles as I lead her to the car.

We arrived at the shelter just in time for the appointment.

"Raf..." she turns to me, her eyes two huge orbs. "What is this?"

"I know we can't have a baby yet. But maybe a puppy could make you happy for now?" I give her a tentative smile.

Before I know it though, she's on me, jumping in my arms and giving me a loud smooch on the cheek.

"This is the best news! Oh my God, I can't believe you planned this!"

"Wait until you see which little guy you're taking home with you."

Taking her hand, I lead her towards the reception where I sign the last papers, and an assistant brings over the small Pomeranian to us.

"You didn't," she breathes in, "God, this is the best surprise ever, Raf," she exclaims in awe as she takes the puppy in her arms.

"You chose great, Mr. Guerra. He was rescued from an abusive home recently, so he could really use the love."

"Isn't that fitting," Noelle giggles, making funny faces at the puppy.

"He's around six months old," the assistant details his life history as well as the injury he'd sustained to the leg and why a lot of people had forgone adopting him because of that.

"What are you going to name him?"

"Hmm," she hums as she cradles the puppy to her chest. "Lovely," she declares. "Because he's lovely in spite of his defect," she beams at me.

"That's a perfect name," I lean in to kiss her forehead.

We spend some time in the city buying everything Lovely needs before heading back home.

The moment we're back at the house though, Noelle lets out a loud squeal as she starts playing with Lovely, effectively ignoring me for the rest of the day.

But how can I be mad when she looks so happy?

"Raf, this is the best gift anyone's ever given me," she gushes as she watches Lovely munch on his food. "Look how cute and lovable he is."

"He is," I agree. Especially as he comes to Noelle's side, patting her on the leg with his little paw and looking up at her with those big, innocent eyes of his.

So entranced I am in the moment, watching them interact with each other, that it takes me a moment to realize my phone is beeping.

Taking it out from my pocket, I see a few missed calls from Carlos.

Frowning, I leave Noelle with Lovely as I step out for a minute, dialing him back.

"What is it?" I ask, thinking he has some news regarding Panchito.

"You forgot, didn't you?" he mutters dryly.

"What…"

"The end of the week, Raf," he simply states, and my eyes go wide.

I've been so lost in Noelle that I completely forgot my predicament, or the fact that she still doesn't know that I'm basically a fancy addict.

"Shit… I didn't think we'd still be here," I confess.

At most, I would have thought that we'd be here a week or so. But we've been having so much fun that I couldn't find it in me to suggest we left.

"What are you going to do? You're not prepared, are you?"

"I have an emergency kit. I always carry one with me," I reply grimly.

Now it makes sense why I've been getting more agitated. It usually happens when my date approaches. Every day until the weekend is going to become increasingly harder to bear. The only positive is that this is just a regular dose, not a readjustment one, which means I won't be going into withdrawal. I will still be under the influence of the drug, however, and I would *never* want Noelle to see me like that.

I've seen videos of my reactions on that goddamn drug, and I know it's not pretty. I become aggressive and unpredictable, and I wouldn't discount harming her. After all, my conscience takes a deep dive whenever the drug takes control. The worst is that all my memories from the time become fuzzy—a mix of hallucination and reality—and I never know what's real and not.

"Raf, I can come up there. It's only a couple hours car ride…"

"No. It would make Noelle suspicious. I'll manage it."

"You should tell her. Maybe she can help you."

"No," I state resolutely. "I don't want her to know."

I don't want her to *ever* know that I'm still a slave to those drugs. I don't want to risk her looking at me like I'm…less. Or God forbid, I don't want her to blame herself for anything.

"I'll deal with it," I tell him before hanging up, not wanting to get into an argument and draw her attention.

Leaning against the door's frame, a smile pulls at my lips as I take in her intoxicating happiness.

I would do anything to protect it—forever.

CHAPTER FORTY
NOELLE

"I'm really sorry, pretty girl. Will you forgive me?" He nuzzles his face in the crook of my neck as he hugs me tightly to his chest.

"You'll only be gone for half a day. I'll be fine," I assure him. I can't begrudge him that when the entire world is still reeling from Michele, and his last stunt had been to get Marcello Lastra arrested for something that happened over twelve years ago.

"But I don't want to leave you alone," he pouts.

"I'll be fine, Raf. I'm serious. Besides, I have Lovely to keep me company. I won't even notice you're gone," I wink at him.

"Is that right?" he drawls, raising a brow at me. "You won't notice I'm gone?"

Leaning down, his breath is on my cheek as he starts skimming his lips over my skin.

"Those are dangerous words, Noelle," he warns, his tongue sneaking out to lick my earlobe.

"How..." I gulp down, a tremor going down my body. "How dangerous?"

I don't know why I'm riling him up now that he's about to leave, but I can't help myself.

On one hand, I know he needs to go back and deal with some urgent business. After some thorough investigation, Raf and Carlos suspect they have finally found the mole who'd leaked information to Michele, and Raf had wanted to be present there for the confrontation.

Although he promised he wouldn't take too long, I'm already feeling the separation.

Now that we've spent so much time together it's hard to imagine being on my own again.

I've been on my own for too long before.

There's something utterly comforting knowing that there's someone I can lean on. Raf's support has made me slowly come out of my shell, and for the first time in too long, I feel like myself again. Or, maybe, I'm *just* finding myself.

"You'll need to wait and see," he taunts, his proximity caressing my body with the promise of future bliss.

"Yes," I breathe out. "I'll wait for you."

My eyes widen as I hear an echo in my brain.

I'll always wait for you.

Shaking myself, I give him a tight smile as I lead him to the car.

"I'll make dinner," I tell him as I lean against the car door. "I'll prepare something extra special," I bat my lashes at him.

He stares at me for a moment before groaning, bringing his hand to his head to massage his temples.

"How am I supposed to leave now? You're not playing fair."

"Well, you weren't playing fair either," I shoot back, chuckling. "Now go. The sooner you leave, the sooner you come back to me."

"Yes, captain," he imitates a salute, starting the engine of the car. Before I can pull away from the window, his hand is on my nape as he brings me forward for a deep kiss.

"I'll be counting down the seconds," he whispers against my lips. I stumble back, my fingers going to my lips as he maneuvers the wheel.

Reeling from the kiss, I can only watch as the car makes it out of the gates, an odd feeling settling deep in my stomach at being alone.

Smoothing down my dress, I take a deep breath, resolving to find some things to do on my own until he returns. Besides, I do have some things to prepare for tonight.

A blush envelops my face as my thoughts stray towards *that*.

Hurrying inside the house, I head straight for the bedroom, getting the boxes I'd stuffed under the bed.

I'd ordered some stuff off the internet and I'd told Raf that they were all for Lovely when he'd questioned me about them.

Lovely finds that exact moment to make his appearance, shakily jumping on the bed and woofing at me.

"You want to see what I got?" I ask him, and he extends his tongue out as he gives a yap. "I'm curious too, so let's see," I bring my hand over his soft fur, giving it a quick pat.

He releases a soft squeak, running around the bed in excitement.

Focusing on the box, I tear at the plastic surrounding it, opening it up and taking out the contents.

A few pieces of clothing have been neatly folded inside, all thoroughly wrapped so they don't reveal what lies inside. Tearing through the packaging of the first one, I spread out the material, my eyes widening in the process.

A deep red lacy one piece, it gapes around the stomach, leaving absolutely no room for imagination.

"That's a lot less fabric than I imagined," I mutter to myself.

I'd wanted to surprise Raf with a set of lingerie, but since I've never worn anything like it, I picked the most popular options from the website. Now, looking at what had arrived, I wonder if I should have spent a little more time browsing it.

Unwrapping the other pieces, I start noticing a pattern. Though the lace covers the skin, everything is visible through it. For a moment I'm reluctant to go through with it, since that little fabric makes me a little uncomfortable. But just as the thought arises, I realize that Raf's seen me wear less. It's not going to be the end of the world if I wear something this revealing.

My mind made up, I start with the one piece. Taking my dress off, I put it on, surprised at how nice it feels on my skin. The lace is surprisingly soft, molding to my body like a second skin. But as I go to the mirror to look at myself, my face falls.

The stomach gaping reveals most of my scars and places an off-putting emphasis on them. My lips purse as I continue to peruse my body. The shape isn't bad, and if it weren't for the empty space around the stomach area, I would love it. As it stands... I don't think I can wear something that will make me continuously self-conscious of my defects.

I release a deep sigh as I turn to go back to the bedroom, intent on trying the others. Surely something must fit nicely.

My spirits are considerably lower than before. Especially since I'd put a lot of hope into this.

Raf has been an amazing influence as he's slowly made me come out of my shell. As such, I'd wanted to be more daring and maybe explore a different side of our relationship.

I've taken an interest in reading books on relationships and communication, wanting to give my best and not give him any reason to get tired of me.

Never having been in a relationship before, sometimes I don't know how to react in certain situations. More than anything, I'm always worried about doing or saying the wrong thing.

There are instances when Raf teases me, or jokes around, and I find myself unable to reply or come up with an idea of my own.

Since researching the topic, though, I've started to understand our interactions better, and I find myself capable of verbally sparring with him too.

But it's not enough.

So many articles talk about spicing up a relationship to keep it alive and make sure it doesn't go stale. I'd read enough to realize I needed to take the initiative more often too—that I shouldn't let him be the aggressor all the time.

When I'd seen that sexy lingerie was an option, I'd immediately gotten on board, already looking forward to Raf's reaction.

But now…

A little upset at the first piece, I try the next one on. Made up of a lacy bra and a thong with a garter, this one is much better.

Looking in the mirror, I try to imagine Raf's expression when he'll see me, a smile pulling at my lips at the thought. To top it off, I also add a pair of heels.

Though I'm a little wobbly on them, as I pose around in front of the mirror, I start getting increasingly confident. And in an act of uncharacteristic braver, I take out my phone, snapping a photo of myself in the mirror as I strike a sensual pose.

Leaning back against the door frame, I arch my back, one leg straight, the other slightly lifted to emphasize the shape of my body. The angle is perfect so that the lingerie peeks through, but one cannot make out the exact model. On the other hand, the shoes are the main attraction, the heels adding an erotic flair to the pose.

I take a few pictures, switching up the angles a little.

When I'm done, I look through them, selecting two that are more flattering and sending them to him.

My cheeks are burning as I press send.

It doesn't take a second for Raf's replies to come through, my phone ringing without stop. I don't get to respond to one because ten more follow it.

What?

What is that, pretty girl? Tell me it's not what I think it is?

Fuck… Now when I'm miles away. Fuck.

You're so fucking hot and I'm on the highway.

Noelle… I'm one second away from turning this car around.

My brows are scrunched up in concentration as I try to type up a reply. Before I know it, though, he's calling me.

"Pretty girl, are you trying to torture me?" He asks, his gruff voice sending a shiver down my back.

"You shouldn't text while driving," is all I manage to say.

"I'm not. Hands free," he says before clicking on the video option. "See? I'm not breaking the law," he winks at me.

"Good. I wouldn't want you to become a criminal," I flutter my lashes at him as I extend my arm so he can see me better.

"Fuck. Me. What are you wearing, Noelle?" He curses out loud. "You're trying to kill me, aren't you?"

"No… Of course not," I chuckle. "I wanted to give you a sneak peek of what awaits you tonight. So you come home faster."

"You succeeded. I'm already close to breaking the speed limit to make sure I get there faster. But until then… Give me a little more."

"More?" I frown.

"Lower. Show me your tits," he barks the order impatiently.

I take my time as I lower the camera inch by inch until he's getting a thorough view of my bra.

"Fuck," he groans. "Where the fuck did you get that? It barely covers your pretty nipples."

"I got it for you," I whisper. "So you could tear it off me," I add daringly.

"You can't say shit like that to me, Noelle. Not when I'm away from you…"

"Go do your thing, and know I'll be waiting for you," I tell him. "In the meanwhile…"

"Don't you dare," he bursts out. "Don't you dare touch yourself while I'm not there!"

"But…"

"That pussy is mine and mine alone," he says in a stern voice, his eyes alternating from the road to the phone. "You won't touch it. You won't even think about it. You're going to wait for me to come home and take care of you like the good girl you are," he purrs the words, his voice enveloping my skin and making me shiver with anticipation. "Focus on that frustration I see in your eyes and hold it in. Because when I get to you…" he shakes his head. "The reward will be much sweeter. That I promise."

"Ok," I whisper, unable to argue with him.

Already, my thighs are clenched together as I try to ease some of the discomfort, so I don't know how I'm going to make it through the day.

"Good," he grunts.

I soon hang up the phone, knowing that the more we draw this out the more he'll be unable to follow through with his plans. Still, the fact that he enjoyed it, albeit only half of the lingerie, heightens my anticipation.

Intent on folding the lingerie away before taking Lovely

out for a walk, I stand up. The action is too sudden, though, and I feel a whoosh inside my brain before my knees give out.

Helpless, I fall down, my knees hitting the carpet, my entire body thrust forward as my eyes roll in the back of my head.

I'm trapped.

Like having no control of my own body, I can only lay there, slow tremors racking my body and sending me over the edge.

All of the sudden the room shifts with me, the images before my eyes changing.

Blinking, I'm no longer in my bedroom. I'm not in the house anymore.

Thick, stone walls surround me, a path forward lit with candlelight. The tunnel is narrow, as if it had been built an eternity ago. A musty, almost rancid smell permeates the air, and I find it hard to breathe as I move forward.

I'm me, yet I am not. I feel like myself, yet I'm not in control of what's happening. Like a movie, I can only follow the images. My will has no effect on this reality.

Is it a reality?

I'm a prisoner in my own body as I watch myself act but unable to do anything about it. At the same time, though, the emotions of the moment seep into my very being, infusing me with fear, anger, and suspicion. I *know* that something isn't right.

I continue moving, attuned to everything around me.

From the structure of the building and to the windy path that takes me lower, I realize it must be underground.

Had there been such a thing at the hacienda?

I can't say for sure. The only memories still remaining are of the inside of the *hacienda*, never outside, or in this case under.

I'm holding a small knife in my hand—my only source of defense. I'd managed to smuggle this one at breakfast one morning, since I'm not allowed to have any sharp object around.

How do I know that?

Increasingly, I can hear sounds. People cheering on, as well as booming voices speaking in unknown languages. My brows furrow in confusion as I can't understand a thing of what's being spoken.

It's not English, and it's not Spanish either. It's something else entirely.

The more I walk, the clearer the sounds are. And just as I take a right, rounding a corner, I come across the source.

A gasp escapes me as I jolt back, fitting myself to the wall in hopes no ones sees me.

There are stairs that lead further down and as I slowly turn my head to peek, I realize there are more entrances just like this one, all leading down to the pit. The room is built almost like an inverted pyramid.

Careful so that I'm not seen, I look around, trying to understand what's happening.

No longer fully made of stone, the room is decorated with panes of black glass. There is a golden throne at the end of the room, elevated from the rest of the features. On the wall behind it, there is a huge jaguar painting on the wall. In fact, the entire chamber has jaguar motifs, all in different stages of attack over its prey.

On the ground, there seems to be a drain system. A huge hole lay in the middle before fracturing into smaller pipes that are strewn all around the room. Around the hole, eight men are in a circle, all chanting the same odd words.

Confusion ripples through me, especially as someone shouts something, making everyone stop. Frowning, I realize I recognize the voice—Sergio.

Immediately, fear suffuses my entire being. I know that if he finds me here, he'll kill me.

Yet no matter how much I will my feet to move, they won't.

I stand, almost mesmerized, as I watch the ensuing events.

The eight people dissipate, stepping back to allow for one of them to drag a struggling person draped all in black. Her cries reach my ears, and in no time she's thrown in the hole. She flounders, limbs flailing as she tries to stabilize herself.

My mouth opens in shock as the black cape is wrenched from her body, leaving her completely naked. Long hair hangs to her back, all beautifully braided despite her haggard appearance.

"The first to go in this new moon," Sergio's voice booms out as he steps towards the golden throne, retrieving a large blade from a support nearby. Slowly, he approaches the girl, all the while swinging the knife around.

What the...

I watch stupefied as everyone starts their chant again while Sergio places the curved blade around the girl's throat.

My breath comes in short spurts as I realize what's about to happen.

And I can't do a damned thing about it.

The girl is struggling again in his arms, her movements languid, but still with some degree of strength because Sergio hits her with the back of his hand, making her reel back and stop moving.

Positioning the blade at her throat again, she seems resigned to her fate.

Her chin is up high, her eyes wide open.

And right in that moment, she looks at me.

I go still.

Shaking my head, I take a step back, knowing I have to get out of here before I'm seen. Before I end up like that girl.

The chanting is getting louder, and as I back away, I will my feet to work as I run at full speed.

"What..." the words tumble out of my mouth as I make contact with a hard surface.

Stumbling back, I fall to my ass, my eyes wild with fear as I look upon one of those men—one wearing a similar mask.

"What do we have here?" he drawls, and I immediately recognize the voice—Fernando, Sergio's most trusted man.

CHAPTER FORTY-ONE
NOELLE

I mmediately I know that I need to run—that I need to get out of here. Bringing my knife up, I'm ready to plow my way through. But as I try to do just that, he easily twists my wrist, taking the knife from me. Then, his hand around the material of my shirt, dragging me forward.

His strength is so great that no matter what I do, I can't dislodge myself from his grasp.

"No, no, please let me go," I beg, but the sound falls on deaf ears.

Even as I try to tear at the material of my shirt—anything to escape his hold—I can't.

And as he reaches the stairs, he merely yanks me forward as he drags my body down the rough stone.

Whimpers of pain escape my lips, and soon, I feel myself numb from it.

But not numb enough for what follows.

"Look what I've found, *jefe*," he says in Spanish. "Una pequeña rata."

Sounds erupt in the room, and as I strain to look towards

the direction of the throne, I see Sergio freeze, his knife still in position to kill the girl.

"Damn, I think we've been blessed tonight," he suddenly says, coming to my side.

Instinctively, I cower back, putting my head down so I won't look him in the eyes—knowing that if I do, he will perceive it as a sign of disrespect and make me pay.

Leaning down, he bends his head enough to whisper in my ear.

"You've been a very bad girl, Noelle. You shouldn't have snooped in something that was no business of yours. What is the saying, ignorance is bliss?" he pauses, feeling me shiver in fear. "In this room, I am not Sergio. I am not your husband and you are not my wife. I cannot help you. You *will* behave as told, or you will die. Understood?" I nod rapidly. "You have one chance to survive," he chuckles. "If you can…"

Stepping away from me, he addresses the other people.

"We have been blessed with another contender on this night. The one who spills the most blood wins, and gets another chance at life."

I blink rapidly, unsure whether I'm understanding it right.

"But first, we need to prepare her," he says right before he turns, going back to his throne and grabbing a mortar and pestle, grinding something inside.

Approaching me again, he pries my mouth open as he sticks two fingers coated in a green substance inside.

"Swallow," he commands, and afraid he will hurt me, I gulp it down.

"What…what is it?" I make the courage to ask.

"You don't need to know," he answers dismissively.

Instructing his men, the chants continue, the position resumes as they circle both me and the girl.

One brief moment of clarity and I realize I need to do something. I can't die here. And I certainly won't sit by to let these weird people have their way with me. Because I truly don't know what's going to happen once…

"The rules are simple," Sergio addresses. "There are *no* rules. Each will be provided with a blade. Let's start, shall we?"

My head is pounding, my vision already swimming. Briefly, I think of what Sergio must have given me.

He drugged me…

I don't get to dwell on it further as the other girl jumps on me, blade out and ready to draw blood.

My eyes widen as my body spurs into action, instinct taking over. Rolling to the side, I barely avoid the blade as it hits the ground.

"Die," she yells at me, her eyes red and glazed over.

Whatever Sergio fed me, he must have fed her too. But she's had more time with it in her system than me, which means… I have an advantage. But not for long.

Looking to the side, it's to see the masked men taking their positions in the circle, the chants louder than ever.

The blade whooshes through the air, barely avoiding my face.

I need to focus.

But how can I when I'm thrust into a life or death situation? When there are people on the sidelines waiting for me to die in a grand show?

Sergio must be counting down the seconds, happy to get rid of his good for nothing wife. Then, I'll have made his job easier, no? That he hasn't killed me until now it's a wonder. But he's certainly tried enough times. After all, it's only fitting for causing his accident and making him lose everything. I have to pay for it *every* single day of my life.

Every fucking day.

He must be smug, no doubt, thinking his meek wife

couldn't possibly defend herself. She's certainly never done so against his fists.

But that thought births a new determination within me.

I'm not going to die today.

I'm not going to die here.

And I'll *never* die by Sergio's hands.

I'd rather do it myself—the only peace I can afford at this point.

But this means I can't give up.

A new focus enters my mind, and I try to banish the fogginess that tries to wash over me as I set my gaze on my opponent.

She's breathing raggedly, her pupils huge as her head bobs from side to side. Her fingers are wrapped tightly around the handle of the knife as she holds it to her front, ready for attack.

I get a better grip on my own knife as I take in my surroundings, regulating my breathing and trying to calm my errant pulse. It's only a matter of time before I become *like her*, so I need to take advantage of my rather intact faculties while I can.

My mind set, I'm no longer on the defensive as I take my first step, switching into a position of offensive.

Stepping from right to left on the raised ridges of the floor, I propel myself forward as I run towards her.

Her sight is lazy and she has trouble making sense of my location. One moment I'm on her right side, the next I'm on the left.

Just as I'd expected, her reactions are delayed, thus giving me the necessary time to get in her personal zone.

One more step.

Just one more step and I'm in front of her.

I blink twice.

This is the moment. I can hesitate, and be killed. Or I can kill and live.

There is no choice.

There never was.

Two seconds before she charges at me, I position my knife with the blade upwards. Thrusting it forward, I impale her in one motion, the knife going right under her chin and into her skull.

Her mouth opens as blood starts pouring out. But she doesn't die immediately. Not for a few more seconds. A few seconds too many as her body jerks, her blade making contact with my lower stomach and cutting a straight line across it.

I gasp.

She wheezes.

More blood spurts out.

My hand goes to my midriff while hers seeks to remove the blade lodged in her skull.

We both move, but hers is her last.

With one tug, rivulets of blood start flowing out of her.

I think I hear a gong. A booming sound echoing across the chamber.

I think someone moves me.

I can't move.

I hear my own heartbeat, the sound deafening. My hands go to my ears, pressing down and trying to shut it out.

But there's no shutting out what's happening before me.

Blinking clarity in my eyes, I realize my reactions must have been impacted by shock. I'm already across the room, sitting on the stairs as I look on to the spectacle before me.

Sergio is holding the girl by the hair above the hole, using his big blade to cut once more across her throat, making even more blood pour out of her and floor the circular indentation.

It flows and flows and flows.

Monosyllabic chants reverberate through the air. Guttural sounds that send a shiver down my back, an ominous feeling enveloping me.

Something's wrong. Something's *very, very* wrong.

I can't even process the fact that I took another life, because the monstrosity happening in front of me is too much to bear—too much for anyone to bear.

Her body's been drained, or as much as they managed to. Placing her body outside the hole, Sergio holds her head over it as he brings the blade down with as much strength he can muster.

Hack. Hack. Hack.

I hear the bone shatter, her cervical spine snapping with every hit. Until… Until her head comes off.

Still holding the head by the braids, he raises it in the air.

Her eyes are still open—empty but open. And as I continue looking at her, it's like I still *see* her.

I *killed* her.

Breathe. I need to breathe.

While Sergio walks around the room with the head, Fernando comes out of his corner holding a big ceramic container.

It dawns on me that he's the only one not actively taking part in the ceremony—merely helping Sergio with his tasks.

But as he starts pouring some liquid into the pipe system, I realize what he's doing.

Phosphorescent light starts emanating from the indents in the ground, almost like a shimmery mess. Since I have a higher vantage point, I can see all the silvery particles as they mix with the blood, making it all look entirely too unnatural.

Mercury.

It's mercury. I'm sure of it.

But what's the purpose of all this? Somehow, I can't wrap my head around anything that's going on.

I can barely feel the pain, though I know the cut she gave me wasn't a slight one. I'm simply numb as I keep on watching. And to my great surprise, everyone gives me a wide berth too. I'm already forgotten as they focus on the dead body, getting it ready for whatever else they have in store.

The headless body is still on the ground. Sergio finally brings a pike, staking the head on it and leaving it in the middle of the room.

One by one, the participants start shedding their clothes, all men stroking their erections.

I freeze.

What...

I'm trembling as I watch them all form a line before the headless woman, the first man grabbing the legs and spreading them before aligning his dick to her entrance, pushing in.

My eyes bulge in my head.

He's... He's fucking a dead woman. He's...

I'm hallucinating. There's no other explanation.

He thrusts into her until groans permeate the air. Pulling out of her, he takes a blade as he cuts himself across the hands before working his dick towards the hole in the ground, shooting his seed into the sea of blood and mercury.

As he's done, he moves aside for the next one to do the same.

He takes the headless woman, just like you would a lifeless doll, and he starts fucking her.

"You need to go if you don't want to be next," a low voice startles me. Looking up, I see Fernando on the stairs, looking down at me.

"Come, we're going back to the house," he jerks me up, pulling me by my shirt as he leads me towards the tunnel once more.

My feet move, but my mind takes some time to catch up

with what just happened.

With the *enormity* of what happened.

"What was that?" I whisper. "That's not normal, is it?"

"Normal?" he laughs at me. "Normal is relative, *chavita*, Your husband is a great man," he says with conviction.

"A great man?" I scoff. "He almost had me killed tonight."

"And by luck you didn't die," he shrugs. "You should thank your gods for that."

"Gods... What are you talking about?" I shake my head, confused.

"Your husband has the favor of the Gods. He is the chosen one, and the reason why this region is so prosperous. *Everyone* owes him. He made jobs for people, he loaned money to los campesinos when there was drought. He is king here." He states resolutely.

I can only stare at him flabbergasted.

I've known from the beginning that Sergio and his acolytes are involved in a drug ring, or something to do with drugs. From what I'd managed to eavesdrop, he has multiple factories where he manufactures novel types of drugs and then smuggles them across the border to the States.

"But what was *that*?"

"That?" He turns to me, his eyes glinting dangerously. "That was him keeping his power. And if you don't want to end up like that girl, I'd suggest you forget everything about tonight."

"Why did you take me away?"

I don't know where this barrage of questions is coming from, but I *need* to know. What the fuck did my family drop me into? Because this is no longer just a fucked up family dynamic where fists replaced words. This is a whole other level of horror show.

"Why do you think?" He asks, his tone suggestive.

"To save me," I answer, but my words don't hold any

conviction.

Because the more we walk away from the horror show from before, the more I get the feeling that another one awaits us.

"Save you?" he laughs. "You know," he suddenly stops, turning to face me.

He's not much bigger than I am, but with the drugs in my system he feels huge.

And threatening.

"*El jefe* told me I could get a reward for providing them with extra entertainment."

Instinctively, I back away.

"What... What do you mean?" My voice trembles as I ask.

He doesn't answer, he merely smiles in a lewd way that makes my insides shrivel.

"Stay away from me," I whisper, shaking my head. "Don-don't touch me."

"I've been eying you for a while now, *chavita*. But *el jefe* forbid anyone from touching you, so I bid my time. I knew eventually he would cave."

My eyes flash at him, fear unlike any I've ever known washing through me.

"Oh, don't look so surprised. You're not the first one," he chuckles, his hands already on his belt.

I still feel woozy from the drugs, but I'm not about to sit by and let this man rape me. Instead, I force a smile to my face as I go closer to him, smoothing my hands over his shirt as I bat my lashes at him.

His brows shoot up in surprise and before he knows it, my knee connects with his crotch. A groan escapes him and he crouches over in pain.

Though I can barely move, I make an effort to run.

The material of my shirt is soaked from blood, but I can't even feel the pain. I just run to the best of my ability.

Hope resurfaces inside of me as I see a light at the end of the tunnel. But before I can cross the remaining distance, though, I'm tackled to the ground, his weight on top of me right as the back of his hand connects with my cheek.

My mouth opens in pain, but I can't even make a sound.

By the time awareness creeps back in I can feel him work his hands on my pants, trying to unzip them and lower them down my legs.

He already has his dick out and...

I can't let this happen.

I won't.

Using all the strength I have remaining, I kick at him, not letting him take my pants off. In my clumsy attempts, I manage to hit him in the face enough to distract him and drag myself from under him.

Yet it's still not enough as he quickly recovers, a murderous expression on his face as he grabs my ankles, pulling me back towards him.

My arms are flailing around as I hope to find some type of support to stop him from getting to me, but it's all in vain. There's nothing but these stone walls that are about to witness the death of my last shred of dignity.

As my hands roam the floor, I feel a sharp edge cutting into my skin.

My knife...

The one he'd thrown out of my hand.

My fingers feel for the handle, and securing it in my hold, I bide my own time, knowing this is a decisive moment.

I can't attack too soon, or I'll lose my weapon. I have to do it at the right time.

He pulls the pants off my legs, discarding them aside before settling between my legs, his hands already on my panties.

But before he can get rid of that last barrier, he looks up at me, a smug expression on his face.

"*Ay que bien te voy a cojer, chavita,*" he adds arrogantly.

But just as he is close enough to me, I bring my knife up, placing all my strength into one thrust.

Just like I'd done to the girl, I push the sharp edge into his throat, nabbing just the right angle for the blood to start pouring.

He coughs on me, splattering me with blood before he collapses on top of me—dead weight.

For a moment, I can't move.

Two.

I killed two people in less than a few hours.

"*Demonios,*" I swear softly, staring at the semi-lit ceiling. "*Quién carajos soy yo?*" I ask the question that's been eating at me all along.

Soon, I'll be able to answer it simply.

Not me.

I ceased to be me the day my brother gave me to Sergio.

Now... I'm what's left.

I don't know if it's the drug in my system that's making me react funny to my current circumstances, but other than shock, there's nothing else.

No remorse.

I can't feel anything.

It feels like forever before I manage to throw Fernando off me, getting into a sitting position and pulling my pants back on. My stomach wound begins hurting in earnest, and I have trouble bending down.

Yet as I stare at Fernando's soulless body, the fact that his dick is still out in the open gives me an idea.

Grabbing the knife, I start cutting.

I might not always be able to defend myself against Sergio's fists. But I can at least show him he can't do whatever he wants with me.

He can't give me to other men.

My fingers close around the puny piece of flesh, and almost in a daze, I find my way out of the tunnel and back to my room.

As I reach it, though, I grab a piece of paper and I write my husband a message.

Vete al diablo.

Then, I simply leave it at his door, dropping the detached dick on top of it.

It's only after that I breathe relieved as I lock my room, not even letting Lucero come in to tend to me.

Lifting my shirt, the wound looks nasty—worse than I thought.

And together with my other scars... I snort as I look into the mirror.

Beaten down, yet not defeated.

If I have to kill everyone who comes at me, then so be it.

And if I get the chance to kill Sergio...

A sick smile pulls at my lips.

I'll do it.

My eyes snap open, my stomach churning from the elusive memory. I barely manage to get up and run to the bathroom before I empty the contents of my stomach. I keep heaving and heaving, the images so insanely nauseating, I can't manage to pull myself together again.

And as I keep replaying the scenes, especially *my* thoughts, I can't help but ask...

Who was I?

Who the hell was I, because I don't recognize that person.

Slumping down on the bathroom floor, my back is against the cold tiles as I look at the ceiling through red tinged eyes.

A killer.

I'm a killer.

Raf was right. I'm a fucking impostor.

Chapter Forty-Two
Noelle

There are times in our lives when we have to take a good look at ourselves and truly *see*. Not the idealized version, not the biased version.

The reality.

I've lived the last couple of years of my life blaming everyone around me and thinking I'd been just a victim. A *meek* victim who'd been persecuted time and time again, first by her family, then by her husband, and then by her family again.

I'd looked, and I'd only seen what *I* wanted to see.

The truth, however, is far from fair. And it's far from pretty.

The truth...will wreck me.

I blink, bringing myself back to the present as I'm greeted by the person staring back at me in the mirror. It's me yet... it's no longer me.

Identity is produced by memories. We are who we are because of the information stored inside and the experiences that have shaped us.

For the longest time, I've been a pianist. And though there

is the inherent talent, I could not call myself one if all my musical knowledge were to disappear.

The same goes for all my other memories.

I'd erased a lot of my memories from before and in turn, I'd erased the person I'd been.

But now?

A sad smile pulls at my lips as I raise a finger to trace my features.

For a few weeks I've been having flashbacks. Sometimes it's just impressions and feelings, and other times it's full scenes, like the one in the tunnels.

Yet the more I see myself through my past self's eyes, the more I start understanding Raf's initial distaste for me.

I wasn't good. I wasn't nice. And at some point...I stopped being able to claim I was a victim.

I see snippets of the past, and I don't like the person I was.

More than anything, she scares me. She'd had no qualms killing to keep herself alive—and then doing it again.

I'd truly thought I would never be capable of murder—no matter the circumstances.

Because good people don't kill. Good people don't lack remorse when they kill. And good people certainly *don't* prepare for the next kill.

That's just the thing though. I *wasn't* good.

"You ok?" I swivel, my eyes wide as I come face to face with Raf.

"Yeah. I was just applying some cream," I lie, forcing a smile.

"This late?" He blinks, bringing his wrist up to check the time on his watch.

"My face felt very dry and I couldn't sleep," I make the excuse.

What else am I to say? That my past is coming back to haunt me?

That my ex-husband was involved in God knows what type of pagan rituals and he was performing human sacrifices? That I watched a corpse being fucked?

Or better yet, that I've killed people.

I've had their blood bathe my skin and drip down my face. And I hadn't blinked.

I hadn't fucking blinked.

The worst, though, is that I *know* I will remember more. And when I do...

"Let me help you," he says as he comes into the bathroom, his hands on my shoulders as he backs me against the tub. "Sit," he orders just as he takes the jar of cream.

"You don't have to. You should go back to sleep. You must be tired after today."

He'd come back in time for dinner—just as he'd promised me.

But instead of finding his sweet wife, he'd found a stranger. One that lied with every word that came out of her mouth.

"I'm never tired for you, pretty girl," he says sweetly, and my heart constricts in my chest.

My cheeks are tight and strained from the fakeness of my smile as I speak even more false platitudes.

Who am I?

"Here," he brings the pad of his finger on my skin, swiping some cream before swirling it around to blend it. His touch is light and gentle, and his eyes are so full of affection —more than I've ever received in my life.

I watch him closely, memorizing every feature.

He can't find out.

I don't think I could bear for him to look at me in disdain. I wouldn't survive.

Instead, I simply thrust everything from my mind, focusing on *him*.

"I love you, Raf. More than anything in the world," I tell him. And in that moment, another certainty washes over me.

I would kill for him.

"You're my heart, pretty girl," he caresses me reverently. "You're everything that's sweet and kind," he continues, those words hitting me in the chest like sharp arrows.

I cough, suddenly out of breath, my eyes moist, my lashes full of unshed tears.

"Easy," he pats me on the back. "What's wrong?"

"Nothing," I shake my head. "Nothing…" I repeat.

"Let's go to bed then," he smiles at me as he swoops me in his arms.

But as he lays me in bed, wrapping me around his body, I can't help but ask.

"Raf," I wet my lips.

My arms are spread on his naked chest, my chin on my hands as I peer at him through my lashes.

"Hm?"

"Hypothetically…" I start, taking a deep breath. "What would you say if I actually harmed someone. If I…killed someone?"

He chuckles.

"There's no hypothetical. You're not capable of something like that," he states with conviction and my heart plummets.

"I may have deluded myself in the past that you were some evil femme fatale," he laughs, "but I know it was my erroneous perception. I *didn't* know you. I only knew *of* you."

I purse my lips at his words, every one of them making me feel even worse.

"You're too kind to harm anyone," he adds.

"But what if," I whisper. "What if I killed people?"

"People? As in multiple?"

I nod.

He looks at me for a moment before laughing.

"You'd never do that, Noelle. I know *you*. I know the woman I fell for, and she could never bear the thought of hurting someone. Even if they deserved it."

"Your view of me is too nice," I murmur, my cheeks red.

"It's the truth. You made me fall for you with your kindness and lack of artifice. Your genuine responses and the way you stood up to me showed me *exactly* who you are. Someone extraordinary. And someone I'd do anything to protect," he bends his head to kiss my forehead.

I smile weakly, getting comfortable as we both go to sleep. But though he manages to fall asleep easily, I don't.

Because how could I when now, more than ever, I know he's fallen for an impostor.

———

"WHAT ARE YOU DOING?" I startle as I feel Raf behind me, the urge to close the laptop overwhelming. But that would mean implying I'm doing something wrong. So I just turn to him, a tight smile on my face.

"Just browsing the internet."

"Aztec human sacrifice," he raises a brow. "Now *that*'s interesting," he notes.

"Do you know anything about it?"

"I took courses on Pre-Columbian Americas," he scratches the back of his head, "and I remember that the heart and the head were pretty important. A lot of facts were exaggerated by the conquistadores when they reached the Americas to justify their actions. That is not to say that sacrifice was not part of the culture. There are a lot of pictograms that depict the practice."

"I see," I nod, raking my teeth over my lower lip as I mull over his words. "But it's an old practice, right? It doesn't happen anymore."

"Of course. Can you imagine anyone performing human sacrifices in this day and age and getting away with that?" he laughs. "Though the belief in the old Gods might still exist in isolated communities."

"Why would they do it, though? I don't understand the allure," I sigh.

"We can't look at these cultures through a western lens. They didn't have the same system of values we have, or the same understanding of right and wrong. A lot of these sacrifices were performed to appease a specific god and to bring some type of benefit to the community. Most of the time, these rituals were done for fertility and to avoid draughts that would affect agriculture."

Immediately, my mind goes to what Fernando had said about prosperity and Sergio taking care of the region. Still, the entire thing seems preposterous.

Maybe it wasn't real.

Yet no matter how much I tell myself that, I *know* it was real.

"Do you know of any ritual with a jaguar?" I ask, thinking back to any clues. I want to add more, like the way the girl had been killed, but that would only raise suspicions.

"Hmm, let me look," he says as he scoots me over so he can join me on the bed. Taking the laptop from me, he starts typing up a few searches before showing me the results.

"This?" He asks as he points at one picture of a stone jaguar, the shape and overall design not too different than the one I'd seen.

"Yeah," I nod.

"It represents the god Tezcatlipoca. His name means smoking mirrors, and he was considered an all-powerful deity for the Aztecs. He also dealt in sorcery and what we might call today black magic," he explains.

"Black magic?"

"Rituals dedicated to him were said to offer the priests in charge powers and unspeakable wealth," he shrugs. "It's all very fascinating. Look at this," he shows me a picture of a skull designed with a mosaic of stones and shells. "This is the representation of Tezcatlipoca, and this," he points to the black glass, "is obsidian."

"Smoking mirror, so *dark* mirror?"

"Right. Since the obsidian is black, and he is associated with it."

"That's fascinating," I breathe out. "And you're so knowledgeable about this."

Everything is interesting, minus the sacrifice part.

"I learned about it in college," he shrugs. "I did my dissertation on minerals and precious stones in Meso-America and their uses as ritualistic tools."

I look at him wide eyed as I process the information. I knew he was smart, but I didn't realize *how* smart. For a moment, I feel ashamed of my lack of education.

All my life I'd had tutors, but never a formal education. The disciplines were chosen for me, but they were basic— enough so I could comport myself in society. After all, when your destiny is to become a wife and a mother, what use do you have of higher education, or of any type of knowledge?

The knowledge I do possess is due to my voracious appetite for media. Since young I've been an avid cinephile, always on my computer in search of my next favorite. Because I was so alone growing up, my upbringings restricting me from doing a lot of things normal teenagers did, I simply lost myself in the wonders of the internet, picking up random facts here and there.

"Now it's your turn to tell me why you were so interested in this," he closes the laptop as he turns to me, an amused expression on his face."

I tilt my head, studying him.

I can't answer the question truthfully when I don't under-stand the past myself. Maybe if I had something more than just a snapshot, I would be able to piece together what had happened and why Sergio had had the equivalent of an inverted pyramid temple under the *hacienda*.

There is also another question... Can I trust my mind? Was what I saw real?

Ceremonies. Human Sacrifice. Necrophilia.

Everything is out of a horror movie.

"I was watching a movie and thought it was very interest-ing. Although the sacrifices were a little gory for me."

"There are countless depictions of them in pictograms, and they are *not* for the faint of heart," he chuckles. "But if you're interested, we can visit a museum that hosts Aztec artifacts. I'll look for exhibitions and we can do a short trip."

"Really? That would be awesome," my lips stretch in a genuine smile.

Twirling my arms around his neck, I bring him to me, kissing his cheek.

"Come here, pretty girl," he says as he swoops me up, laying me on his lap and tugging me to his chest.

His head resting on my head, he brings his arms around me as he hugs me tightly.

"I was thinking we could look into venues so you could perform," he suddenly says. "If you want to, that is," he amends. "But now that we're not tied down by anything, and since there's no more danger..."

"You'd be ok with me becoming a performer?" I lean back so I can look him in the eye.

"I'd be ok with anything that makes you happy. And I know that music is part of you," he says as he brings his hand over my heart. "I would never dream of taking that away from you."

"But that would mean traveling and..." *being away from you.*

"I'd come with you, of course," he retorts in indignation. "You think I would let you travel the world by yourself?" he grumbles under his breath.

"You'd do that for me?" I blink, surprised. "What about you? What would you do? I'm sure you'll have work and..."

"Work can be done remotely too. And I happen to love traveling. Where you go, I go. We're a package deal, the two of us," he says as he flicks his finger over my nose in an affectionate manner. "And if you're happy, I'm happy."

"You're too sweet to me, Raf," I sigh, unable to believe how lucky I am.

But if he finds out...

I quickly thrust that thought aside. There's no way he can find out except from me. And I'm not about to confess out loud that I'm a murderer and that I might have very well killed his first love.

At this point, I'm just happy she's dead. It's so bad of me to even think that, but I can't help it. I'm more than happy, I'm ecstatic that she's dead.

Because he's mine, and only mine.

And if she weren't dead...then I might very well kill her myself.

I inhale sharply, the direction of my thoughts terrifying me.

Who am I?

"You bring out the best in me," he winks.

But he might bring the worst in me...

We spend the rest of the day lounging in bed and watching TV. I know Raf is trying his best to forget what happened in New York and the fact that one of his own friends might have betrayed him. There's also the issue with Marcello and his family... The entire situation is a mess.

"We can go back to the city, you know," I add at dinner. "We've had an extended vacation as it is. I'm fine with returning."

"Are you sure?" he frowns. "I don't want to ruin this…"

"You're not ruining anything. We can return on Monday. How is that? That way we have the weekend to forget about everything and then we go back to the real world."

"If you're sure?" He asks, looking at me with a worried expression. Before I can reply, though, he gets out of his seat, swooping me up and taking my seat before placing me on his lap.

"I'm sorry we have to cut it short. I wanted you to have a good time away from all the mob business, since I know you don't like it."

"Whether I like it or not, it's our life," I tell him gently. "And I know you didn't choose this willingly either."

My brother had been pretty strict about the terms of their agreement, and he needs Raf to be the head of the Guerra family so he can take advantage of its name and resources.

"I promise you I'll do my best to keep you away from the ugly side of it. We'll travel the world together. You'll play the piano, and I'll do all the dirty work," he kisses my temple.

Taking my fork from my hand, he proceeds to feed me.

I giggle at his attempt, but he shushes me.

"I like to take care of you," he whispers in my hair. "Let me do that, please," he says in a low voice.

"You do realize I can eat by myself too," I challenge.

"I know. But I want to take care of every single one of your needs, pretty girl. Because you're mine. And because…" he trails off.

I turn.

"Because?"

"Because this is the only way I can ever make it up to you for how I behaved. By spoiling and pampering you and showing you how much I care about you," he gives me a tight smile.

"Raf…" I trail off, taking a deep breath. "I thought we'd talked about that before. It's time to stop feeling guilty."

"I don't know if I can," he whispers.

"I forgive you. You need to forgive yourself too," I bring his knuckles to my mouth for a kiss.

He grunts, but doesn't let me go, continuing to feed me as before.

Shaking my head with a smile, I accept it as his token of affection since it's clearly important to him to make sure I'm taken care of.

After we're done with our food, we split the cleaning tasks—he washes the dishes, I dry them. But not before he plays some music for us.

We both move to the rhythm as we clean the kitchen up, and I can't help but laugh as he takes my hand to lead me into a spin.

The fun is cut short though when my phone rings.

Frowning, I pick it up to see it's my brother.

"You answer that and I'll be upstairs in the room," Raf says, turning off the music and leaving the kitchen.

Taking a deep breath, I answer the call.

"How is it going, Noelle?" He asks in his usual somber voice.

"Good," I answer in a neutral tone. "We're in Newport," I tell him though I am sure he already knows.

"So I've heard. I hope you have better weather than we do," he chuckles, and my lips flatten into a thin line at his attempts at small talk.

"How is Yuyu and the baby?"

"Great. She's recovered well, and he's getting bigger by the day," he adds proudly.

There's a pregnant pause as neither knows what to say.

"We'll be coming home soon. I thought I'd give you a heads up. We won't be staying there long, though."

"You're moving for good?"

"We've decided to take a trip to Italy, tour the boot so to speak."

"Are you thinking of moving there permanently?"

The situation had only gotten tenser as past enemies had resurfaced for both Cisco and Yuyu after the reveal of her identity. I know that they've been extremely careful now that they had the baby to think about too.

"Maybe," he answers flippantly.

"Is that why you called?" I roll my eyes.

"I wanted to check up on you and make sure Rafaelo is treating you well."

It's on the tip of my tongue to shoot him a sarcastic retort.

Now you care?

Instead, I take a deep breath, and I reply civilly.

"Yes. He's treating me very well, Cisco. You don't have to worry." *As if you ever did.*

A brief pause and I can hear him breathing on the line.

"Good. I'll see you in New York then," he says before he hangs up.

To say that I'm surprised that he'd inquire into my well-being is, well, an understatement. Shaking my head in amusement, I head upstairs to our room.

We'd planned to continue our marathon of horror movies well into the night, so I'm excited for that.

The door to the room is wide open, and I get this crazy idea to surprise him with a jump scare. Abandoning my slides, I tiptoe barefoot on the floor as I attempt to stealthily enter the bedroom.

I'm barely inside when I frown. He's holding something in his hand, his expression melancholic. But as soon as he spots me, he throws the item into the drawer, pretending he wasn't doing anything wrong.

"What was that?" I ask as I reach his side, bummed that he'd seen me before I could scare him.

"Nothing," he smiles. "Just my watch," he lies.

I blink in surprise.

"I'll go take a shower and then we can get back to Saw," he winks at me as he jumps from the bed, heading straight into the bathroom.

A little unsettled, I spend two minutes staring at the floor as I try to make sense of what just happened and the fact that he lied to me.

His watch was still in the kitchen when I'd left, since he'd taken it off while washing the dishes.

But why would he lie to me?

My eyes skitter to the drawer, and something inside of me compels me to see what it is.

I extend my hand to open the drawer, before putting it down, scowling at myself and lack of trust.

I shouldn't snoop around.

But he lied.

Why did he lie?

A few more attempts at opening the drawer end in failure and I end up taking a deep breath and making my mind.

I want to see—I need to see.

Straightening my back, I look in the direction of the bathroom, satisfied that the sound of the shower is still on, and I slowly open the drawer, reaching inside.

My fingers wrap around a small stone dangling from a thin chain. And as I lift it up, it's to realize what it is…

My eyes close on a tired exhale, and without even thinking, I drop it back, closing the drawer and trying to put it out of my mind.

Why?

Why does he still have the necklace? And what is he doing with it *here*?

It's been months since he stopped wearing it, so why now? Since then, I haven't even seen it around—not even at home.

But for him to have it here?

I try to regulate my breath, but it's becoming increasingly harder not to give in to the panic attack threatening to overtake me.

Why?

I'm not even angry. I'm...sad.

Betrayed.

He promised me she was in the past. He promised that she...

I shake my head, my heart pounding in my chest.

Why?

Am I not enough? Why else would he need a reminder of her?

He loves me. I try to tell myself that he loves *me,* that he's married to *me* and that she's already dead.

But that's the crux of the issue, isn't it? How can *anyone* compete with a ghost?

He loves me.

The words become a small chant in my head as I try to convince myself of the fact—as I tell myself that the necklace doesn't mean anything.

But it does.

I bring my fist to my chest as I bang against it in an attempt to settle my errant heart.

He loves me.

Does he, though?

Panic bubbles inside of me as I mentally go over every single interaction we'd had.

Has he ever said the words?

I tell him I love him every chance I get, but his reply is always the same.

I adore you.

You're my heart.

I care about you.

It's not...love, is it?

My lungs constrict and I feel like I can't breathe. Dashing to the window, I push it open as I take big gulps of air. Yet no matter how much I inhale, or exhale, I still feel like I'm suffocating.

My hand goes to my throat as I massage it, willing it to open up and let me breathe normally.

But the more I think about it, the more agitated I become.

He's *never* told me he loved me. He used any other word, just not love.

No, it can't be right.

I refuse to believe that he doesn't love me. He's shown me repeatedly how much he cares about me.

But is that love?

Hasn't he reiterated time and time again that he feels guilty about the way he treated me? So is that all it is? The fact that he feels sorry for me? Am I just a pity fuck? Is that it?

There's this tiny voice inside my head that won't let me be. It contradicts every little explanation I might come up with, making me face the dire fact that he...

"No, no, no," I whisper, my voice ragged.

"Noelle?" He calls my name out, and in my panic I haven't heard the bathroom door open.

Closing my eyes, I count to ten before I slowly turn, plastering a fake smile on my face.

He has a towel wrapped around his waist, and nothing more. His skin is glistening, small droplets of water dripping down his hard chest.

He's mine.

I refuse to believe he's anything but mine.

He's never even slept with Lucero. I'm the only one who knows him intimately. The only woman he's ever been inside.

But is that enough?

"Are you feeling ill? You look a little pale," he says as he comes to my side, the back of his hand on my forehead as he checks my temperature.

"No," I shake my head, "I'm fine," I lie.

Taking a step forward, I open my arms as I hug him, holding him tightly against me.

"I love you, Raf," I tell him, awaiting to see his answer.

There's the barest pause, but it's there, and my heart drops in my chest.

"I adore you," he murmurs softly.

My eyes go wide, and I do my best to keep myself from breaking down.

Instead, I ask the question in a roundabout way.

"You're the only person who's ever loved me," I add, waiting for his reply.

"You have no idea how much I care about you, pretty girl," his arms come around me, the heat from his body transferring to mine.

But why does it feel like I'm freezing?

He doesn't admit, nor deny it.

Whether I want to or not, I have to concede that he's never uttered the word *love* to me. He's *never* used it.

Chapter Forty-Three
Noelle

That night, for the first time, I block everything, my body almost on autopilot. He's his usual attentive self, kissing every inch of skin as he seeks to wring pleasure from my body.

Yet I can't.

I lay there, my mind a whirlpool of confusion, and I can't feel anything. I let him make love to me, but instead of joy and excitement, I feel an overwhelming sense of bleakness.

He entices me with his mouth, teasing and nibbling, and I can't react.

I simply can't.

And for the first time ever, I fake an orgasm, wanting everything to be over—wanting him to get away from me. Even as he thrusts into me, what I would have otherwise welcomed more than anything, now feels like the worst type of stabbing pain.

He seeks my lips, brushing his against mine in a sweet kiss before leaning back to watch me.

I blink back tears as I realize I can't even look at him. Instead, I ask him to switch positions—take me from behind so I won't have to see him and his expression. So I won't fool myself when it's becoming increasingly clear that I've been blind to his affection the entire time.

He cares for me. I won't deny that. But you care for a sister. You care for a friend...

You don't *care* for your wife.

I lay on my belly, his grunts in my ears as I just wait for it all to end. One more thrust and he empties himself into me, collapsing over my body as he breathes harshly against my skin.

"I'll go clean up," I murmur, disentangling myself from him.

I spend more time in the bathroom, knowing it won't take long for him to fall asleep. Only when I know he's out do I join him in bed, staring at the ceiling and realizing fairytales aren't real. Muffling the sound of my cries, I tell myself that I can take anything he gives me. That I can love him for the both of us.

But I fear it's just another lie....

The following morning, I'm up before him, taking Lovely for a walk and trying to clear my head. I won't be able to solve anything if I keep everything bottled inside. More than anything, I know the issue will continue to bother me if I don't address it with him.

I *need* to know why.

My mind made up, I go back to the house just in time to find him building a dog house for Lovely.

As if he couldn't imprint himself even more in my heart...

"Raf?" Holding Lovely in my arms, I head to his side.

"There is our little baby," he says as he gets up, coming closer to lay a kiss on top of Lovely's head. "You're a good fur mamma, pretty girl," he winks at me, and immediately I feel my cheeks heat up.

"Thank you," I whisper, trying to look away from him.

He's wearing a tank top that displays his muscular arms, sweat clinging to him and glistening in the sun—all making him look like a golden Adonis.

Scooping Lovely from my arms, he places him at the entrance of the mini-house.

"What do you think?" He asks, amused.

Lovely limps inside, immediately curling down on the cushion Raf had set for him. He gives a cute woof before snuggling closer.

"He likes it," I add, a genuine smile on my lips

"You like it, don't you?" he pats him on the head playfully.

"Raf..." I take a deep breath. "Can I see you in the bedroom in five minutes?"

He frowns at my words but eventually nods.

My fists clenched, I head back to the house first, going straight for the room and opening the drawer. Sure enough, the necklace is still inside.

Taking it out, I palm it, an odd sensation enveloping me as I touch it. The stone is yellow-brownish, the sun hitting it and making it sparkle. Though I am mesmerized by the sight, I refuse to look at it more than I need to. After all, it's a reminder that he's *not* mine—at least not fully.

"Pretty girl?" His voice echoes in the room as he steps inside.

His eyes widen as he spots the necklace in my hand.

"What..."

"Why do you have this, Raf?" I do my best to control my voice, but it still comes out shaky.

He wastes no time in striding over to me, grabbing it from my hands.

"It doesn't mean anything," he says, though he won't look me in the eye.

"You said you got rid of it."

"I said I stopped wearing it, not that I got rid of it."

"But... Why? Why would you still keep it?"

"Why would I throw it away?" He counters.

"You said..." I take a deep breath. "You said she was in the past. But how can I believe she's truly in the past if you have her necklace hanging around."

"This was originally *my* necklace," he explains. "My mother gave it to me on my eighteenth birthday," he continues, and I frown at the explanation.

"But..."

"You don't have to worry about it, I promise you." He drops to his knees in front of me, one hand cupping my cheek as he turns me to face him. "It's just a memory."

"I don't want you thinking about her," I whisper, biting my lip.

"She's dead, Noelle. You're here, with me. *You* are my wife."

I blink.

His voice is full of conviction, yet why do I feel like I can't trust his words?

"That's the issue, Raf. She *is* dead. You never got any closure and I worry that in time you'll keep yearning for her."

He shakes his head vehemently.

"No. I told you, pretty girl. She's my past and you are my future. There's nothing else to it."

His tone suggests that he wants me to drop the issue. Yet how can I when I feel like he's not telling me everything? When I can see that no matter how many assurances he gives me, a part of his heart might be forever out of reach to me—forever hers.

How can I sit still, even knowing that?

"Why did you lie to me, then? Why did you say it was your watch when it wasn't?"

My eyes on his, I note the sudden tension in his features.

"I didn't want you to worry," he replies in a low voice.

"You *lied*," I repeat, my voice breaking.

"I'm sorry," he says quietly. "I really didn't want you to think too much of it. It wasn't with ill intent."

"I want to believe you. But I don't want to be second best to a ghost, Raf," I whisper.

"You're not. God, you're not," he groans, bringing my face closer to his for a kiss. "You're not," he repeats against my lips.

I don't reply, merely nodding and forcing a smile on my face.

He takes me in his arms, murmuring sweet words in my ears as he slowly undresses me.

He makes love to me like he *does* love me.

But he never says the words.

———

I GASP FOR AIR, my eyes snapping wide open as I take in my surroundings.

I'm home. I'm safe. I'm not…

For a while now, it's always been the same dream.

I'm standing over a bloody corpse, a knife in my hand as I look smugly at my surroundings. I know it's *me*, yet it doesn't feel like it.

My entire body is covered in sweat as I drag the sheet off my body. But as awareness creeps in, I realize I'm *alone*.

Alone in our room.

"Raf?" I call out, thinking he's in the bathroom. "Raf, it's not funny," I add just in case he's trying to play a trick on me.

Since the confrontation earlier in the day, things have been slightly strained between us, but I can see him trying to make it better. Until we'd gone to bed, he hadn't left my side, doing everything in his power to make me comfortable.

If only he understood that he could do it with three words.

If he just told me he loved me, he'd put my doubts to sleep once and for all.

Grabbing my robe, I shrug it on and tie it around my middle. Knocking on the bathroom door, I open it to realize it's empty.

Where is he?

Thinking he might have gotten hungry, I go downstairs, checking the kitchen and the ground floor. But it's in vain. There's absolutely no sign of him *anywhere*.

"Raf?" I call out again, this time my voice echoing in the house.

The nightly breeze brushes against my skin, making me shiver as I pull my robe tighter around me. He has to be somewhere around.

A little worried, I start looking in every room on the first floor. Yet it's soon clear he's not in any. What about... The second and third floors?

But what would he be doing there when they haven't been cleaned, the rooms dusty and stale from unuse?

I become a little uneasy as I make my way up the stairs, first checking the second floor.

Nothing.

Yet it's as I go up to the third floor that I start hearing little sounds—something akin to harsh moans.

Led by those sounds, I put one foot in front of another as I head towards the source—a room at the end of the corridor that looks to be locked from the inside.

Placing my ear to the door, though, I listen to signs of life.

"No!"

I recognize Raf's voice as he yells.

My eyes widen, my mind coming up with the worst scenario. Without even thinking, I dash downstairs to the pantry where there is a spare chain of keys for the entire house. I quickly grab them, running back to the third floor and trying one after another until I get the right one.

Luckily, he hadn't left the key on the inside, so I'm able to push the door open.

But as I do, it's to be struck by the surroundings. The room is tiny, yet clean, as if it had been prepared in advance. There's a double bed in the middle, the sheets crisp and clean. But what shocks me the most is the sight of Raf.

He's on the bed, one wrist chained to the bed as he writhes in pain, his hand pulling at the shackle in an attempt to free himself. A thin sheet barely covers his naked body.

"Raf," I close the door shut behind me as I hurry to his side, assessing him from head to toe.

My first thought is that someone had done this to him, but it's soon clear that he's done it himself.

"Raf?" I bring my hand to his forehead to find it slick with perspiration. He's moving around wildly in bed.

Yet as I call him out again, this time louder, his eyes snap open.

His irises are a stormy blue, his pupils out of proportions. And as he looks at me, it is as if he can barely recognize me.

"Raf, what the hell is happening," I mutter to myself, immediately spotting the key to the handcuffs hidden under the nightstand.

Grabbing it, I quickly undo his cuff, throwing it aside.

"Are you ok? What happened?" I ask, gently massaging his wrist.

He's not answering, merely tilting his head to the side to study me.

"Raf," I take a seat on the bed next to him as I palm his cheek.

He looks...high. There's no other explanation.

"Let's get you back to our bedroom and I'll make you some tea," I offer, not knowing what I can do in this case.

Still, to think of Raf on drugs... It's almost preposterous to consider such a notion. He's lived with us for months, and never once did he give the inclination that he was on drugs.

Except...

My eyes widen when I recall the first time we'd met in my piano room—a time that he hadn't even remembered.

His eyes had been the same as now, his pupils huge and lacking recognition.

"Let's go," I urge him gently, grabbing his hand and pulling him off the bed. "You'll feel better in our own bed."

The words are barely out of my mouth when he pulls me to him, the action rougher than what I'm used to from him.

I fall on top of him, my breasts against his hard chest.

Still, he doesn't say anything as he regards me curiously, his other hand coming up to trace my features.

"It's me, Raf," I tell him.

His nostrils flare as he looks at me, his brows pinched in a frown.

Before I can say another word, both his hands grab at my robe, tearing at it and pulling it away.

"Raf," I breathe in, surprised at his sudden aggression.

Yet I don't get a moment of reprieve as my nightgown soon follows until I'm standing naked against him—just like he is.

Bringing his nose to the crook of my neck, he inhales deeply.

"Mine," he whispers.

One hand snakes around my waist, and in no time I find myself on my back, the breath knocked out of me.

Spreading my legs, he settles himself between them, the head of his hard cock bumping against my core.

"Raf, what are you doing?"

His eyes closed, he hovers over my face, almost as if he's breathing me in—savoring me in a primitive way. Moving lower, he makes his way down my body, his tongue making contact with my skin as he trails it between the valley of my breasts and all the way down my stomach until he reaches my pussy.

There's no gentleness as he dives between my legs, lapping at me like he can't get enough. He uses the flat of his tongue to lick me thoroughly before pushing the tip against my opening.

Though surprised at the turn of events, I can't help the way he brings my body to life, my eyes rolling back in my head as he makes me climax with just a few strokes of his tongue.

But he doesn't stop.

Again and again, he drinks me in until I'm screaming his name.

"I can't..." I whimper, my body too spent.

Bringing my hands to his hair, I tug him up, trying to get him to put me out of my misery.

"Please, Raf..."

Rising up, he still has a blank expression on his face as he comes back to me, his lips on my neck as his fingers dig roughly into the flesh just above my hip bone.

His cock is at my entrance, the head barely inside as he half-thrusts into me before retreating. I arch my back, my arms around his neck as I open up for him, urging him to take me—slake his need on my body.

He surges within me in one go, the power of his thrust making me reel.

My mouth opens on a silent moan, my head thrown back as my nails lodge into the skin just below his shoulder blades. And as he pulls all the way out before sliding in again, I can't help the sounds I'm making—the way I'm mewling and crying out, shouting his name loud enough to be heard in the entire house.

He's rough—rougher than he's ever been. But it's appealing in a way I'd never thought possible, each stroke of his cock hitting a spot deep within me and making me gasp both in pain and in pleasure.

"My Raf," I bring him to me for a kiss, my mouth opening for the thrust of his tongue as it aligns with the thrust of his cock. "Yes, fuck me," I whisper against his lips. "Fuck me, destroy me, do whatever you want to me but love me," I cry out my plea, my lashes damp with tears of exertion and too much emotion. "Please love me," I whisper on a ragged breath.

"Mine," he rumbles, the only thing he's said so far. "You're mine," he nibbles at my lips, his eyes cold yet *warm*.

Without warning, he turns me around, dragging my ass towards him as he plows into me—faster, harder, deeper. His fingers find their way in my hair, digging painfully in my scalp as he yanks my head back, his teeth scraping at my earlobe.

My body starts shuddering, my pussy gripping him tightly as my channel tries to squeeze him dry. I barely contain a moan as my muscles tense, my orgasm rolling through me.

His mouth trails down my neck before he clamps his teeth down on my shoulder, biting into my flesh. The gesture is animalistic, the initial pain giving way to a surprising plea-sure as he licks at the wound. I'm pretty sure he's drawn blood, but at this point I revel at every sensation—be it pain or pleasure.

"More," I whimper, and I suddenly find myself face down on the bed, his hand moving from my hair to my nape as he holds me tightly, his fingers digging into my skin and almost cutting my air supply. He pushes me harder into the mattress just as he increases the speed of his thrusts, the force doubling.

Muffled sounds of flesh slapping against flesh, as well as my ragged breath and his own harsh one echo through the room.

He surges into me so violently, I can barely make a sound as he pins me down even harder.

The corners of my eyes fill with tears, the pressure inside of me building to such a painful crescendo, it erupts into a multitude of flashes that dance before my eyes. For a moment I can't make sense of him, or me, or how we are two separate entities.

There's just *feeling*.

This joining that's wild and feral and so exquisitely addictive it's making every single atom in my body hum in pleasure.

He's inside of me—so deep inside I wish he'd never leave. But more than anything, I feel him in my heart.

His hold on my throat starts to weaken as he slows his thrusts. His cock pulses inside of me, the swollen head bumping against my G-spot and eliciting a moan from me as I wrap my fingers in the sheets, trying to ground myself.

My walls close in on him, sucking him in and squeezing him dry as he climaxes. His warm release floods my insides, the feel unlike any other.

"Fuck," he curses as he collapses on top of me, his arms coming around as he secures me under him, not giving me any chance to escape. "I love you," he whispers in my hair.

My eyes go wide at his words.

Turning my head to the side, sweat clings to my skin and hair as I take a big gulp of air.

"I love you too, Raf," I tell him with as much emotion as I can muster. "I love you more than anything," I confess.

"*Luz*," he murmurs, and I frown. "*Mi luz*," he continues, peppering kisses all over my back.

My heart stops in my chest.

Light. My light.

"*Te amo. Te quiero tanto, mi luz.*"

I blink, unable to move. My entire body is frozen as my brain processes what he just said.

I love you. I love you so much, my light.

Chapter Forty-Four
Noelle

My breathing intensifies as dry sobs rack my body. I keep on gasping for an air that won't come. Just like before, I feel like I'm slowly suffocating, my throat closing up as shudders go down my spine.

From unnatural stillness, I go to an aggression that's uncharacteristic of me as I push and push against him, needing to get as far away from here as possible—as far away from him.

How could he...

He falls on his back, a small groan escaping him. Yet he's barely aware of what's happening—of the fact that he just ripped my heart out of my chest and trampled on it.

Pulling myself together, I stare at his form, shock slowly washing through me. Tears are streaming down my cheeks and I can't stop the way my body is seemingly breaking down. Stumbling out of the bed, I fall to the ground, my knees making contact with the hard floor. Pain radiates from the injured area, but I can't register it. I can't register any outside stimuli when my insides are crumbling.

My sight foggy, my throat clogged up, I push myself up,

somehow making it out of the room and down the stairs. I don't know what I'm doing. I don't know where I'm going. I just know I need to be away. Taking a few steps at a time, I start running, tripping on my feet and falling at the base of the stairs.

More injuries. More physical pain. Yet I no longer feel it.

I breathe and breathe, my mouth wide open, but air just won't fill my lungs. Even as I fall, and even as I get up, the pain is but an echo in my body, my own *feelings* the harrowing source of my physical pain.

Hearing her name… Hearing her name on his lips when he'd been inside me. Telling her he loved her…

I barely make it in time to the bathroom as I empty the contents of my stomach. Slumped over the toilet, I replay everything in my mind, hoping—needing—to believe I heard him wrong.

But it wasn't wrong.

He'd called me *luz*. Light. Lucero.

Bringing my fist over my heart, I keep hitting my ribcage in an effort to alleviate the hurt inside.

He'd called me luz…

Why?

On shaky legs, I barely get up, washing my mouth with some water as I stare at the mirror. I take in my disheveled appearance, the redness of my eyes and the crusted tears on my cheeks.

Bringing one hand to my puffy lips, I can only ask myself how I got here. I've been through more things than a normal person has, yet until this moment I didn't know how it felt to die inside.

Te amo, mi luz.

All this time and he…

My voice cracks with the power of my sobs.

Is this the first time, or has it happened before but I just never realized? In my bid to have someone to love *me*, have I overlooked the obvious signs?

Was I that oblivious?

I purse my lips as I continue to stare at myself—at the stranger in the mirror.

Was I so desperate for any crumb of affection that I created an alternate scenario in my head? Did I distort reality?

One after another, the questions flood my brain.

All this time, did he imagine it was her instead of me? When he was fucking me, was he fucking *her*? When he was kissing me, was he remembering the way her lips tasted?

The what-ifs are killing me, my hands going to my ears in an effort to stop the errant thoughts from making me go even more insane than I already am.

He never gave me the words, yet he whispered them to her so easily…

I've fallen for a lie.

And the truth is staring me right in the face. I've been her replacement all along. Spurred by his guilt towards me, he decided I would do. Sure, he's attracted to me. But other than that… He can't have her, but he can have me, isn't that right?

I hate her. I hate her with everything I have in me.

"I hate her," I yell, my throat hurting as the rough sound comes out.

From the beginning, I should have seen this coming. I should have fucking paid attention to the signs.

Because how does one go from hating someone so much for allegedly killing the love of his life to *this*? He was willing to do whatever it took to ensure that Lucero's tormentor got her due. He was willing to do *everything* for her. How could I have been so dumb as to think he could suddenly change his affections so easily?

He's loved her for years. He's only known me for months.

In his mind, she's his unfulfilled love. She's an ideal—a wasted potential.

How could I ever compete with that?

He put her on a pedestal. Compared to her, I'm just... human. I have faults where she has none.

There's no comparison.

I blink, the realization startling.

I've been lying to myself from the beginning, haven't I?

I wanted him so much, I was willing to overlook every red flag. I was willing to put aside the past and just look at the future. But the past can *never* be overlooked, since it dictates the future.

That was my first mistake.

My second was being too desperate for anyone to see me as more than a lunatic. To see me as a human being—a woman. A flesh and blood woman, with wants and desires. A woman worthy of love...

It was all a lie.

My gaze hardens, and before I know what I'm doing, I bring my fist against the mirror.

I'm not strong. I barely have any strength in my limbs.

Yet as my knuckles connect with the mirror, a loud bang erupts in the room before shards of glass shatter everywhere.

Blood pours from my hand and into the sink, and I can only watch as it washes down the drain.

I stare at the red liquid, and all I know is that I *hate* her. I hate and resent her so much, that if she'd been here, before me, I would have used one of the sharp edges of a shard to cut her throat. Then it would be *her* blood I would watch dripping down. It would be *her* suffering that would finally give me some sort of peace.

Just as that thought arises, I reel back, my entire being thrust into the past. And as I open my eyes to look around me, I see my former room at the *hacienda*.

My entire body is shaking with pain—so much pain that I'm barely able to stand upright. One hand clutches at my midriff, and I feel like my womb is about to fall out.

Though I feel on the brink of death, there's a steely determination that brings me here, to this spot. I know what I must do, and nothing will stop me.

My fingers feel the outline of a key in my other hand, and with wobbly movements, I bring it to the keyhole, stabbing it inside and twisting until I hear the click of the lock.

Limping away, I see myself head to the stables, grabbing a large canister of gasoline.

My thoughts are too messy to make sense of them. More than anything, I feel like a spectator in my own body as I watch myself *act*.

Walking around the house, I'm having a hard time carrying the liquid with me as my body is slowly dying of pain. But beneath it all, there's unwavering conviction.

I'll do it.

I may die trying, but I'll do it.

I'm bleeding. From what part of my body, I don't know. Or maybe, the blood is pouring from *everywhere.*

Every breath I take feels like my last, but I push on.

Tilting the canister, I let the flammable liquid pour on to the ground. I walk all around the corridors of the house before circling the entire place on the outside.

When there's barely anything left, I dump the container.

And as I stand in front of the entrance, I know I don't have much time left to live.

But one thing is for sure. If I'm going to hell, I'm taking everyone with me.

My gaze blank, every cell in my body disintegrating, I bring a shaky hand up.

Once, twice, three times. I bump the match against its case, hoping a flame would flicker to life soon.

And when it does... I simply let it fall.

I jolt back to the present, the enormity of what I just witnessed washing over me.

I killed her. I actually killed her. I killed everyone!

Bringing my bloody hand to my face, I drag it down my face, smearing the red liquid everywhere. Tilting my head to the side, I let my eyes roam over the little reflective shards still in place.

I killed her.

And for the first time since seeing scary flashbacks into my past, I'm not horrified at what I've done.

I'd do it again.

My God... Who am I?

My fingers still on my cheek, I tug at the corner of my mouth, forcing it into a smile. Blood touches my lips, streaming down my chin, yet I can only force my mouth into a wider smile—wide and wider. My brows are pinched in a frown, my eyes close to tearing up at the pain. But just as I'm about to give in, bawl my heart out, a light giggle escapes me. Instead, my cries are mingled with laughter, my tears complimenting my strained grin.

I'm sick.

I'm sick because I would do it again. I would kill her all over again.

I don't even know why I did it in the first place, but right this moment, I would *slaughter* her.

"What is wrong with me?" I ask with a straight face once my fit of laughter subsides. "What the hell is wrong with me?"

Maybe that's just the answer—everything.

From the beginning, everything's been wrong with me.

Everything.

Cisco was right. Everyone was right.

I am mad. I'm fucking insane.

Insane…

My eyes rove around the mess around me, settling on a larger shard of glass. Wrapping my hand around it, I hold tightly, reveling in the sting of the sharp surface.

Without even realizing what I'm doing, my feet carry me up the stairs. There's a disconnect between my brain and my heart—between my brain and my body.

I'm no longer lucid as I step into the room, the sharp object in my grasp.

He's still on top of the sheets, naked.

With slow but precise movements, I climb on top of him.

"Why?" I whisper, staring at his serene face.

He's so beautiful my heart aches.

"Why couldn't you love *me*?" I ask, more tears falling down my face.

Bringing the shard over his chest, I trail it down his pecs and to the square of his abdominals.

It would be so easy… So easy…

I nip a bit of skin, blood flooding to the surface. Swiping it with my thumb I bring it to my lips, closing my eyes as I sigh at the taste.

He's not mine. He'll *never* be mine.

And if he's not mine…

Raising my arms over my head, I position the tip of the shard over his heart, ready to bring it down with full force—end this forever.

I'm in position. I only need to move.

Yet the more I stare at him, the more I realize I can't.

I can't kill him.

Killing him would mean killing my own heart. And I'm not brave enough to dig my own heart out of my chest.

Instead, I linger. Weapon raised, I linger.

"Why…" I shake my head.

Right at that moment, his eyes snap open, and in the next

second I find myself under him, my back hitting the sheets, my breath knocked out of me.

His eyes meet mine, but it's just as before. He's not present. It's him, yet it's not. And in a way, *this* is the real him. The version that doesn't lie, deceive, or disillusion. This is the truthful version.

He peruses me, his gaze settling over my bloody hand still clutching at the shard of mirror. Slowly, he disentangles my fingers from around it, taking it from me.

I don't know what he means to do, but as the weapon switches owners, I take hold of his wrist, bringing it to my throat and willing him to do it—put me out of my misery.

"Do it," I whisper.

He tilts his head, his eyes narrowing at me.

Instead of going through with it, he imitates my previous movements, bringing the sharp edge of the mirror over my naked flesh before cutting just above my breast.

I gasp at the sudden sting. But just as it flares, it's gone, warm lips surrounding the battered spot.

On my back, I turn my gaze to the ceiling, staring at it.

I couldn't kill him.

He couldn't kill me.

Where does that leave us...

But like the sick masochist I am, I need the confirmation. I need to hear it once more for my heart to break for good —forever.

"I love you," I whisper, focused on one spot of mold on the ceiling. "I love you, Raf," I tell him, waiting for the confirmation of all my fears.

His tongue swirls at the cut before he trails it up my neck, his warm breath fanning on my skin and sending me back to comfortable memories—of being, of belonging.

To the illusion of belonging.

He nibbles at my earlobe, before he whispers in the sweetest voice.

"I love you, too. So much…"

Closing my eyes, I wait for the pain to hit.

He's between my legs, pushing himself into my body.

Still, I wait.

"I love you so much," he repeats on a harsh intake of breath, thrusting in and out of me.

Squeezing my eyes shut, I palm the sheet beneath my body, holding on to it for support.

"You're my eternal love," he rasps. "*Fuck, te extraño, mi luz. Regresa a mi!*"

I bite my lip in pain as I turn my head to the side.

In that moment, my soul truly splinters.

Why? Why did I need to hear it again? As if it didn't hurt enough the first time. Now…

But I needed it. I needed to hear it again—to know it wasn't just my erroneous perception at the time.

"This is goodbye, Raf," I tell him gently. There's no other way around it.

His brows furrow in confusion.

"No," he grits out. "You're not leaving me. Not again," he states vehemently as he wraps his arms around my torso, holding me captive to his chest.

A sad smile plays at my lips.

Now that my slight maniac episode wore off, I can see things more clearly—including what I need to do.

But for the moment, I indulge him, closing my eyes and pretending for one last time that it's me he loves. Because in the morning…

Chapter Forty-Five
Noelle

"I'm one hour away. I should be there soon."

"Thank you for coming on such short notice, Amo. I really appreciate it."

"Does Cisco know?"

"No. And I would appreciate it if you didn't tell him. At least not yet. I'll talk to him soon."

"Fine by me," he says before he hangs up.

Surveying the packed bag at my feet, I take a deep breath, doing my best to keep my head high and not devolve into a crying mess.

On the inside, I'm already dead. But at least on the outside I can preserve some of my dignity.

Lovely snuggles comfortably in my arms and I hug him tighter, the heat of his body giving me a modicum of control.

Raf still hasn't come down—likely hasn't awakened yet.

I'd left him just as he'd fallen asleep again, and if my plan works accordingly, I won't see him before I leave.

Maybe it's a coward's move, but I don't know how I can face him again after last night. After I became so pathetic I let him use me while he was thinking I was another woman.

Instead, I wrote him a letter.

It wasn't easy to lay out all my thoughts on paper, but I did my best. After all, I know that if I don't do this now, it's only going to get worse.

I'll hold everything in until I'll resent him and I'll resent myself even more.

Like this, we can go our separate ways while on good terms.

I won't have to live with the perpetual reminder that he's not over Lucero and he won't find out that I killed her. He won't find out anything about the past, and he won't look at me any differently.

Because if he ever does...

I could stand his second-hand affection. I could even stand his indifference. But his contempt would break me.

It would...annihilate me.

Total annihilation of the heart.

I scoff at the term my brother had used, because ulti-mately it had become the truth.

What's worse is that now that I'm starting to remember bits and pieces of the past, I realize that they were all right.

I'm too unstable.

I *am* insane.

There's no other explanation, because as it stands, I *would* kill Lucero again. But this time, it wouldn't merely be a fire.

No, I would...

I shake myself. I need to get a grip on reality. But how can I when I feel so disconnected to my surroundings? When I feel like I've been dumped into the wilderness with no instructions and I'm fair game for everyone to take a stab at me?

Maybe I *do* belong in a mental facility... They would be able to figure out what's wrong with me, wouldn't they? Why I've suddenly become this *stranger*—this sick person that rejoices at others' misery and doesn't bat an eye at mass murder.

My hands are stained with blood—so much blood—and I know that when the rest of the memories will return I'll just spiral further into madness.

He can't know!

He can *never* know the extent of what I've done. If he finds out that he'd been right all along—that I *am* a murderer and that I killed his beloved... I don't think I could bear to see the change in his regard.

He would look at me as I rightly deserve—like the deranged woman that I am—and I could never recover from that.

I can go on knowing he at least holds some affection for me. But to have him *hate* me?

I'd rather die.

Isn't that terrifying? The fact that I value his opinion more than my own life.

My throat trembles with unreleased laughter about the irony of the situation.

That's exactly why I've come to this decision.

I can't be his second best. But I also can't be his worst enemy. If I were to choose... I'd rather be a pleasant yet distant memory—like I know he'll always be for me.

Lovely's soft bark gets me back to the present, and I pat his head lightly, putting his leash on and getting ready to leave.

I drape my bag over my shoulder and go downstairs.

Every step I take leads me further away from him, and my insides burn at the thought.

It's for the best...

"Noelle! Noelle!" His voice rings out in the house.

I'm almost at the entrance when he strides down the stairs, a crazed look on his face.

"Thank God," he exhales in relief as he reaches my side. "Thank God, you're ok."

"What are you talking about?" I frown.

"I woke up and there was blood and..." his eyes widen when he sees my bag. "Where are you going?" he demands sharply.

"Amo is coming to pick me up in a bit," I shrug, my gaze bleak.

"What? Why? Where are you going?"

"I'm going to stay with him for a while," I simply answer.

"Noelle, this isn't funny," he rasps, his hands on his hips as he stares down at me, unabashed by his own nudity.

I will myself to seem indifferent as I ask.

"Do you remember what happened last night?"

A guilty look crosses his face, and biting his lip, he gazes down at his feet.

"I didn't hurt you, did I?" he inquires in a soft tone.

I don't answer. He did hurt me. He hurt me more than if he had physically assaulted me.

He doesn't take well to my silence, taking one step forward and seeking to pull me into his arms.

I flinch, my entire being rebelling at being close to him again. Without even thinking, I slap his hand aside, backing away.

"Noelle..." he whispers, shocked at my reaction.

I swallow hard, and taking a deep breath, I face him.

"You lied," I simply state.

"If it's about the drug I can explain. I swear I just didn't want you to worry..."

"It's not the drug," I cut him off, though his lack of trust in me hurts, too. I'd pondered about his high state and why he'd taken drugs in the first place. But then I remembered the *hacienda* and the fact that they pumped him so full of drugs I doubt he can ever be fully free of them. Still, he never once mentioned it. He never once tried to tell me that those drugs might still be an issue.

"You lied to me, Raf. You told me you were a one woman type of man and you *lied*," I say pointedly, my voice almost cracking with each word. I'm beginning to see that he's lied to me about *many* things.

"What..." He regards me with confusion.

"You're not a one woman man," I add accusatorily, his promise from before still ringing in my ears. I'd believed him then. Against my better judgment and my fears, I put my trust in him.

And he betrayed it.

"How can you be when there are two currently residing in your heart? You told me you were over her. That she was the past and I was the future. You *lied*," I emphasize the word, biting back tears as I recall again the events of the previous night.

"I didn't lie to you, I swear, pretty girl. Whatever it is you're thinking, we can talk it out. I promise you there's no one else but you," there's no trace of deceit in his tone, but I've already learned my lesson.

He tries to take another step towards me, but I don't let him.

"No. Stay there," I put my hand up. "Do you know what you called me last night?" I ask, and for the first time I see realization seep into his face.

He looks guilty. Shocked. Aghast.

"You called me *mi luz*, and you told me how much you loved *me*," I laugh at the irony. "But it wasn't me, was it?"

His cheeks color in shame.

"It was the drugs. I'm never in my right mind when I take them," he tries to explain, but my ears close up. He speaks, yet I'm past listening.

I shake my head at him.

"You never told me you loved me, Raf. *Never.* You found ways around it. You told me you cared about me, that you adored me. But *never* that you loved me," I pause, taking a deep breath. "And like an idiot, I bought it."

"Pretty girl, it's not like that..." he frowns.

"That's just the thing. It *is* like that. Do you think of her when you're with me?" I ask on a whisper. "Do you imagine it's her when you make love to me?"

"God, Noelle," he threads his fingers through his hair in frustration. "I swear to you it's not like that. I told you what I had with her and what I have with you are two completely different things."

"Different," I scoff. "There are degrees of comparison to *different.* And it's clear that you still love *her,* while you only *care* for me."

"That's not true," he refutes my statement, moving closer. "I've *never* felt for her what I feel for you, Noelle. How many times do I have to tell you that?"

I squeeze my eyes shut, his excuses bruising my already broken heart even more.

"I love you, Raf. I do. But I can't continue knowing you're thinking about her when you're with me."

"And I'm telling you I'm not," he spits out, exasperated. "I've never *once* thought about her when I was with you. Pretty girl, you're the only one for me, I swear."

"You called me her name," I gulp down the nausea threatening to overtake me. "You called me by her name while you were inside *me.* Do you think I can ever sleep with you again and not wonder if you're thinking about her?"

His eyes flicker with emotion, his face pale as he listens to my words.

"So what if you've never had sex with her," I give a dry laugh. "You could very well imagine it's her you're fucking when you come to *my* bed."

"I'm sorry. I'm so fucking sorry. But I promise you it was the drugs. This always happens..."

"Why? Why does it happen, Raf, if some part of you is not still hung up on her?" I raise a brow as I dare him to answer.

He's silent, merely looking properly chastised as he keeps trying to shorten the distance between us.

"No. Don't come any closer."

"You're mine, pretty girl, and I'm yours. That's the only thing that matters."

I close my eyes, a wave of pain hitting me straight to the chest at his words.

He's not mine, and I don't think he's ever been. And *that* hurts so damn much.

I inhale sharply, setting my severe gaze on him.

"I'm yours and you're mine, but you've never told me you loved me," I challenge.

"But I do. You know I do."

"Tell me. Tell me you love me."

"I..." he stops, blinking as he realizes his inability to spell out the word love—at least not in the same sentence with me.

This is why I hadn't wanted a confrontation. Because every little thing he says or does just augments my pain.

"You're breaking my heart, Raf," I tell him brokenly, bringing my fist to my chest. "I gave you all of me. I gave you the love I've never shared with another and you. Broke. Me," I enunciate each word, banging over my heart.

Already my eyes are swimming in moisture, and I can't stop my tears from rolling down my cheeks anymore. No matter how much I'd like to look strong, I can't...

"I'm so sorry, Noelle. I swear to you I didn't mean to let you think you weren't enough, or that I didn't care. What I feel for you can't be quantified. It's so much more than words can encompass..."

I can't help myself as I burst into laughter. He frowns, regarding me as if I'd sprouted a second head.

"Yet you can't even bring yourself to say love, can you?" I shake my head, still laughing in spite of my heart breaking into even smaller pieces. "Why did you lead me on?" I ask in a low voice. "Why did you have to give me hope to just squash it in the end?"

"I didn't. I never led you on," he counters. "You mean the world to me, pretty girl and I'd do anything for you. I swear to God, I've never lied about that."

"Then tell me," I push my chin up, taking a step forward for the first time. "Tell me you love me," I dare him, though deep down I know the outcome.

I wait.

He waits.

His Adam's apple bobs up and down as he swallows uncomfortably, his eyes on me as his mouth opens to speak.

But the words never come.

He stares at me yet he's unable to form the words.

I close my eyes, inhaling deeply.

Then I simply turn, walking out of the house.

"No, no, pretty girl. Don't!" He yells, chasing after me.

This time, he doesn't care about my request that he keep his distance. He crashes into me, hugging me from behind. His arms come around my waist, his chin on my shoulder as he keeps me to his side. He seeks to fit his cheek to mine, gently brushing his skin against mine.

"Don't leave me, please," he whispers in a broken voice. "Please don't leave me, pretty girl. I can't imagine life without you," he says raggedly, his breath on my face as he breathes heavily—almost as if he'd run a marathon.

"Lucero's death hit me hard, it's true. But you... Not having you in my life would truly end me. You're my other half, Noelle," he confesses, his lips against my skin.

My heart does a flip in my chest at his words. Yet in spite of his admission, I don't find myself wavering. Not when the words from last night echo in my mind—they will probably never cease to.

"You called her your eternal love," I barely manage to speak, choking on each syllable that comes out.

"Noelle..."

"You can't even bring yourself to tell me you love me yet you called her your eternal love. I'm sorry, Raf, but I just *don't* believe you."

I push my hands against his arms, getting out of his hold and continuing forward. I keep my head high, simply placing one foot in front of the other.

A small thud startles me, and turning around, it's to see Raf on his knees, tears coursing down his cheeks.

"Please don't leave me," he whispers brokenly. "I'll do better. I promise I'll do better," he repeats.

My own tears start falling again.

"There is no better," I walk in front of him, stooping down and brushing my fingers against his cheek. "You can't force feelings, Raf. I love you too much and I know I would be miserable staying with you and knowing you'd never be able to return my feelings."

"But I..."

I bring my finger to his lips, shushing him. I don't want to hear any more platitudes coming from him. Not when they hurt the most.

"I don't want to be second best. I don't want to always wonder if you love her more. It would be torture for both of us and we would end up resenting each other. Let's end this while the memories are still pleasant."

He shakes his head at me.

"I can't do this, Noelle. I can't do this without you. Please... I swear to you, pretty girl," his voice cracks as more tears accumulate at the corners of his eyes. "I'll do anything... Please, just don't leave me."

"I'll have the papers for the divorce drawn up and I'll send them with a lawyer," I tell him softly. "I'm sorry," I whisper, ready to get up.

But he won't let me.

He's holding on to my dress, his fists wrapped in the material as he keeps on begging me to reconsider—to not leave him.

I swallow hard, his urgency slowly getting to me.

But I can't let myself be swayed by pretty words. Not anymore.

Getting him off me, I simply bring my lips to his forehead, stunning him with the gesture.

His hands fall limply by his side as he holds himself immobile.

"Maybe in another life you would have met me first instead of her. And maybe you would have fallen in love with me first," I whisper the words with a sigh.

He's stunned to the spot as I finally get up.

Without looking back, I pick up Lovely's leash, tugging him towards me just as I put my bag over my shoulder again. And as I walk away, step by step, I'm leaving crumbles of myself behind.

When I see Amo's car at the gates, I simply put on a fake smile, assuring him everything is ok.

It's not.

"Talk to me, Noelle. What's going on? Did that bastard do something to you?" He asks as he spares me a glance.

I shrug, hugging Lovely to my chest as he stares out the window in wonder.

How I wish I could see the world through his eyes...

"Nothing. I've realized we don't suit each other."

He frowns.

"What did he do?"

"He didn't do anything," I reply, rolling my eyes. "Differences of personality and all that," I wave my hand dismissively.

Can't my brother see I don't want to talk? Can't he take a clue from my tear-streaked face or the fact that my entire palm is bandaged and in pain?

"I'll fucking kill him," he mutters.

"No. You will do nothing of the sort," I tell him in a stern voice.

Now he cares?

"It's between me and Raf. End of discussion. Now can I get some sleep? I'm a little tired."

He purses his lips but eventually nods, leaving me alone.

My lids feel heavy, but I know I won't be able to fall asleep.

If before I had severe issues with insomnia, now I know it will only get worse, the images in my head *not* likely to let me get a wink of sleep.

I'm patting Lovely's head absentmindedly as I look out the window.

Out of nowhere, though, something collides with our car, hitting it in a T right on the driver's side.

Reeling back, I quickly grab the top handle as the car is driven off the road.

"Amo," I call out, worried since he'd been hit directly.

"I'm fine," he groans, trying to get control of the car.

We move haphazardly until we hit a tree, smoke coming out of the hood of the car.

Luckily, though, we are both relatively fine.

"Wow, that was a close call," I breathe out relieved when Amo tells me he's ok.

"Lovely is also fine," I let him know as I unbuckle my seatbelt, ready to get out.

I barely get to open the door to the car as the smoke makes its way inside, making me cough. Still, the sound of a gun going off is unmistakable, as is my brother's shape as it sways in the air before hitting the ground right as he's about to get out of the car.

"Amo!" I yell, bolting to go to his side.

One step, though, and I come face to face with the barrel of a gun.

"Nice seeing you again, sweet sister-in-law," Michele drawls, trailing the gun down my face and positioning it under my chin. "I think we have a lot to catch up on, wouldn't you say?"

I FEEL my way around the dark room, trying to map out my surroundings.

Michele had taken me to a foreign location an hour or so away from the accident site. To my everlasting relief, when he'd forcefully led me to his waiting car, I'd managed to see Amo still moving.

At least he's not dead.

To say that I've been shocked to see Michele still alive had been an understatement. But I'm starting to find out that nothing is out of bounds with him.

It's been two hours since he left me in this room.

There are no windows, no lights, *nothing*.

No doubt, he's trying to intimidate me with the light deprivation. I almost roll my eyes at that, since it's not going to work on me—not when I've had enough training at the *hacienda*.

I occupy my time by walking around the room, my hands on the walls as I measure the distance—anything to build an image in my head.

A while later, though, he decides to grace me with his presence.

Opening the door, he strides inside confidently, a twisted smile on his face as he regards me.

"Ah, but that look on your face when you saw me," he shakes his head in amusement. "*Priceless.*"

"Where is my dog?" is the first thing I ask. Knowing Michele, I'm sure he *would* stoop so low as to hurt an innocent animal. He's *that* vile.

"Safe. For now." His lips pull up in a fucked up grin.

At least he hasn't killed him. *Yet.*

"What do you want with me?" I raise a brow at him, my expression bored in an effort to show him I'm not falling for his tricks.

"Just trying to play a little with my brother," he chuckles. "Nothing more."

"Well, you chose the wrong person for that," I grumble.

"I'm sure," he laughs. "I'm going to have so much fun watching him flounder when he can't save the love of his life. Maybe this time I'll switch up the script though. Hmm, let's see..." he strokes his jaw pensively.

He's not taking this seriously, that much is clear.

With faking his death and now suddenly reappearing just to mess with us, it's quite obvious that what he wants isn't just clear cut revenge—he could have had that on the roof. No, he wants chaos. He wants to see Raf on the brink of misery.

Not to worry, though, I don't plan on letting him get away with it.

Raf may not be able to return my love, but that doesn't mean mine automatically ceases to exist. I'll love him to my dying breath, maybe even beyond.

"You chose poorly, Michele," I roll my eyes at him.

"Right," he scoffs. "Please spare me the speech that you're

not that important to him and blah blah blah," he brings his fingers together as he imitates a person talking. "I've watched that movie and it's booooooring."

"What are you, a child?" I mumble under my breath.

He doesn't hear me as he goes on and on about his plan to make Raf suffer.

"I'm sorry to rain on your parade, Mr. Baddie, but you got the wrong person," I give him a strained smile. "My husband happens to be in love with another woman."

He raises a brow, leaning back and regarding me skeptically.

"How convenient," he eventually laughs.

"It's true," I shrug. "So you're quite wrong about me being the love of his life."

"And why should I believe you? You'd say anything to get away now," he narrows his eyes at me.

"Well, imagine my surprise when my husband was fucking me and all of a sudden called me another woman's name."

"Right," he mumbles, unconvinced. "Let's say I believe you. Who is that woman?"

"She's dead."

"Well, isn't that even *more* convenient? We're done with this," he snaps as he takes a step towards me.

"Her name was Lucero. He met her at the *hacienda*, and she died in a fire." I'm not sure why I'm continuing with this. It's clear he's not going to believe me.

"I'm sure she did," he laughs. "I don't care about whatever ghosts you're inventing, Noelle. My brother cares about you, and he will no doubt care even more about what I'm going to do to you."

My eyes flash at him.

"What are you talking about?" I take a step back.

"Take off your clothes."

"What? No!"

"Take off your clothes, or I will. And I won't be as gentle," he smirks as he lifts up a knife, letting it glint in the dim light coming from the doorway.

My eyes skitter between him and the door, and I do a quick calculation of what would happen if I ran away. He'd catch me and…

"Off. Now," he grits out angrily.

Chapter Forty-Six
Rafaelo

Pebbles gnaw their way into my flesh as I let my weight rest on my knees, simply staring ahead. A bleakness unlike anything I've ever experienced washes over me, my body frozen on the spot and unable to do anything.

I keep looking ahead, willing this one moment to be just a bad dream.

You lied to me.

I did lie to her. But I never lied to her about the most important thing.

She *is* my heart. She is my *everything*.

There's absolutely no way to quantify what I feel for her, or the fact that she's so deep within my soul that I no longer see myself as a separate being from her.

But now that she's gone...

I gulp down, squeezing my eyes shut and praying it's just a bad dream.

Carlos was right. I shouldn't have done this on my own, leaving myself open and vulnerable—for her to see just how pathetic I am.

For the entire period of my captivity I'd been fed countless drugs, the moments of lucidity few and far in between. During that time, Lucero had been the only thing keeping me sane, tethering me to the real world when my consciousness was about to slip from me.

Maybe that's why whenever I return to that state, her name is the only one on my lips.

I've seen tapes of myself in the throes of my hallucinations. I've seen how aggressive and out of control I'd been. And all for one reason—because she wasn't there.

But this... to call *her* by Lucero's nickname... There aren't hell fires hot enough to punish me for my stupidity and for my fucking mouth.

How the fuck...

I shake my head. Eyes closed, features tense, I can only replay the events in my mind as I remember them.

The night is a blur—as it always is. When I'd woken up uncuffed and seen a piece of glass around, as well as stains of blood on the sheets, I'd known something must have gone wrong.

Oh, something went *very, very* wrong.

In the distance, I can still spot her figure as she opens the gate, heading for the car just outside.

That image is enough to pull me out of my shocked state and give me the spur I needed to finally move.

I order my limbs to obey, my mind solely recovering and honing in on one purpose.

I can't let her go.

I'll do whatever it takes. I'll fucking chain her to my bed until I can convince I speak the truth—that she's the only one in my heart.

She's the only fucking woman for me. Now or ever.

And nothing and absolutely *no one* will take her away from me. Not even her.

I can't let her leave me.

More than anything, I don't think she understood just how true my words were. I couldn't go on without her. Because without her I have *nothing*.

No family. No happiness. No purpose.

In such a short period of time, she'd become my everything.

My resolve strengthening by the moment, I put one foot in front of the other as I start sprinting, bursting through the gates and running after the car.

I don't care that I am butt naked, or that there are some old ladies staring at me from the sidelines. I simply dash forward.

"Noelle," I yell her name, running at full speed and hoping I can catch up with the car.

I'm barefoot, and the debris on the ground is already making a mess of the soles of my feet. Still, I push forward, unable to imagine *not* getting to her.

"Noelle! Come back," I keep yelling.

A few seconds and I think I am getting closer to the car. Raising my arms up, I wave them around, hoping she'd see me in the mirror and tell her brother to stop.

It's not her that sees me though. It's her brother.

And as he makes a quick U turn, he changes gears as he goes on to the highway. No matter how much training I've had, and no matter how steely my resolve is, there's absolutely no way I'm going to catch up with them.

And he's never going to stop.

"No!" I sink to my knees, yelling at the top of my lungs.

My entire being is rebelling at the thought of Noelle leaving me.

She wants to divorce me...

Well, she might as well try. I'm *never* going to sign my name on that piece of paper.

When she married me, she married me forever.

Until death do us apart.

And If I have something to say about it, not even then.

If she thinks that leaving me now means she can leave me for good, she's wrong. I don't care what I have to do to prove to her that I'm sincere and that she's my only one.

I'll fucking do it.

Realizing I need to pick my battles carefully, I slowly trudge my way back to the house, careful to avoid detection. The last thing I need is for someone to call the cops on me for public indecency.

Spotting a cardboard by the side of the road, I grab it and place it in front of my crotch, pushing my chin up as I walk back, avoiding to meet the inquiring stares of the grandmas by the side of the road.

"Fuck it," I mutter softly under my breath as I finally close the door behind me, stepping inside the house and looking at the vast emptiness with an equal empty heart.

I went and did it this time, didn't I?

I limp around the house as I find some clothes to put on before getting my phone.

All along a side of me has been going mad with worry that I would fuck something up—that I wouldn't be worthy of her. And the truth is, with that fear foremost in my mind, I'd put on my best front. I'd shown her my good side while carefully stashing away the bad. I'd done my best to paint myself as the good guy, earn her trust and make her see me as her protector rather than her tormentor.

In the process, I lied to her.

I lied about my past, and the fact that I have more blood staining my hands than anyone—Michele included, since I'd been the catalyst for his fall from grace. If anything, everything he's done is on *me* because I'd been too cowardly. Too wrapped up in my own perfect world that I hadn't deigned to imagine his wouldn't be equally as perfect.

I lied about the fire, and I never openly told her I'd been there that night.

But more than anything, I lied to her about my nature.

Knowing her past and trauma, I only showed her my caring and gentle side. I did everything to make her comfortable and get her to open up to me—get her to trust me. To do that, though, I suppressed everything *more* that she awakens in me.

Aware of her issue with violence, I suppressed my unnatural urge to do harm to anyone who dares to look at her the wrong way. Instead, I pushed everything down, wanting to avoid another incident like the one at the amusement park.

Then there's also her need for independence, and the fact that she's been so smothered by her family that she craves to make her own decisions and feel like she's taking her life in her own hands. For that, I've had to push down my need for her—this unnatural need to *own* her that I know it's not normal.

But as I've realized *since* her, nothing about her is normal.

She makes me act in ways I've never thought possible— ways I've previously thought inconceivable.

I remember a couple years ago when Sisi was telling me about her relationship with Vlad and the ways he made her feel—like they were one half of the same whole. I'd thought it preposterous back then, because how can one being depend so much on another? Their codependency had struck me as silly, and in my head, I'd thought it would never happen to me.

I thought myself impervious to that.

Yet it took only *one* woman to shake me—one slip of a woman who challenged me at every turn but sought comfort in my arms in times of danger. That dichotomy soon proved to be my kryptonite.

She could go toe to toe with me and hold her own

ground, but she could also display an addictive vulnerability. She touched something primal inside of me. She activated sides of me I never even knew I had.

And because of that I *know* no other woman would do —ever.

I clench my fists by my side, breathing through my nose as I try to calm myself.

Instead of giving in to my rage and destroying the entire house, I dial up Carlos, needing some friendly advice. In my current state, I can barely think properly, and I know that to win her back I'll need all my wits about me.

"Don't say I didn't tell you," Carlos mutters when I give him a rundown of the events.

"I didn't think... Fuck," I curse.

"You knew how you react to the drug, but you still preferred to *not* tell her about it. You're a fucking idiot, my friend."

"Don't I know it," I sigh. "I'm wrapping things up here and I'm coming back to the city. Noelle said she's staying with her brother, Amo. Can you check where that is? I want to know all her moves, at all times."

"Right. I'll see what I can do about that, but Amo isn't that easy to pin down. He has houses all around the country, and often likes to switch things up at the last minute. But I'll get some eyes on him, don't worry."

"Good. I'll see you in the city then," I say as I hang up.

Packing everything up, I linger as my fingers brush against the garnet necklace.

Another tidbit I'd avoided telling Noelle is that having the necklace with me when I'm in a drugged up state helps me. It calms me in a way that little else does.

But admitting such a thing would have meant opening myself up to even more questions. Ultimately, she would have wanted to know why it's *her* necklace that calms me of all things. And even I don't have an answer to that.

It simply does.

Maybe I *should* have gotten rid of it...

In theory it would be so easy. In practice though...

I shake myself, pocketing the necklace and getting everything to the car.

The ride to the city is smooth, and it takes me a couple of hours to get to the brownstone.

To my everlasting surprise, though, I come face to face with Cisco, his wife and their newborn.

"I didn't expect *you* here," I mumble.

He frowns.

"Didn't Noelle tell you? We're staying in the city until our flight to Rome in a couple of days. On that note, where is she?" He asks as he looks behind me.

"She's with Amo. We had a small squabble and she's staying with him for the time being."

"A squabble?" He narrows his eyes at me.

Just at that moment, though, his phone rings.

"Yes? Yes, this is Cisco DeVille. He what?" a brief pause before he nods. "I see. I'll be there soon."

Hanging up, he sets his mismatched eyes on me, the lighter one glinting in the sunlight as he stares at me for a moment.

"That was the police. Amo was rushed to the hospital with a gunshot wound to the head. He's in emergency surgery."

My eyes widen at his words, my heart stopping in my chest.

"Noelle?" I ask on a whisper.

"No sign of her. There was a car accident and they found him alone at the site."

I take a deep breath.

Missing means she's alive—captured.

Not dead.

This is good…

Fuck!

I take a deep breath. In and out as I dim my feelings in favor of my brain. I need all my faculties about me to get to the bottom of this.

"I'm coming with you," I tell him as he walks towards the living room where Yuyu is seated on the couch with her infant son.

"*We* are coming with you," she notes, getting to her feet.

"You heard?" Cisco asks in a tight voice, and Yuyu nods.

"Noelle couldn't have just disappeared. Someone must have taken her," I interject.

"I agree. And until we have more information, we can't do anything. Amo is the only one who might know what's going on, and he's…"

"It will take time," I curse. "One moment," my voice breaks. "One moment I'm away from her and *this* happens…"

Shaking my head, I pivot as I take out my phone, calling everyone I know and asking for help.

And as we head to the hospital, while Cisco and Yuyu talk with the doctor, I am on the sidelines interrogating the police.

"And there are *no* cameras on that highway?"

"Not in that spot. There is one a few meters away…"

"I want to see it."

"We can't just…"

"I want to see it," I reiterate, more forcefully.

My heart is clamoring in my chest, my brain overheating at the mere thought that something might have happened to my pretty girl.

No, that's unacceptable.

Noelle is fine and I will find her.

Even if I have to fucking kill everyone who stands in my way.

A heated discussion with the policeman in charge and I'm led to the station. Cisco and Yuyu stay behind to wait for the diagnosis in Amo's case, but they promised to let me know if they have any news.

In the meanwhile, I manage to get access to the footage, and as I scour every camera near the site at the time of the accident, I notice something.

"That," I point towards a black car. "It's the only one with tinted windows."

"It's not that uncommon."

"No, but in this case it is," I mention. "We've watched out for every other car, and while the camera does have blind spots, it gives us a pretty good idea of who's inside the car," I explain with a sigh.

I would have preferred not to involve the police in this, but the only one who could have accessed the feed is Panchito. As it stands, I still don't fully trust him. There might not be any obvious signs pointing towards him aiding Michele at that time, but my gut tells me something else. And if his loyalties are questionable, I can't in good faith count on him to find Noelle's location—I don't know how I could trust that.

Instead, I make do with what I have—intimidation and the reputation of my family's name. That and Cisco's own influence with the police seems to have worked wonders in coaxing them to pull up the feed from the highway.

"Can you run the car plate?"

The officer operating the computer gazes up at me, his brows furrowed.

Not having enough patience, I tell him his superior has given me carte blanche to their system. Well, I might be exaggerating just a little, but time is of essence here.

He works on the plate while I try to rack my brain and come up with *anyone* who would have a grudge against me.

With Michele out of the picture, there isn't anyone that comes to mind. But it could be anyone with a grudge against Guerra or DeVille.

"It's a rental," the officer's comment gets my attention. "It was returned a little while ago too. The client paid cash."

"Any description of the client?

He gives me a short description that could be literally anyone, and I already feel like I'm losing my mind.

"Thanks," I say as I leave the station, already on the phone with Carlos to see if he'd had more luck than me.

"If this was a kidnapping, they will contact you sooner or later," he tells me, and *that* doesn't warm me in the least.

By then, they will have had access to Noelle for hours. They could...

I close my eyes, panic unlike any I've ever known bubbling inside of me. And as I get behind my wheel, I realize I can't move.

My hands are trembling, my entire field of view is foggy and I can't help the tears that start pouring down my face.

My fault. This is all fucking my fault.

I bang my hands against the steering wheel, the tension in me mounting to an unbearable crescendo.

"I'll get you back, pretty girl," I promise, both to her and to myself. "I swear on my life that I'll get you back or I'll die trying."

Because without her... I have nothing.

I blink my tears away, staring into the distance as I watch people walk up and down the street, going about their regular day.

How I wish we were like them too. That we didn't have this much fucking baggage behind us.

But the more I stare, the more *her* words echo in my brain.

Maybe in another life you would have met me first instead of her. And maybe you would have fallen in love with me first.

What if something happens to her… What if something happens to her and she'll die believing I didn't love her. That I…

I bring my fist to my mouth as it opens on a soundless moan, my shoulders slumping with the magnitude of the emotions I'm feeling.

I love her. I love her more than anything. But why the fuck couldn't I say the words? If only I'd done that, none of this would have happened.

It's all my fucking fault.

If she'd heard me say those three words, she wouldn't have left. And now, she wouldn't be missing.

I'm losing it.

I know I am.

My brain cannot cope as I remember word after word of what she said. But most of all, it hurts that she was right.

I loved Lucero, that's true. But I loved her with the innocent heart of a first love. She was my haven when my life was pure hell. In her I found the briefest respite from my torment and I was able to borrow strength from her when I had none.

With Noelle, however… There's no comparison.

She makes me feel *everything* a thousand times stronger. With her, everything is more potent—my senses themselves are overtaken by her.

Scent. Sight. Hearing. Smell. Taste.

Everything converges in *her.*

I used to consider my condition a burden before—it made me different, and it made me perceive the world differently.

Not in this case. It allows me to explore her in ways that are not possible without linking all those senses together. When I'm with her, they meld together in an intoxicating combination that makes me so full of her, we're no longer two different beings.

Her essence is everywhere within me. She permeates every atom of my being, until all I know is her sweet, heavenly taste.

How does one compare that to...anything?

Starting the engine, my hands are still trembling on the wheel as images of my Noelle battered and hurt cloud my mind.

I'm not in my right mind to drive.

Leaving my car behind, I end up taking a cab back to the house—because it's not home anymore if she's not there.

Cisco and his wife are still at the hospital, so as I climb the stairs, I'm relieved that I won't have to deal with anyone else. I don't think I could bear to do that now.

Heading straight to the piano room, I take a seat on the bench, running my fingers all over the keys.

"Fuck," I curse out loud, my helplessness getting a rise out of me.

How am I supposed to simply wait until whoever took her reaches out to make demands? How?

Knowing they might...

I close my eyes, a sigh escaping my lips as I bring my head down on the keys, a deep sound reverberating in the room.

Still, it warms me like nothing else, because I feel *her.*

I feel her in the simple action of sitting by the piano, feeling it's planes and angles and imagining *she* was here. It was her beloved space after all—her passion.

And seeing her play... I don't think I've known greater joy than hearing those notes as they envelop my entire body, encapsulating me in her thoughts and feelings. Her music simply brings me to heaven.

Taking a deep breath, I straighten my back as I tentatively

bring my fingers on to the keys. My mother taught me the basics, but it's been years since I attempted anything on my own. Yet it's the thought of her *piece*, the one she'd written specifically for me, that spurs me into movement.

I lay a finger down, marveling at the sound that comes out. I repeat the action until I manage to string together enough notes to create a pleasant melody. It's not hers, but it's the only thing that connects us now.

I've never had a passion before—not like her—just like I've never had a goal.

All along I've been merely existing and reacting to things happening to me.

Until her.

In my teenage years, I did my best to go under the radar. There was no time for hobbies when my entire existence was centered around keeping my disguise in place. My guilt had wrecked me so much I'd stopped dreaming.

I went to college because it was expected of me, and to my mother's dismay, I chose to study geology. I liked it well enough, I suppose, but nothing more than that.

Maybe when I was younger, I had aspirations. Maybe... But that's a lifetime ago and a lot of things have changed since.

She changed me.

She opened my eyes to *living* and for the first time I experienced pure happiness.

That also meant she became the center of my world—my passion. She's the only reason I want to do better, to plan and to dream.

And if she's gone...

I continue playing, the notes awkward from my unpracticed hands. My eyes are foggy, and I can barely see in front of me.

If she's not there, then neither am I...

In such a short time she's become so essential to my being that if anything happened to her, I would *not* survive.

I lose track of time as I continue to fiddle with the keys. My phone blares to life next to me, Cisco's name on the screen.

Immediately, I pick up, knowing it must be something related to Amo.

"How is it?"

"He's out of danger. Just waking up."

"And? Did he say anything? Did he see who took her."

"That's just the thing, Raf. He did…"

"And?"

"He said it was your brother," Cisco replies.

I pause, unsure I heard him right.

"My brother?" I repeat.

"Yes, he said it was Michele who crashed into their car."

"You do realize we *both* saw him die. Is Amo ok? He just survived a head wound, maybe he's talking shit," I say a little more aggressively than I would have wanted.

"No, he is sure," Cisco sighs. "Look, we were both there. But we were also concerned with Noelle. Maybe…"

"He died, Cisco. I saw him fucking get shot before falling off a building. He doesn't have nine lives," I mutter.

"No. But if he had inside help to figure out our plans, couldn't he have made a plan of his own?" He counters.

I bring my hand up, massaging my forehead.

"He's sure?"

"Positive."

"Thanks."

Hanging up, I head out, going straight to the warehouse.

CHAPTER FORTY-SEVEN
RAFAELO

"Look who's here," Thomas whistles. "Didn't think I'd see you anytime soon, mate."

He's sitting at his desk, feet propped in the air, newspaper in hand.

"Panchito. Where is he?" I ask, looking around.

I know Carlos isn't here yet, since he'd promised me he would look into the rental place on the downlow.

"He should be in the back with Anita. Why?"

I ignore his question.

After we'd started suspecting Panchito of being the mole, both Carlos and I had started surveying his movements very closely. We hadn't told anyone else in the crew in case our suspicions ended up being unfounded.

Since he was our friend, we didn't want to jump the gun and accuse him of something so foul as betrayal.

But that was before, and this is now.

I don't care who I have to go through to get some information, and if Panchito knows something about Michele...he better talk.

I crane my neck, releasing some of the tension in my tendons before stalking to the back of the warehouse.

Panchito and Anita are lounging on a couch, playing video games and laughing.

Laughing while my heart is missing.

My mind goes blank as my hand shoots out, wrapping itself around Panchito's throat. His eyes go wide when he sees himself off the ground, my fingers locked tightly against his airways.

Looking him straight in the eye, I utter only one thing.

"Michele."

He blinks at me, but his face turns a deep shade of red—a sign of his guilt.

At this point, I don't care about excuses. I don't care about anything but the truth and any information that might help me find Noelle.

Flinging him to the side, he hits the ground, his right shoulder bearing the brunt of it as he moans in pain.

"Raf, what the hell is wrong with you?" Anita shouts, going to his side.

"Stay out of this. It doesn't concern you," I tell her as I stride to Panchito's side, grabbing him again and dragging him towards the fighting area.

"I'm sorry," he whispers repeatedly.

I wince, the confirmation jarring to my ears.

"Talk," I order as I shove him on the mattress.

When he doesn't make any effort to open his mouth, I simply uncuff my shirt, rolling my sleeves up before stepping forward.

He's prepared for the first punch, and he manages to duck. But he isn't for the second. Or the third. He's definitely not prepared for me to pummel away at his face.

Vaguely, I hear Anita calling out my name before yelling for Thomas. But that doesn't stop me from going even harder at him, all the while asking him about my brother.

"I can't..."

"You can," I say resolutely.

"Raf, what the fuck," Thomas jumps in the ring as he grabs me from behind, pulling me off Panchito.

Bloody and beaten to a pulp, he just lays there. His guilt is written all over his face, and that makes me even madder as I stare at him.

"You betrayed us," I yell. "You fucking sold us out."

He tips his chin down, avoiding my stare.

"Pancho, what's this about?" Thomas asks, looking between the two.

Anita dashes to Panchito's side with a wet towel in her hands as she tries to clean the blood off him.

"Tell them it's not true," she whispers, her tone full of disappointment.

"I'm sorry," he whispers.

My blood boiling, I start struggling in Thomas' hold.

"You..." I see red, suddenly realizing that everything until now had been because of him. "Get the fuck off me, I'm going to kill him," I keep kicking until Thomas has a hard time holding me.

Just in time, though, Carlos arrives at the scene.

Instead of helping me out though, he helps Thomas to restrain me further.

"Not you too," I spit, looking between all of them. "He knows something. He must know something..."

"And he will tell us. But he can't do that if he's dead, Raf," Carlos shakes his head at me. "Look, I get you're suffering. I get that," his hands on my shoulders, he positions himself in front of me, a buffer between me and Pancho. "But if you kill him, you're not going to get any answers."

"He won't talk," I grit out.

"Did you even let him?" He rolls his eyes at me.

"Try," I tip my chin at him. "Try and see if he talks."

"Hold him," Carlos barks the order to Thomas, who secures his grip on me, taking a step back and putting more distance between me and my object of destruction.

Carlos walks to where Anita is tending to Pancho, kneeling down and looking at him.

His expression is severe—entirely unlike the Carlos we all know. Most of the times he's like the bigger brother we've all never had. But now... Now he looks like a disappointed father.

"We know it was you who messed with the computers, Panchito. You can stop lying."

He blinks, his eyes swollen as he flinches at Carlos' words.

"Why now then? Why didn't you say anything before?" he whispers, his words barely audible.

"We wanted to do a thorough investigation. We didn't want to accuse you without all the proof. We also wanted to give you a chance to come to us of your own volition. Why did you think I mentioned the incident so many times?"

Panchito shakes his head, wrenching his gaze away.

"Will you kill me?"

"Yes," I grit out at the same time Carlos says, "No."

"What?" my eyes widen, and I give Thomas a hard shove. The big guy has me well and truly caught, though and it's all in vain.

"Tell us what we need to know and we won't do anything."

Panchito dares to look at me. Upon seeing the anger in my gaze, though, he addresses Carlos.

"I didn't want to do it," he starts, telling us how Michele had monopolized the supply of medicine Anita needs for her genetic condition.

"You know it's the only thing that keeps her alive and *living*," he pleads.

"Go on," Carlos mentions, sparing me a glance.

"Initially he only asked me to give Raf false info about his whereabouts."

"So the reports were all fake?" I narrow my eyes at him.

"Semi," he sighs. "He didn't go out much, that was true. But the few instances he did, I kept from you. That and..." he promptly shuts his mouth.

"That and what?" I demand, coldness seeping through me at his declarations.

"He was seeing someone and he didn't want anyone to know."

I frown, remembering some texts we'd read—texts Panchito had supplied, so I ask him exactly that.

"Yes. He wanted it to be found out eventually, but not in the beginning," he explains.

"Who was she?"

Panchito purses his lips.

"Venezia Lastra."

I blink, wholly taken aback.

"You mean..."

He gives a brisk nod.

"Since when?" I ask on a groan, already feeling a headache forming.

"A year? Around a year," he says in a dejected tone.

"A year?" The disbelief is written all over my face, mainly because Venezia just recently turned eighteen. But that's not even the worst, because if Michele is Nicolo's biological son, that means...

"Fuck," I curse out loud.

Now everything makes sense. The revenge porn. Marcello's sudden stint in prison. Everything makes fucking sense because there's only one person who would be fucked up

enough to do that—and also have the resources and motiva-
tion to do it.

"All this time we've been trying to work out the situation
with Lastra and you fucking knew?" I spit out, my rage
mounting by the moment.

He has the decency to look ashamed. Still, I'm not
appeased.

"You were my *friend*, Panchito. You fucking sold me out."

"It wasn't like that," he briefly protests before Carlos gives
him a stern look.

"You could have come to us about the medicine problem.
You could have reached out," Carlos shakes his head.

Meanwhile, Anita is staring at Panchito open mouthed.
It's clear she had no idea what he'd been up to, and her
expression is one of absolute desolation.

"How could you," she whispers, her voice breaking.

"I'm sorry," he takes a deep breath.

"What about Noelle then?" I ask, since *that* is the only
thing I need to know.

"I had no idea. I didn't even know he was going to strike
so soon."

He gives us a short account of what he'd gathered about
his plan at the piano concert, and how he hadn't ended up
dead.

The more I hear, the more I can't believe this is the same
Michele I knew growing up.

In our teenage years, he was the absolute prodigal son—
drinking, whoring and engaging in every vice possible. If
there was a party in the city, he was there.

He never struck me as the cunning, or wildly intelligent
type.

I was wrong.

Because if what Panchito is saying is true, then Michele
isn't just intelligent. He's a fucking genius.

And he's been one step ahead of me this whole time.

"He wants to make you suffer," Panchito suddenly says. "But it's not the physical type of pain he's interested in."

"Emotional warfare," I grunt.

"He's only using Noelle against you because he saw how much you care about her. But if there's anything we've learned about him, it's that he's *not* who we think he is. And because of that, it's almost impossible to predict how he's going to behave." Carlos adds thoughtfully. "We need to approach this carefully. Panchito," he turns to him, studying him from head to toe. "Are you willing to help us out?"

"You're going to trust him?" I glare at Carlos, the idea preposterous.

"Do you have another alternative, Raf?"

I curse under my breath. He's right. As much as I don't want to count on Panchito right now, he's the only one who could point us in the right direction.

Right at that moment, my phone rings in my pocket. Still holding me back, it's Carlos who comes to my side, taking it out.

"You have a text message," he frowns. "Number unknown." He pauses as he looks at me. "If Thomas releases you, are you going to behave?" He raises a brow at me.

"Fine," I mumble, and the moment my hands are free, I snatch the phone from his hand.

But as I open the text message, it's to feel my entire world come crashing down on me.

It's Noelle. Naked.

I take a deep breath, a wave of nausea rolling through me.

On her chest, someone had painted one word in a white, viscous substance—semen. And it spells *used.*

"I'm going to fucking kill you," I burst out, dropping my phone and jumping on Panchito once more, not caring about anyone else around me or the fact that I'm completely out of control.

"Restrain him," Carlos yells.

Before I know it, I find myself cuffed to the bars of the fighting ring, everyone staring at me with odd expressions.

"What the fuck, Raf. What's wrong with you?" Thomas' wide eyes meet mine as he shakes his head in disbelief.

"What's wrong with me?" I get the urge to laugh. "What's wrong is that my fucking lunatic of a brother probably..." I trail off, barely able to say the words. "He probably raped her," I hiss brokenly, "and I wasn't there to protect her."

Tears sting my eyes at the thought of Michele anywhere near Noelle. But to have laid a hand on her. To have...

It makes me ill just thinking about it.

Fucking hell, how is my pretty girl doing? How...

"Let me go," I tell him, my voice unyielding. "I need to see the photo again."

They are skeptical about my quick change of attitude, but a little coaxing, and Carlos releases me again. Grabbing my phone, I zoom in on the picture, wanting to study every inch of it in search of a clue.

But just as I think it's useless, just as I think grief is about to overwhelm me, I see it.

Above the *d* on her chest there is a small, curved line under which lies a barely discernible dot.

All at once, my shoulders sag in relief.

She's fine.

"She's good," I say the words out loud, explaining she'd placed a strategic *fermata* over the word—the musical sign for stop, or pause.

This means that she'd been the one to write the words on her own chest and *that* means she might not have been harmed. Or at least that's what I keep telling myself. Because to picture otherwise... I don't know how I would make it.

"You want to help?" I take a step towards Panchito. Everyone tenses, ready to move to hold me back in case I jump on him again. "Get me the coordinates from where this picture was taken." I tell him.

He nods effusively, immediately getting to work.

An hour or so later, though, he has grim news.

"He altered the metadata. I can't trace it. I'm sorry."

"Damn," I swear, and Thomas is immediately at my side to ensure I don't kill Panchito.

"Fuck. Fine. Fine. I'll behave. But you," I point at him, "are going to tell me everything from the beginning. Every single interaction you've ever had with my brother. And don't you dare leave one thing out."

Panchito ends up telling me everything, including how Michele had approached him and threatened him with Anita's safety. It's been an open secret for a while now that he's had feelings for her, so it doesn't surprise me he would jump at the opportunity to save her.

After all, wouldn't I do the same?

I'd fucking move mountains for my pretty girl. Yet now I find myself unable to do *anything*.

"He's going to contact you again," he suddenly says. "But not immediately. He wants you to despair, and only then will he contact you with his terms."

"You seem to know him pretty well," I lift a brow.

"He's trying to wear you out emotionally," he shrugs. "He's very manipulative. You have to be careful of that."

I grunt.

"That doesn't mean I forgive you."

"I know," he gives me a sad smile. "And I'm sorry for what I did. But I know if you were in my shoes you'd have done the same."

"And that's the only reason why there isn't a bullet in your skull right now, Pancho," I tell him grimly. "I know far too well the pain of losing someone, so I will spare you this time. But that doesn't mean…"

"That doesn't mean we're back to what we were," he interjects and I nod.

"The trust is broken. And if there's no trust, there's nothing."

His shoulders sag in disappointment but he nods at my statement, taking his laptop and limping away. Looking at his shape, it seems I got him pretty bad—not that I regret any of it.

A short conversation with Carlos later, and I return home.

Cisco is in his office, a glass of whiskey in his hand as he stares at the night sky.

I give him a brief update about what I'd gathered, but he only nods, barely acknowledging me.

It's only when I'm about to exit that he speaks.

"We'll get her back. And we'll get her back alive," he says, his voice distant.

"We will."

I'm about to head to the piano room, knowing I would not be able to sit still anywhere else, when the sound of a sweet melody beckons me to the living room.

Yuyu is comforting her son, rocking him softly in her arms as she increases the volume on the television.

I freeze as I recognize this as one of Noelle's pieces—her style unmistakable. And as the camera focuses better on her, she looks younger. Her expression is light, her smile intoxicating as she plays to her heart's content.

"She's got a unique talent, doesn't she?" Yuyu suddenly speaks.

Her son seems to have fallen asleep, yet she keeps swaying him in her arms, the gesture soothing for the infant.

"She does," I reply in a low voice, not wanting to wake him up.

"Don't lose hope. We'll get her back, one way or another."

"I know we will," I give her a strained smile.

Yet the question remains... *At what cost?*

Either something will have happened to her, or it will happen to me. It's unavoidable.

At the same time, even knowing I might be going to my own death, I'll do whatever it takes to get her out alive and well.

"You know," Yuyu starts, her eyes still glued to the television. "When she's with you I get glimpses of the old her. The one before..." she trails off, swallowing hard.

"Before Sergio."

She gives a brisk nod.

"We were wrong to agree to the match. We were so wrong," she shakes her head.

I don't reply, merely leaning against the door frame as I wait for her to continue.

"Do you know how it all came about?"

I shake my head, and on a sad note she starts talking.

"Cisco was supposed to marry Sergio's sister. Obviously, he didn't," she gives a dry laugh. "Sergio was incredibly pissed about it. He kidnapped our son in retribution, and safe to say, Cisco was forced to sign the marriage contract."

She takes a deep breath.

"Maybe we should have found another way around it. Maybe *I* should have killed him. But we had no idea he was such an evil man," she shakes her head, bringing a finger to her eyes to remove a tear. "No one knew anything until we got that call from the hospital. That they'd found her—the only survivor in that entire goddamn place. We heard the extent of her injuries and that's when we knew we'd fucked up."

"Does she know?" I ask quietly. "Does she know *why* Cisco agreed to the marriage contract?"

Yuyu shakes her head.

"He never told her. He's stubborn like that," she chuckles. "He wanted her to hate him so she could pull herself together."

"He succeeded."

"He's never forgiven himself." She half-turns to me, her expression melancholic. "He's *never* forgiven himself for it. It may not seem so," a strange smile pulls at her lips. "But my husband is a complicated man. He doesn't open up to people and is ok with everyone believing the worst of him."

"Not you," I raise a brow.

She shakes her head, an amused expression on her face.

"He's an extension of me, just like I am an extension of him. But I reckon you know the feeling," she tilts her head to the side, studying me.

I nod.

"We've wronged her all her life. I'll leave it to you to make it right, Raf. Make her happy," she pauses, her tone sad. "I doubt she's ever been."

"I'll get her back. And I'll make her the happiest woman alive," I tell her sincerely.

"I'm glad we have an understanding," she smiles warmly, lowering her head to press a kiss to her son's forehead.

I pivot, ready to head upstairs when something stops me in my tracks. Slowly, I turn around to watch the screen.

"You guys came," a young Noelle remarks, a precious smile on her face.

"We told you we wouldn't miss the show," Yuyu replies, going forward to hug her.

"You did well, Noelle," Cisco praises in his usual nonchalant fashion.

"It's my newest composition. I spent months perfecting it," she adds, an effusing bliss imbuing her words.

It's not her intoxicating happiness that strikes a chord in

me. It's not her youthful beauty and her unspoiled innocence. It's the *cadence* of her voice.

So light and carefree. So…

My eyes close as I let it wash over me, a soothing taste of vanilla custard settling on my tongue. It speaks of comfort and shelter in the middle of the storm—of inconsolable nights made bearable only by the sweetness of that tone.

The shock that should have overtaken my body is replaced by an unexpected calm as all my senses reel into alignment. A startling tranquility starts at the base of my skull and travels down my body, all the pieces slowly fitting together.

As much as my brain reacts to the new information as it would any shocking revelation, my entire being slowly becomes used to the idea as if I'd known it from the beginning. The signs converge into one single conviction.

Fate.

It was fate.

She was my light all along—*mi luz*.

Noelle smiles at the camera, waving enthusiastically, and my heart tugs painfully in my chest.

"I love you, pretty girl," I whisper, saying the words out loud for the first time.

Under any name, or identity, it's her. It's always been her.

The only woman I've ever loved—the only woman I'll *ever* love.

TO BE CONTINUED

Made in the USA
Middletown, DE
20 August 2023

37058731R00342